5 Rounds

THE FIGHT GAME: BOOK ONE

NIKKI CASTLE

Cover Art: Dark City Designs
Editing: NiceGirlNaughtyEdits

❀ Created with Vellum

To my Tristan, whose teasing makes me want to both punch and kiss you on a daily basis.

1

REMY

I'm being evicted.

I'm really being evicted. This is actually happening. *How is this happening?*

"I'm really sorry, Remy, I wish there was something I could do," my landlord continues on the other end of the phone. "But they're my family and I can't leave them stranded. They can't afford to go anywhere else. I promise, if I had any other choice, I wouldn't ask you to do this."

I close my eyes and rub my temple, the beginnings of a headache already forming. "I get it, Dan. I understand," I say into the phone. And I do. "I would do the same thing for my family. It sucks, but I get it. I have thirty days, right?"

"Yeah," he answers, and I can almost hear his wince. He's a good guy so it's really hard to fault him for any of this.

I pause as I picture a calendar. "So that puts me close to the end of the month, right? Is there any way you can give me an extra week so I can move out at the end of the month?"

But I know the answer before he even says it. If it were up to him, he'd give me as much time as I needed, so the fact that he said thirty days means his sister and her family absolutely need the apartment as soon as possible.

"No, I'm sorry," he sighs, confirming my thoughts. "As it is, they'll be staying with me for two weeks. They were given two weeks to evict so they basically need the apartment as soon as possible. I'm really sorry."

I exhale a heavy breath. Not only do I have to scramble for a new apartment, but getting kicked out halfway through a month means I have only three options: either I get lucky and find a place that's available immediately, or I overpay on an apartment for two weeks—which also means finding the place immediately—or I'm homeless for two weeks and wait to move until next month. None of my options are pretty.

"Okay, I'll be out in thirty days," I grumble, rubbing my eyes. "If by some miracle I can be out earlier I'll let you know."

"Thanks, Remy. And again, I am so sorry. I hate that I have to end your lease like this. You were such a great tenant. If you ever need anything, just let me know."

A sad smile stretches across my face. I know he means that. "Thanks, Dan, I appreciate that. We'll talk later."

I hang up and immediately throw myself on a barstool at my kitchen island. I groan as I drop my head onto my crossed arms.

Just then, I hear a key in the lock at my front door. The door opens and my sister walks in.

"I can't tell you how excited I am to finally try this Latin restaurant," I hear her chirp happily as she walks into the kitchen. "I heard it's amazing—whoa, what happened? What's wrong?"

I raise my head to see her frowning at me.

Hailey is four years younger and the polar opposite of me. Where I am brunette, she is blonde. Where I am fit and strong, she is model-thin. Where I am loud and headstrong, she is quiet and thoughtful. The only similarities we share are that we're both short—we're 5'2" on a good day—and we both share our mother's good looks. Though she's considered much more beautiful since it couples with her perfectly tiny frame.

She's also my best friend in the world. We were always close growing up, and have gotten even closer since she moved to the city three years ago. I even moved her into my townhouse that I shared with college friends after she graduated high school. My friends loved her just as much as I did, despite her being several years younger than them. She was kind and funny and unproblematic, and she fit into our circle immediately. Somehow even though she was the youngest of all of us, she was the one we all went to for advice.

Which is exactly what I need right now.

"Dan just evicted me," I groan. Her eyes widen at my news. "His sister's family just got evicted from their apartment for not being able to pay rent and he has to move them into my place. I have thirty days to find a new apartment."

"Damn," Hailey mutters. I can see the wheels turning in her brain, trying to figure out how to help me. "I guess I understand, since it's family, but that still sucks. What are you going to do?"

"Find a new place, I guess." I grimace and rub my temples. "Why does this have to happen now?"

Hailey shares the same pained look on her face. "I guess it's pretty shitty timing that I moved in with Steve this year. If I was still living at my old place in Fishtown, I would've just let you stay with me."

"I'll figure it out," I sigh. "Maybe I'll ask Jax if I can crash with him for that week."

Hailey lets out a loud laugh. "That would also mean staying with Tristan. Are you sure that's worth it?"

"Maybe I can convince Jax to kick him out," I think out loud. "Or maybe I can just tell him to stay with whatever brainless bimbo he's currently screwing? I'm sure sex would sway him. Because there is not a chance in hell I'll be able to live with him for that long."

Hailey shakes her head, chuckling. She hands me my purse and pushes me out the door.

A few hours later I'm pounding on Jax's front door.

"Let me in, asshole, I need to pee!" I shout angrily. A young couple walking on the sidewalk shoots me an annoyed look. I stare right back. Despite this being Queen's Village in the nice, hipster part of South Philly, it's still Philadelphia. We're expected to be loud assholes.

Just as I'm trying to decide which alley I'm going to sneak down to relieve myself, the door opens to reveal a smirking Tristan West.

I have a lot of thoughts about Tristan, but the one thing I can't deny is that he's gorgeous. He's over six feet tall and a solid 200 pounds of muscle. I know him from the MMA gym I joined because of Jax in college—and it's an understatement to say they both look the part of a fighter. Tristan is the pretty boy of the two, with just-woke-up tousled, dark brown hair and piercing blue eyes that always feel like they're staring straight into the secrets of your soul. His jawline is defined and he's got just enough stubble on his face to give him a rugged look, but not enough that it comes off as a scruffy beard. His skin has a warm tan, most likely from all the shirtless runs he does around the city for his cardio workouts.

I also know from my time at the gym that he's completely shredded from his training. Every pound of him has a purpose, his body built to be an efficient fighting machine with a low body fat percentage and muscles defined not by lifting weights, but by training with a real purpose and a fuck-ton of hard work. His dedication to the sport is unrivaled and it definitely shows in his appearance. I've never met a man as comfortable in his body as Tristan, and that fact coupled with the physical result of his work-outs gives him an air of confidence and raw masculinity.

Basically, an effortless Adonis.

He's also a total ladies' man and a shameless pig. Or maybe that's just to me, since I assume there's a reason why women all fall into bed with him. Either way, he and I have been at each other's throats since the first day I stepped in the gym and he gave me directions to the ballet studio down the street.

"Of all the women I know, you're easily the least lady-like," he drawls.

I glare at him and push past, heading for the bathroom. "I guess that's really saying something, huh? God knows you've been with half the women in this city," I throw over my shoulder.

By the time I come out of the bathroom, he's sprawled on the couch and is back to watching whatever MMA fight he was analyzing before I pounded on his door.

"Where's Jax?" I ask as I plop onto the loveseat next to the TV.

"Still out at happy hour," Tristan responds without even looking at me. I notice he's watching a UFC title fight, most likely analyzing the champ's fighting style for his own arsenal of skills.

I glance at my phone. "Jesus, still? It's 9pm. How much do those corporate assholes drink?" I throw my head back with a groan.

"Look, Remy—" I immediately growl at the condescending tone, knowing I'm not going to like what's about to come out of his mouth. "I don't mind if you hang out until Jax comes back, but could you be a doll and shut the fuck up? I'm trying to work." He smiles sweetly. "Actually, I take that back, I do mind. Can you just wait for him in the kitchen like a good woman? Maybe make me dinner while you're in there."

I glare and launch a pillow directly at his head—which he deflects easily.

"I can't believe chauvinists like you still exist in this day and age. Hasn't the women's movement stomped you out yet?" Then I pause, thinking of something. "Actually, what surprises me the most is that you still find women to sleep with you. Although I doubt the women you fuck even know the definition of chauvinist, so maybe that's my answer."

He chuckles and gives me an exaggerated once-over. "Everybody knows your hatred for me is just a cover for how badly you want to be under me," he says with a smirk.

I exaggerate gagging at his words. "No thanks, I'd rather take a beating from the guy on the screen than entertain the idea of you flopping around on top of me for thirty seconds." Tristan bursts out laughing. "Actually, I'd rather take that beating than sit here with you right now. I'll just wait for Jax in his room." I stand up and head for Jax's bedroom upstairs.

I've barely reached the stairs when I hear, "Don't pull another New Year's and mistake my room for his again, or

I'll assume you've decided against your women's movement and want to be under me, after all."

This time, my pillow hits him directly in the back of the head.

"That was *one time!*" I screech. "One time that I got drunk enough to pass out in your bed instead of his. It's hardly proof that I'm secretly salivating over you."

I ignore his amused chuckle as I stomp into Jax's room.

I'm sitting on the bed scrolling through my phone when Jax finally gets home. I wince when I hear him shout Tristan's name—he's definitely shitfaced.

Sure enough, he has a giant grin on his face when his door swings open.

"Remy baby!" he shouts gleefully. He throws his suit jacket on his desk chair and then immediately launches himself at me on the bed. I grunt at the impact.

"Get off me, you big oaf," I grumble as I try to shove him off of me.

Where Tristan is a shredded 200 pounds, Jax is a massive 230. They're both just as muscular as the other but Jax has about four inches over Tristan and loves to do strongman workouts and eat everything in sight. With his massive stature and dirty blonde hair, he practically screams Viking descent. The fact that he works in corporate America as a sales guy for a tech company has always made me laugh. Even with custom suits and perfectly gelled hair, he'll always be an overwhelming presence in any room. But with his contagious smile and affable personality, it's easy to get over the feeling of intimidation and fall in love with him.

He's also been my best friend since middle school. My parents moved us into the development where his family lived and—being the crazy tomboy that I've always been— Jax and I became fast friends. People always teased us about dating, but it only took one awkward kiss when we were seventeen to realize just how gross that idea sounded. He was my brother, my protector, my friend. We did everything together in high school, to the point that we couldn't fathom going to college in different cities. So although we attended different schools, we both moved to Philly our freshman year.

I also joined the MMA gym because of him. I was looking for a new sport after I couldn't get rid of the Freshman 15 and by that point, he was already deep into his obsession with MMA. It was an easy choice since he and Tristan were constantly watching and talking about fights—and I'll be honest, I was coming off of a bad breakup and *really* liked the idea of punching guys in the face. But it quickly became so much more than that. I learned valuable self-defense and became the healthiest that I've ever been. And while I never fought like the guys did, I was obsessed with taking classes and learning the techniques.

Now, three years after college, the boys are living together and working separate jobs. Both boys have gone pro, though Tristan truly lives, breathes, and sleeps MMA. Most of his income comes from private lessons and teaching classes. He's so focused on becoming the next world champ that his entire schedule revolves solely around his training.

Jax works his 9-5 at the tech company and trains at night. Secretly I think he's nearing the end of his career after five years. He's had plenty of fights, but I don't think he loves fighting enough to make the commitment of pushing it to the next level. Plus, he's flying through the ranks at his post-college job and seems to enjoy life the most when he's not in fight camp and can take advantage of time off and life in the city—as evidenced by tonight.

"Tristan said you were mean to him," Jax teases drunkenly, weight still fully on top of me.

I give up trying to push him off and roll my eyes at his comment. "More like he was mean to me for no reason. When have I ever been the first to throw a punch?"

"Last week at the gym," he chuckles, probably remembering when I lost my temper with a drop-in fighter and popped him in the face for not listening to our coach.

I scowl and cross my arms. "That guy was an idiot! He thought he was too good for Coach's drill. And the move was to defend your partner's jab, so technically I did nothing wrong."

"You didn't have to make his nose bleed." Jax's amusement has now escalated to rumbling laughter.

"Whatever, he still deserved it," I grumble. "But I'm telling the truth about Tristan. He's an ass—he always rips into me for no reason. That's why I was waiting for you up here."

Finally, he lifts his head off my stomach and sits up. "Why are you here, anyway? Not that I don't enjoy your company when you don't need something." He grins knowingly. We've been friends for long enough that he can sense when I'm about to ask him a favor.

I fidget nervously, eyes in my lap. I've never been good at asking for help.

"I'm being evicted," I mumble quietly.

"*WHAT?*" Jax yelps loudly. "How the hell did that happen?!"

I sigh and recap what happened with Dan earlier today.

"I'm going to start looking for an apartment tomorrow, but I'm not sure I'll find anything available that quickly at this time of year." I look at Jax with pleading eyes. "Worst case scenario, I'm homeless for about a week next month and need someplace to crash. I just need to know if I can consider your couch my Plan C."

Jax frowns when he seems to think of something. He grabs his phone and scrolls through it before looking up with a big smile.

"This actually works out perfectly," he says excitedly. "I have to be in San Francisco for work that week and I was going to go early and stay late so I can hang out with Jordan and the guys at the gym out there. So, you can even take my room." He grins, proud of himself. "See? Problem solved. You're welcome."

I let out a relieved breath and give him a small smile. "That's such a huge weight off my shoulders, you don't even know. Thank you. I'm still going to see if I can find an apartment next week but if I can't then I'll let you know, and we'll bank on me staying here." I pause—and cringe when I realize the worst part of this plan. "Fuck, that means I'd be living with Tristan." I turn toward Jax with a sweet smile. "Any way we could kick him out by then?"

He laughs and pulls me up off the bed. "Not a chance, sweetheart. But you can break the news to him by ordering us dinner tonight and then maybe he won't hate us as much." He pulls me toward the stairs and shouts, "Hey, *Tristan!* Guess who's coming to live with you?"

"She's *WHAT?*" I hear Tristan yelp from downstairs.

I wince as I follow behind Jax. This is going to be a long few weeks.

After ten minutes of walking, I finally reach my car. I get in the driver's seat and slam the door behind me. I sit quietly for a moment.

And then I scream—for a solid three seconds.

This is now the sixth apartment I've looked at and each one seems worse than the last. This one has zero parking, so I was forced to park way too far from the building.

Other issues today have included: a studio that would be small for even NYC, a crack house for neighbors, and windows that don't even close. Just for starters.

I rub my temples tiredly. I'm having zero luck finding an apartment that's in my budget and available within the next week. By number five I realized what I already knew in the back of my mind—that I'll need to wait until next month to move. Which also means I'll be living in Jax's house for a while.

I groan and lean my head back against the seat. I have two more apartments to see today and I'm the opposite of thrilled to see them.

I dial my sister on my cell. Miraculously, she actually picks up.

"Holy shit, you answered your phone," I exclaim. "It's a Christmas miracle."

Hailey's laugh rings out through my car speakers. "What's up? How's the apartment hunt?"

"Atrocious," I groan. "I have two more to see today and I am this close to bailing on the realtors. They were on the bottom of my list as is and if they're worse than the ones I've seen today then I think I'm actually a little scared."

"That bad?" she asks softly. I wince and rub my temples again. "I guess it makes sense. This isn't a good time for apartment hunting right now. All the college kids probably just took up all the decent spots, and the rest I assume are in shitty areas of Philly."

"Can you come with me to see the last two?" I plead. "I can't handle any more of these on my own."

"Yeah, sure," she responds instantly, and I think I love her for it. "I'm at Steve's, can you come pick me up?"

"Thank God," I tell her gratefully. "I'll be there in ten minutes."

Having Hailey with me at the next hellhole makes the task a little more bearable, but the place is still a major pass. I've had enough of living next to frat houses for the next few lifetimes.

"Okay, last one," I cringe. "Then we get plastered at the Irish Pub."

The next apartment isn't too far from Jax and Tristan's house, and we actually manage to find parking in front of the building. I get out of my car, already skeptical.

The street is pleasant enough. We're on a side street in South Philly and I see young couples and an occasional baby stroller when I look around.

"This is too good to be true," I mumble.

The realtor is waiting for us on the steps of the apartment complex. It's a somewhat newer building, which explains the price compared to what this area should be going for. They offer cheap prices to get people into the apartments immediately.

When we walk into the one bedroom that I called about, I realize with a sinking feeling that something must definitely be wrong here. It's very clearly too good to be true.

The door opens to a little hallway, at the end of which is the bedroom and bathroom. Both are a great size. But it's the kitchen and living room that really take my breath away.

The kitchen is cozy—not overly large but with enough counter space that even I nod in approval. There's an island in the center with two barstools. Another huge checkmark on my list. I like to host, and I always prefer entertaining guests at an island while I prepare the food.

But the biggest selling point of this apartment is the living room that the kitchen opens into. Not because of the size or shape, but because the far wall is made up entirely of oversized windows.

I walk over to the windows and peer down to the street below. I can only imagine how beautiful the city's lights shine in here at night. I sigh and ready myself to be disappointed.

I turn back to the realtor. "It's incredible," I breathe. "What's the catch?"

He looks startled. "There's no catch," he assures me. "It's a one bedroom, $1,400/month, just like you asked for. And it's ready next month."

I groan. There it is.

"I needed it next week," I say, dejected.

He frowns as he looks down at the paper in his hands. "I'm sorry, I must've misheard you on the phone. I thought you were looking to move in next month. This building won't be ready until then so unfortunately I can't get you in here next week."

I sigh and pinch the bridge of my nose. I figured this was coming anyway, so I shouldn't really be surprised.

"I'll take it next month," I say. "Just send me the paperwork and I'll get everything signed. Deposit is first, last, and security, right? So, three months' rent?"

He nods, still looking guilty. I smile weakly at him. "Okay, thanks for showing me around. We'll be in touch."

He leads Hailey and I back to our car and shakes our hands goodbye. When I slide back into the driver's seat, I pull out my cell and type a single message:

Remy: Guess I'm moving in with Tristan for a week

Twenty minutes later, Hailey and I are tucked comfortably in a booth at the back of the Irish Pub. It's the oldest Irish bar in the city and was Hailey's first job when she moved here, so we always get the VIP treatment.

"There you are. I thought I heard a little birdie whisper that you're here tonight."

We look up to see her old manager. Hailey's face breaks into a smile as she stands up to give him a hug.

"I thought I'd stop in to say hi since it's been a while," she says warmly. I wave politely at him.

"I'm glad you did, it's always good to see you. Shots are on the house. Tequila?"

I grin and nod. "That'd be awesome, thank you. This day's been dog shit, so tequila sounds like the only acceptable finisher."

He laughs and gives us a thumbs up. "Double shots it is. I'll be right back, ladies."

Hailey sighs. "I can't say I miss dealing with drunk assholes in here, but I do miss these particular assholes." She turns back to me to finish the conversation we had started on the way over here. "So, will you just leave all your furniture and boxes at Mom and Dad's house? I can't imagine it would make sense to get a storage container for less than a month."

"Yeah, I guess that's the easiest choice. God knows their basement is big enough for all my shit." I rub my eyes tiredly. "I can't get over how annoying this whole thing is. I'll have to rent a U-Haul twice instead of just making one move from one apartment to the other. Ugh, stupid Dan's family..."

Hailey laughs. When I glare at her for finding my misfortune amusing, she holds her hands up in a gesture of surrender. "Hey, at least that new apartment is stunning," she points out. "I'm jealous. New buildings are definitely the way to go. They're always so cheap."

"Yeah, except their timing is subpar," I grumble.

"Except that," she concedes. "But Jax gave you the okay to stay at his place for that week? The timing of his trip works out pretty perfectly."

I wince and sip my beer. "Tell me about it. I was not looking forward to sleeping on a couch for that long. At least this way I actually have my own space and can hole up when I need to. Which I assume will be almost the entire time, since I'll be sharing a house with Tristan." I groan and drop my head onto my arms. "Why does he have to be Jax's best friend? Why can't Jax live with a nice, intelligent gentleman?"

"It looks like these shots really are coming at a good time," I hear someone murmur above me. I look up to see my sister's old manager holding three shot glasses. "For whoever needs a little extra," he explains, nudging the extra shot toward us.

"You're a godsend," I groan, reaching for one of the doubles. "Thank you."

"Anytime," he grins. He looks at Hailey. "I wish I could stay and chat but it's obviously a little crazy in here. Catch me before you leave. It was great to see you again." His eyes light with a mischievous twinkle. "And you know anytime you need a job you have a spot waiting right here for you..."

Hailey laughs and shakes her head. "Not gonna happen, but I always appreciate the offer. Thanks again for the drinks."

At the mention of it I throw back a double and wince as it burns my throat. I sigh and settle back in the booth, waiting for the calm that alcohol always brings over me.

This day's been so horrific that I figure it can only go up from here.

I would be very wrong in that assumption.

"So, I hear we're going to be roommates."

I freeze when I recognize the voice. Slowly, I turn to glare daggers at Tristan standing in front of our booth.

"Trust me, it's not my first option," I growl. "Or my second. I hate this just as much as you do, so let's just set some ground rules right now and start off on the right foot."

He raises an eyebrow at me. "You're going to set ground rules in my house?"

"Yes," I snap. "Otherwise, I'm not sure we'll both survive."

He rolls his eyes but makes room for himself on my side of the booth. I scowl as he hip checks me to move over.

"Okay, rule number one," I start. "We stay out of each other's rooms. I know you like to barge into Jax's room and borrow his shit so that stops for the time that I'm there."

"But what if I'm out of condoms and need the stash in his dresser?" he whines dramatically.

If looks could kill... Tristan wouldn't have a pulse.

"Then I guess there will be one less notch in your bedpost," I snap. "Which brings me to rule number two: I do *not* want to hear you railing some idiot sophomore that doesn't know any better in the middle of the night. I wake up early like any decent adult, so quiet time starts at 11pm." I glare at him pointedly to make sure I've made myself clear. "And on a similar note, I don't want to walk into the house to see you fucking anyone, either. So, no sex outside of your bedroom."

Tristan finally shakes his head with a chuckle. "You've obviously put a lot of thought into my sexual activities. Are you sure you're not just trying to limit the amount of women in my life because you're secretly jealous?"

Hailey lets out a loud laugh. I glance at her, startled. I completely forgot she was here. I glare at her then return my attention to the smirking asshole next to me.

"You keep telling yourself whatever you need to in order to feel better about the fact that I won't sleep with you," I snort. I consider something, then ask, "Am I the only girl to ever turn you down? Oh my god, I am, aren't I? Wow, that explains why I get under your skin so much." I laugh delightedly.

But the laughter dies in my throat when I feel him press his lips against my ear. "Sweetheart, I've never asked you," he whispers condescendingly. "I hate to burst your bubble, but you always just assumed."

I can feel my cheeks burn red. I glare at him and shove his body out of the booth. He laughs triumphantly as he stands up.

"See ya later, Remy baby," he taunts as he walks away.

I'm seething as I grab the other double shot and down it without so much as a wince.

"Well, this is going to be interesting," Hailey murmurs.

2

REMY

I wake up to the delicious smell of eggs and bacon wafting through my apartment. I groan happily, thinking for the millionth time how grateful I am that my sister is a brilliant chef.

Sure enough, when I shuffle into the kitchen with bedhead and a sleepy smile, I see Hailey at the stove with a skillet in her hand and a dish towel thrown over her shoulder. She flips the omelet as I plop down on the bar stool behind the island.

"I don't know how you do it," I mumble. "It's 7am and you're already dressed for work looking perfect, making a breakfast that would've taken me an hour to figure out."

"That's because your cooking skills are so bad that you have to pore over every line of a recipe and then look up what 'mincing' means," she laughs. I glare at the back of her head—even though she's spot on. I actually burned water once.

"Not the point," I grumble. "I think the joke about you being dropped off by the stork might have some truth to it, since no one else in the family is even close to being an early bird. I don't know where you got it from."

She shrugs as she slides the omelet onto the plate in front of me. My mouth immediately starts watering. "I have a lot to do today," she reasons. "I'd rather get to the café early and get everything done so I have time to make Steve dinner before he gets home."

I pause my chewing as I consider my next question. I've sensed something is off about my sister's relationship recently, but she hasn't seemed eager to talk about it, so I haven't pushed. But my sister spidey senses are starting to go from tingling to fire alarms and I feel like I need to start pushing a little bit.

"You can always sleep here if you don't want to go home," I tell her softly. "I know you guys have been a little off lately. Maybe you need some space. Like more than a night."

Her shoulders drop and I can practically feel the sadness in her stance. "No, it's okay. I want to see him tonight. He already texted me this morning that he misses me and can't wait to see me. I'm just going to head home after work." She looks up at me with a fake smile plastered on her face. "All good. What's your day look like?"

Her deflection isn't fooling anyone but I decide to drop the subject anyway. I dig back into my omelet.

"I have back-to-back meetings with some of the Subject Matter Expert engineers today," I say around a mouthful of egg. "I read over what they wrote and now I have to sit down with them and basically translate their techy speak into normal person speak. It's great. I get to be looked at like I'm an idiot all day long. I'm living the dream."

Hailey shoots me a pitying glance. I don't even have it in me to jokingly wave it off.

"Thanks for the omelet," I say with a mouth full of bacon. "This is one of your best."

"Bacon crispy enough for you? I practically turned it into charcoal."

I glare at her smug face, both of us remembering the time she *actually* burned my bacon to charcoal so she could prove to me that there was such a thing as 'too burnt.'

"Yes, it's perfectly crispy," I snap as I shove another piece of bacon in my mouth.

She laughs as she dumps her dishes in the sink and finishes the rest of her coffee. Slipping on her pea coat, she grabs her tote bag off the island. "Okay, well, I'm out. Thanks for letting me stay over. I'll call you tomorrow to figure out the plan with Jax for the fights this weekend. Which I'm actually looking forward to, by the way. I can't remember the last time the three of us hung out with just us."

I smile when I realize she's right. Once Jax and I went off to college, it was rare that the three of us managed to get our schedules to match. This Saturday will be the first time in a while that we'll all be together.

"Okay, have fun at work," I tell her as I happily crunch through the last piece of bacon. "And let me know if Steve acts up. I've been itching to introduce him to Bennie."

She lets out a loud laugh. "Let's not bring Bennie the Bat into this just yet."

I grin triumphantly at the fact that I made my sister laugh. "You just tell me when you're ready for him. Bennie hasn't seen any action since your high school boys."

"Nuh uh, you said you brought him out when that guy in your hall thought he could follow you into your dorm room."

"Oh yeah, I forgot about that guy." I frown. "Guys are fucking morons."

She laughs again and I swear it's the happiest sound in the whole world.

I turn back to my plate with a sigh, a small frown crossing my face. I love my sister more than anything and it kills me when she's not happy. From the age of fourteen she's been a supremely independent person, doing what she needs to do to be successful and creating her own happiness —she's never been reliant on another person for either of those things. Jax and I have known her current boyfriend wasn't going to be the one, for the sole reason that he doesn't drive her to be better and doesn't particularly add anything to her life. But we never thought he could actually drag her down. We just always assumed Hailey would cut any guy the second he started giving her more bad times than happy ones.

Right now, it definitely seems like he's making her more unhappy than happy. And I can't for the life of me figure out why Hailey would keep him around if that's the case.

I huff in frustration and finish the last few bites of my omelet. I can't help my sister until she wants to be helped so in the meantime, I've got my own problems to deal with.

I think about the meetings I have scheduled today while I get dressed. As much as I would love to be the kind of writer that works from home wearing leggings and the messiest of messy buns, somewhere along my career I've become the kind of writer that exists in Corporate America. I open my closet, looking through my clothes for something that says, 'professional and beautiful but not looking for attention or like I'm trying to sleep my way to the top.'

I never thought there would be such a fine line.

In the end I settle on a black pencil skirt that reaches my knees and a dusty pink patterned blouse that I tuck into the skirt. I twirl my hair into a low bun at the nape of my neck, laughing to myself when I think about how Jax calls it my 'bitch bun.' I briefly debate pulling on heels, but when I remember that my first meeting is with Paul 'the Ass Man,' I grab my flats instead.

I complete the look with mascara and a swipe of lip gloss and then I'm grabbing the tote bag with my laptop and walking out the door.

Two hours later and with my second cup of coffee, I'm thanking all the deities in the world for my sensible shoe choice.

For one, Paul only paid attention to half of our meeting, spending the other half acting like I didn't see his constant glances at my legs. If I had worn heels, it's likely the whole meeting would've been a waste instead of just half of it. Even still, I'll be working late tonight trying to write the datasheet that Paul should've drafted before our meeting. But for another, sore feet are the last thing I need on this already-shit-at-10am workday.

I wince as I rub my temples. I have four more Subject Matter Expert engineers to meet with today and it's rare that these particular meetings are ever enjoyable. Where my job is to simplify and clearly market our company's software, the engineers that I meet with can't understand how anyone could possibly not understand what they're talking about. They're so wrapped up in their world that they're subconsciously assuming everyone has their engineer brain and can comprehend the level at which they're speaking. And in my effort to simplify their content and put it into layman's terms for a datasheet that will be used for marketing, they always end up looking at me like I'm an idiot.

I growl into my coffee, remembering Paul's shocked, 'what do you mean you want me to say it another way? I just explained it very clearly, I can't possibly simplify it any more.' Knowing he's the easiest of the engineers I'm meeting with today does nothing for my shit mood.

With impeccable timing, Cassandra appears next to my cubicle. I can tell without her even saying a word that she's in a hurry and wants to get this over with as quickly as possible. I groan inwardly, knowing that will make this even worse.

"Hey, Remy, want to grab a conference room? I have a hard stop at 11:00 so we might need to speed this up a little."

Consciously ordering my brain not to roll my eyes, I nod stiffly. "I booked Montgomery for us. Let's meet in there." Without a word, she spins and walks toward the conference room.

I gulp down the last few swallows of coffee, hoping some extra caffeine will save me from the disaster I'm about to experience.

"I have a thousand important things to do today so let's get this over with," she starts without hesitation. "I wrote up the datasheet for you. It should be in your inbox."

As I open her document on my laptop, I yet again marvel at the ridiculous expectation that 22-year-old Remy started this job with: the assumption that in Corporate America, everyone is a professional, responsible adult that can be pleasant while also having their shit together in order to get their work done.

Apparently, Cassandra didn't get the pleasant memo.

And looking down at her "document"—which can barely be classified as a rough outline—I realize she didn't receive the "get your shit done" memo either.

"Okay, this is a great start," I fumble awkwardly, trying to keep a cordial tone. *It's barely a start.* "I do have a few questions, though."

"About what?" she practically sneers. "It's all right

there. What else could you possibly need? Just use your pretty words and make it sound marketable. Isn't that your job?"

I swallow roughly as I try to remind myself that responding in the same snappy tone will only make this situation worse. "It is, but I need a little more information than what you have here. This probably seems clear for an engineer, but I'm not a technical person so—"

"You don't need to be technical to understand what I wrote," she snaps, cutting me off. "It should be perfectly clear what the new software does. Anyone with half a brain could figure it out and write a few measly sentences about it."

I stare at her in disbelief, not knowing which of her sentences to argue with first: the fact that what little she wrote is *not* clear, that a six-page requirement is hardly "a few measly sentences," or that she just flat out insulted my intelligence.

Deciding to ignore the blow to my intellect, I try one last, self-deprecating tactic, in the hopes that I can appeal to her pity. "I'm sure this seems simple to you, and I apologize for making you feel like I'm wasting your time, but if we could just spend a little bit of time reviewing the technical points, I'd feel more comfortable writing the document. I'd rather have you go into too much detail than not enough and risk me writing something incorrect—"

"That's your problem, not mine," she interrupts again. "I don't have time to train you on the technology. You should have knowledge about the company's software, otherwise how else could you write this stuff?"

"Technically, I'm not supposed to be writing anything," I finally snap. "My title says I should be proofreading your work, not writing it. You can call this a document all you want but you and I both know this is barely a bullet point list of fractured phrases."

Her eyes widen in shock. I don't even care that I've just shot myself in the foot in the hopes of Cassandra ever being helpful again. I refuse to sit here and be shit on just because some alpha bitch wants to take out all the sexism she's dealt with on another woman.

"I think we're done here," she hisses, standing up. Without another word, she tucks her laptop against her inappropriately exposed cleavage and angrily strides out of the conference room.

I walk back to my desk—stopping to grab a third cup of coffee—and begrudgingly settle into my research on the product Cassandra was supposed to write about. Instead of an hour edit of what was supposed to be a finished document, this has now become a four-hour job of research, writing, and then proofreading.

I wince, rubbing my temples again. Today just got a whole lot longer.

A few hours later, after one meeting with an actually nice—but idiotic—engineer, followed by yet another pervy one, I'm engrossed in more product research when my stomach rumbles loud enough to startle my coworker in the cubicle next to me.

"Whoa, hungry much?" he laughs. "Is that an 'I forgot to eat lunch' rumble or a 'lunch wasn't enough and now I need a snack' rumble?"

I smile sheepishly. "Forgot to eat. I lost track of time and didn't realize it was almost 3:00. Guess I better go heat up my lunch, so my obnoxious stomach doesn't continue to distract you."

"I appreciate that," he chuckles as he turns back to his screen. He's a nice man, very quiet and always focused on his work. I'm lucky if I get more than a brief conversation out of him every few days.

I sigh and lock my computer screen before heading toward the kitchen. As always, I have some form of healthy, prepped food ready to be heated up. Once I started training, I realized how much better both my mind and body feel when the majority of my meals are meat and vegetables. Lunch especially turned out to be an important meal, since it would either fuel me to finish work and an evening work-out, or make me feel sluggish and cause me to crash on my couch as soon as my workday was over. I prefer feeling energetic.

As I warm up my chicken and broccoli dish, I think about the work I've done today and what I still have left to do. I groan when I realize my fruitless meetings have ensured a late night. Before I realize it, my brain starts going down a rabbit hole of unhelpful—but very accurate—anti-work thoughts.

I'm not happy. I don't like my job here. In fact, most days I hate it. I hate the people I have to work with, I hate that I'm doing things that I wasn't hired to do, and I hate that I'm in a position where I have to do the work anyway. All of those things make me a very unhappy employee.

But mostly, I hate the fact that I somehow ended up so far away from what I actually want to be doing.

When I became an English major in college, I was enthralled with every single one of my classes. I loved reading every form of literature. I loved my creative writing classes. I even loved writing fifteen page research papers analyzing a single theme in a book. I loved everything about my studies.

I never admitted it to myself in college, but I picked my major because I wanted to one day become an author myself. I wanted to write something that would change people's lives.

The only problem was that dream fell very flat the summer after I graduated.

I dabbled in writing my whole life, but I had never seriously sat down to actually finish something that wasn't a required college essay. Somehow, I never realized how difficult the process actually is. Nothing that ended up on paper ever sounded as profound as it did in my head, and I could never bring myself to actually write an entire book. Somehow, in all my years of reading and writing, I never realized how hard writing actually is.

It took me a single anxious and depressed summer of half-assed and incomplete writing to come to the conclusion that I needed to wake up and find a real job. Being a writer was not something I was ready to do.

So, I found a job that was technically in my field that paid a decent amount of money. Actually, it paid more than a decent amount of money. Corporate America pays very well. Which only made me feel guiltier about my choice, because I knew the money would be very hard to walk away from. It only took me a few months to realize that money is a very big reason that people stay in this world, even if it means wallowing in depression until retirement.

Three years later, I'm still sitting in the job that was only meant to be a temporary stream of income until I wrote something. Three years later, I still haven't written anything of substance.

Suddenly, I feel like wallowing in the same sadness I used to mock other cubicle employees for sitting in. I pick at the chicken on my plate with a frown. Despite the healthy meal in front of me, I find myself wanting to go home and crash on my couch.

That thought is enough to shake me out of my depressed stupor. I've noticed in the past that the times when I least want to get a workout in are the most important times to get one in anyway. I scarf down the rest of my meal and decide to fly through the rest of my work as quickly as possible. It's still going to be a long day in the office but if I can be done by 6:30, I can still make it to the gym for class at 7:00. God knows a date with a heavy bag sounds way better than my original plan of running a few miles in an empty office gym.

The rest of the workday seems to both drag and fly. It flies because it's 6:30 before I know it, but I also had so much technical research and writing to get through that at the same time it feels like I've been sitting at my desk for thirty-six hours. I grimace when I finally straighten to stretch my back.

"You're still here, Remy? I thought I was the only workaholic in this office."

I smile tightly at my boss, Brian. I'm often the last one to leave the office and I can confirm that he is very rarely still here at 5:00.

I don't think you can call yourself a workaholic if you leave before your paycheck says you can leave.

"I'm heading out, too," I respond politely. I quickly shut down my laptop and stuff it into my tote bag. "Have a good night. Don't stay too late." He grins at me, seemingly satisfied that I bought into the ruse of his 'late night' at the office.

Thankfully, the gym is only a fifteen-minute walk from my office. I got really lucky that the two places I frequent in my life are so close to each other, and I try to take advantage of that fact as often as possible. I try to make it into the MMA gym three or four times a week, using the remaining days to rest or just run and stretch. Typically, I wouldn't be heading to the gym tonight, but I can feel that my brain is in desperate need of it tonight.

I see Jax as soon as I walk in. He's leaning on the front desk, casually talking to a woman about signing up. I know without a shadow of a doubt that he'll have her sold on a membership before she leaves here today.

A small frown appears on his face when he sees me. He knows I don't usually come in on Thursdays. I smile and wave him off, conveying without words that I'm fine and that he should continue his sales pitch. The frown doesn't leave his face, but he turns his attention back to the woman in front of him.

"Hey, Remy!" my friend Lucy calls from across the gym. I turn to where she's already stretching on the mats. "What're you doing here?"

I shrug as I drop my bag on the side of the mats. "Just wanted to get an extra session in. Had some time tonight."

"Oh. Cool. Let's pair up, then."

I nod. "I just need to change out of this ungodly outfit, I'll be right back." Grabbing my workout clothes from my bag, I start walking toward the changing rooms at the end of the hall. I'm almost to the women's room when the door to the men's room opens and Tristan steps into my path.

I grunt as I run into a solid wall of muscle. I stumble back—yet again priding myself on not wearing heels today —and feel myself steadied by two strong hands as Tristan grips my waist.

My eyes widen as I look up at him. He's looking at me with his usual gaze of stoicism, and I realize suddenly that at some point I had braced my hands on his chest. I pull away as if electrocuted. He holds onto me for a second longer, then lets go and allows me to take a step back.

"You should probably watch where you're going," he says dryly, expression unchanging.

I snap back to reality and aim a glare at him. "Hey, *you* stepped in front of *me*. It wasn't my fault."

He only raises an eyebrow in response.

I huff and roll my eyes. "Whatever, I don't have time for this." I turn to lean down and pick up my clothes that dropped out of my hands during the collision. When I straighten back up, I catch Tristan's gaze quickly snapping back to my face.

My eyes narrow suspiciously. "Are you kidding me?! What is wrong with people today? It's just a goddamn skirt. You'd think I was walking around in lingerie or something."

Tristan's eyebrow quirks again, but he still doesn't say anything. At my insistent glaring he finally shrugs, not at all looking embarrassed by the fact that he just got caught staring at my ass. "An ass is an ass. Even yours." A smirk lifts one corner of his lips. "You should be thankful for the occasional attention. God knows you don't get it when you're not dressed like that."

My glare intensifies. "That's not even a little bit true," I huff, planting my hands on my hips. "I get plenty of male attention. And even if I didn't, I'm not going to sit here and be 'thankful' that some guy is staring at my ass, or that his body is naturally reacting to my body being good breeding stock. Get your caveman head out of your ass."

By now his smirk has grown into a wide grin. I haven't even heard what he's thinking yet, but I can already tell it's going to be condescending. "I don't think I would classify you as good breeding stock, though I'm interested to hear that's how *you* think of women. Wouldn't you need to have big tits and the ability to cook to be valuable to the classic male?"

I ignore the dig—I can't do anything about my cooking but I'm damn happy with my perky B cups.

Ladies, don't ever let a man tell you that size is more important than shape.

"And tell me, what exactly makes you think you're the ideal male?" I ask instead.

"Classic male," he corrects. "But good to know you think I'm the ideal." He cuts off my squeak of protest by continuing, "For one, I'm skilled at combat and could easily protect a partner. I can also hunt for food. But mainly I happen to be exceptionally talented at procreating."

I stare, unblinking, at the grinning man in front of me. Finally, I shake my head and pinch the bridge of my nose. "I've definitely had too much of the male population today," I murmur. "I think I need to go punch things now." I push past Tristan, making sure not to touch him again.

"Try not to think of me when you do it," he calls after me.

"Not a single ounce of me can make that promise," I respond without turning back.

The hour-long Muay Thai class is exactly what I need. I'm so focused on learning the striking combinations that I forget all about my shitty day and the shitty men and women that filled it. Plus, as a bonus, it's an exhausting workout—by the time I'm done, I know I'm going to pass out the second I get home. I pack up quickly after the class is over, wanting to give my body what it's screaming for.

"Remy, are you going to the fights on Saturday?" Lucy asks me as I pull my sweatshirt on.

I nod. "Yeah. Hailey will be there, too."

Lucy perks up at that news and nods her approval. I once again think about how grateful I am that my friends love my sister enough to be happy when I bring her along.

"Nice. Let me know if you guys want to pregame before

you head over. I'm probably going to have people at my house early and then we'll walk to the arena together so text me if you want to come."

"Will do," I respond as I swing my bag over my shoulder. I'm officially itching to be home in my own bed, so I wave at Lucy and start walking toward the exit.

"Have a good night, Remy," Tristan drawls from behind the front desk. "I would tell you not to tempt any other men on your way home, but I think that outfit is doing a decent job of that on its own."

I scowl, looking down at my raggedy college sweats. "Like you don't have old ass Temple University gear still in your closet," I snap.

He grins. "I don't, actually. Because I'm an adult now who actually cares how I look in public. You should try it sometime."

I hear Lucy snicker behind me. Throwing a glare in her direction, I turn my back on the exhausting, meaningless interaction that is every conversation with Tristan and continue towards the exit. In the process I make eye contact with Jax walking out of the heavy bag room on the far side of the gym.

"Remy, you heading out?" he calls to me. "I can give you a ride, I'm leaving now, too."

I nod gratefully. Jax grabs my bag and throws his arm around my shoulders as we walk through the front door. "Let's get out of here. Also, why are you wearing your Temple sweats? That set should've been burned a long time ago."

Tristan's raucous laughter follows us long after the door slams closed behind us.

3

REMY

"Pass me that tequila, Remy baby."

I glare at Jax for using the ridiculous nickname—as well as the fact that he's already drunk, since using my nickname is his dead giveaway that he's not sober.

"I think you should probably cool it, Don Julio," I growl, clutching the bottle of tequila. "I don't need a repeat of the last fight night. Hailey and I could barely carry your big ass out of the arena."

He rolls his eyes but takes a seat at the island anyway, conceding defeat.

Hailey grabs the bottle from my hand and pours two shots, one for each of us. I raise an eyebrow in surprise.

She shrugs. "I feel like drinking a little. Sue me. I haven't been to a fight with you guys in forever, so just do a damn shot with me. You know you want to."

I chuckle and reach for the glass. "Cheers, motherfucker," I chant, grinning at our classic cheers mantra. We clink glasses and down the liquor. And while I barely flinch at the taste, Hailey sputters a little and grabs the coke out of Jax's hands.

He takes turns glaring at both of us. "I hate you both. I'm not even that drunk!"

I cross my arms and glare at him pointedly. "Oh yeah? What starts with 'B' and ends in 'rewery'?"

His nose scrunches in concentration, and I almost laugh out loud at the attempt I know he's about to make at pronouncing the word—the word he's incapable of saying when he's drunk. "Bewery. Wait no, brerry. Fuck. Beerary?"

This time I don't stop the laugh as it bursts from me. Hailey chuckles next to me, too. Jax has so many tells when he's drunk that it's a miracle any of his clients take him seriously during happy hour.

"Fuck you guys. Again. I'm just trying to enjoy my not-in-fight-camp time when I can actually drink."

I roll my eyes. "Being able to drink does not equate to getting so drunk that you try to pick up every girl between our seats and the exit." He chuckles at the memory, clearly proud of the fact that he did actually get a few numbers that night. "And anyway, why aren't you cornering the fighters tonight? Why didn't Coach put you to work?"

He shrugs. "Since Dane's opponent dropped out it's only Max fighting tonight. Tristan's there, obviously, and he wanted Aiden to get some practice cornering, so the three of them have it covered. I wasn't needed. I was given a free pass to watch the fights and *get drunk*." He glares pointedly at me.

I sigh and slide the tequila across the counter. He grins like a kid in a candy store and grabs the liquor, taking a shot straight from the bottle.

"God, men are gross," Hailey groans next to me. "Remind me to never drink anything from this house ever again." She winces and turns back to the tequila soda she poured during Jax's temper tantrum.

I grin as I look over my sister. Sometimes I forget how

ingrained I am in the guys' testosterone-filled world—how much of a tomboy I really am. I don't even notice half the gross boy behavior anymore. As close as she and Jax are, she's too feminine to ever be as close to him and his world as I am. She likes fighting enough to occasionally go to fights with me, but she's never shown any interest in training.

Plus, she's too busy being engaged in the exact opposite sport of fighting: dancing.

She does occasionally work out with me at the gym, though. I'm adamant that the women in my life know some self-defense. It always cracks me up watching her move around because she's got such a dancer's body—skinny but lean, lithe in all her movements—that everything ends up being more graceful than powerful. But she knows enough of the sport, and enough of the fighters, that she fits in with us just fine during our fight outings. For the most part.

There were only a few instances in the very beginning where Jax needed to use his overprotective big brother voice to make it crystal clear to every guy in the gym that she should be seen as their little sister—and to be very much left alone.

I look over her outfit and wonder if drunk Jax will need to issue another reminder tonight. Hailey is wearing black leather pants with a dusty pink spaghetti strap top, complete with black high heeled boots and a long gold necklace that's settled between her breasts. Her blonde hair is long and straight and so shiny that it makes your fingers practically itch to touch it. Her leather pants alone are enough to make her attractiveness stand out, and that's not even taking into consideration that we'll be in a drunk, male-dominated arena tonight.

I look down at my own outfit and once again laugh at how stark the contrast is between us. Hailey looks girly no matter what she wears, whereas I look like a fit chick that would drop kick anyone that looks at me—or more accurately, looks at anyone I love—the wrong way. My black jeans are ripped and distressed along the entire front, and I've paired them with my trademark combat boots. Even though I've topped it with a simple white tank top, I've attempted some femininity by cutting it to end above my stomach. I work hard in the gym and I enjoy showing off my flat stomach and curvy hips when I get the chance. I've taken down my brown hair from its usual messy bun and let it lay naturally straight.

"We should get going soon," Hailey says, interrupting my thoughts. She finishes the last of her drink and then rifles through her purse for the lipstick that I know she wants to touch up before we leave. She finds something and stops, looking up at me.

"You should try this dark burgundy lipstick I just bought," she says, extending the tube in her hand toward me. "I think it's too dark for me but it would look really good with your outfit. Very vampy and badass."

I hesitate before accepting the lipstick. Other than mascara and an occasional winged eye, I rarely apply anything more than a nude lipstick. A dark lip would definitely be a new look for me.

"Ah, fuck it." I walk toward the hall mirror and unscrew the liquid lipstick. I swipe the dark color onto my lips and immediately decide this is going to be my new patented look.

I turn back to my sister with a grin. "I like it. I'm keeping this."

She snorts and rolls her eyes. Grabbing her purse, she nudges Jax and tilts her head in my direction. "How does she look, big bro?"

Jax grunts a half-assed approval. I chuckle, knowing it's the closest thing to a compliment that I'll get from him in regard to my appearance. One of the things I know Jax has appreciated in our friendship all these years is that I've never rubbed it in his face that I'm female. It's also one of the things that's helped me to exist in a male-dominated sport.

"Let's get out of here," Jax says after a final swig of the tequila. He raises an eyebrow and offers me the bottle, which I take with a shot of my own. From the corner of my eye, I see Hailey shudder.

I grin and smack her ass as I walk past her toward the door. "Let's go watch some fights."

The arena is buzzing with excitement. Even though we've arrived fairly early, the building is already half full of drunk fans that are eager for some fights. A few sections have been taken over by a group of people in matching fighter T-shirts, waiting for their friend or family member to make their appearance in the cage. Occasionally a fighter with taped hands can be seen weaving through the crowd, trying to kill their nerves by killing time with their friends. The air smells like sweat, Vaseline, and leather.

"What's our section number?" Hailey yells over the crowd's noise.

Jax, tall as he is, looks over the heads of everyone in front of us and around the arena for anyone from our gym. He spots the group quickly, and grabs Hailey's hand to drag her along behind him in the path that his large frame clears. I chuckle—not for the first time—at the massive size difference between Jax and my little sister.

There are a handful of people already sitting in the section that is saved specifically for our gym. I smile at the girls and give the boys fist bumps.

For the next few hours, we drink beer, watch fights, and talk about training. Fight nights are my favorite nights because my teammates are my best friends and watching fights with them is like the best kind of party. I always think my jaw is going to fall off by the end of the night from laughing so much.

When the lights dim for the announcement of the last fight, everyone in our section stands. My skin prickles with nerves and anticipation and I wring my hands anxiously as we wait for Max to appear. I don't understand how anyone can deal with the nerves before a fight—I can't even handle being nervous for someone else's fight.

The announcer calls Max's opponent first. Our section stays quiet, refusing to boo like some drunk fans like to do when an opponent is called. Instead, I study the guy that steps through the smoke and makes his way down to the cage. I notice that he's tall for this weight class, which immediately makes me nervous because Max often struggles with sparring taller people. In the back of my mind, I wonder if that's why Coach lined up this opponent for him.

"And now introducing his opponent, Max Davis!"

At the announcer's words, our entire section erupts in screams. We make as much noise as humanly possible, cheering Max on as he emerges from the smoke and heads down the walkway. He winks at our group when he passes by, which I take as a good sign of his confidence level going into this fight.

Behind him, Tristan and Aiden are walking with towels and a bucket of supplies. Their faces are masks of complete focus and concentration.

"Where's Coach?" I ask Jax incredulously. "He's not cornering?"

He leans down to talk in my ear. "I heard him say something this week about wanting Tristan to lead more, and that he might put him in charge of the corners tonight instead of just assisting. Guess he actually decided to do it. I've always thought it would help Tristan to see fights from a coach's eyes, instead of just a fighter's. I have a feeling this will be good for his fight IQ."

I watch Tristan as he settles in his chair beside the cage. He places the bucket by his feet and gestures for Aiden to sit in the chair next to him, all the while keeping his focus on Max in the cage. At one point Max turns to look at his cornermen. Tristan seems to give an instruction, followed by a firm nod with a set jaw. Max's eyes blaze at the encouragement and he nods hard in response.

"Ladies and gentlemen, this is a Middleweight matchup and your final fight of the night! Fighting out of the red corner we have..."

I tune out the announcer's booming voice as I continue to wring my hands nervously. After what feels like an eternity, the ref brings the two fighters to the center of the cage and indicates they should shake hands and "fight clean." I watch with wide eyes and bated breath as Max finally backs up to his corner again.

"*Fight!*"

As soon as the two fighters begin circling each other, it becomes apparent that my height analysis is just as big of a factor as I thought it would be. Max's opponent from the red corner is several inches taller, and his limbs are longer. He snaps out a few straight punches to test the distance.

Max slips out of the way, getting a feel for his own distance, as well. He knows he's going to have to get close to land any shots, which means he'll need to avoid any punches thrown his way as he steps in. He aims a few leg kicks at his opponent's long legs, testing his defense.

At one point the fighter in red steps in with a lightning-fast series of punches, stunning Max into falling back a few steps. Red moves to close in on him but Max's movement is slick, and he manages to step out of danger. Red tries again to land his long punches but Tristan is screaming so loudly for leg kicks that Max doesn't hesitate before kicking his opponent's leg just as he steps in to punch.

I look at Tristan, still sitting in his chair and loudly yelling simple, clear instructions every so often. Subconsciously I think about how perfect this role looks on him: not only does he have a great voice for yelling directions over an obnoxious crowd, but he also does so with a confident and knowledgeable tone. Everyone at the gym knows his experience speaks to a very high level of proficiency in the sport, but he also delivers instructions in a calm and steady manner that you immediately know you can trust in. The man was built to be a leader.

I'm distracted, studying Tristan's coaching style when the bell rings to signal the end of the first round. He grabs his stool and jumps in the cage to give Max a place to sit. A very wide-eyed Aiden scrambles in behind him with the bucket.

As Aiden holds a bag of ice to the back of Max's neck, Tristan stands in front of him and begins explaining what he needs to do in the next round. It's a safe guess that Max's opponent won the first round, simply because of the hard combination that landed mid-round. Max was countering Red's long punches with great leg kicks, but it's clear that in this second round Max really needs to get in closer and land some punches of his own.

A sound indicates that the coaches need to leave the cage. Tristan gives Max one last sip of water before smacking him in the shoulder and hustling back to his chair outside of the cage.

The second round starts at a higher pace than the first one did. Red is clearly feeling more comfortable with his long distance and is starting to loosen up and throw more punches. At first, I think Max is struggling with the increased stream of attacks, since he doesn't try to step in closer. But then I spot Tristan's strategy at the same time that Max does.

During the last round as Red threw more and more shots—thinking his pressure was overwhelming his opponent—Tristan must've noticed that each punch got sloppier than the last. Because Red is so much taller than Max, he has to punch down when he throws. Now with every additional punch, Red's hands drop and his shoulders droop. His chin is wide open when he's attacking.

"*Now,* Max, throw it *NOW!*" Tristan bellows. The whole arena vibrates with his urgent command.

At the same time that Red throws a sloppy jab, Max slips to the side. With his opponent's hands and shoulders down, it only takes one big overhand right to the chin for Max to drop his opponent to the canvas. The ref jumps in to stop the fight before Max can jump on him and continue his onslaught.

The crowd *screams* in pleasure at the beautiful knockout. The sound is so deafening that you can't even hear the bell signaling the end of the fight. Everyone around me is shouting and jumping around, giving each other high fives and celebrating the huge victory. I think I'm screaming too.

I look toward the cage and see Max and Aiden hugging, their grins so big it looks like the stretch might actually hurt their cheeks. Tristan stands off to the side with a slightly more composed—but no less excited—look on his face. He grins at a laughing Max and gives him a fist bump. He looks like a proud papa.

Our section can barely quiet down enough to hear the announcer declare the official winner. When he calls Max's name, we erupt in screams all over again.

By the time everyone has cleared out of the cage and Max has disappeared back to the locker rooms, I'm convinced I'll never again have full use of my hearing. I make a mental note that another reason Jax shouldn't be drunk at fights is because he yells too damn loud.

"All right, where's the after party?" he asks us, clapping his hands together with a grin. "Frankie's? First round is on me." His words are met with a loud cheer.

Some people split off to head home, and the remaining dozen start walking toward the nearest exit. Twenty minutes later—which probably would've only been ten if Jax hadn't stopped to get the phone number of a woman we passed—we're all crowded around some high tops at the back of Frankie's.

"I can't believe Max actually knocked that guy out."

"It was like a real-life David and Goliath!"

"It must feel so satisfying to finish a fight like that."

"I'm glad he won. Coach would've put us all through the wringer next week if he had lost."

I sigh contentedly, loving the sounds of happy chatter around me. Obviously, it feels great when a teammate gets a win, but I would've been happy even if we were gathering after a loss. It's the comradery and family aspect that I love about this sport. It's an odd feeling to be a part of a team in what is clearly an individual sport, but until we're standing in the ring with only our fists and our strategy, it's our teammates that are helping to lead us to that point. Regardless of age, gender, or experience, the only requirement to join the team is work ethic and a willingness to help others. We win together and we lose together, and at the end of the day we're just as invested in everyone else's success as we are our own. We're a family.

I look at the people around me. Hailey and Lucy have their heads together and are chatting animatedly about something, so lost in their conversation that everyone else looks completely shut out from their world. The guys are laughing and ripping on each other with no mercy. I see one of them shove another and then immediately crack up, as if it was the funniest thing in the world. Chuckles ripple around their circle.

Jax has one of the newer fighters, Dane, pulled off to the side and is having a serious conversation with him, likely about Max's fight. Jax is gesturing wildly, talking a million words a minute, but Dane is nodding furiously and hanging on to his every word.

"Poor Remy, you look so lonely. No one wanted to talk to you?"

I startle and turn to my right. Sure enough, Tristan is standing next to me, already nursing a beer.

"How did you get here so fast?" I blurt, shocked that he a) got out of the arena this quickly, and b) is here at all. Tristan is well-known for limiting his time with the fighters outside of the gym in a non-professional environment. He likes to keep his distance from his students.

He raises an eyebrow in question, disbelief marring his features. "That's the best question you could come up with? No wonder no one wants to talk to you."

I snap out of my shock and scowl at Tristan before

taking several big gulps of my beer. I can already tell I'm too sober for this conversation.

"What'd you think of the fight?" Tristan asks in an even tone. I take another sip of my beer to try to cover my surprise at his attempting a normal conversation.

"I think it was a good matchup," I respond honestly, looking out over the bar. "I assume Coach took that fight for Max to test his distance and footwork, since that's what he's been trying to fix for months. It was an ugly start, but it looked like Max executed the game plan. The fakes to get inside looked good. And not much actually landed from the other guy, so his stance and footwork is definitely getting better, too."

Out of the corner of my eye I can see Tristan studying me. I'm not sure how much he thinks I know about fighting —especially having never fought before—but it feels like he's impressed with my analysis. After a breath he nods once, then turns back to his beer.

I debate for a moment if I want to say what's on my mind. But then I decide *fuck it, if he can be decent then so can I.*

"You looked comfortable in the coaching seat," I say without making eye contact. His eyebrows shoot up in surprise. "It seemed like you were motivating Max while still keeping him calm. Those guys trust you." And then since it feels like I'll vomit from the sweetness of giving Tristan a clean compliment, I add, "Plus you have a ridiculously obnoxious voice, which means Max could've heard you from the other side of the arena."

Tristan doesn't respond but smirks at my comment. When I turn to smile cheekily at him, our eyes lock. His eyes flit down to my dark lips.

I can't help but squirm under his intense gaze. He's locked onto my mouth for several long seconds, and when he finally looks back to my eyes, I'm wide-eyed and blinking hard. I'm frozen, and for some reason I can't think of a single snarky comment.

Just then, a loud shout goes up behind us. When I turn toward the sound, I see Max walking into the bar with a big grin plastered on his face. He spreads his arms to welcome the cheers that are now rolling through our group and around the bar. His name becomes a chant that even the other bar patrons pick up.

I smile as I watch people approach him with eager fist bumps and claps on the shoulder. The biggest testament to our gym's family feel is everyone's reactions to a fighter's performance. If they put on the performance of their lives and win a belt, we celebrate as if we were the ones that won —and if they suffer a horrible loss, we drown our sorrows at the bar right there next to them. We train as a family; we fight as a family.

"Overhands for days, baby," I grin when I finally reach the man of the hour. He squeezes me in an excited hug, keeping his arm around my shoulders even after he lets me go.

"That is the greatest fucking feeling ever," he says excitedly. "It was so insane, Remy. I actually watched his eyes roll in the back of his skull. I don't think even a good fuck can compare to that feeling." He looks around the bar with a grin. "Not that I wouldn't love one of those tonight, too."

A loud, happy laugh bursts out of me. "Let's get you a beer, hotshot."

I order Max his favorite IPA and then stand quietly next to him at the bar while he regales his fight to our team-mates. Even people that we don't know are listening to him, all of them fascinated by our excitement and interested in hearing about fighting. I smile into my beer, content to watch Max bask in his glory.

After a while I let my gaze wander around the rest of the bar. Hailey is still locked into her conversation with Lucy, and most of the other guys are still glued to Max.

My attention snags on Tristan in the far corner of the bar. He's leaning on a high top, his gaze focused on the cute brunette in front of him. I can't see her face, but I have a perfect view of Tristan's. He's wearing his trademark bad boy smirk and blatantly looking over her body, and I can tell it's having the intended effect because I see the girl giggle and touch his arm, pressing even closer to him. His grin grows.

I turn my attention back to Max, not wanting to stare at Tristan's pickup attempt. I try to focus on whatever weight cut story Max is entertaining the group with.

Barely a minute later, I see Tristan's companion turn away from him out of the corner of my eye. She starts to walk toward the back of the bar, seemingly heading for the restroom. When she turns, I get a look at her for the first time.

She's short, and undoubtedly cute, but only one thing catches my attention: she's got dark red lips.

I can't stop my startled glance toward Tristan. I find him staring at me, eyebrow quirked in question. My own eyebrows shoot to my hairline in surprise.

He grins and finishes the last of his beer, at which point I hurriedly turn away from him and back to my own group. I force myself not to look over at him again.

But when I sneak a glance back a few minutes later, Tristan is gone. I sigh in relief.

Although the feeling of relief is short-lived, because it's not long before I hear Hailey yell, "Remy, come get your man. He's one shot away from once again trying to prove he can shotgun a beer bottle."

I sigh into my beer. Downing the last of it, I leave the bottle on the bar and step into my role of Jax's babysitter.

I groan as I blink my eyes open. Despite only having a few drinks last night, I've always been susceptible to headaches the morning after a night out. I press my hands to my forehead with a wince.

I hear a resounding groan from next to me and turn to see Jax emulating my hands-in-face position.

"The next time you grumble about me taking the tequila from you during the pregame, I'm going to remind you of this very moment," I growl at him. He only grunts and pulls the covers over his head.

I unwind myself from the sheets and slowly stand upright. When my headache doesn't intensify, I pull my sweatshirt over my head and quietly walk out of the bedroom.

I've lost track of the amount of times people have reacted in disbelief when Jax and I have admitted to sleeping in the same bed. Like they can't believe a guy and girl could possibly sleep together without *sleeping* together.

The thought always makes Jax and I cringe.

It doesn't happen as much anymore—only occasionally when Jax gets too drunk, and I want to be sure he makes it to his bed. But it was a frequent occurrence when we were in college. Since we attended separate schools, we wanted to spend as much time together as we could when we actually did meet up, so I often stayed the night at his house. Not once did it ever feel weird or like we wanted to do anything other than sleep.

Sometimes we would joke about how that wouldn't have been possible without the awkward—and cringe-worthy—kiss we shared when we were seventeen.

It probably helps, too, that Jax doesn't have any problem finding a girl to actually sleep with if he wants to. Girls flock to his massive muscular form and charming personality.

I make my way downstairs to the kitchen for a bottle of water. As I turn the corner, I see Tristan straightening from where he's pulling something from the fridge. I balk when I realize he's only wearing boxers.

"Christ, it's too early for this," I squeak, covering my eyes. "Can we tone down the bachelor pad for just long enough for me to get out of here? My eyes are burning."

When I peek through my fingers, Tristan is staring at me with an amused look on his face.

"You know, I'm still not entirely convinced you're not a virgin," he drawls.

"Trust me, I'm no virgin," I mutter under my breath. I see Tristan's eyebrow quirk in response. "I just don't feel like being accosted by borderline nudity from anyone I don't want to fuck."

"Oh, honey, you don't know what you're missing," someone purrs from behind me. I see a self-satisfied smirk stretch across Tristan's face just before I spin around.

And come face to face with the cute brunette from the bar last night.

My eyes widen as I take her in. She's dressed in the same outfit as last night, but her hair is rumpled and there's no sign of the dark lipstick she was wearing. Ignoring my speechlessness, she walks over to Tristan and presses a chaste kiss to his lips. "Call me," she says with a smile, before turning around and walking out the front door.

Tristan's grin seems to grow as my silence stretches on.

"Are you kidding me?!" I finally explode. "You were at the bar for like, fifteen minutes. You actually managed to pick her up?"

Tristan's smile doesn't waver as he shrugs.

I shake my head in disbelief. "Unbelievable," I mumble. "I will never understand what women are thinking."

Finally, Tristan turns away with a chuckle. He grabs his water bottle and steps around me to head back up the stairs. "Regardless, you better get used to it. If you and I are going to be roommates, then you're going to be seeing a lot of it."

I glare at his retreating back. "About that. We still need to set our ground rules. I don't want to deal with a revolving door of women while I'm here." He doesn't respond, which only annoys me further. "Tristan. *Tristan!* I'm serious!"

His chuckle floats down the hallway.

4

REMY

I'm surrounded by bubble wrap and moving boxes when Hailey walks into my apartment later that day. She stands in the doorway and looks around in shock.

"How do you have so much kitchenware for someone that can barely make a grilled cheese?"

I glower at her as I clear yet another drawer. "Very funny. We can't all be Gordon Ramseys, you ass. And I'm perfectly capable of following any intermediate recipe, hence the many kitchen appliances. Now grab some bubble wrap and make yourself useful."

She rolls her eyes and takes her sweatshirt off. She grabs a box and helps me pack the last few drawers in my kitchen.

"How was Jax feeling this morning?" Hailey asks me as we move to the cabinets.

I roll my eyes. "How do you think? He didn't leave his bed until 2:00, and even then, it was just to pay the Chinese delivery guy." I shake my head, remembering the image of an ogre-sized Jax hidden under a blanket opening the door to a wide-eyed Chinese restaurant employee. "I will never understand how he's so bad at drinking when he does so much of it at work conferences and happy hours. How does he keep his shit together for work the day after a bad party night?"

"Your guess is as good as mine," Hailey chuckles.

I reach for the mugs in my designated coffee cabinet. "You seemed pretty buddy-buddy with Lucy last night," I comment. "What were you guys talking about?"

Out of the corner of my eye, I catch Hailey's flinch. I straighten with a frown and turn my full attention toward her.

Recognizing that I'm now expecting a real answer, she starts to fidget with the bubble wrap in her hands, avoiding making eye contact with me. After a long few moments, she takes a deep breath and meets my eyes. "We were talking about long term relationships," she mumbles.

My frown deepens. "What about them?"

Hailey turns back to look at what's in her hands again. "Just about what changes are normal when you've been with someone for a long time. Lucy's been in long term relationships and has seen both good ones and bad ones, so I picked her brain for most of the night." She pauses. "There have been a few things that feel different with Steve lately, and I just wanted to get her opinion on whether or not I should be worried."

I grimace, turning back to the cabinets in an effort to hide my reaction from her. We've always been close to each other and have never hesitated to share something, so the fact that she's talking to someone else hurts me a little. But I want to be sensitive about this, so I don't want my discomfort to make her feel guilty about going to someone else.

Still, I can't help but ask, "Why didn't you want to talk to me about it?"

She finally looks at me, the guilt clearly showing in her

eyes, and I've already decided I can't be mad at her. For anything. "It's not that I didn't want to talk to you, I just... Lucy has experience with this kind of stuff. And you... I know you say you can know everything about your compatibility with a guy in a few months but that doesn't exactly make them long-term relationships. I just didn't think you'd have anything to say. I'm sorry." She hangs her head in shame.

I sigh and climb off the ladder so I can drop myself into the pile of bubble wrap next to her. We're not exactly an affectionate family, but we're open enough to give each other our undivided attention when we talk like this. I want her to know I'm here for her and that she can talk to me about anything, even if she thinks I'll have nothing to say. We know from watching our family that keeping shit bottled up only makes problems worse.

"Do you want to talk about it now?" I ask her softly, punching her lightly in the leg. Mock violence is the extent of any affectionate contact in our family.

She cringes but gives me an honest answer. "Not really," she says softly. After a moment she punches me back. "I'm just really confused and kind of embarrassed about the whole thing, so I didn't want to tell you. But I also don't want to keep you in the dark since I know it's not fair to talk to other people and not you."

I don't say anything. I just wait patiently, giving her time and space to share what she wants.

"Things are just... weird right now," she explains, nervously wringing her hands in her lap. "I can't really pinpoint why. That's why I was talking to Lucy. I was trying to figure out what things are usually like after the honeymoon phase."

I wince and pull my knees up, wrapping my arms

around them. As much as I want to tell Hailey she should break up with the guy if she doesn't want to be with him anymore, I also recognize that she's the only one that can make that decision. If I give her my honest opinion, she'll probably just interpret it as me doing my usual jump-ship routine.

"Are you unhappy?" I finally ask her.

She sighs and leans back against the cabinets. "That's the thing. Not really. I'm happy like 85% of the time. The other 15% I just feel kind of moody and uncomfortable. Which doesn't sound like a bad ratio when I say it out loud. I mean, no relationship is perfect, right?"

"I don't know, Hailes," I tell her honestly. I tighten my arms around my legs and study her thoughtfully. "The only thing I know is that you deserve all the happiness in the world, so if he's not giving you a massive amount of that then he isn't good enough for you."

I see her swallow roughly as she nods and looks down at her hands again. I can sense she wants the conversation to be over, so I try one last shot at honesty.

"But what do I know, I'd jump ship the second Bennie the Bat entered my mind," I shrug.

Hailey laughs and I swear that sound makes my heart happier than any other.

Still chuckling, she reaches for the box that she's been packing my kitchen utensils into. I take her cue and stand to finish my own boxing.

"So, when are the movers coming?" Hailey asks as she tapes up the box, ending our heart to heart. I let her, knowing it's not the last we'll talk about it, but also that I won't push until she makes her own decision.

I can't help the laugh that bursts out of me. "Movers? I practically live at a gym full of massive men. I have the pick of any muscle I want." I reach for the half-filled box of plates.

She flashes a big grin at me. "Yes, you do."

I glare at her over a stack of boxes. "Don't even start. Jax will lose his shit if he hears you're ogling any of the guys again."

"Trust me, I know," she mutters.

"Plus, I'd rather just pay the guys," I continue. "Aiden and Dane are both college students so I know they could use the money. They're coming on Saturday to move most of my shit to a storage locker, and a few boxes over to Jax's place. Once I have the keys to the new apartment, I'll pay them another few hours to move it all." I roll my eyes, once again reminded how inconvenient this whole double-move thing is. "Again."

Hailey winces when she has the same thought. "Hey, at least you got a great deal on your new apartment. Your new place is so cute, I'm actually jealous that you found it so cheap."

I sigh, propping my hands on my hips and looking around my apartment. "Yeah, but I think I'm going to miss this place. This was the first apartment I ever got on my own. It's weird to think I've been here for almost three years. I feel like these walls have seen the biggest phases of my life: post-college existential crisis, moving from the arts to Corporate America, God knows how many shitty boys, all of it." In a moment of uncharacteristic emotion, I pout at the sudden sadness that overcomes me from reliving those memories. "Fuck, I really am going to miss this apartment. Goddamnit, Dan."

Hailey stops wrapping bubble wrap around the mug in her hands and gives me a sympathetic look. "Just think of it as a new chapter. A better one. You've always said your life gets better with every year, maybe what comes next will be even better than the memories you have right now. Starting with that insane kitchen and the wall-to-wall windows in your new apartment."

I sigh and drop my hands in defeat. "I hope so," I mutter.

A week later, I'm parking in front of Jax's house and dragging my last suitcase behind me.

I stop in front of the door and take a deep breath. "It's just ten days," I mutter to myself. "I can do this."

When I finally push the door open and walk in, I immediately hear that the guys already have the fights on. They've also started drinking, which means they're both *screaming* at the TV.

"Ah come on, I saw that head kick coming from a mile away! I can't believe you just got caught with that!" Jax throws a hand up in annoyance. He chugs the rest of his beer and slams it on the side table, which is littered with empty beer cans.

I roll my eyes at their dramatics as I hang my jacket up and walk into the kitchen. "You want another one?" I ask Jax over my shoulder. For the first time in a while, it's only the three of us. Typically, there's a whole horde of fighters lounging on the couches.

"Yeah, thanks," he mutters, distracted.

"You're not going to ask me if I want one?" Tristan teases. "If we're gonna be roommates then we should at least be amicable."

I glare at the back of his head as I grab two beers from the fridge. "As far as I'm concerned, you and I will live entirely separate lives for the next ten days and will try as hard as we possibly can to ignore the other's existence." I walk around the kitchen island and hand Jax his beer. "Basically, every man for himself," I declare as I throw myself on the couch.

Tristan grabs the beer from my hand. "I don't know if I can abide by those rules," he grins. "You're way too fun to infuriate." I try to take the drink back from his hand but he's too damn long for me to even come close to my target.

I scowl and cross my arms over my chest. "How is it possible for you to be this much of a child?" I jump over the back of the couch with a huff and stomp into the kitchen for another beer.

"*I'm* a child?" Tristan says, his hand placed mockingly over his heart. "I'm the one who's trying to put our differences aside and be civil to each other!"

I hear Jax groan and drop his head into his hands. Honestly, I feel the same way. Both of us can see right through Tristan's charade. There's not an ounce of him that actually wants to be friends, he's just enjoying pissing me off.

"Sorry, asshole, that ship has long sailed," I snap as I drop back onto the couch—this time as far away from Tristan as I can be without actually sitting on the armrest. "You said goodbye to our friendship the second I walked into the gym and assumed that just because I was a girl, that I was lost."

He chuckles, probably remembering how mad I had gotten. "In hindsight, I don't know what I was thinking. There's no way your body frame could be a ballerina."

Jax yelps in surprise. "Tristan, are you *kidding* me?!" he yells at his best friend. "This is how you want to start with her? Dude, she's going to *kill* you!"

I shrug off Tristan's comment. Weight and body type are common topics at martial arts gyms, since weight classes are a very large part of fighting. I'm not nearly as sensitive about my weight and muscular frame as I used to be. As it turns out, my ass and thighs are actually a benefit to my fighting style—especially when it comes to wrestling and jiu-jitsu.

"My *body frame* has gotten me five gold medals in local jiu-jitsu tournaments," I grind out.

Tristan smirks and takes a swig of his beer. "You would have a lot more if you'd get out of your head and stop losing to girls you have no business losing to."

My eyes narrow as my body starts to bubble with anger. He's not wrong, but it's annoying that he's noticed my main training flaw.

"I could still submit *you* in under one round," I snarl at Tristan.

His eyes light up in gleeful surprise. "Did you get punched in the head too many times this week? In what world do you really believe that's true?"

Without a word, I stand up and cross my arms—offering a clear challenge.

His face splits into a wide grin. He hands Jax his beer, who is now cringing at what he knows is about to happen.

"You two have exactly *one round*. Joe's fight is starting soon," he mutters to us.

There's a reason the guys don't have a coffee table in front of the TV. Because inevitably during fight nights someone will decide they want to fight. Whether it's wanting to try a move or simply to get out aggression, their friends always end up rolling around on the ground at some point.

MMA is made up of several martial arts: boxing, Muay Thai, wrestling, judo, jiu-jitsu, and a dozen others. We train mostly Muay Thai—which is basically kickboxing with knees and elbows—and Brazilian Jiu-Jitsu at the gym. Jiu-jitsu is a mix between wrestling and chess with the human body. The goal is to use your and your opponent's body to force a submission with either a chokehold, an armlock, or a leglock. It's the ultimate self-defense sport because by definition, size and strength don't matter. Technique is the only thing that matters. It's also very low risk because there are no punches or kicks being thrown, which is why it's the go-to activity whenever people want to fight in the house.

Tristan and I square up in our wrestling stances. I haven't trained with him in a while since he's switched to training during the day, so I'm not actually sure what I'm in for right now. Obviously, I know that he's a pro fighter, so way more skilled and dedicated than me, but I also have faith in my own skills. And my scrappiness.

We circle each other and fake a few shots at a takedown. The grin on his face grows and I realize my face has probably morphed into an expression of sheer focus and determination. He knows he could destroy me at any point but he's enjoying playing with his prey a little longer.

Sure enough, when he shoots for a real takedown, he gets it pretty easily. I land on my back but recover my guard quickly, wrapping my legs around his waist to keep him from being able to pull away. He tries to create space but my 'non-ballerina frame' makes it hard for him to unlock my legs.

As I think about what I know of his fight game—and what I could possibly beat him with right now—I realize that he's still just playing with me. He's very clearly not taking me seriously. He's making rookie mistakes, moving slowly and leaving his arms out for me to easily trap.

Anger starts bubbling through my veins.

In a quick motion, I put one foot on his hip and push off so I can swing it around to trap the arm that he's lazily left out. I grin triumphantly because I can instantly feel that it's a solid attempt at an armbar.

The grin drops from his face and I see his eyes flash in surprise. It takes him a few moments, but he manages to free his arm from my grasp.

Not to be deterred, I use his escape to immediately swing into another submission attempt. This time I trap his other arm and wrap my legs around his neck and shoulders, effectively working to strangle him with my legs.

This chokehold isn't as close of an attempt as the armbar was, but I'm still pretty proud of the speed at which I flipped from one move to the other. I always loved that jiu-jitsu is so strategic—to win you have to anticipate your opponent's moves and be three steps ahead.

It doesn't take Tristan long to escape this submission, either. He shifts toward the side of my body and pulls himself out of my trap. Except now, he's in an even stronger position on top of me because I don't have my legs controlling him.

He quickly manages to throw his leg over my waist and straddle me. In jiu-jitsu this position is called the full mount —and it's undoubtedly the worst position to be in.

Tristan sits up slightly and grins when he sees my angry expression. He knows he's in the best spot to finish our little match.

In a final attempt at a Hail Mary, I trap his hands and bump my hips up as hard as I can. Since he doesn't have his arms to brace with, my motion rolls us easily. And now I'm the one on top of him.

"All right, assholes, round's over," Jax calls. "Joe's fight is starting."

I grin triumphantly down at Tristan. I know technically

neither of us won, but a part of me feels smug seeing the shock on Tristan's face. He almost looks impressed.

"You're too cocky for your own good," I smirk. "If that was a points match, I would've won. That's what you get for not taking me seriously." I stand up without offering him a helping hand. Grabbing my beer, I curl happily into the couch to watch the fight starting on the TV.

I hear Jax snicker. "She's right, dude, you could've beaten her if you weren't playing around the whole time."

Tristan glares at his best friend and stands up. But he doesn't look even a little bit embarrassed. He just shrugs and saunters over to his spot on the couch with the same cocky smirk he had on his face a few minutes ago.

We watch in anxious silence as our friend Joe appears on the TV screen. It's Tuesday night and we're watching an MMA reality show where fighters compete for a contract in the UFC: the biggest MMA organization in the world. Philly is finally starting to make its mark in the sport, which is why we were all so excited to hear Joe got the call to be on the show.

None of us say a word throughout the entire fight. Jax is definitely the closest to Joe, so I know he's concerned for his friend's success. The guys at the gym like to joke that watching each other fight is actually worse than the nerves of their own fights. Which seems absolutely bizarre to me, though I know it's true because I see how they all act with each other.

I can tell Tristan is watching the fight from a fighter's point of view. He's analyzing the strategy, the style, everything that makes the big leagues different from the local circuit he's currently running in. Being undefeated and the champion in one of the local organizations, it's no secret that he's eagerly waiting for his call from the UFC. He gets closer with each victory but for now, he continues to study the televised fights.

Joe ends up submitting his opponent in the third round with a chokehold. It's a great fight, and we all breathe an audible sigh of relief.

"Thank God," Jax mutters. "The gym would've sucked tomorrow with a loss hanging in the air." He yawns, then turns to us. "Okay, I'm going to bed. I grabbed an early flight tomorrow, so I'll be gone by the time you two wake up. Remy, I'll try not to be too loud in the morning."

I snort, both of us knowing there are very few things in this world that can wake me from a dead sleep.

Jax takes turns glaring at Tristan and I. "Okay, then I will say this one time and one time only." He points an angry finger at us. "I love you both, and I really, *really* don't want to come home to a funeral, or the house in pieces. Neither would make me happy. So, if you could somehow find it in your hearts to keep the soul-piercing barbs to a minimum, that would be great." He smiles, the look of a scolding parent now gone. "Other than that, enjoy your time together."

I roll my eyes, knowing that is the opposite of what I'll be doing while I'm here. I glare at Tristan, conveying my displeasure with my eyes. I nudge him angrily with my foot.

"Get up, I want to go to sleep," I growl at him. Since Jax is still here tonight I decided I'm going to sleep on the couch, which means I need Tristan to leave. "And don't you dare try any stupid pranks while I'm out in the open like this because I swear to god, I will make your life a living hell for the next week and a half."

He lets loose a bark of laughter but stands up anyway. "I'm not sure why you think I'm going to abide by your made-up rules in my own damn house, Remy," he says, shaking his head.

"Oh, dear god," Jax mutters, rubbing his eyes. "This was the worst idea ever." With a final glare in our direction, he says, "Don't make me regret this."

He starts up the stairs, Tristan right behind him, when Tristan turns around to wink at me. "Goodnight, Remy baby."

I launch a pillow at his head. "Goddamnit, stop calling me that!" I shriek. He chuckles and disappears up the stairs.

I settle back on the couch with an angry huff. Pulling the blanket up to my chin, I think about how I'm probably going to be throwing a lot of pillows for the next ten days.

5

REMY

The next morning, I wake up to a quiet house. Jax is already gone, and Tristan is probably at the gym. I smile and stretch my arms over my head, happy to have the house to myself for an hour before work. Sitting down with a cup of coffee and a good book is my own form of morning meditation. I glance excitedly at the espresso machine sitting on the kitchen counter.

I swing my feet off the couch—and freeze.

There is whipped cream all over the floor.

There is whipped cream *all over the floor*.

There is *whipped cream all over my feet*.

A red haze begins to cloud my vision. I know in an instant that Tristan did this. He actually *pranked* me.

I grab a pillow and scream into it.

I stand up but fall right back down when I slip on the slick floor. The red haze grows.

I stand again, carefully, and take a few tentative steps toward the kitchen. There's so much whipped cream on my feet that I leave several slippery footprints behind me. I'm seething by the time I reach the paper towels on the counter.

I quickly wipe the whipped cream off my feet. I grab the whole roll of paper towels and set to cleaning up the trail I left, then eventually the origin of the mess. It takes several minutes and several sheets of paper before the evidence of Tristan's prank is gone. I grab the mop to get rid of any remaining residue on the floors.

By the time I'm finished cleaning, I've already planned out Tristan's murder in my head. I grab my phone to compose a text.

Remy: You know, I would've bet money that you'd at least make it to day five. Who knew I'd have to off you the very first day.

My phone lights up with a text reply almost instantly.

Tristan: New rule: no making rules in my house. Because you won't like the ones I come up with.

I furiously type out a response.

Remy: You're an ass. I'm not engaging in a prank war with you just to appease your childish inability to be a decent person. You remember what happened the last time we did this.

Tristan: I still cringe when I see a hair trimmer. But that was a while ago. You wouldn't win now.

Tristan: But I won't continue without your retaliation, or at least without any newly declared "rules."

I angrily throw my phone on the couch. Any semblance of a peaceful morning has completely vanished, leaving me irritated and unhappy. I discard my plans of lounging around with a book and instead stomp upstairs to take a shower and get ready for work. Getting a head start on my workday is better than sitting around here and fuming.

It's a shitty start to an increasingly shitty day. It takes me twenty minutes to catch a bus to work, and then when I finally get to the office, I realize there's construction going on in the building right outside my window. The sounds of machinery give me a migraine that only gets worse throughout the day. That coupled with the fact that the company's engineers have apparently taken asshole pills today, and my whole day has become an increasingly frustrating hump day.

My only savior is knowing I'll be able to punch my frustrations out at the gym later. I leave the office late, so I only make it in time for an hour cardio bagwork class, but it's better than nothing.

I leave everything on the mats. I put my anger into every punch, every kick, until I'm drenched in sweat and struggling to catch my breath.

"Damn, girl, who pissed you off?" Aiden grumbles next to me.

I shake my head, too tired to answer. But then I hear Lucy start to laugh. "She's pissed because she's stuck in the same house with Tristan for almost two weeks," she laughs.

The guys around me look startled. "Tristan? Why?" Aiden asks.

I aim a glare at Lucy for finding amusement in my pain, but answer Aiden's question anyway. "I'm in between apartments for a little bit so Jax offered me his room while he's traveling for work. Unfortunately, that also means dealing with Tristan's annoying ass." I pause, then grumble, "He sprayed the floor with whipped cream this morning so I'd step in it when I woke up."

The gym fills with raucous laughter.

"I'm glad you guys find it funny," I snap. "I hate all of you."

"Can we take bets on who's going to make it out alive?" Aiden grins.

I scowl at my so-called teammates and stomp toward the showers.

It's almost 10:00 when I finally get home. I'm exhausted after my less-than-stellar day, and all I want to do is eat my dinner and go to bed.

I drag myself into the kitchen and onto one of the barstools. I stopped to grab a burger at one of my favorite burger spots in the city and I groan happily when I'm finally able to bite into it. A little bit of joy seeps into my atrocious day.

I'm barely three bites in when I realize I can hear voices coming from upstairs. I pause my chewing and strain my ears to listen.

It only takes a moment for me to realize that what I heard... is exactly what I thought it was.

The red haze from this morning clouds my vision again.

This motherfucker actually has a girl over right now.

I'm fuming when I hear the girl's laughter drift down the stairs. The sound is clear enough that I have a feeling Tristan's bedroom door is wide open. Which he only would've done if he wanted to make this even more awkward for me than it already is. He's probably trying to piss me off by making me stay downstairs until he's done, since there's no way to get to Jax's bedroom without passing Tristan's first.

I let loose a low growl. I cannot *believe* he could be this infantile.

It only takes me a second to decide that Tristan can no longer go unpunished. I tried to be nice—even my house rules were meant to make it easy for us to avoid each other

—but between this and the morning prank, I've had about enough of his games.

I can play games of my own.

I walk quietly up the stairs so they can't hear me coming. Just before I reach Tristan's bedroom, I plaster a shell-shocked expression on my face.

"Oh my god, *Tristan!*" I shriek. "What are you *doing?!*"

They both jump when they hear me come through the door. Tristan is sitting on the edge of his bed, shirtless, and a half-naked girl in only her bra and panties is straddling him. They're both openly staring at me.

I cover my face with my hands and cry loud, fake sobs. "How *could* you?" I cry. "You said I was the love of your life!" I gesture angrily at the girl who has now jumped up and is looking back and forth between Tristan and I. "Who is this bitch? Is she who you've been fucking behind my back?"

Tristan is still staring at me, slack-jawed.

"I—I didn't—" stammers the poor girl. "I didn't know he —I sh-should go." She quickly grabs her clothes off the floor and pushes past me toward the stairs.

"Babe, wait!" Tristan finally says, following her path into the hallway. "She's not who you think! She's—" But to her credit, the girl is already gone.

I chuckle and cross my arms. "Babe?" I mock. "Is that what you call them when you can't remember their names?"

I watch Tristan slowly turn back toward me, anger radiating from every inch of his body.

Every inch of his perfect, muscled body, I realize, as it registers in my brain that he's still half-naked.

I swallow roughly, trying very hard not to let my eyes wander.

"*You,*" he growls. He inches closer to where I'm standing

against the doorway. "Does it make you happy to ruin my fun?"

My nerves fade in the face of his anger. I glare daggers at him and step forward, putting myself right in his face. "*Your* fun?" I shout. "I don't give a shit about your fun! Not when you're trying to make my life a living hell! I was going to be an adult and let this morning's incident slide, but did you really expect me to wait downstairs like a blushing nun while you finished with your sorority girl?"

Despite our height difference we're barely a breath away from each other, both seething through clenched teeth and squeezing our hands into fists. I can actually see the anger flashing like lightning in his eyes. I can feel the fury radiating off of him in waves, can see how badly he wants to throw me out for ruining his night. But I'm just as angry, and there's not a chance in hell that I'm going to roll over and let him keep playing me.

Neither of us wants to be the first to back down.

Suddenly the anger drains from him, to be replaced with his typical cocky grin. His eyes trail across my face, down to my chest that's practically pushed against him because of our closeness, then back up to my scowl.

"Jealous, Remy baby?" he taunts. "You can admit that's why you got rid of her. I would completely understand."

The red haze clouds my vision again—for the fourth time since I moved into this house twenty-four hours ago.

"Hardly," I snap. "She should be thanking me for saving her from a night of subpar sex."

Tristan's white teeth flash in a grin. "Subpar? Hardly," he chuckles. His eyes shine with his arrogance.

He takes a step forward, forcing me to take a step back. With another step he's backed me against the wall. My eyes widen when he braces his hands on either side of my head, trapping me in place. I know I should push him away, but I can't quite catch my breath enough to move. This feels so different from when we train at the gym. Now, there's no purpose for our closeness. Now, there's just emotion and intimidation and... tension. I'm shockingly aware of the fury in his gaze that's cooled to annoyance, and the angry warmth that's still radiating from his bare skin.

We're not breathing from physical exertion; we're gasping from the growing heat.

"Beg me for it and I'll prove it to you," he purrs. "I promise I can fuck you better than whatever nerds you usually sleep with."

A flash of unexpected lust rushes through me and I bite my lip to keep a gasp from escaping. His eyes dart to my lips —and immediately darken when his pupils dilate with that same lust.

"I don't fuck nerds," I say weakly. "I just happen to have a different type than 'arrogant womanizer.'"

He rips his eyes from my lips and grins at my response. His arms drop and he steps away from me.

"You don't know what you're missing," he says. He steps through the doorway to his bedroom but pauses before he actually shuts the door. His eyes pass over my body again. "Actually, you should probably stick with whatever your loser type is. It would take too much time to break you in for my tastes."

He slams his door and I feel my heart drop into my stomach.

It takes me forever to fall asleep that night.

The next day is marginally better than the previous one. I made sure to lock Jax's door before I fell asleep—to ensure no hidden pranks were pulled in retaliation for chasing away Tristan's booty call—and he was already gone by the time I woke up, so I did actually get to enjoy my coffee with a book in the morning.

Work flies by. I barely notice the construction today since I'm buried in documents all day. I've got a few deadlines coming up on Friday and I'm so distracted by the amount of editing that needs to be done that I do a double take when I realize it's almost 6:00.

I curse mentally. I'm meeting Hailey for dinner tonight and our reservation is set for 8:30. I was really hoping to get a workout in before we gorged ourselves at the new Italian restaurant but now that it's so late, I'll probably only have enough time for a quick run.

I clean up my desk and pack my bag, grumbling to myself the entire time. I decide to head down to the gym in the basement to get a treadmill run in before I go home to get ready.

My four miles fly by quickly. I think females have decent cardio to begin with but couple that with my workouts at the MMA gym and my weekly runs, and I'm in the best shape I've ever been in. Even as a teenager, I preferred to be strong and healthy. MMA was the perfect sport for me in that sense.

The physical exercise puts me in a happy mood. Although today's been an uneventful, decent day to begin with, a rush of endorphins always puts me in a great mood. I typically cool down with stretching that doubles as meditation, but I don't quite have enough time for that today. Instead, I grab my stuff, throw on my hoodie, and call an Uber as I walk outside. Fifteen minutes later I'm already walking into the house.

I see Tristan standing in the kitchen as soon as I open the door. He's got an empty plate in front of him and he's holding a half-empty water bottle in his hand. But after one glance at him it takes everything in me not to let my jaw physically drop to the floor.

I can't decide which I want to focus on first: the black suit pants that are tight enough to showcase his strong thighs and grabbable ass, or the white button-up shirt that's stretched across his massive chest and rolled up to his elbows to expose his muscular forearms.

He is... heart-stoppingly sexy.

It takes me a second to figure out why he's dressed up. I heard Jax mention a few times that Tristan will occasionally work a nighttime security shift, but I never really considered what that would look like. Although now that I think about it, security guards do typically dress like he is now.

I just tend to picture them as fat old men—not stunning young sex gods.

I internally shake my head to clear my traitorous thoughts. I force myself to remember how furious he made me yesterday with his stupid games, and how frustrated I had felt after he cornered me against the wall.

Okay that thought process isn't helping to steer me away from my inappropriate thoughts...

Luckily, he interrupts my inner turmoil. "Well, well, if it isn't Ms. Cockblock," he taunts.

I shoot a glare at him as I throw my bag on the couch— any expression that isn't open-mouthed staring. Walking around the island, I open the fridge to grab a water bottle of my own, trying to avoid any further eye-fucking.

"You deserved it," I snap. I turn to face him and lean

against the counter as I take a sip of the water. The cold is shockingly refreshing and seems to calm my nerves.

"Consider us even," I continue. "Now can we go back to the rules I kindly suggested in the very beginning? Just call a truce and go back to ignoring each other?"

He crosses his arms and stares at me for a moment, but he doesn't answer my question.

I roll my eyes. "Whatever. I don't have time for this. I'm going upstairs to shower."

A smirk finally curls the corners of his lips. "Want me to join? You're clearly enjoying my appearance tonight. I assure you I look even better in the shower." The smirk stretches into a wide grin. "I'll even help you pick out the right outfit after."

A furious blush lights my cheeks at having been caught checking him out. My embarrassment causes me to lash out. "Don't flatter yourself," I snap. "It's just weird seeing you dress for a job that doesn't involve rolling around with sweaty men." He doesn't react to my taunt, just continues leaning against the counter with his arms crossed over his chest and a grin on his face.

Feeling both flustered from Tristan calling me out and panicked that he'll continue his teasing, I hurry from the kitchen and head upstairs to get away from him as quickly as possible. I select an outfit for dinner tonight and head to the bathroom to get ready.

A minute later, I'm standing under the rainfall shower and exhaling the tension I didn't realize I was holding onto. I mentally slap myself for letting myself be so affected by Tristan.

It's never really been like this with him before. Sure, I always knew he was attractive, but that's about all that was likeable about him. He was too arrogant and too selfish for me to be interested in him in any real capacity. Other than Jax, the only thing he ever seemed to give a shit about was fighting, which meant even women didn't matter to him beyond being a good fuck. And since I'm not interested in sleeping with a coach that I'm going to have to see every day after he tosses me to the curb, sex has always been completely off the table. Which just leaves the option of friendship.

That, obviously, hasn't worked out either. I'm not sure he even knows how to be friends with a woman. So instead, we've been insulting each other for three years and trying not to kill each other for Jax's sake. It's never gotten so bad that one of us has actually hurt the other, but it's clear to anyone that sees us interact that we really don't like each other. I can count on one hand the amount of positive interactions we've had over the years. Jax tries to keep us apart as much as possible but between training at the gym, fight nights at the house, fights at the arena, and the average house party between the gym family, it's pretty much impossible to keep us apart entirely. Over the years we just had to learn to deal with each other.

But there's never been a sexual undertone like there is now. Tristan has never flustered me as much as he has this week. I can't figure out if it's the forced proximity or the absence of Jax, but ever since I ran that sorority chick out of his bedroom, it's like there's a charge between us. I'm not sure if it's an "I wanna fuck you" charge or an "I'm minutes away from killing you" charge, but it's definitely there. He's thrown me off my game this week and flustered me way more than I'm comfortable with. Not to mention I'm noticing his physical appearance now, which is absolutely unacceptable.

I shudder, remembering how he looked at me after he

had backed me into the wall last night. Hours later, I still couldn't stop thinking about what it felt like to have his heated gaze on me. I tried—and failed—to keep my brain from imagining what it would be like to lick his lips. To be caged underneath him. To feel him take his anger out on me. Even now, my brain is caught up in the image and my hand is trailing down my stomach...

I growl in disgust at my own thoughts and reach forward to turn the water to cold. I can't keep thinking like this. Tristan is an ass, and off-limits, so anything happening between us is a huge no-no.

That is, if he would even have me. I haven't forgotten his words last night. No, the only solution is to continue ignoring him and hope he gets tired of his games.

A small thud interrupts my thoughts. I frown, straining to hear what the sound was.

Eventually I decide it was probably the front door slamming shut as Tristan left for work. I turn back to the loofah in my hand and set to washing the rest of my body under the cold water.

Thoroughly chilled and with thoughts of Tristan banished from my mind, I turn the water off and reach for my towel.

My hand meets only air.

I pull back the shower curtain with a frown and look to where I had hung my towel up.

It's not there.

I look around, my frown deepening. My clothes aren't where I left them on the sink, either.

My eyes go wide. Suddenly I realize what's happening—what the sound was that I heard.

"*TRISTAN!*" I scream.

He's already there on the other side of the door, chuckling.

"Are you *kidding* me?!" I shout. "You *stole* my *clothes?!*"

I can practically hear the smirk in his voice. "I'm sure I have no idea what you're talking about."

I let out a low growl and start pacing the bathroom. "Come on Tristan, I don't have time for this! Just give me my clothes back! Or at least give me a towel, damnit."

He chuckles again. "Nah, I think I'd rather watch you fumble your way through this." He laughs again. "You know, I did offer to help with your outfit. Maybe next time you'll take me up on it instead of getting defensive and yelling at me. Now you're stuck with an outfit that I *know* you're not happy with."

"*Fuck you*, Tristan!" I explode, trembling with fury. I hate, more than anything, when men hold power over me. And right now, standing wet and naked on the cold porcelain tile, I feel as powerless as I have in a long time. "I would rather go through my entire day naked than shower with you."

This time he lets out a loud, raucous laugh. "You wouldn't be saying that if you knew what it looks like when water is running down my naked body. You'd actually be drooling at the chance." I don't even have to imagine the smug look that I know is on his face.

A shiver runs through my body and I'm so glad he can't see me right now. He would never be able to miss the way my nipples harden at that thought.

"You just keep telling yourself that," I snap. "Whatever keeps your precious ego inflated."

I keep pacing, trying to figure out how the hell I'm going to get out of here. "You know you really are the worst kind of asshole," I growl through clenched teeth. "Either you make me sit in here, wet and cold, until you take pity on me and let me out, or you make me suffer the humiliation of walking out of here naked. Either way, I repeat: you are an *asshole*."

I can easily picture his quiet grin on the other side of the door.

"Oh my god," I realize quietly. I stop pacing and stare, dumbfounded, at the door. "You really don't think I'll do it."

"I know you won't," he mocks. "That's why this is fun."

If it were anyone else, or any other situation, he'd be absolutely right. I would never let someone see me naked like this. It's not that I'm ashamed of my body, because I'm not—I work hard in the gym and I'm proud of the way my body looks. But seeing me fully naked is an intimate thing, something that only one other boy has ever seen. Other boyfriends only ever saw me in the dark, or partially clothed. I never wanted to give them the space or time to see my body. It felt like an intimate secret that I didn't want to share with just anyone.

Despite all of that, there's one difference in this situation: I hate seeing Tristan win. I have no problem showing myself if it means beating him at his own game. Hell, of all the reasons to show off my naked body, this is probably at the top of the list.

And all of a sudden, I'm the one who's grinning.

I straighten up and lift my chin. Before I can think too hard about what I'm about to do, I open the door and step out into the hallway.

Tristan is leaning on the railing, arms crossed, with a giant smirk on his face. He's enjoying my torture way too much. But when he sees me step out of the bathroom, his entire demeanor changes. His eyes go wide.

Then his gaze begins trailing down my body. I can feel the blush light my face on fire, but I don't break my stare—I won't give him the satisfaction of my embarrassment. I keep my focus locked on his face as I walk slowly toward him. His eyes snap up to meet mine once I'm standing in front of him.

His shock over my action and obvious appreciation of my body immediately inject me with confidence. I push my breasts forward and cock my hip to the side to accentuate my curves. Of all the power games we play, in this moment, I know I've won this round. And I want nothing more than to make sure he knows that.

I smirk at his expression. "You know," I purr, tracing my finger down the front of his shirt, "it's not exactly the best proof of your social prowess if you have to trick a girl into getting naked and wet for you."

I saunter down the hallway to my bedroom and slam the door behind me.

6

TRISTAN

Damn, she has a great body.

I mean, I always figured she did, but I had no idea she was hiding all *that* under her clothes at the gym.

I wasn't wrong about her body not being the ballerina-type—it's better. She's thin but toned, with subtle muscle definition everywhere I look. Her abs are flat and tight. At the sight of her perfectly shaped tits and the water drops that tease me as they run over every mouth-watering curve of her body, I'm pretty sure I totally fail at not gawking at her. And when she turns around to walk back to Jax's room, I definitely can't help staring at her perfect, round ass.

I honestly didn't expect her to meet my challenge, but I can hardly say I'm disappointed.

Remy Porter is nothing if not exciting.

I'm gone long before she finishes getting ready. Part of me wonders if I don't trust myself not to pounce on her if I see her again tonight, since two nights of teasing and no action can make a guy a little hard-up.

Even last night had been a challenge to tear myself away. The sorority girl—whose name I had indeed forgotten—

was partly a booty call but was mostly invited over to piss off Remy. I had only wanted to establish that she wasn't allowed to set rules in my house.

I didn't anticipate her fighting back and driving the girl off.

It was actually impressive. That she came up with the idea so quickly and managed to get the girl out without even a hiccup was almost admirable. Unfortunately, it left me with a hard-on that I later had to take care of myself.

What made the situation even more annoying was the fact that I wanted to take it out on Remy.

I always knew she was hot, but she spent so much time glaring daggers at me and spitting hateful words that I never really felt the need to look at her as anything other than Jax's annoying little friend. Being shit on doesn't exactly make me want to take a girl to bed. Plus, I'm pretty sure Jax would kill me if I ever made a move to. Between her smart mouth and the constant presence of Jax, it was easy to ignore even the fleeting thoughts of wanting a hate-fuck.

She's always come off as a bit of a bitch to me. Maybe even a little pretentious. I've never blamed her for thinking I'm a womanizer—because I *am*—but that's hardly a reason to think you're better than someone else. I don't get the feeling she acts that way because I'm a fighter, since she's obviously fine with Jax being the same, so I'm not sure what makes her look down her nose at me. Possibly the fact that I'm not using my business degree or working in an "acceptable" career—my parents love that excuse. But with Remy, I could never be bothered to find out. In general, I don't give two shits about what people think about me.

But even if I could get past all of that, I'm also fairly certain she's a prude. Which is yet another reason I've never shown her a sliver of interest. She hates the mention of sex, and she actually seems to hate it when I'm not clothed. Most girls smile or fawn when they see me shirtless, but Remy's never done either of those things—she just gets flustered or, more often than not, angry with me. I've also heard from Jax that she's only ever dated nerdy types for a few months at a time, which I consider another clue that she's probably inexperienced or a prude. None of which align with my specific sexual preferences. So, I definitely never looked at her with any interest.

Until she moved into my house.

In only two days I can already feel that she's beginning to burrow under my skin. The sudden close proximity from being in the same house is forcing us to interact in ways that we've never had to deal with before.

And it's starting to get my dick hard.

Before long, I'm too tired even for thoughts of Remy. Training killed me today and it's taking everything I have to stay awake for tonight's security job. It's a good gig to have on the side but right now, all I want to do is go home and pass out.

It's 4:00 in the morning when I finally crawl into bed, fully clothed. And it feels like only five minutes later that my alarm is ringing, waking me up for the early classes that I have to teach.

The only thing that gets me through the morning is years of training that have taught my body to function normally even under extreme exhaustion. Still, I exhale a sigh of relief when the gym empties out between morning and afternoon classes, finally giving me enough time to take a nap.

I dream of a naked, wet brunette.

When I wake up, I'm even crankier than before. The last thing I need in my life right now is a distraction—

especially if said distraction has an attitude the size of Texas.

Thankfully, Aiden notices my grunts of frustration and asks if I want to grab a drink after class. I nod stiffly. A drink would probably calm me down.

An hour later, Aiden, Max, and I are crowded around a high top at one of Center City's best hole in the wall bars. It's Friday night so there's a decent amount of people around us. Even the music is louder than normal, with several people milling about on the makeshift dance floor.

I take a long sip of the whiskey in my hand, already feeling the tension start to ease from my shoulders. Between being left high and dry two nights ago, and Remy's teasing performance yesterday, I've been unusually wound up for the past few days. I probably just need to get laid so I can chill out again.

I shake the sudden thoughts of Remy from my head. Even if it's just a physical attraction, I definitely need to stop thinking about that girl—nothing good could possibly come of anything happening between us. That is, if she even wants something to happen between us. God knows she seems to hate my guts.

I shake my head again. Surely there's a hot blonde some-where in here that can ease all my frustration. I turn to scan the bar.

And immediately lock eyes with Remy Fucking Porter.

I scowl. This is now the second time in a month that I've run into her at a bar, and it's starting to piss me off.

The guys spot her at the same time that I do.

"Hey, Remy and Lucy are here," Aiden says from next to me. "Let's go say hi."

He and Max start to head over to where Remy and Lucy are leaning against the bar. I scowl again but follow behind them, realizing that hanging behind would be even more awkward than just acknowledging her.

I scan her from head to toe as I walk closer. Her outfit is simple—ripped skinny jeans with her trademark combat boots and a strappy black top that shows off her small but perfectly shaped tits. Her hair is loosely curled and falling over her shoulders, looking so shiny that I feel the sudden urge to wrap it around my fist. That urge is only slightly beat out by the temptation of her full, pink lips.

She looks fucking delicious.

I growl internally at the memories that flood back of her naked body standing in front of me yesterday. Even just the glimpse of her cleavage now is reminding me how perky and pink her nipples are, how much I'd wanted to fall to my knees so I could lean forward and taste them.

She seems to be remembering the same thing.

Even in the dim lighting of the bar, I can see the pink that now tinges her cheeks. This is the first time we've seen each other since the "shower incident"—as my brain now refers to it—and she definitely looks embarrassed. For how cocksure she seemed strutting out of the bathroom yesterday, she doesn't look nearly as confident right now.

Her unease helps me regain some of my own control. I grin as we reach the bar.

"Hi, ladies," I drawl. "Fancy seeing you here."

She glares at me—per usual. "What are you guys doing here?" she snaps.

Aiden chuckles under his breath and shoots me a knowing look. If he didn't understand my foul mood before, Remy's extra snappy tone probably just connected the dots for him.

"We just wanted to let off some steam after the gym," he answers smoothly. "What about you two? Stressful week?"

If looks could kill...

Remy's eyes burn with her barely-concealed hatred. They hold mine, unrelenting. "You could say that," she growls.

I grin, loving the effect I have on her. I've always thought she's sexy when she's angry, even before this week. That's why I always loved to rile her up. "Why don't we buy you two another round?" I offer innocently. I can't help the taunt that slips from my lips. "We'd love to *shower* you with our attention tonight."

If she wasn't seeing red before, she definitely is now. I notice her knuckles turn white on the glass she's holding, and my grin widens.

"Thanks, but no thanks, asshole," she spits. She grabs Lucy's arm and looks apologetically at the two guys beside me. "Sorry guys, we'd love to stay and chat but if I don't get a bar's worth of distance away from Tristan, I might become responsible for the derailment of your golden boy's career. Have a good night." And without a second's hesitation, she pulls Lucy to the other side of the bar. I vaguely register Lucy grumbling something about "so much sexual tension."

"Damn, dude," Aiden mutters next to me. "What the hell did you do to her?"

I laugh and take another sip of my drink. "If I tell you, she'll definitely derail my career."

For the next hour, we mingle around the bar, talking to friends that we run into and chatting up a few girls. Both Aiden and Max are clearly athletes that radiate single vibes, so girls tend to gravitate toward us. At one point we manage to capture the attention of a very drunk, very horny, bachelorette party.

I politely chat with the bride herself, trying my best to ignore the blatant bedroom eyes she's throwing my way. I'm not a fan of the cliché pre-wedding infidelity in general but I'm also just not interested in the pretty blonde. She's so obviously throwing herself at me that it's actually a turn-off. I find myself wishing she would at least give me the illusion of a chase, maybe push back with a joke or a snarky comment.

My eyes scan the room, landing on Remy sitting at the bar. She's sitting sideways on the barstool, laughing loudly at something Lucy just said. There's no trace of the anger or resentment that she wears when she talks to me. She actually looks... happy.

I glance down at the glass in her hand and notice she's drinking a clear liquid on the rocks. I vaguely remember Jax telling me she's not really a drinker but that when she does, she goes for tequila. Which immediately makes her very, very happy.

I'm barely aware of the bride droning on about some crazy college experience that she had, completely clueless to the fact that I'm not listening. Instead, I study Remy's body language. Her shoulders are loose, her smile happy. She's animatedly telling Lucy a story about something, her hands gesturing wildly to emphasize whatever it is she's talking about. And when she hears a certain song come on, she gasps and grabs Lucy's arm. She pulls her friend onto the dance floor and they start dancing to the upbeat tune.

If any part of me was paying attention to the bride in front of me, it definitely isn't now.

I can't take my eyes off of Remy. I've never seen her dance before.

It's fucking mesmerizing.

Her hips move from side to side, her movements fluid and comfortable. She's always been graceful at the gym— light on her feet and in total control of her body—so it makes sense that she's the same on the dance floor. She raises her hands above her head as she continues to roll her hips.

I probably would've been lost in her trance for hours if I didn't notice the guy slide in behind her.

Without any word or introduction, he slides his arms around her waist and pulls her tight to his body. His jerky hip movements are cringe-worthy.

All happiness drops from Remy's face. She scowls, her brows furrowing more than they ever have with even me, and she tries to push his hands off. But the asshole isn't loosening his grip.

It looks like she says something to him because he grins, the smile stretching across his face in what seems like victory. He lets her turn in his arms to face him.

She points a finger threateningly at him. When he doesn't respond, she puts her hands on his chest and tries to shove him away again.

The whole thing seems to happen in an instant. It takes me a second to register what's happening, and a few more seconds to stride across the bar.

I shove the guy away from Remy, fury boiling in my veins.

"She said, *back off*," I bark. I hold my ground between Remy and the asshole.

"Yo, man, we were just talking," he snaps at me. "Get lost, this doesn't concern you."

I step closer—almost close enough for our noses to touch—and let loose a low growl. "Unless you want me to make your nose splinter into your skull, I suggest you turn around and get the fuck out of this bar," I snarl. "*Now*."

If my tone wasn't enough to convey my message, I straighten up to impose my height over the five-foot-something prick. That coupled with the fact that he looks like Remy can lift more than he does, and the decision should be an easy one.

The asshole glances away nervously and takes a step back. "Fine," he eventually mutters. "Fuck you both." Then he turns around and shrinks out of the bar.

As soon as he's out of sight, I turn back to Remy.

She shoves me, a scowl on her face. "I didn't need you to save me," she snaps. "I could've gotten rid of him on my own!"

I ignore her comment. I still feel the anger lingering in my chest, so I send some of it her way. "You shouldn't be dancing by yourself," I bark at her.

At some point in the past few minutes Lucy must've left Remy to get them another drink at the bar, which is why she seemed vulnerable enough for the guy to come onto her. "At least keep Lucy with you, otherwise guys are never going to stop coming onto you like that." My eyes drop to her exposed midriff and heaving chest. "Especially if you're wearing that."

Her jaw drops in shock. But she composes herself quickly, crossing her arms over her chest as she glares at me. "So, it's *my* fault that guy is a piece of shit that can't keep his hands to himself?!" she yells in disbelief.

I wince and look away. "No, of course not," I grumble.

Obviously, everything that just happened is one hundred percent that douchebag's fault. But I'm flustered from not being able to control my anger—flustered from the appearance of it at all. Even though I can hear myself being a dick, I can't stop myself from snapping, "We should just go home. I have an early day tomorrow and Jax would kill me if he knew I left you here after what just happened."

Remy is back to looking shocked again. "I'm not leaving,"

she says, disbelief and anger still warring in her eyes. "I don't need you to look out for me. If you want to go, then go. But you can't just order me around, Tristan." She hisses the last part, and it takes everything in me not to just grab her and throw her over my shoulder.

"Fine," I snarl. I turn around and stride back to the high top where I had been standing with the guys, the bridal party nowhere in sight. I barely register that Aiden and Max are a step behind me, having appeared as silent backup during the altercation. I remind myself to thank them once I'm calmer.

When Remy realizes I'm not leaving, she turns back to the bar in a huff. Every few minutes she glances my way, then scowls when she sees I'm still there, still watching her.

But I meant what I said. Jax would be pissed if I left her here so I'm not leaving. I just need to wait until she finishes her temper tantrum and realizes that if it weren't for my comment, she would've left already anyway.

She gets angrier with every glance my way.

Suddenly, she turns to the guy next to her. He's been sneaking glances at her for the past few minutes, but she's had her back to him—until now.

He eagerly starts a conversation with her. She laughs easily, touching his arm when she does, and leans in too close. She angles her head so he can talk into her ear, over the music. Every movement, every touch, is intimate.

I would've bought her little performance if she didn't lock eyes with me the next time he whispered in her ear. I force a wide grin on my face and wink at her, signaling that I know exactly what she's doing.

She scowls and tugs the guy a little closer.

It's the moment I finally give up.

I turn to Max and Aiden and notice with surprise that

they're talking to two cute girls. I've apparently been oblivious the entire night. "Sorry to interrupt, ladies," I drawl, "but I'm going to head out. I'll see you at the gym tomorrow. Have a good rest of your night." I give the guys a fist bump and flash a quick smile at the girls.

I was willing to wait around while she hung out with Lucy, but I'm not third wheeling if she wants to bring a guy home. Even Jax's wrath isn't worth that ego hit. She's a grown ass woman that can make her own stupid decisions.

I don't even glance in Remy's direction as I leave the bar.

7

REMY

I watch Tristan leave the bar, surprised to feel a pang of guilt in my chest.

I hate leading on the guy next to me—Chris, I eventually figured out—but I'm furious at Tristan for trying to order me around. Who the fuck does he think he is? I don't need his protection. I fight guys for fun, for God's sake. I'm not the kind of girl that needs to be coddled.

Still, I can't shake the twinge of guilt I feel for driving Tristan away because of my stupid game. I hate playing games. I should've just ignored him and left when I wanted to leave. But he made me so angry that I couldn't stop myself from trying to piss him off further. I don't know if he thinks I'll sleep with this guy, but I seem to have convinced him enough to get him to abandon his alpha male efforts.

So now I'm left with a hopeful, clueless guy at the bar and an angry Tristan waiting for me at home. *Fuck.*

I briefly contemplate following Tristan home and giving up on my game entirely. But then I remember his face when he all but ordered me to go home with him, and I quickly wave that idea away.

Instead, I spend another twenty minutes politely chatting with Chris, making sure not to touch him anymore. Maybe if I wait long enough, Tristan will be asleep by the time I get home. Eventually, I turn to Lucy with pleading eyes. She hides her smile, knowing exactly what I'm silently begging her for.

"Remy, we should get going," she says, shooting Chris an apologetic glance. A slight frown crosses his face. "We have an early session at the gym tomorrow and it's getting kind of late."

"You're probably right," I agree. I turn toward Chris with a smile, trying to hide my guilt at leading him on as best I can. "It was nice to meet you. Thanks a lot for the drink." I stand up off the barstool.

Chris blocks my path, his body angled in front of me, and one arm braced on the bar. I'm not completely blocked in but he's definitely too close for comfort. My eyes widen in surprise.

"I'd love to see you again sometime," he says, pulling me in by my wrist. "Can I get your number?"

I lean back, trying to recapture some of my personal space. I'm shocked that Chris is bold enough to try something like this, since he was too nervous even to say anything to me before I initiated the conversation. This must be his Hail Mary.

Unfortunately, all it succeeds in doing is pissing me off.

"Sorry, no," I say firmly. "I don't think that's a good idea. But again, thank you for the drink." Without waiting for a response, I grab Lucy's hand and pull her out the door.

We stumble out to the street. "Jesus, you've got everyone fawning over you tonight," Lucy laughs. "Two strangers at the bar and now you've got Tristan waiting at home to spank you." Her grin is downright evil.

"Lucy!" I yell in horror. "Tristan is *not* interested in me! What would possess you to say something like that? Did you not see how much of an ass he was tonight?"

"Girl, all I saw was a very protective, very angry Tristan who did not want any guys anywhere near you tonight. That translates to being interested."

"He's just being protective because he knows Jax would kick his ass," I mumble.

Lucy chuckles and shakes her head. "You tell yourself whatever lie makes you feel better."

I glare at her as I wave down a taxi but give her a hug anyway. "Thanks for tonight," I say. "I'll see you at the gym in the morning."

"Yup, see you then. Have a good night." She aims one last mischievous grin my way before the taxi pulls away from the curb. I flash a less-than-ladylike gesture at the retreating car.

It takes me a minute to flag down my own taxi and less than ten minutes to pull up in front of the house. I gulp nervously as I get out of the car. It's been a while since Tristan left the bar so I'm really hoping he's already asleep.

He's not.

He's sitting on the couch flipping through the TV channels. He's wearing sweatpants and nothing else.

As in, he's *shirtless.*

I almost fall over my feet as I walk into the house. I've seen him shirtless plenty of times at the gym—it's undeniably sexy there, too—but there's something so much more erotic about seeing him lounging shirtless in the comfort of his own home. He's so fit from fighting that he doesn't even have to try for the eight pack, or for the V on his hips that drags my attention down...

"Look who decided to finally make the walk of shame," he taunts without looking away from the TV, effectively interrupting my very inappropriate and unhelpful train of thought.

I scowl and cross my arms. "Not that it's any of your business, but I did not fuck that guy."

He chuckles. "Yeah, Remy, I know you. You're too much of a prude for a quick fuck in a bar bathroom."

Any guilt I feel for tricking Tristan tonight flies straight out the window. My control snaps.

"I'm not really sure why you think you know *anything* about my sexual proclivities—and frankly it's a bit creepy how much you *think* you know—but I assure you, Tristan, your sources are sadly mistaken. Maybe I would've gone home with him if he hadn't—if he—never mind..." my voice trails off because I realize I don't want to admit how my interaction with Chris had ended.

In an instant, Tristan is on his feet. Before I even realize he's moved, he's standing only a few inches away from me and holding my wrist in an iron grip. His other hand grasps my chin and lifts my gaze to meet his. His eyes are burning with the same fury that I saw in them earlier tonight, except now it looks like there's a sort of panic mixed in them, too. "What happened?" he demands. "Did he touch you?"

"N-no, of course not," I stammer. "Nothing happened—"

His fingers tighten on my chin. "Don't lie to me, Remy," he growls.

The accusation snaps me from my nervous haze. "I said nothing happened," I snap, tearing my face from his grasp. "And anyway, how is this any different from what that guy did to me tonight? You're just as much in my space as he was."

I ignore the part of my brain that's screaming this feels *nothing* like the other encounters.

The anger dims in his eyes. Instead, I see a flicker of

something else, just as a cocky smile slides across his face. He leans forward to whisper in my ear, brushing his lips lightly over my skin and causing a shiver to ripple through me. The lingering smell of whiskey entwines with his male scent and envelopes me in an intoxicating bubble.

"The difference is, I know for a fact that you like me being this close to you—that you're actually soaked right now," he purrs.

I can't stop my sharp intake of breath. As if on cue, my cunt starts throbbing. Suddenly all I can think about is how badly I want him to bend me over and fuck me until the sun comes up.

He pulls back and stares in amusement at the expressions flitting across my face. He knows exactly what kind of war he just started in my brain. He always knows. And he always enjoys it.

"That's pretty self-assured, even for you," I manage to say. "Unfortunately, it's a ridiculous theory."

His grin spreads wider. He reaches up to run a fingertip lightly down the side of my face. "Prove it," he says in a deep voice. My heart is beating so hard that I'm sure he can hear it.

"I'm not going to sleep with you," I blurt.

He tilts his head and studies me with a curious expression. "Okay," is all he says. He shrugs and runs his finger down the side of my face again. As if my blatant rejection doesn't bother him at all.

He trails his finger from my cheek to my lips, his touch feather light. He slowly, gently, traces my lips with his thumb. He pauses at the center of my bottom lip.

His smoldering gaze feels like it's cutting through all my secrets, yet I can't bring myself to look away. Just when I start wondering if it's possible to combust solely from eye contact, he pulls his finger from my lips and sucks it into his mouth.

It's like a direct line to my aching core. When I catch a glimpse of his tongue wrapping around his finger, my breath catches and wetness pools between my thighs. That feeling only multiplies tenfold when he growls, "I knew you would taste like cherries."

His face leans closer to mine and for a second, I think he's going to kiss me. I feel my heart rate spike to unhealthy levels.

But he just brushes past my mouth and presses his lips against my ear. "I think you're going to change your mind," he whispers. "And I don't think I'll be able to stop thinking about it until you do."

I can't stop the shiver that runs through my body. He notices and pulls away with a grin. Stepping back, he lets go of me completely.

"Goodnight, Remy," he says smoothly. Then he walks up the stairs, leaving me in a puddle on the floor.

The next morning when I wake up, the house is quiet. Tristan is notoriously an early bird, so I realize quickly that he must already be at the gym. I groan when I remember our interaction last night.

I briefly debate skipping the gym today. Saturdays are the only days that my and Tristan's schedules overlap, so I know I'll have to interact with him this morning. And after last night it might not be a bad idea to put some distance between us.

But I quickly shake the thought away. I love training for more reasons than one, and I refuse to give up even a day of it because of a guy. I'll suffer through a class with him if I need to. I'll just make an effort to ignore him entirely.

The more I think about it, I realize I should probably keep away from Tristan for the rest of the week, not just today. He's been near me too much lately and whenever he's that close, it feels like I can't pull myself away. Because of that I feel like I've been two steps behind in our games all week—he's clearly been the one in control.

As I throw the covers off myself and pull a sweatshirt over my head, I make a decision: keep as much distance between us as possible for the rest of the week.

I take my time getting ready. I've never been the type that could train on an empty stomach, so I make some scrambled eggs and brew a cup of coffee. I hum happily as Frank Ocean plays in the background. After I'm done eating, I settle into the couch with my coffee and a book.

An hour later, I've changed into my workout clothes and grabbed my gym bag. Twenty minutes after that I'm walking up to the gym, taking a deep breath to steel myself for whatever side of Tristan I'm about to experience.

When I walk in, that breath rushes out of me as I automatically and immediately relax. This place is like a second home to me. Everyone is practically family, and the environment itself feels like a sanctuary. Whenever I have a bad day, regardless if it's from work, friends, or family, this place is here to welcome me with open arms. I can pound my frustrations into a heavy bag or grab a partner to drill some techniques and take my mind off my problems. This gym is better than any therapist.

I smile at some of my teammates as I walk through the first mat room. I make my way to the bag room in the back, where all the heavy bags are and where my first class will be held. This morning I'll start with a cardio bagwork class and finish with a few rounds of jiu-jitsu during the gym's open mat hour. It's my favorite way to double up sessions because tiring myself out with a mindless cardio workout always produces my best rolls during jiu-jitsu. Something about being exhausted makes me forget about perfect technique and allows me to just *roll*.

"Hey, Lucy," I greet my friend. She looks up from wrapping her hands, a huge grin splitting her face.

"Hey, yourself," she teases. "How was *your* night?"

I roll my eyes and try to busy myself with unraveling my hand wraps, so as not to let her see the blush that I'm sure just crept across my cheeks. "You're ridiculous," I murmur. "I told you nothing would happen. I went to bed as soon as I got home."

"Oh yeah?" she challenges. "Tristan wasn't waiting up to chastise you?"

I glare at her as I wind the wraps around my hands. "No. Next topic, please. Before someone overhears your outlandish ideas and drags my good name through the mud."

She laughs but drops her line of questioning. "Okay, fine. Do you know who's teaching this morning? I didn't see Danny here, so I assume someone is covering for him." We both look around to see who our designated drill sergeant will be this morning.

Right on cue, we hear a deep voice boom across the gym. "All right, sweethearts, I don't care if you're hungover this morning, I want to see everyone *haul ass!* Ten laps around the gym, *NOW!*"

My stomach drops when I recognize Tristan's voice.

"Fuck," I hear Lucy mutter next to me. We exchange pained glances before breaking into a run. We both know the hardest classes are the ones that are run by the pro fighters—they hold every student to a professional-level work ethic and inevitably run us into the ground.

Sure enough, Tristan shows no mercy. Only twenty minutes into a forty-five-minute workout and every single person is struggling to put any power into their punches.

"Come on, my six-year-old cousin can kick harder than that!" I hear him shout at someone. "Put your hip into it!"

I grunt through the combo, willing myself not to slow down. My T-shirt is completely sweat-soaked and I'm breathing so hard that I can barely catch my breath. This is easily the hardest workout I've done in a very long time.

The bell sounds loudly. "Give me fifteen pushups and fifteen squat jumps during the rest period, then right back to that same combo!" Tristan yells. I groan. Even the rest periods aren't easy.

"What was that, Remy?" I hear from beside me. I startle, not realizing he was so close.

"Nothing," I grumble as I continue my pushups.

Tristan drops down to lie on his stomach in front of me. He watches me closely as I stare straight ahead and try to ignore him.

"Excuses and grumbles won't help you here," he scolds with a smirk. "The only thing that matters is hard work."

I open my mouth to snap at him—then stop myself when I realize that he's expecting my backtalk. I close my mouth and stand up with a growl, launching into my jump squats.

His face splits into a wide grin. He must be satisfied with my non-answer because he stands to go hound someone else.

The next fifteen minutes go by agonizingly slowly. It feels like Tristan gives us longer and harder combos every round. By the end, half the class barely has any power left in their shots. Which, of course, only antagonizes Tristan more.

"You should be getting *stronger* with every round, not *weaker*!" he yells. "Every round you should be giving your opponent a harder fight than the last. Pick it up! *LET'S GO!*"

I grunt and throw myself into the combo with renewed aggression. I'm so tired that I think my body has thrown caution to the winds and is now running purely on the fumes of my will.

"Okay, last round coming up! We're going to do a burnout round. That means you can throw whatever you want, but I want everything thrown *hard* and I *do not* want to see you stop. Does everyone understand?" I hear weak groans of acknowledgement. "Good. So any combo you want, but *constant* and *as hard as you can throw*. Three minutes. *LET'S GO!*"

The room erupts into sounds of leather being pounded with fists, kicks, knees, and elbows. Everyone is grunting with the exertion.

I grit my teeth and throw everything I have into my punches. For just three minutes, I force myself to tear down any limitation my body thinks it has—I throw as hard as I would if I were fresh and it was the first round. My muscles are screaming in agony and my lungs are desperate for air, but I ignore both.

"Let's *go!* Last round is the best round!" Tristan yells. "However hard you're working now, your opponent is working harder! Pick it up! I want *winners* in this room, *NOT* quitters!"

The first bell rings, signaling ten seconds left in the round. I throw every remaining ounce of energy into my last few shots.

The final bell rings right as I whip a head kick. "*TIME!*" Tristan calls.

Everyone around me collapses to the floor. Groans reverberate throughout the room. I make eye contact with Tristan as he raises an eyebrow, watching to see what I'll do.

I stay standing. My lungs are desperately gulping air and every muscle in my body is screaming, but I refuse to drop. I straighten my shoulders and stare straight at Tristan.

He grins and seems to give a quick nod of approval—then turns and walks out of the room.

"Oh Lord Jesus save us all," Aiden wheezes next to me. He's managed to get to his feet, but he's still bent over, hands on his knees, trying to compose himself. "That was the hardest workout I've ever done. By, like, a lot. Who peed in his cereal this morning?"

Lucy shoots me an accusatory look. I scowl. "I actually think that's him in a good mood," she says to no one in particular. "I think it makes him happy to run us ragged. Fucking psychopath..." A few people grunt in agreement.

After a few minutes, we've recovered enough to head back to the main mat room. Where the bag room is filled with heavy bags hanging from the ceiling, this room is devoid of any type of equipment. The only thing it has is a massive amount of mat space for sparring and jiu-jitsu. It's also where the benches and gear cubbies are, which means it's the room where everyone congregates.

As we walk into the mat room, I hear Coach ask us, "Who's staying for open mat? Does anyone want to roll?"

"There is not a single ounce of me that has any energy left after that bag workout," Aiden tells Coach honestly. Everyone nods in agreement.

I look around the mat and realize that it's mostly filled with advanced students. A lot of people only do jiu-jitsu, so they wouldn't have come in for the Muay Thai workout that we just did. For them, this is their first workout—which means they're fresh and full of energy. Everyone around me has multiple advantages over me before I've even stepped on the mats.

But a part of me hates leaving when there's such a good group of people here. A lot of the best guys only train in the mornings, so by the time evening classes roll around, class is filled mainly with beginner students. And though I'll never say I'm too good for anyone, I also can't say no to getting my ass kicked by the guys that are better than me. It's undoubtedly one of the best ways to learn.

"I've got a few rounds in me," I tell Coach. "Just give me a second to get changed."

I'm not certain, but out of the corner of my eye I think I see Tristan's head snap up in surprise.

I ignore the wide-eyed stares of my teammates next to me. They already know I'm a pit bull by nature so I'm not sure why they're surprised. I take a swig of my water bottle before rummaging through my bag for a rash guard.

Since jiu-jitsu is body-to-body contact, it's not enough to train in a T-shirt—we have to wear spandex on both top and bottom. I don't bother changing the leggings I'm already wearing but I do need to swap my soaking wet, now-baggy T-shirt for a skintight rash guard. I peel my shirt off and toss it in my bag.

As I stand there in my sports bra trying to slide my sticky arms through the tight clothing, I notice Tristan looking at me from where he's warming up. I see his eyes travel over my sweat-covered body.

Suddenly I remember that Tristan has already seen me completely naked—what he's looking at now is tame compared to how I looked coming out of the shower. I duck my head as a blush flames across my cheeks. I quickly tug the rash guard over my head and yank it down over my stomach. I take another swig of water before rushing onto the mat.

Coach nods in approval at the fact that I'm staying for another session. He calls me over for the first round.

The bell rings to signal the start of the five-minute round. We start standing but, just like with Tristan earlier this week, I quickly end up on my back. I make a mental note to work with more wrestlers so that I'm not so easily knocked over.

Coach doesn't destroy me, but he also doesn't give me an easy round. For five minutes we alternate positions—sometimes advancing, sometimes losing ground. Both of us attempt several round-ending submissions. I tap out once when he catches my arm in an armlock that I can't get out of. Overall, it's a great round with a lot of back and forth action.

I do three more rounds with other teammates. The minutes are hard, with everyone applying a lot of pressure, but the flow and rhythm is so good that I don't even mind the extra exertion. I was already exhausted when I stepped on the mat, so my body has automatically forced itself into fight-or-flight mode. I'm so far past my energy limitations that I don't have any left to overthink or worry about perfect technique. I just... roll.

"Remy, I've got you next round."

Breathing heavily, I look up to see Tristan is beckoning me to his side of the mat. And because I'm too tired to even argue, I crawl over without a word.

We shake hands to begin the round. I try to catch him off guard with a reach for his legs, but he sidesteps easily and ends up beside me. Before I can even react, he's wrapped his arms around my waist and lifted me off the ground.

If this were a real fight, he would slam me into the ground and probably knock the wind out of me. But because we're training—and because it's common etiquette when you outweigh someone by seventy pounds—he drops me gently. I've barely touched the ground before I'm scrambling to try to face him. The worst position you can be in is having someone behind you, when you're blind to their moves and they have all the control.

But no matter how hard I try to move, Tristan is not letting go of my back. Eventually he slips his forearm under my neck and applies a chokehold that has me instantly tapping in defeat.

I jump back to my feet, annoyed and ready to start over. We shake hands and go again.

This time he's the first to attempt a takedown. He tackles me easily. The second my back touches the ground I wrap my legs around him in an effort to control his position. But as soon as I move one of my legs to attempt a submission, he uses the opening to spin to a more dominant position. Not long after that, he's used his position to isolate my arm and force me into an armlock submission. I tap again.

I'm silently fuming at myself. I'm not under any delusion that I'm even close to Tristan's skill level but I thought I could at least hold my own. So far, we're barely two minutes into the round and he's already submitted me twice. As we stand and start again, I study his face to look for any signs of egotistical motivation. It's not uncommon for guys to want to assert their dominance just because they feel threatened by women in martial arts.

But Tristan's face is completely expressionless. He's not submitting me for any other reason than he's training hard and giving me a good, honest round. Which is the best thing anyone can do on the mats—it shows respect.

We shake hands and go again.

A minute later, he's submitted me with an ankle lock.

Two minutes after that, he gets another chokehold.

The bell rings to signal the end of the round but I barely hear it. "Again," I bark at Tristan.

Still expressionless, we shake hands and start again. He submits me with a toehold.

"Again." This time, it's a kneebar.

"Again," I pant. My muscles are shaking with exhaustion and I've given up playing my usual game of chess-like strategy. I've been reduced to using blatant physicality to try to survive.

But it's still not enough. Tristan is just too good. He shows no mercy, submitting me with another armlock and yet another chokehold.

"Again," I rasp as I roll away from him.

"No. You're done, Remy," I hear my coach call. I look over to see the entire gym is staring at Tristan and I. Aiden and Max are standing with their mouths gaping in shock.

I glance at Tristan. I note with satisfaction that he's breathing heavily, too. Even though he just kicked my ass for —I look at the timer and blanch—fourteen minutes straight, I at least put up enough of a fight to make him tired. It's a small consolation but a consolation nonetheless.

"You did enough today," Coach continues. "Good work. But you're done."

I peek at Tristan again, then look back at Coach. I nod weakly—and then immediately collapse onto my ass.

"I'm exhausted just from watching that," I hear Aiden mumble. "You two are nuts."

It takes me a good five minutes to peel myself off the

mats. Lucy is waiting for me with my water bottle like the brilliant friend that she is. I smile gratefully when I reach her.

"For the record, you're insane," she says bluntly. When I only glare at her she shakes her head with a grin and continues. "But on another note, do you want to come out with us tonight? I meant to ask you earlier. Me and the guys want to check out that new bar on 8th Street. Ask Hailey if she wants to come, too."

I nod as I gulp down more water. "Okay, I'll call her when I leave here. Is that the place that's kind of upscale compared to the typical hipster bars in that area? Do I need to dress up?"

"It's not upscale but yeah, it's not an oversized tee and beanie kind of place. Just wear your usual jeans and combat boots but pick a sexy top or something. You don't have to go crazy."

I nod. "I can do that. What time are you going?"

"Let's just say 9:00. Does that work for you?"

I nod again. "I'm going to go home and take the world's biggest nap and then I'll get Hailey and meet you there."

"Perfect." She pauses and then glowers at me. "And tell Hailey it would be great if she didn't show us all up with her perfect outfits for once. It's not fair that she demands all the male—and female—attention in the bars. She already has a boyfriend, she shouldn't even need the attention."

I chuckle, shaking my head. "That's like telling her not to breathe. She can't even help it, it's disgusting. But I'll try to get her to tone down the unassumingly gorgeous vibe." I roll my eyes, already knowing that task is a nearly impossible one.

Lucy grins. "That's all I ask."

I lean down to grab my bag with a groan. "I might regret

this. Let's hope my nap is a miracle one that reinvigorates my body and soothes all of its aches and pains."

She claps me on the back, ignoring my sound of protest. "You're fine. Just throw down a couple of tequila shots and you'll be good as new."

A few hours later I've showered, eaten, and napped. I feel like a brand new person.

"I will never understand how naps act like an elec-troshock for you," Hailey grumbles from where she's sifting through the closet. "You close your eyes for fifteen minutes and down a Red Bull and it's like you got a full eight hours of sleep. It's inhuman."

I take a sip of said Red Bull and lean back against Jax's headboard with a content smile. "What can I say, it's a gift."

As Hailey shakes her head in disbelief, her attention seems to lock on something hanging in the closet. She pulls out a little black dress.

"This is perfect," she decides with a smile. "Simple, subtle, but sexy as fuck. You can wear those black heels you have from Ally's wedding."

I look suspiciously at the dress she's holding. It really is a simple and beautiful black dress: it's got thin straps, a neck-line just scandalous enough that it will show the curve of my cleavage, and it fits tight against my body until it reaches the top of my thighs. It's the perfect LBD.

"Lucy said I should just wear jeans and a nice top," I argue. I wear enough skirts at work that I try to dress comfortably when I'm not in the office. Jeans and combat boots are my preferred outfit.

Hailey rolls her eyes. "Lucy doesn't know what she's

talking about. Either that, or she thinks that's the extent of you dressing up."

I sigh. "Probably the latter. Okay, I'll wear it. But there's not a chance in hell I'm doing heels. I'll wear my combat boots."

Hailey shakes her head as she turns to hang the dress on the closet door. "Fine, but wear the high heeled combat boots instead of your normal flat ones. You could afford to at least try to look like a woman instead of a KGB spy."

I raise an eyebrow and point to the dress. "That dress is barely long enough to cover my ass. I assure you, I will look like a woman regardless of the height of my shoes."

I hear her chuckle even as she pulls her own outfit from her bag. I peek curiously at the clothes she pulls on.

She's wearing black high-waisted jeans and a dark gray long sleeve shirt that has extra fabric connecting the arms to the body of the shirt. It's thin and flowy and would look cute if it was tight, but it's so loose that it looks more like a poncho than a top. Between the dark colors and the fit of the clothes themselves, Hailey's body is completely hidden. The icing on the cake is when Hailey hides away her beautiful hair by pulling it into a ponytail.

I bite the inside of my cheek as I think about how I can ask my next question without sounding like a total judgmental ass. "That's... pretty conservative for what you usually wear when we go out. What's going on?"

Hailey fidgets with the zipper on her bag, avoiding eye contact. "Steve's not really comfortable with me wearing what I usually wear," she finally mumbles. "I figured I'd tone it down a bit and cover up more. No big deal."

My frown deepens as her words sink in. I'm all for toning down the hooker outfits once a girl has a boyfriend, but Hailey's never dressed provocatively. She's just naturally so beautiful that any nice outfit she wears automatically makes her beauty stand out. Right now, it seems like she's actually trying to cover herself up. The only thing more conservative would be a turtleneck.

My eyes widen when a thought occurs to me. "Did he tell you that you could only go out if you cover up?"

Hailey's head snaps toward mine, her eyes wide. "N-no, of course not," she stammers, and I immediately see through her lie.

I can feel my fury start to boil in my veins. I always had a suspicion that Steve was controlling, but this is now officially at an unacceptable level. I've noticed changes in my sister over the past few weeks, changes in her confidence and how she spends her time. She barely sees her friends anymore and where before she was a strong-willed, independent woman, she now seems to need Steve's input for everything. I knew he was changing her even before she described their issues to me; this just confirms it.

I take a deep breath to calm myself. I myself have never been in a controlling relationship, but I've known plenty of strong women that have found themselves in similar situations. There's something about manipulative men that can get through to even the strongest women, so I know it can happen to anyone—even my sister.

"Hailey," I start softly. "You know I love you, and I'll support any decision you make. But Steve shouldn't be giving you ultimatums. You should be able to wear whatever the fuck you want."

I try not to sound patronizing or accusing, but she still gets defensive at my words. She glares at me. "He's not giving me ultimatums. I'm just being understanding of his concerns. We can't all just do whatever we want in relationships and not give a fuck about the other person."

I swallow and look down at my hands. I know she's just lashing out, but her words still hurt. I've always been the one to wear the pants in my relationships, partly because I'm an assertive bitch who knows what she wants, and partly because I've always been the one to care the least. Boyfriends have often accused me of being selfish and heartless.

Although if I'm being honest with myself, I've always thought it was just because I have yet to find someone worth caring about.

"I just don't want you to be unhappy," I say quietly. "You deserve the best, and I want you to be with someone that pushes you to go after your dreams, that makes you happy, that lets you be every bit of the confident, beautiful, intelligent woman that you are." I look up to see her eyes have softened. "If Steve is that for you, then I'll shut up. But I'm here if he's not."

She sighs and comes over to sit next to me on the bed. "You don't have to worry about that. Steve is good for me, and I'm happy. I'm just trying to compromise with him so we're both happy."

I nod, sensing that the conversation is over. I won't get any more out of her until she herself realizes that he's not who she thinks he is. Or maybe I'm wrong and they're actually good for each other. Who knows? I'd love to be wrong about this.

In a normal lovey-dovey family, I'd probably give her a big hug, but we're not that. Instead, she punches me in the arm. "Go get your curling iron. I'll grab the tequila and make us some drinks so we can start pregaming."

I grin at the word 'tequila' and bounce off the bed. I practically skip down the hallway to the bathroom.

But I pause when I pass Tristan's room. His door is wide

open, and my gaze is drawn to his unmade bed. Suddenly I'm flashing back to the night that I caught him with a girl, when he was sitting half naked at the edge of said bed.

I feel my heart rate pick up. I can't help remembering his toned chest, or the way he had been gripping the girl's waist. I can't help thinking about what they would've been doing a few minutes later if I hadn't interrupted them.

Then I remember his words to me that night. *I promise I can fuck you better than whatever nerds you've slept with before.*

I shiver at the memory. I know Tristan's reputation and I know the way my body reacted to him that night—I have no doubt that he could keep that promise.

I clench my legs against the growing ache between them at that thought.

I jump when I hear Hailey pass by me. She pauses at the top of the steps, her hand on the railing, and looks at me with confusion. "All good?"

I mentally shake myself out of my stupor. "Yeah, I—I just thought I left the curling iron in my room for a second."

She frowns. "No, I just saw it in the bathroom."

"Oh. Okay." Hailey starts down the stairs again as I turn toward the bathroom.

I spare one last glance at Tristan's room, banishing all thoughts of sex with him from my brain.

8

TRISTAN

I'm still breathing heavily as I roll away from Remy. Coach waves me over to do a round with him, and I mentally thank my strength and conditioning coach for driving me through his cardio workouts from hell to ensure my stamina is always next level. Fourteen minutes straight with Remy was no joke.

I had no idea she was so good. Even though I practically live at the gym, somehow our schedules never really align, so we rarely ever train at the same time. It's probably been close to a year since I've done jiu-jitsu with her, and back then she was still a white belt. Clearly, she's made big strides with her skills during that time.

I could feel that she knew what she was doing when we had the play match at the house before Jax left. Not only was she technical, but she actually implemented her techniques with aggression. Most of the time people are one or the other: either technical but too nice, or aggressive with no sense of grace or skill. It's always impressive when an athlete is able to combine both.

Or maybe she just hates you and wants to maim you.

I chuckle at the thought. Remy has always had violent tendencies toward me—ever since we met and started off on the wrong foot. I've always thought her threats were amusing. It also seems she's never been able to master the ability to be in my presence and *not* threaten some kind of bodily harm.

In all honesty I didn't think she'd have enough energy to actually threaten me. I'm surprised she even stepped on the mat. I always make it a point to put students through the wringer when I teach the cardio bagwork class, and this morning was definitely one of the harder workouts. I had fully expected everyone to be crawling out of the bag room.

But somehow, Remy not only stayed standing when everyone else collapsed around her, but she volunteered for another workout with students that were fresh and energized. That's the kind of fighter spirit that I rarely even see in, well, fighters. I know grown men who fight professionally that half-ass their workouts and talk more on social media than they put in real work. With what she showed today, Remy would put most grown men to shame on the work ethic scale.

I shake my awed thoughts of Remy and try to concentrate on the black belt that's currently working to rip my arm off. Even though I don't have a fight coming up, I still need to put 110% effort into my training in order to stay ready. Not falling into the mythical trap of "off season" is one of the reasons my name is launching through the ranks right now. Hopefully my next matchup is one that, when I win, will finally get me that call from the UFC.

I do a few more rounds before people start to call it quits. I roll until there are no partners left for me, and then I head to the treadmills in the corner to run three miles as fast as I can, burning every last ounce of energy in me. End of workout burnouts are undoubtedly some of the hardest workouts—they're specifically designed to force you past every mental barrier that screams bloody murder at you to 'stop, please, for the love of God just *stop*.'

But I don't. I push harder every time my brain says I can't. With every step past where I want to stop, I further condition my mind and body to accept a newly calibrated limit. Humans can go so much further than their brains think they can.

My lungs are on fire and I'm starting to get tunnel vision by the time I reach mile three. I sprint an additional quarter mile for good measure before slowing to a walk, desperately gulping deep breaths of air and trying to slow my heartrate back down.

Other than my legs still trembling from the brutal workout, my body's almost completely recovered by the time my phone rings. *Mom* lights up on my screen.

With my headphones already in my ears, I swipe the answer button. "Hey, Mom."

"Hi, honey. What are you up to?" she asks cheerfully.

"I just finished my workout. I'm about to head home."

"Oh, perfect. Why don't you come to the house? Your brother just stopped by so I thought it'd be nice if we could have everyone over, even for a little bit. What do you say?"

I wince and rub my temples. Spending time with my brother—and my dad—is not my idea of weekend relaxation.

But underneath everything I'm still a mama's boy at heart, and I can't ever refuse a request from my mother. Especially one to spend time with her.

"Yeah, okay, I'll come," I respond with a sigh. "Let me just shower and then I'll head over. I should be there in about half an hour."

"Great!" she chirps happily. "It makes me so happy when I have both you and your brother here together. He's going to be so excited to see you."

I roll my eyes. I can never tell if she recognizes her own lie, or if she's just oblivious to the tension between my brother and I. Either way, I'm sure my brother doesn't give two shits about whether or not I come over.

"I'll see you soon, Mom."

"See you soon, honey. Drive safe."

I hang up the phone with a frustrated growl. Spending time with my family, even for only an hour, is not what I had planned for today. It's rare that I don't have private sessions scheduled into the afternoon on Saturdays, so I had been excited to nap and watch some fight footage today. So much for a relaxing Saturday.

I sigh and shut down the treadmill. I grab my gym bag and head toward the showers to clean up.

Thirty minutes later, I'm walking into my parents' house on the outskirts of the city. Everyone is in the formal sitting room, and they all look at me as I enter.

"Tristan, there you are!" my mom calls, clapping her hands together and rushing over to give me a hug. I squeeze her back, a small smile stretching across my face.

That smile quickly falls when I look over her shoulder to see my dad and brother staring at me with matching frowns. They're perched casually on the furniture across from each other, my brother very clearly the spitting image of our father.

"Tristan," my dad nods by way of greeting. My brother merely smirks at me.

"Hi, Dad." I walk over to sit on the other end of the couch from my brother, my mom once again taking up her place next to her husband.

"Scott and I were just talking about you," my dad drawls, staring directly at me. Without even hearing the words, I know what he's going to say. I can tell just by the condescending look in his eyes, the slight curl of disgust in his lip.

I guess we're jumping right into the usual fight, then.

"There's an opening in your brother's company for a financial analyst," he starts. "It's a new job posting, and they're probably looking to hire internally, but Scott can put in a good word for you and get you bumped to the top of the list. If need be, I can call the CEO, as well. He and I went to college together and still connect occasionally."

I exhale an angry breath and awkwardly rub the back of my neck. I know exactly how heated this argument is about to get, but I always think I can keep things calm if I can just answer politely.

"Dad, I'm not looking for a job," I say quietly. "I have a job. Several, actually. And I'm making good money. I probably make as much as Scott does."

My brother laughs from his spot on the couch next to me. He's lounging comfortably like he always does, one ankle resting on his opposite knee and his arms splayed out along the back of the couch. I don't think I've ever seen him tense or uncomfortable. Only obnoxiously arrogant.

I ignore his reaction to the thought that we might make the same amount of money doing such vastly different things—and with very different amounts of hard work.

My dad studies me with his usual frown. I can never decide what answers he's looking for when he glares at me like this. *Why I don't want to follow in his footsteps? How I could possibly like fighting? How he failed so miserably with me?*

I swallow roughly when I realize it could be any of those.

"When are you going to be done with this karate bullshit?" he finally asks me.

I can't help the wince that flashes across my face every time my father makes the cheap comparison. I never know if he does it intentionally or if he really thinks of me as the fucking Karate Kid.

"Not anytime soon," I say bluntly. I can feel myself nearing the end of my rope a lot sooner today than I usually do.

His lip curls in disgust as he shakes his head and looks away. That look hits me directly in the chest every time I see it—regardless of how many times I've been on the receiving end.

Like clockwork, my mom jumps in to try to ease the tension. She hates when Dad is irritated, and she always takes on the role of peacekeeper. Though I don't know if you can be considered a peacekeeper when you're very clearly supportive of one side and against the other. "Honey, wouldn't you rather have an easy 9-5 job where you're home at a normal time and you don't have to get hurt? You know it kills me when you get injured." She clasps her hands in her lap and looks at me with hopeful eyes.

I wince and lean forward to rub my temples. As much as I would love to have this out via a screaming match, I know that would break my mom's heart. For her, I try to gentle my words again. "Mom, I know you think that's the ideal job, but that kind of life is not for everyone. I would hate sitting on my ass and running numbers all day. It's just not for me. Can't you just accept that I love something you don't under-stand and support me for it anyway?"

"No, because we're your parents and we know what's best for you," my dad snaps. "We're not going to stop pushing this until you come to your senses and leave this ridiculous, barbaric hobby behind."

I aim a cold stare—the one I inherited from my father—

at the man that I sometimes can't believe is really a parent. "It's hardly a hobby, Dad. I'm one of the best fighters in the Northeast."

Scott lets out a snort from next to me. "Nobody even knows who you are."

I turn my piercing glare to my brother. "Tell me that again in a year. I'll be in the UFC and you'll still be getting drunk on golf courses with your shitty frat brothers."

"Enough," my dad snaps. "Your brother is following the career path that *you* should be following and he's doing a damn good job. He'll be a Chief Financial Officer one day."

I smother the delirious laugh that threatens to break out of me. My brother does bare minimum in every aspect of his life—he'll never even get close to a C-level title.

I turn back to my dad. "Regardless, I'm not looking for a job. I'm perfectly happy right where I am. It's a completely pointless conversation. Do you want to keep talking about it or should we change topics?" I look at where Mom is nervously wringing her hands. "How are you, Mom? How are your friends doing at the country club?"

She casts a nervous glance at my dad, but I know she can't resist sharing gossip from their country club. They've only been members for the past three years, ever since Dad really hit his stride at work and got a big promotion and pay raise. As much as I hate the pressure he puts on me to follow in his line of work, I can't deny that he's become very successful at what he does. He's a hard worker and it definitely shows. The long years he had put in at his company finally paid off with the promotion and at that point my parents' lifestyles really changed—Mom retired from her occasional substitute teaching job, they bought a new house and made some rich friends, and they joined their most sought-after status symbol: the country club.

Three years ago is when Dad really started pushing me to fix my career choice.

They weren't supportive of fighting even before that, but the pressure got really bad after Dad saw the life they could have with a well-paying corporate job. He managed to instill the vision in Scott, but he's never stopped trying to do the same with me.

And based on today's conversation, that's not stopping anytime soon.

I half-listen as Mom drones on about some lady at the country club supposedly having an affair with another member's husband. I can tell none of us are listening, but we all know it makes her happy, so we let her speak. Scott looks bored and Dad is stuck in his scowl, most likely stewing over our conversation. I'm counting down the minutes until I can get out of here.

The rest of the night goes by with only a few passive aggressive digs aimed at me. Mom serves dinner while Dad and Scott tune me out by talking about work. I know they do it on purpose but I'm actually thankful for the reprieve because not having to talk means there's less chance of me losing my cool. As it stands, I'm still eager for dinner to be over so I can get the fuck out of here.

The second Mom finishes her after-dinner coffee, I push my chair back and stand up. "I have to get going," I announce. I lean over to kiss Mom on the cheek. "Thanks for dinner, Mom. I'll call you next week."

"Thanks for coming over, honey," she says with a small smile.

Dad is still glaring at me—I'm starting to think that's the only way he's capable of looking at me. I give him a tight nod. "Dad. Thanks for the career advice." I don't even look at Scott as I say, "Brother, it's been a pleasure. As always."

I don't expect a response from either of them, so I turn around and make my exit. It isn't until I'm sitting in my car that I let out the agitated breath that I've been holding for what feels like several hours.

I take a few deep breaths, but it does nothing for the anger simmering in my veins. With a frustrated growl, I grab my phone to make a call. I need a drink.

"Aiden, where you guys at tonight?"

9

REMY

"So, Hailey, what's with the outfit?"

My sister chokes on her drink at Lucy's words. I can't help my grin—we've been at the bar for almost two hours and the whole time I've been waiting for when Lucy would comment on my sister's conservative attire. Apparently, it took a few drinks for her tongue to loosen.

Hailey glares at my teammate. "There's nothing wrong with my outfit," she growls. "I always dress like this."

Lucy grins, very much enjoying tormenting my sister. "No, you usually dress like a model. Right now you look like a repressed only child that got sent to a girl's boarding school for kissing the neighbor boy."

Hailey's glare is momentarily replaced with a look of blinking surprise. "That was... very descriptive."

Lucy shrugs. "I dated a girl that had that vibe going on. I actually only approached her because I wanted to see if it was all a ruse or if she really was a prude."

I smother the laugh that wants to break out of me at watching these two polar opposite women tease each other.

"And what was the verdict?" I manage to ask without laughing.

At that, a devious grin slides across Lucy's face. "Total ruse. That girl was the freakiest bitch I ever got with."

I can't contain the laughter anymore—it bursts out of me, loud and happy. A group of guys next to us turn in our direction with raised eyebrows.

Hailey is back to glaring at Lucy. "Are you saying I look prude, sex-crazed, or ugly? Because it's hard to keep up with so many insults, Lucy. "

Lucy lets out a loud laugh. "Okay calm down, I'll stop teasing. You just... you look... not as hot as you usually do." She holds her hand up in surrender when Hailey's glare intensifies. "You know what I mean. You just seem... conventionally dressed. I know I told Remy to ask you not to be at full hotness-capacity tonight, but this is overkill. Even Remy did up her outfit tonight." She casts an appreciative glance at my dress. "Girl, you look hot as fuck. Well done."

Smirking, I stick my hip out in an exaggerated pose and flip my hair over my shoulder. But as I turn my head, I lock eyes with someone across the bar. The grin immediately slides from my face.

Tristan is standing at the bar next to Aiden and Max, staring straight at me. I saw him walk into the bar about an hour ago and beeline straight to the bar for a drink. Anyone could see the frown on his face and tension in his shoulders so I'm assuming alcohol was needed for whatever his problem was.

That tension is nonexistent now. He's leaning casually on the bar top and lazily spinning his whiskey glass. He's wearing dark jeans and a tight black T-shirt that accentuates every single mouth-watering muscle on his upper body. The tattoos that I know run over his chest and shoulder peek out past his sleeve, running down to his elbow. His dark hair looks as sex-tousled as it always does, and the bright blue of his eyes clashes perfectly with the permanent smirk on his lips.

He is the picture of male arrogance.

Slowly, shamelessly, his eyes rake down my body, spending extra seconds on the shortness of my dress and the way my heels lengthen my legs. I swallow, my throat suddenly feeling very dry.

Just as slowly, Tristan's eyes move up the length of my body to meet mine again. When he grins, a rush of desire floods my core. Suddenly, I'm transported back to last night —to Tristan's body pressed against mine, his lips touching my ear and whispering dirty things. The flame of my lust increases tenfold at the memory.

"Earth to Remy!"

I snap out of my lust-drunk haze and turn toward Lucy. "Sorry, what?"

Her eyes narrow suspiciously. "Where did you just go? We were talking about that new Netflix show with Chris Hemsworth, and you totally zoned out. You love Hemsworth, I don't know how you weren't paying attention."

I wince. "I just... remembered something that happened at work and got distracted. Sorry. What about the new show?"

With a sigh, Lucy launches back into whatever she was talking about. I chance a look back at Tristan, but he's already turned back to Aiden. I try to focus on Lucy's latest Netflix-obsession.

Suddenly, I see Hailey's eyes go wide as she looks over my shoulder. I spin to see what's caught her attention, and realize Steve is heading straight toward us. He's not smiling.

"Did you know he was coming out?" I ask Hailey. She shakes her head, seemingly frozen in shock. I frown and take a step closer to her.

Steve finally pushes through the crowd and steps up to Hailey. Based on his furious expression I expect him to grab her, but he only glares at her and ignores the rest of us.

"Why haven't you been answering my calls?" he demands. "It's late, you were supposed to be home by now."

Hailey's cheeks light with an ashamed blush as she looks down at where her feet are shuffling nervously. She mumbles something that we can't hear.

"Steve, she probably didn't hear her phone," I say gently, trying to deescalate the situation. "It's loud in here. And it's only midnight. Not that late to be worrying that something happened."

He spins around, fury blazing in his eyes. He opens his mouth to snap at me, but then seems to realize who he's talking to. He visibly softens. His posture slouches a little bit, and he forces a tight smile onto his face.

Can't make an enemy of the girl's family, after all, I think bitterly.

"Hey, Remy. Sorry, I didn't see you there." He steps closer to Hailey and takes her hand, stroking it lovingly. I look at their entwined hands, a deep part of me wishing he would've just been forceful about it so I'd have a reason to throw him out of my sister's life. Instead, I have only his fake words to react to.

"I'm sorry, baby," he tells Hailey tenderly. "I just get so worried about you. I know it's not that late yet, but you said you were going to text me when you were getting ready to leave here and when I didn't hear from you, I panicked. You know I worry about you partying in the city."

I roll my eyes at the comment. My sister is the definition of a responsible adult, and she rarely ever has more than a drink or two. Being worried about her 'partying' is ridiculous. And clearly just a way to spin his possessive feelings.

Hailey doesn't notice the tactic—or she ignores it—and instead looks up at him with a grateful smile. "I know, I'm sorry," she tells him. "I was just having a lot of fun and must've lost track of time. But you're right, it's late. We should get going."

Steve visibly relaxes at her concession. He smiles again and gives her hand a squeeze.

But then the smile freezes in place. Slowly, his eyes rake over Hailey's outfit.

"What is that?" he asks tightly. The disdain practically drips from his voice. I look around to find what he could be talking about.

"My shoes?" asks Hailey, sounding just as confused as I feel. I look down at her tan wedge sandals. They're high because Hailey's always been self-conscious about her height, but they're otherwise modest, cute sandals. They're about the only cute thing Hailey's wearing right now.

"Why would you wear those?" Steve spits through clenched teeth. "They're practically hooker heels."

I can't hear Hailey's response over the roaring in my ears. My vision floods with a red haze at the degrading insinuation, and I open my mouth to finally tear into Steve. I don't care if I'm butting into my sister's business—right now it feels like I need to protect her from herself.

"Everything okay here?"

I turn, startled, to find Tristan standing behind me. His stern gaze is focused on Steve.

"We're fine," Steve snaps as he turns back to Hailey.

"I wasn't asking you," Tristan responds coldly.

At that, Steve turns back with surprise, his angry mask cracking to reveal the insecure boy hiding underneath.

Tristan brushes by me to stand directly in front of Hailey, effectively stepping in between the couple and forcing Steve to drop her hand. He visibly becomes even more frazzled. Hailey stares up at Tristan with a wide-eyed, awed expression.

"Hailey, you okay?" he asks again.

Hailey swallows nervously but nods. "Yeah, I'm okay. Steve is my boyfriend. He was just coming to pick me up, we were about to leave."

Tristan doesn't let any reaction show on his face. He stares at Hailey for a moment longer, until she's squirming under his all-seeing gaze. "And you're sure you want to leave with him?"

At that, Steve finally snaps out of his nervous stupor. He glares at the back of Tristan's head and steps around him to grab Hailey's hand again.

"What kind of question is that?" he snaps. "She just told you I'm her boyfriend. Of course she wants to leave with me."

Tristan ignores his comment and waits for Hailey to answer.

"Yes, I'm sure," Hailey confirms, her voice sounding stronger now. "I love him."

Tristan doesn't react but he doesn't ask her again.

Seemingly annoyed with the line of questioning, Steve tugs at Hailey's hand to try to move her toward the exit. "Come on, babe, let's go home." She smiles at Lucy and I by way of goodbye and turns to follow her boyfriend.

Except, Tristan steps into Steve's path before he can take more than a step. Steve stares up at the very tall, very intimidating man in front of him with more wide-eyed shock.

"I know what you are," Tristan says simply. "If you hurt her, I will know. So I suggest you don't."

We all stare at Tristan in stunned silence. Even though Steve doesn't know Tristan very well, the words are said in such a way that it's very clearly not an empty threat. Hailey just looks stunned, like she can't believe she's witnessing a fight break out over her.

"I don't know what you're talking about," Steve finally stammers. He goes to step around Tristan and, when he doesn't meet more resistance, pulls Hailey out of the bar with him.

Tristan watches them leave, his expression still not giving away any reaction. Finally, he turns to Lucy and I. "Your sister should break up with that guy," he says before walking away. Lucy and I follow his path back to the bar with wide eyes.

"Damn, I thought he was only protective yesterday because he wants to fuck you," Lucy mutters. "Guess he's just protective, period."

I whip my head around to glare at Lucy. "I already told you he doesn't want to fuck me," I growl.

She raises an eyebrow at me. "No, he definitely still wants to fuck you, but I'm saying that's not why he almost broke that guy's neck yesterday. Apparently, Tristan has as much of a mama bear streak as you do."

I frown and turn again to study my current roommate. He's joined Aiden and Max at the bar and is listening to whatever inane argument those two are currently involved in.

I never would've expected Tristan to be the protective type. In fact, he's always come off as the opposite: selfish, worried only about his career, and ignoring everyone else around him. I knew he had a soft spot for Jax, but I figured that was a reflection of the type of loyalty my best friend commands, not of Tristan himself. Apparently, I was wrong.

"I guess I should go thank him," I mutter to Lucy. With a nod and a swat to my ass, she wanders off to go find someone else to talk to.

I take a hesitant step toward the bar. Then it becomes two, and three, and the next thing I know I'm standing in front of Tristan.

He turns his even gaze toward me and raises a brow. I open my mouth to say something, but it's at that moment that Aiden notices me standing there.

"Hey, Remy!" he chirps happily. He stands up from where he's sitting at the bar and offers me the barstool. "I assume you want to ream Tristan out for whatever he just did. Here, take my seat. Max and I are heading back to the rest of the group now anyway."

I chuckle uncomfortably. "Uh, thanks." By the time I take the seat and turn toward Tristan, the boys are gone. "I, um, just wanted to say thank you for what you did. And said."

I stumble over the words. It feels awkward to aim them at Tristan.

He stares at me with his usual unyielding gaze, letting none of his feelings show. After a few moments, he asks, "Is she safe with him tonight?"

I turn my attention back to the cocktail I've been nursing for the past hour. I take a quick swig when I remember its existence. "Yeah," I answer easily and honestly. "They live together. And he's not abusive—or at least not physically. He's just kind of mean. I don't think she realizes the effect he has on her. But he would never hurt her. I'd never let him." Then something occurs to me, and I chuckle. "Plus, that crazy bitch has too many daggers in her purse to be in any real danger."

Tristan's in the middle of gesturing at the bartender when he turns back to me with a startled look. "Seriously? She carries daggers?"

I grin. "And a few knives. It's been a while since I've seen what's in her purse."

Tristan's lips twitch into a grin, then he nods in approval. "Smart girl," he mutters. "I figured she was okay, since I doubt Jax would let her be around anyone that's actually dangerous. But when I saw him with her, I just wanted to make sure."

I nod, nervously spinning the drink in front of me. "Well, thank you anyway," I murmur. "That was... really nice of you. You know, to threaten him and all."

The usual cocksure grin appears on Tristan's face. It will never not be disconcerting that he has only two expressions: arrogant and stoic. "What good is all this muscle and talent if I don't use it to boss people around once in a while?"

I roll my eyes at his arrogance finally making an appearance. I let out the tight breath I was holding, feeling much more comfortable with this version of Tristan that I know so well.

Just then, the bartender appears with two shots of tequila. I look quizzically at Tristan.

"Isn't tequila your preferred drink?" he asks, sliding one of the shots in front of me. "I figured we both need it after that bullshit."

I bark out a laugh and grab the shot glass. "You're not wrong." I raise the glass and turn toward Tristan. "What are we cheers-ing?"

He stares thoughtfully at the clear liquid, then turns his soul-piercing gaze back to me. Without breaking eye contact, he lifts his glass and says, "To being willing to gut anyone that fucks with the people we care about."

A shiver runs through me at the possessiveness of his words. In the back of my mind, it occurs to me how different this possession feels from Steve's.

We both throw our shots back. I cringe, then sigh happily at the warm feeling that flows through me with the aftertaste.

I fidget nervously with the shot glass as I try to think of something to say. Now that I've said my thank you, I'm not quite sure how to keep being around Tristan.

"So, uh, any fights coming up?" I ask awkwardly.

Tristan is silent for a moment, then he chuckles. I twist my head toward him. "What?" I snap.

His arrogant smirk is back in full force as he motions to the bartender again. "You really don't know how to have a normal conversation with me, do you?"

I squirm under his curious gaze and turn back to my shot glass. "Nice Tristan is unnerving as fuck," I eventually mumble.

He barks a laugh at my admission. "I can go back to being an asshole if that would make you more comfortable," he grins. "I could tell you that dress is way too short because your ass is too big."

My head snaps back toward him again, this time with the deadliest glare I can muster. "You can go fuck yourself," I grumble. "My ass is fantastic."

I don't miss his lazy, lingering glance down to the bottom of my dress, across my exposed thigh. I tug at my dress self-consciously.

He doesn't miss the motion. His eyes dart back to my face, grin still firmly in place. "Okay, so no-go on that idea, too. We can figure this out, Remy." He turns his body to face me fully and leans his elbow casually on the bar, cocking his head slightly. "How about this: I'll let you be your usual, charming self and give you full reign to insult me however you want. Assume whatever you want about me and I'll tell you if it's true or not."

My eyes narrow as I study him suspiciously. "How would I know if you're telling the truth?"

He nods at the bartender delivering the tequila shots before sliding one over toward me. "Guess you'll just have to trust me," he answers with a grin. He lets me glare at him for another moment before grabbing his shot and nodding at mine. "What's it gonna be? Wanna play with me?"

I turn toward the new shot glass to hide the blush that flames across my face at his bold words. "If you think I'm going to hold back, you're delusional," I grumble.

His grin widens. "I would expect nothing less." My breath catches as he leans in closer. Clinking his glass to mine, he whispers, "Do your worst, Remy baby." Then he slams the shot without even a grimace.

I throw one last glare his way before downing my own. I can feel the alcohol buzzing its way through my body and I can already tell it's about to loosen my tongue more than it ever should around Tristan. But right now, I can't bring myself to give a fuck. I welcome the return of my confidence. Turning my body completely toward him and taking my time crossing my legs, I lean against the bar and study him thoughtfully. I smirk when he tries to hide his glance at my legs.

"The fighting and arrogance are an overcompensation for a tiny dick," I start with a straight face and way too much confidence.

Tristan's eyes widen in surprise for a split second before he bursts into laughter.

"I'm not sure why I expected anything different," he says with a chuckle after he's calmed down. I raise my eyebrow, waiting for his answer. The cocky grin on his face appears right back where it was a moment ago. "No, I do not have a tiny dick. But good to know that's the first part of me your brain goes to."

I roll my eyes before waving at the bartender for another order of shots. I ignore Tristan's amused glance.

Turning back toward the focus of my assumptions, I take another guess. "Your older brother got all the love in the family, so you got used to demanding attention by being obnoxious and arrogant."

This time he's the one that rolls his eyes. "Again with the arrogance," he mutters. But I frown when I notice the sudden tightness in his body and the lack of his usual flighty grin.

"Not true," he finally answers. But when he doesn't offer an explanation, I decide to take the obvious cue that I've struck a nerve and move on.

"Jiu-jitsu is the biggest weakness in your fight game," I guess again.

I'm rewarded with the return of his trademark smirk. "Not true," he says again.

My eyes narrow suspiciously. "Wrestling is the biggest weakness in your fight game."

He sighs in resignation. "True. But don't be calling my competition with this information."

I smirk in victory just as the bartender appears with our third round of shots. "Just keep putting them on his tab," I tell the guy with a coy smile. I hear Tristan snort as he shakes his head. I slide one of the shots over to him, thoroughly enjoying the comfortable buzz that's now running through me. One more drink will put me at my favorite level of just barely drunk.

I clink my glass against his and throw back the shot

without a second thought, sighing contentedly at the burn. I ignore Tristan's appreciative glance.

Once he's taken his shot, I take another guess, emboldened even further by the alcohol. "You don't actually enjoy drinking. You only do it for one of two reasons: to shove down negative emotions or to make sex more enjoyable with the plastic fuck bunnies you love so much."

His eyes widen again at my bluntness. Either that or I nailed it again with my first assumption.

He ignores the first one and instead focuses on the second, a grin once again stretching across his face. "You seem to love asking about my sexual activities, Remy. Why is that?"

I glare at him, refusing to dignify that with an answer. "Just answer the question, Tristan," I growl.

If possible, his grin actually grows in its smugness level. "True. I have my reasons for drinking. And amplifying the pleasure of sex is one of them." His eyes drop down to rake across my body, from the subtle exposure of my cleavage to the very exposed length of my legs.

My breath catches at his heated glance. I squeeze my thighs together, desperate to tamp down on the rush of lust that runs through me at the obvious direction of his thoughts.

Something's changed between us in the past few days—Tristan no longer looks past me. Where before I was just Jax's annoying childhood friend, the shower incident seems to have reminded him that I'm a woman. I should've known his male brain would be that predictable.

And although I see him as exactly the same arrogant womanizer that I always have—except maybe a little more protective than I anticipated—I also can't deny that having his undivided sex-gaze on me ignites something deep inside me. I've always known he's ridiculously hot; his athletic body and piercing blue eyes, coupled with his cocksure attitude, melts the panties off of women for a reason. But I've never had the full force of it directed at me.

It's making me squirm.

I draw in a ragged breath, starting to second guess my decision to ask sexual questions in this game. It's getting harder to hide how affected I am from Tristan's blatant once-over.

"Why so interested in my sex life, Remy?" he purrs, leaning closer. His gaze darts across my face, and lands on my lips. "You can say it."

"I'm not," I blurt out. "I'm just playing your game."

A smile slowly slides across his face. "I'm beginning to think you might actually know how to play," he murmurs. And I think I might combust from the heat in his words.

At that moment I think the last shot finally makes its way through my body because a surge of confidence drives a feline smile onto my lips. "You have no idea how well I can play," I purr.

His eyes widen in delighted shock.

Taking advantage of his momentary speechlessness, I push away from the bar and step off the barstool. "Order another round. I'm going to use the bathroom and then maybe you can do me." I grin when his eyes go even wider. "Make assumptions about me, I mean."

I turn away before he has the chance to say anything else. I couldn't stop the extra sway in my hips even if I wanted to. I'll just blame it on the alcohol.

I take my time in the bathroom, using the extra minutes to touch up my makeup but mostly to get my heart rate under control again.

As much as I know nothing can happen between us, I

can't deny that exchanging drunken banter with Tristan is entertaining. Of course, the clear attraction of a hot guy is a boost to my ego, but there's something extra appealing about that attention coming from the bane of my existence who's only ever looked at me like a little girl. I send a mental thank you to Hailey for my outfit.

As I walk back toward our spot at the bar, I realize from across the room that my seat has been taken over by a very attractive blonde—that is now hanging all over Tristan.

I frown. I was only gone for a few minutes, and he's already replaced me? Annoyance starts to sizzle in my veins, despite knowing that Tristan can't help that he's a magnet for women, especially in bars. It makes no difference that we were actually having a decent conversation.

I study the girl. She's easily one of the prettiest girls in the room, with a model's body and the tiniest silver sequin club dress to show it off. Her long legs are further elongated by the stilettos she's wearing. Her makeup is perfect, with dark vampy lips and sultry, smoky eyes, and her blonde hair is pulled back in a high pony that exposes her long neck and thin shoulders. She's taken over my seat and is currently leaning so far into Tristan that her breasts are pressed flat against the side of his chest. She has one arm wrapped around his neck, her other hand tracing patterns on his forearm. She whispers something into his ear.

Tristan whips his head to the side before she can kiss him—and immediately locks eyes with me. I realize then that his body language is stiff—he's not touching her at all —and that he's actually trying to lean away from her and back against the bar. When his eyes meet mine, they almost seem to be pleading.

My frown deepens as I look between the two of them. There's something off about her...

And then it hits me. It's his recent ex, Sabrina. The one that's still not over him and that runs into him a little too often for it not to be suspicious.

I rack my memory for what I know about her. I vaguely remember Tristan telling Jax about how she was great in the beginning: she understood that he wasn't looking for anything and was content with just a physical relationship. He liked that she wasn't trying to "tame him" like most girls do. But after a few weeks it turned out she was actually playing a very different game. Instead of trying to lock Tristan down, she was trying to hang on his coattails until he made it to the UFC, where she was planning to find a "real fighter" to seduce. She just wanted to be a WAG. Tristan broke it off with her after he overheard her telling a friend as much.

From across the bar, I watch her press against Tristan, and I realize that she clearly hasn't given up on that idea.

He looks at me again, still pleading. When he mouths 'help me,' I roll my eyes and throw my hands up in defeat.

I don't know if it's because I feel grateful for how he protected Hailey or if I just hate the sight of Sabrina hanging all over him, but I decide to play along.

I saunter up to Tristan. Ignoring Sabrina completely, I straddle Tristan's hips and wrap my arms around his neck.

"Baby," I pout dramatically. "I thought we were leaving."

Tristan's expression is equal parts shock and amusement, but he contains himself enough not to let it show. He slides his hands over my hips and pulls me a little closer, forcing me to arch my back. A smirk tugs at the corner of his lips.

"I'm sorry, *baby*," he responds, and I can hear the sarcasm in the endearment. He knows I'm the last girl to ever call a guy baby. "You're right, I promised I'd take you home."

I smile seductively and lean forward, brushing my lips against his cheek. "Good, because there's something I want to try tonight," I purr, just loud enough for Sabrina to hear. I hear Tristan's sharp intake of air and feel his grip tighten on my hips. I smirk and lightly nip his earlobe before pulling away.

His eyes still sparkle with delight but now there's an intense fire smoldering behind them, as well. His stare tries to burn through my charade to see what's behind it, and for a moment I forget that I'm faking it all. I get lost in his gaze. For a few seconds, it feels like we're the only two people in the entire bar.

"Umm, who the fuck are you?" I hear from beside me. I turn startled eyes to a very angry looking Sabrina. Her arms are crossed and she's willing me to drop dead with her eyes.

"Oh. Hi. I'm Remy," I offer sweetly. "His girlfriend."

Her eyes narrow and I can practically see the steam coming out of her ears. "He's never mentioned you," she says tightly.

I shrug and turn back to Tristan with a sexy smile. "It's a new thing. But when it's this good..." I purr softly as I shift closer to him, "...you forget about everyone else."

As I watch, the fire in his eyes becomes a blazing inferno.

"Listen, slut—" Sabrina starts. But without waiting for the rest of her threat, I unwind myself from Tristan and step back. I grab his hand and tug gently.

"Come on, baby, let's get out of here," I whine. "The vibe in here is way too plastic." Tristan is one joke away from outright laughing at my poorly concealed insults, but he stands anyway.

Sabrina, on the other hand, reaches a whole new level of infuriated when I cut her off. She rips our hands apart and steps between Tristan and I, putting herself right in my face.

"You have no idea who you're dealing with," she snarls. "He would never pick an ugly dyke like you over someone like me. Just stop embarrassing yourself and go home."

Over her shoulder I see Tristan's nostrils flare with anger. He opens his mouth to say something, but I stop him with a slight shake of my head.

A crazy smile stretches across my face—as if I'm happy for the confrontation. "I know exactly who I'm dealing with," I tell her. "You're hardly the first attention whore that's tried to attach herself to his career. And trust me, honey, you're going to need more than fake words and a plastic rack to keep his attention." I hear snickering from around us. Shocker—our cat fight has drawn some attention. "I would recommend trying for one of the idiot narcissists in the amateur circuit. They're probably the only ones your act can fool."

Sabrina's eyes flare with anger and she opens her mouth to snap back at me. But once again I cut her off. "Stay the fuck away from Tristan," I snarl. "I don't want to see your desperate ass stalking him ever again. And if I do, or if you ever lay a hand on me again..." I step close enough to her that our noses almost touch. I don't even care that she's a few inches taller than me—I know how to straighten my shoulders to make myself seem dominant, even from below. Her eyes widen in fear. "...I will fuck you up so bad that you'll never be pretty enough for anyone, ever again."

I hold her terrified gaze, waiting patiently for her to look away first.

She takes a shaky step away from me, her eyes darting between Tristan and I. Then with a final attempt at appearing dignified, she straightens with a huff before turning and walking away. I watch her leave with a victorious grin plastered on my face.

"Holy shit," I hear Tristan whisper in shock. He looks at me with awe. "You actually got rid of her. I've been trying to do that for weeks."

I roll my eyes and take my seat at the bar again, trying very hard to forget how close Tristan and I were just a few moments ago. I try to will my heartrate to slow down. I even flag the bartender down for two shots, hoping that'll do the trick.

"Poor Tristan," I coo mockingly. "Too many women fawning over him." I flash a tight grin at his scowl.

"It's not funny," he grumbles. He sits down on the barstool next to me. "She was awful. I couldn't figure out how to get rid of her without an actual restraining order." He grins at me, still looking impressed. "I had no idea I just had to sic Remy on her. I might need you to do that for a few other girls, too."

I glare at him before downing the double shot of tequila that just appeared in front of me. "You're a pig," I growl, wincing at the feel of the liquor's comforting burn. "I should've just let her have you."

I feel Tristan's body shift to face me. "Yeah, why didn't you let her have me?" he muses. "That's now the second woman you've driven away from me. If I didn't know better, I'd say you were jealous."

I don't know if it's a placebo effect or if the tequila really has hit me already, but the extra dose of alcohol settles me into the category of perfectly tipsy—which is my favorite level of drunk, since I just end up happy and unable to give two shits about anything else.

Emboldened by the buzz running through my veins, I

turn to study Tristan thoughtfully. "Maybe I was just trying to repay you for helping my sister," I answer honestly. I lean a little bit closer to whisper, "Maybe, out of the two of us, I'm not the one that's doing the chasing."

There's no longer any amusement in his eyes—the inferno from only a few minutes ago is back in full force. I suck in a breath at the intensity of being enveloped by his fire, unable to look away.

His eyes dart to my lips. The hunger in his gaze makes my heart start to beat faster.

I try to say something, anything, to break the spell, but no words come out. I lick my lips and try again.

At the sight of my tongue running along my bottom lip, a low growl slips from Tristan. His grip tightens around his shot glass. My breath catches when he starts to lean in.

"Damn, you two are just magnets for bar drama."

I jump, startled. Tristan and I quickly pull away from each other as we turn stunned eyes toward a very drunk Aiden.

He just chuckles. "First that guy went after Remy, then today Tristan's stalker shows up. You guys should be each other's bodyguards." And with that, he claps Tristan on the shoulder and walks away, completely oblivious to his interruption.

Fortunately, his intrusion is enough to shake me from whatever spell I was just under. I glance nervously at Tristan as I stand up. I'm about to be actually drunk in a few minutes and I feel like I need to get out of this bar.

"I'm going home," I announce, looking everywhere but at Tristan. "Aiden's right, I've had enough excitement this weekend. I'll just see you... around the house." I turn to search the bar for the remaining friends in our group.

I feel Tristan gently grab my wrist before I can walk

away. "I don't want you out there alone," he says gruffly. "I'll take you."

I finally turn to look at him. I don't know if it's the alcohol that's driven away my need to fight, or the protective tone in his voice, but I nod my acceptance.

Without letting go of my arm, he downs the remaining double shot before pulling me after him. "Let's get the fuck out of here," he murmurs.

We quickly realize that Aiden and Max are the only ones left from our group. They're both heavily invested in a drunk debate—most likely about boxing versus wrestling, if I know those guys at all. Only an attractive, single female could tear them from their conversation.

Instead of interrupting them, we pay our tabs and head outside. I stand awkwardly on the sidewalk as Tristan calls an Uber on his phone. And I suddenly realize: I have no idea how to act around him right now. I feel like I have whiplash from the evening as a whole, and when I said I was leaving it was mostly because I wanted to come outside for a breath of fresh air and to clear my thoughts for a minute. But now Tristan is with me and I feel like I can't accomplish either of those things.

Between him protecting Hailey and then what happened with Sabrina, are we supposed to be friendly now? I feel like we had a comfortable, not-quite-aggressive flow going with his game at the bar before the fake-girl-friend act completely threw me off of that. I don't know if Tristan's gotten sexier or if I'm just tipsier than I realize, but either way I can still feel the taste of desire choking me. I can't even look at him without blushing from the memory of his hands tightening on my hips and pulling me closer.

As I'm standing on the sidewalk waging an internal war with myself, I notice a familiar face out of the corner of my eye. I turn slightly and realize Sabrina is on the other side of the street with a group of her girlfriends.

She sees me at the same time that I spot her. Her eyes dart from me to Tristan and I realize with a jolt that what she thinks she's seeing is Tristan taking me home for the night. And even though we'll both get in the car and we really will be going home to the same place, my fake girlfriend story from earlier probably won't sell very well if I'm standing awkwardly to the side with my arms wrapped around myself. If I were his girlfriend with the promise of sex, I'd most likely be all over him.

I only hesitate for a heartbeat before I grit my teeth and steel myself for what I'm about to do. I make a quick wish that my drunken attraction to Tristan doesn't carry me away in my performance this time.

I step up to stand in front of him and nervously wrap my arms around his waist. I tilt my head up to appear like I'm demanding his full attention.

Tristan looks up from his phone in surprise but moves his arms out of the way so I can move my body closer to his. My skin tingles even through my dress where the hand not holding his phone comes to rest on my hip. He looks down at me in confusion, and I can't help but feel the same way, even as I feel a comfortable warmth being this close to him. It vaguely registers in the back of my mind that this is now the second time tonight we've been this intimate, and neither of us has seemed very put-off by it.

"I... um... I thought..." I stutter. I have so many things I should be saying right now. I want to tell him that Sabrina is watching us and that I assume he'd want me to keep the charade going—that we should probably try to look like we're going home together. But the tequila is running through my veins now and I can't tell if I'm feeling drunk or just drunk on his closeness. Suddenly every single thought flies out of my mind, and all I can think about is that his blue eyes are boring into mine and his lips are only a breath away.

At that thought, my gaze drops to his mouth. My heart starts beating so loud that I'm afraid he'll hear it, but I don't think I could avoid the pull of my body to his even if I wanted to.

My gaze darts back to his eyes to see him studying me, looking equal amounts surprised and hungry. That look is what gives me the confidence to push up on my toes and press my lips to his.

My eyes close at the contact. His lips are soft and warm, and a comfortable buzz runs through my body. I feel Tristan's hand tighten on my hip as his mouth starts to move against mine. I sigh and settle into the kiss.

I gently kiss his top lip, then his bottom. I pause, feeling unsure of myself for only a moment before I open my mouth to deepen the kiss. Our tongues touch and my breath catches at the sensation.

It seems to affect Tristan, too. The moment our kiss intensifies and our tongues begin to tangle, a deep groan rumbles through his chest. His grip tightens on my hips and he pulls me forward so that there isn't an inch of space between us. He tilts his head and greedily demands control of the kiss. I give him that power with a grateful shiver.

He licks my lips, coaxing them to open further. Every swipe of his tongue drives a bolt of lightning through me, another rush of liquid heat to my core. It doesn't take long for the power of this kiss to destroy me so thoroughly that my head spins and my knees grow weak, and I'm left breathless and clinging to Tristan's waist.

I somehow manage to end the kiss before I demand he

drag me down an alley to finish what I started. I pull back just far enough so I can look at him and tell him... something that I need to tell him but can't quite remember right now.

He's just as breathless as I am. We stand there, completely oblivious to the fact that we're blocking the sidewalk and forcing people to walk around us, and stare at each other as we suck air into our lungs and try to make sense of what just happened. He looks completely confused, but his hands stay holding my hips, as if he doesn't want to give me more than an inch of space.

Because he looks like he wants to go in for round two.

We're shocked out of our mess of thoughts when Tristan's phone rings. He looks down at the phone in his hand as if he's never seen one before and is now trying to figure out what to do with it.

The shrill sound snaps me out of my trance. I shuffle out of his embrace, still dizzy from the tequila or lust-drunk haze. I feel my senses come back to me along with the memory of what I was trying to tell Tristan. "Sabrina was watching us," I tell him hurriedly. I'm not sure why I need him to understand that there was a reason for what I did but I suddenly feel the need to explain my actions.

He raises his eyebrows in surprise. Then his eyes dart around, looking for the girl in question, and it seems like he finds her because his gaze immediately hardens and a scowl forms on his face. I think it's intended for Sabrina but when he turns back to me, that angry expression grows even angrier when it's aimed at me.

He finally answers the phone with a terse, "Hello?" He looks away from me and down the street.

I swallow roughly as my face flames with embarrassment. I thought I was helping the situation by kissing him but based on his reaction, it seems I've misjudged everything. I step further away from him.

After a short phone conversation, he turns back to me, jerking his head over his shoulder and signaling the car that's currently pulling up in front of us. "That's us. Get in," he says gruffly. There's definitely a bite in his tone.

The ride home is a quiet one. The last shot from the bar seems to have finally made its way into my bloodstream because despite my lips still tingling and the feel of Tristan's fingers imprinted on my hips, my shoulders relax, and I forget about the scowling man sitting next to me. I even forget about the sudden desperation to escape Tristan that shot through me when he became angry after our kiss. I can see the rigid set of Tristan's jaw out of the corner of my eye and the tense way he's gripping his thighs. If I were sober, I'd probably try to figure out how he went from seductive gentleman to his usual emotionless, pain-in-the-ass self in under a minute. But I'm not, so instead I sigh and close my eyes.

When we pull up to the house, Tristan thanks the driver and gets out of the car. I follow quietly behind him as he starts walking toward the house. We're almost to the door when I trip—on thin air, like a cliché drunk—and fall forward.

Tristan catches me before my face can meet the pavement and pulls me upright. "Jesus, watch it," he barks, steadying me on my feet. "Can you not be a klutz for just one second?"

I study him for a moment, then sigh and decide not to fight him. I blame—or credit?—the alcohol for my lack of anger and aggressive comebacks. Instead of feeling defensive, I realize suddenly that I just don't care.

Without thinking about what I'm doing, I step closer to

him and run my fingers through his hair, trying to understand the sudden shift in his mood. His eyebrows shoot up in surprise, but he stands still and lets me play with strands of his hair. Without the tequila coursing through my veins, I never would have let myself touch him like this. But right now, I can't find it in me to care.

"It must be exhausting being so mean all the time," I observe thoughtfully. Something flashes in his eyes, but I can't put a name to it, and then it's gone just as quickly.

I turn away from him, completely oblivious to how much I just overstepped our normal boundaries. "Not to mention you would be so much hotter with just a little less snark," I call over my shoulder. I'm too busy drunkenly fumbling with my keys in the lock to notice his eyes widen at my honest comment.

"Ha!" I exclaim triumphantly, pushing the door open and stepping inside. But before I can take more than two steps in, I feel myself being pushed to the wall, Tristan's body pressing tightly against mine. "Hey!" I cry. His moody expression is gone, replaced with the smug face that I know so well.

"You would hate me if I was a nice guy," he drawls.

I roll my eyes at him, trying to push him off me. "Guess we'll never know, because you being a nice guy is as likely as me using the word 'literally' wrong." He grins, knowing how much I hate when girls use the word to describe something that is very clearly not literal.

"Admit it," he says softly, pushing me harder into the wall with his body. My breath catches as his face nears mine. "You like me the way I am."

"I—I don't—" my brain no longer seems to be able to form a coherent sentence. All I can do is stare into his hungry gaze and try not to picture what it would feel like if he fucked me against this wall right now.

His lips brush against my cheek, at the same time that he kneads my hips with his fingers. Every touch, every whisper of his breath, is further uncoiling the heat that's growing between my legs.

"You don't want someone to pull your chair out for you, or ask you what you want to eat," he continues. "You want someone that doesn't need your permission. Someone that will call you on your shit." He tangles his fingers in my hair and pulls my head back. I gasp in surprise. "You want someone that will spank you when you're acting stupid."

I can't contain the whimper that slips from my lips. I squeeze my legs together, trying to think of a response but failing. When he pulls back to wait for my reply, I know that no words could answer his unspoken question.

There are so many things that I hate about this man— he's arrogant, and selfish, and rude. He's a player that uses women for sex, and the only thing he actually gives a shit about is fighting. He's the definition of self-absorbed. I should be shoving him away from me, telling him to fuck off and to stay on his side of the house for the rest of the week. I shouldn't be thinking about what he tastes like, or how his cock might feel inside of me. I shouldn't be wondering how hard he could make me come.

But his words remind me that the same alpha qualities that make me hate him... are also the ones that are making my knees weak.

I realize in that moment that every insult, every prank, every teasing comment, is exactly what ratcheted up our sexual tension this week. His alpha personality is what drives the fire between us. We couldn't have one without the other. And I am so desperately, achingly, tired of fighting that fire...

So, whether it's the tequila or the need to finish the kiss that we started, I decide I don't want to fight it anymore.

I learn forward and roughly press my lips against his, my hands fisting in his shirt. I press my body as close to his as possible—suddenly, I can't seem to get close enough. The tension between us steals my breath away. It feels like every place we touch is on fire. I part my lips, my tongue darting forward to stroke his.

He groans and opens his mouth. He pushes me harder against the wall—it feels like he can't get close enough, either. His kiss is brutal and aggressive, and I know my lips will bruise but I don't care. In this moment, I want all of his roughness.

As if reading my mind, his hand shoots up to grip the front of my throat and push my head back against the wall. I moan in pleasure. He grins at my response and kisses me again.

"You might regret what you just started," he growls against my lips. "Hate sex can be intense. And with the way you and I feel about each other, I might actually kill you with pleasure."

His arrogant promises make my cunt pulse, because I have zero doubt that he is going to do exactly as he says.

"Just shut up," I snap—and pull his lips back to mine.

10

TRISTAN

It feels like my body is operating on its own accord because I still can't make sense of the fact that she's kissing me. This whole night has been a clusterfuck of emotions, and I think it's taking a minute for my brain to catch up. But the one thing that's undeniable is the fact that I've been hard for Remy since the moment I saw her at the bar. I've seen her in skirts for work, but I've never seen her dressed up like she is tonight. I damn near lost my mind when I looked across the bar and saw her in this tight little dress.

I wasn't going to do anything about it, though. I wasn't even going to approach her tonight. I was content to just watch her in her element, tipsy and happy and having a good time with her friends. I realized that I only ever see her serious or angry—but happiness looks sexy as fuck on her. I just wanted to watch her a little bit.

But then that asshole put his hands on her sister, and I couldn't not get involved. People might think I'm a woman-izer but one thing I will never fucking allow in my presence is any sort of disrespect or violence against women. Or anyone I care about, really, but especially a woman like

Hailey who doesn't seem to see the abuse for what it is. I am nothing if not protective of the people around me.

I also felt a thrill of pleasure when I saw Remy about to step in just before I did. I've known that she's fiercely loyal to the people she loves but it's another thing to see that she really would've thrown down with a grown ass man for her sister, consequences be damned. If I wasn't so furious at that shitbag her sister calls a boyfriend, I may have sat back with a drink to watch her hand that guy his ass.

I was impressed, and that feeling multiplied tenfold when Sabrina joined the evening's events. Remy had no obligation to help me get rid of her, but fuck, am I glad that she did. That girl has been nothing but a headache since the very beginning. Yeah, she was good in the sack, but from the first time she tried to convince me she didn't want anything from me, I could tell there was something off about her. The fact that she couldn't leave me alone when I broke it off with her and kept "accidentally" running into me in the city was just further proof that my gut instincts were right. I really thought I was going to have to get a restraining order at some point.

I like to think Remy helped me out because she felt some respect for me tonight, too. Not just because I helped her sister, but also because I managed to make her feel comfortable around me with that ridiculous assumption game we played at the bar. Maybe she's finally starting to see that I'm not as much of a bad guy as she always thought I was. Maybe she's realized that I'm not just a selfish bastard, but a loyal and protective one. The same way I'm starting to realize she's not as bitchy as I once thought she was—she just comes off that way when she's defensive. But whatever it was that opened her up to helping me, I felt instantly grateful the second she straddled my lap. Grateful... and other things.

I knew she was only doing it because Sabrina was standing next to us but holy *shit* did she feel right in my arms. I couldn't help tugging her closer any more than I could help the fact that my breathing sped up when she started whispering in my ear. I tried so hard to see if there was any part of her that was enjoying the closeness as much as I was, but I had no way to tell while Sabrina was still there.

I thought I got my answer when she kissed me on the street. I thought she was acting on the heat that I know she felt between us at the bar. And goddamn, did that heat explode when she kissed me. I'm not typically a huge fan of kissing—it feels more intimate than a lot of other sexual activities—but in that moment, it was all I wanted to do. I couldn't get enough of Remy's lips. I felt such relief that she was feeling the same things I was. And when she pulled away and told me she only did it because Sabrina was watching, that relief morphed into anger and humiliation on a scale that I've never felt before.

But by the time we got back to the house, I managed to calm down enough to realize that it couldn't possibly be all in my head. I couldn't be the only one feeling the sexual tension between us. And even if it was purely physical, even if Remy still didn't like me, I knew she wanted to give in to this thing between us. It's been growing for days, probably years—we just didn't know what it was because we hid the truth with our verbal sparring.

But no more. No more dancing around this tension. No more hiding behind sexual innuendos, or pranks, or conde-scending digs. By the time she pushed into the house, I had decided she was going to have to make a decision: either admit she felt it too or reject me to my face.

I needed her to make the first real move. Not only because she'd been drinking but mainly because I wanted her to want me. I wanted her to show me that she needs me just as much as I need her. And now that she's kissing me, I don't think I'll be able to stop.

It feels like there are currents of electricity running through my body. Right now, as my hand is curled around her throat and I'm nipping her jawline, she's running her hands up and down my lower back. Energy emanates from every place she touches me. As I hit a particularly sensitive spot on her neck, she digs her fingers into my hips and presses herself tighter against my body with a moan.

I growl as the motion causes my dick to get even harder than it already is. My jeans are cutting into me and I'm already past the point of feeling uncomfortable. If I don't get my dick out and inside her soon, I think I might actually lose my mind.

But even in my feelings of horny desperation, I want Remy to come first. I *need* her to come first. I'm obsessed with the thought of her spasming around my fingers, my tongue, my cock. Ever since last night—when I almost kissed her after she came home from the bar—I've been dying to know what she looks like when she loses control. Despite my better judgment, I actually let myself jerk off to the thought of her coming on my fingers. And right now, with her under my hands, her pleasure is the only thing I give a shit about.

I lick back up her neck until I'm teasing her lips again. I can still taste a hint of her cherry chapstick, though it's not as overwhelming to my senses as it was when she kissed me on the street. It's faded enough so that it's her natural, sweet taste on my tongue now, mixed with the subtle sting of tequila. It's an intoxicating combination, and I'm thrown right back into what damn near destroyed me earlier tonight. My head spins with how much I want to touch her, taste her, consume her. I slide my tongue in her mouth with a groan.

She surrenders in my arms. Almost immediately, she begins desperately tugging at my shirt, trying to speed up our dance.

I chuckle and shake my head. "Not so fast, Remy baby," I tease. "I'm going to take my time with this." Grabbing both of her wrists, I pin them above her head with one of my hands.

She frowns at my scolding and begins weakly struggling against my grasp. But as soon as I'm kissing her jaw, her neck, her collarbone, she shivers and stops fighting.

"Good girl," I whisper. "What's the rush? We have all night."

Then, slowly, I begin tracing my other hand down her body. She's still wearing her little black dress but it's so tight that it's not leaving much to the imagination. It's also cut low enough that her breasts are perfectly in my view, and all I can think about is how I can't wait to strip them completely bare so that I can marvel in their every detail.

I gently trace the curve of her breast before moving lower, down her side, further still until I finally reach the top of her thigh and the edge of her dress. I begin softly caressing her thigh. I'll be rough later, but for now, I'm enjoying teasing her with light touches. Then I'm slipping a finger underneath the fabric of her dress, continuing to stroke her soft skin.

I capture her gasp with my lips. I take the opportunity to slide my tongue inside, caressing her tongue the same way my fingers are caressing her skin below. I can't get enough of the fire between us when our mouths collide.

I grab a fistful of her dress and pull it up a few inches. I'm dizzy with the thought of finally being able to touch her, to see how wet she is. It was all I could think about when she was straddling me at the bar. Without a second thought, I grab her panties and rip them from her body. A whimper escapes her, and she drops her head forward as she begins to pant against my lips, her long, wavy hair falling forward to frame her face, adding to her look of dishevelment. I can practically feel her body start to vibrate with need. I move my hand to her thigh and begin sliding up, and I can hear her breath hitch as I come close, so close. But I still don't give her what she wants.

"Tristan," she hisses through clenched teeth. "If you don't touch me in the next two seconds, I swear I'm going to hit you with that knee you taught us today."

I chuckle at her desperation, continuing to touch her everywhere but where she wants me to. I stroke the inside of her thighs, her lower belly, sometimes getting dangerously close to her damp heat but never giving her what she's really asking for.

"You won't," I murmur in her ear. "Because if you do, what will I fuck your sweet pussy with?" And then just as she groans at my dirty words, I slide my fingers between her lips and spread her wetness along her slit. Once my fingertips are drenched, I drag them up and start lazily circling her clit.

Her groan deepens and she drops her head against the wall, her eyes closing. I continue my assault on her engorged clit, still using a slow pace because I know it's driving her absolutely crazy.

Once I'm satisfied that she's accepted this is my game

and that she won't try to rush me again, I push a finger deep inside her. My thumb stays pressed to her clit. I slowly start to push into her.

"Tristan," she whimpers. "I—I can't... it's too slow..."

Before she's finished her sentence, I've added another finger and quickened my pace. My desperation is also building, and I can't hold back much longer. I kiss her lips hungrily as my fingers push deeper into her.

She starts trembling, and I know she's close. I can feel it in her moans. She's soaked and getting wetter by the second. I can hear the sound of my fingers moving in and out of her and it drives blood straight to my already-hard dick. She's trying to open her legs further to give me more access—so I can give her more of what she needs. Her body is desperate for release. She's going to come any second.

And when I bite down on her pulse point, she does.

She gasps as her orgasm hits. Her body begins spasming, and I tighten my grip on her hands above her head to keep her from falling. I continue pushing in and out of her. Through her waves of pleasure, I can feel her walls squeezing my fingers, over and over again, making me groan as I marvel in the feeling of her.

Eventually, I feel her body stop shaking. I let go of her hands and instead wrap my arms around her waist—I can feel her coming back to herself and steadying her legs. She blinks her eyes open as if she just woke up.

Holding her eyes, I lift my hand to my mouth and slowly suck her taste off my fingers.

"Just as sweet as I knew you would be," I mutter.

She looks at me, stunned, and whispers a simple, "Fuck."

I chuckle and kiss along her jawline. "That was just the first one, *baby*. Better buckle up."

She blushes at my words and fists her hands in my shirt,

pulling me closer. "I still hate your fucking guts," she murmurs before pulling my mouth down to hers.

I smirk against her lips. "I would expect nothing less."

As she's kissing me, she starts to unbutton my jeans. "Remy..." I growl. I try to knock her hands away since this is my game to play, but she's adamant now about what she wants. She's already pushed my jeans and briefs over my hips enough that she can now free my dick. I groan as she wraps her hand around me.

"My turn now," she whispers against my lips. And before I realize what she's doing, she's sliding down the wall to kneel before me.

I brace my hands against the wall in front of me and gawk at the sight below me. There's something so provocative about this woman at my feet, made even better by the fact that she's now wedged between my cock and the wall.

She wastes no time licking the pre-cum from my tip. I hiss at the sensation, already failing at trying to hide from her how much she's affecting me. With a final smirk thrown my way, she covers me with her lips.

It doesn't take her long to work her mouth down my shaft, inch by inch, until I'm balls deep in her throat. She doesn't even flinch, just pulls back to the tip and then dips right back down until my length has disappeared in her mouth again. She tightens her lips around me and sucks hard as she bobs forward and back.

"*Fuck*, Remy..." I grit through my teeth. She's way too fucking good at this.

She ignores me and continues her furious pace, moaning every time my hips twitch and I drive deeper into her mouth. It almost seems like she's forgotten I'm here, like the only part of me that she's focused on is getting as much of my dick in her mouth as possible. The thought makes me want to come on the spot.

It registers in the back of my mind that Remy is very, *very* far from the prude I once thought she might be.

After only a minute, I realize I can't take any more. Her mouth is just too fucking perfect. "Enough," I snarl, stepping back and pulling her to her feet. I barely recognize my own raspy voice. Her body is pressed tight to mine, my arm automatically wrapping around her back, and I'm once again reminded of how easily she fits against me. "If you keep doing that we won't get to the fucking part."

She ignores my comment and instead grabs my hand, pushing it against her warm cunt.

"Feel how wet that just made me," she purrs against my lips. And I do. She's drenched. She's even wetter now than when she came on my fingers just a few minutes ago.

Did she really just get that turned on from sucking my dick?

Fuck. I am so fucked.

I suddenly have zero interest in teasing her or taking things slowly. I walk into the living room, pulling her behind me. Games and fun are over. I need to fuck this girl before I lose my mind.

I spin her to stand in front of me at the edge of the couch. With her back to me I place a hand on her stomach, pulling her flush against my chest. The other hand grips her hip possessively. I nip at her neck, loving how she shivers at my touch.

"I've been thinking about bending you over this couch all week," I growl in her ear.

Before I lose too much of my head, I pull a condom from my pocket and toss it on the armrest. I'm just about to push her down when she grabs the foil and twists her head to show it to me.

"I'm on the pill," she says matter-of-factly. "And I hate condoms. I also know you're religious about using them, which means you should be clean. I am too. We're not using one now."

I blink, stunned. But she's waiting for my answer, so I nod, once—and then swallow nervously as I realize just how badly I wanted to fuck her bare.

I take the packet from her hand and chuck it across the room. And before she can say anything else, I grab the back of her head and push down, folding her over the armrest.

She catches herself with her hands and automatically pushes back into me. I groan as she rubs her ass against me. But I feel like I need to regain the power in our dynamic right now, so I step back and drop a slap onto her exposed ass cheek.

She yelps in surprise, then immediately spreads her legs a little wider, pushing her dress further up her hips and revealing more of her perfect ass. She's so horny she can't even control how her body is reacting to me.

I debate dropping my pants and impaling her right then and there but decide I need to make her come one more time first. I drop to my knees behind her and lick the length of her slit.

And immediately groan when I taste how perfectly sweet—and *drenched*—she is. Tasting her on my fingers was nothing compared to the experience of dipping my tongue into her. I hungrily trace over the length of her again.

She moans at the contact and buckles, barely catching herself before she drops onto the couch. I grab her thighs in a punishing grip and start teasing her with my tongue.

Fuck, she tastes so good. I could spend the entire night

right here behind her. I alternate between lapping at her wet cunt and sucking on her swollen clit, and when I spear her entrance with my tongue, I feel a whole body shiver run through her.

I'm no longer taking my time. We both sense each other's feelings of desperation and I'm setting a rapid pace to match it. I can tell she's getting close by the way she's breathing. She's panting, pushing her soaking pussy into my face and begging for more friction. Just as she's about to explode, I press the pad of my thumb against her asshole.

She screams as her release tears through her. She's shaking, whimpering, as I continue to lazily tongue the bundle of nerves above her pussy. I slowly ease off as I feel her coming back down.

But before she's fully recovered, I'm already standing and pushing my pants to the floor. I grab her hips and slide in deep.

She gasps at the sudden intrusion—then immediately starts meeting my thrusts, pushing her ass back and begging for more. I groan and drive in even harder.

I can't stop staring at the view in front of me, at the sight of my dick covered in her orgasm and sliding in and out of her tight pussy. Even with her dress still on, I can see the perfect curves running from her tiny waist to her plump ass. Her cheeks shake tantalizingly with each thrust. I slap one, hard, and relish the sound of her gasp-turned-moan.

"You're so deep," she whimpers. I see her hands start to scrabble at the couch, as if she's trying to find something to hold onto. The vision just makes me growl and hit even deeper. "Oh my god, *Tristan.*"

I throw my head back with a slew of muttered curses as I feel my release growing in my balls. I knew as soon as she was bent over in front of me that this wouldn't last a long time, but I still need her to come again before I can finish.

I lean forward until my chest is pressed against her back and my lips touch her ear. "Such a good fucking girl," I whisper. "You take my cock so well." My hand slips around her waist and slides down until I'm massaging her clit again.

"God yes," she moans. "Don't stop, I'm s-so close..."

"I know you are," I growl, rubbing her a little faster. "I can feel how drenched you are, how much your pussy is tightening around my cock and getting ready to come again. You feel fucking amazing."

I let my tongue slide along her neck, nipping her skin and looking for the sweet spot that will make her go crazy. "You love being fucked like this, don't you? You love how deep I can get, how rough I can take you. I can fuck you as hard as I know you like to be fucked."

She whimpers at my words, which is as much of an admission as I need that I have her pleasure pegged perfectly. I find the spot along her neck just below her ear that makes her knees buckle again when I bite and suck at the skin. I wrap my other arm around her waist to keep her from falling and increase the furious tempo of my fingers on her clit. I'm craving her release more than I can ever remember wanting it from a woman. If I don't feel her waves of pleasure around me soon, I might actually lose my goddamn mind.

Suddenly, I'm ready to end this. I move the hand that was gripping her hips up to wrap around her throat. I squeeze. "I need you to come on my cock, Remy. *Now*. Come for me."

At my grip and my words, she explodes beneath me. I feel her pussy squeeze me, hard, as her orgasm shakes her whole body. My release is only a few seconds behind hers—

there isn't a chance I would've been able to get through the feeling of her coming on my cock without exploding myself. I groan, spilling inside her.

I lean against her back, my cheek pressed to her shoulder. Our breaths are both ragged and I can feel her shaking from the aftershock of her orgasm.

Not wanting to crowd her with my weight for too long, I straighten up and step back. I readjust my pants as I watch Remy out of the corner of my eye.

She stands up and quickly tugs her dress down to cover herself. As she smooths her just-fucked hair, I can tell she's avoiding my gaze. She's spent so long hating me that she doesn't know how to react to this change in our relationship —or what it means.

I don't know either but what I do know, without a shadow of a doubt, is that I won't be able to stop after one time. I rack my brain for something to say that can ease her nerves.

"Remy, I—" I start, but she cuts me off, finally looking up at me.

"It's okay, you don't need to do that," she says quickly. "Let's just... forget it."

I don't know if she changed what she was going to say or if she's telling me to forget what we just did, but before I get a chance to ask, she's grabbed her ripped panties from the hall and rushed up the steps.

And I'm left standing in shock, trying to make sense of what just happened.

Fuck. Jax is going to kill me.

That's my second thought after waking up the next

morning. The first is that last night was hands down the best sex I've ever had. My dick is still rock hard hours later from just the thought of Remy's pussy wrapped around me.

I groan and drag my hand down my face.

I know I should regret it, for a number of reasons. For one, Remy hates me. Giving her a few orgasms won't change that. For another, she's basically Jax's little sister. He never explicitly said I couldn't pursue her, but that man is insanely protective of her and he is definitely not going to be happy when he finds out what happened. And the last thing I need is any kind of bad blood with my best friend.

But *fuck*, I couldn't help myself. This whole week has been one long game of foreplay. In all honesty, it's probably been years of foreplay, ever since we first met. I've never denied that Remy is hot, and even hate is a form of passion. Our sarcasm and barbed insults have only fueled the fire between us. And then after everything that happened last night, there's not a chance in hell I would've been able to say no to her. Last night, I needed Remy more than I've ever needed any woman.

I groan again at the memory of what it felt like when we both finally gave in. I know she must've been trying to fight the temptation the same way that I was—I could see the turmoil in her eyes the entire time we were at the bar. I know she didn't want to admit to liking me and I know she would never want to do anything to hurt Jax. But this... *thing* that's been brewing between us this week was just too much. I don't think either of us could've resisted when we were finally alone.

And giving into that temptation resulted in one hell of an explosion. I have never, in ten years of fucking, ever had chemistry like that with a woman. It was like we both knew exactly what the other wanted without ever having to say a word. First time sex is usually tame at best, and awkward at worst.

Last night put that theory to shame.

Watching how responsive Remy was to my touch was mesmerizing. It was like I knew exactly what she wanted, and her body would immediately reward me for giving it to her. I'm pretty sure I have her turn-ons pegged perfectly, and I definitely could've pushed it last night to expose her true desires, but I was so desperate to be near her that I couldn't catch my breath enough to think past the singular thought of fucking her into the closest surface. After all these years of winding up the tension between us, combined with the physical closeness in every situation last night, it's a miracle I didn't explode the second I touched her.

Although with the level of chemistry that we clearly have, there's a part of me that worries that might be a possibility anytime I touch her.

I frown at that thought. Fucking Remy once was probably a mistake, but twice would definitely be a bad idea. I might be able to convince myself that last night was a result of booze, the thing with Sabrina, and hate-induced passion, but I wouldn't be able to explain another night. For so many reasons, Remy should be off limits.

I force myself to accept that fact as I climb out of bed and get ready for the gym. As much as I'd love a repeat performance of last night, I don't need to overcomplicate things by getting involved with my best friend's childhood best friend. I need to just write off what happened as a one-time thing that will never happen again. I can't say I won't tease her mercilessly for letting her body admit that I was right about her always secretly wanting to be under me, but I can keep my dick in my pants until Jax gets home. I only have one more week with Remy living in my house—surely,

I can keep my shit together for that long. After that, we can go back to only seeing each other when there are other people around, where there's no risk of us accidentally crossing this line again.

By the time I'm done getting dressed and throwing a change of clothes in my gym bag, I feel better than I did when I first woke up. I feel good about this resolution. As much as I shouldn't have let last night happen, I can keep it from getting worse. I can keep my hands to myself.

No matter how badly I want to bend her over again.

I open my bedroom door to leave, but the second I hit the hallway I realize that Remy is only as far as the other side of my wall. Immediately I'm hit with visions of her smooth skin, her firm ass, her silky brown hair. I remember the way her skin flushed pink after I spanked her, the way the aftershocks ran through her body when she came on my fingers. Her whimpers when the pleasure was too much for her to stay quiet. How tight she felt around me—

I groan as I feel my cock immediately harden. *Fuck. I am so fucked.*

11

REMY

I wake up to sunshine and the sound of the city. The feel of a no-alarm Sunday morning in a city I love is enough to let me ignore the alcohol-induced headache that's currently tickling my subconscious. I snuggle back into Jax's pillows with a small smile.

But then the memory of last night comes back in full force, and my subtle headache becomes a very large, very obnoxious one.

Fuck. I had sex with Tristan last night.

I groan and duck my head under the pillow. *What the fuck was I thinking?!*

The answer is that I wasn't. The answer is that I let my lust-fueled brain finally act on my attraction to him. And now he'll never let me hear the end of it.

I cringe when I think about the fact that I just became another one of Tristan's conquests. All the shit I talked on the women that have fallen into bed with him, and now I'm one of them. Seduced by his arrogance and that goddamn smirk.

Another groan falls from my lips. Not only do I have to

deal with his smugness probably showing tenfold now, but I also have another week with him here. Alone. With the memory of being bent over that couch floating through my brain every time I walk downstairs.

Fuck. This is so bad.

Not to mention, what will Jax say? Do I even tell him? Will Tristan tell him?

I frown, assuming the answer to that last question is probably a no. I doubt Tristan has a death wish, since telling Jax that he fucked his basically-sister is a good way to get a beating. But the only way he won't figure it out is if nothing changes between Tristan and me.

I sigh, knowing that's probably the best way to deal with this entire situation. It's not like it'll ever happen again. Partly because Tristan is a once and done kind of guy, but also because God knows I never need to let that happen again. So the best thing to do is to just act like it never did.

I sit up in bed, mentally steeling myself. I can do this. I can treat Tristan the same way I always have. I just need to glare at him and yell a few insults. Easy. Maybe after ignoring him for a few days, I'll be able to get the image of him pulling a screaming orgasm from me with his fingers out of my head. He practically lives at the gym anyway; it shouldn't be too hard to avoid him for a few days. And if I do see him, I'm just going to act like nothing ever happened. No problem.

And I'm just going to ignore the fact that it was the best goddamn sex of my life.

I groan and fall face first back into the pillows.

I manage to avoid him for almost two days. Miraculously, he's already left the gym when I show up on Monday night, so I fully expect him to be passed out by the time I get home. I even linger with Lucy in the parking lot after class to make sure I get home as late as possible.

Instead, I open the front door to see him sitting at the kitchen island. I freeze.

"Hey," I force out.

Fuck. I really did not want to have this conversation now.

He looks up from his phone with a lazy smirk. "Hey," he says.

"I thought you'd be asleep already," I stammer awkwardly as I force myself to walk into the kitchen to make my dinner.

The grin on his face grows. Of course he can tell I'm flustered. "Hoping to avoid me another night?"

I glare at him and start digging through the cabinets. *What's the quickest protein-dense meal I can make in about ninety seconds? I need out of this room.*

I spot the peanut butter and decide this is going to be a PB&J night. *Good enough.*

"So how long are you planning on ignoring me? Forever, or just until Jax gets home?" he asks, returning his attention to his dinner but keeping that stupid grin plastered on his face.

"I'm not ignoring you," I snap. "But what we, um... did the other night..." Fuck, I'm stuttering. "It doesn't mean I like you all of a sudden. I don't want to hang out with you now." I fumble with the peanut butter jar, trying to rush out of here as quickly as possible.

"Remy, we fucked," he says bluntly. "You can admit you liked it. We both know the truth, anyway. You can even admit you're a little obsessed with me now." If he grins any harder, I think his face might split in half.

"Don't flatter yourself," I snarl. I turn my attention to spreading the jelly on the piece of bread in front of me. "I was drunk, and horny. You could've been any guy." I stop, the anger causing my nerves to dissipate and making me feel more in control. I glance at Tristan. "To be honest, the whole night was pretty mediocre. Not quite obsession-worthy."

I'm lying through my teeth, but there isn't a chance in hell I'm going to admit that to him. He doesn't need to know that I haven't stopped thinking about that night. That I've touched myself three times since then to the thought of him fucking me. That I caught myself touching my lips a few times, remembering how electric his lips had felt against mine.

No, he doesn't need to know that. He can go on thinking I was unimpressed, that our relationship is the same angry, insult-fueled one that it always has been.

"You're a liar," he whispers in my ear. I yelp. I didn't even notice him come around the island.

His hands grip the counter on either side of my arms, effectively caging me in. He's not touching me, but he might as well be—I'm aware of every inch of his body that's close to mine. The fire between us pulses and I shiver as I feel his breath on my exposed neck.

"You can try to lie to yourself but we both know that night was hot as fuck," he breathes against my skin. "I still remember how wet and tight you felt when I bent you over the couch. My dick's getting hard just thinking about it."

I bite my lip to keep a moan from slipping out. I squeeze my legs together and try to ignore the heat growing between them. How is it possible for someone to make my knees weak with just his dirty words?

With his finger he scoops a bit of jelly out of the jar in front of me. Before I realize what he's doing, he spreads it on my lower lip, letting his touch linger for just a moment.

My tongue automatically darts out to lick it off. He growls at the sight. "I can't wait to have that mouth on me again," he mutters darkly.

I turn in his grip to face him, fury burning in my eyes. "Fuck you," I snarl angrily. "I am not one of your brainless fucktoys. Just because I drunkenly fucked you one night does not mean you can now have me in your bed whenever you want. I still hate you just as much as I did last week—probably more. So, if you think I'll ever let you in my pants again, you are out of your goddamn mind. One mistake was enough."

To my complete chagrin, his smile grows. He leans forward, lips almost touching mine. But I won't give him the satisfaction of backing away.

"We'll see," he whispers, just before his tongue slides across my lips and licks the remaining jelly off. With his smirk still fully in place, he turns and walks upstairs.

I'm still fuming about the run-in with Tristan when I wake up the next morning. I frown and curse my way through the morning, unable to stop his cocky words from replaying in my mind as I get ready for work.

So much for acting like nothing happened.

I should've known he wouldn't be able to let it go. He's too arrogant for his own good, and as much as I want to pretend our sex wasn't hot as fuck, there's no denying for either of us that it was.

I wonder briefly if the sex is that good with every girl he

sleeps with. Does he give all of them the best sex of their lives? Was Saturday even good for him?

I scowl at the direction of my thoughts and go back to styling my hair. Thinking of how I compare to the many women that have been in Tristan's bed is definitely not a productive use of brain power. Plus, it's sex—guys love sex regardless. And it was obviously good enough for him to think about during the following days, or he wouldn't have admitted to it. Well, that and the fact that he can't wait to do it again.

Which will definitely *not* be happening.

Nothing good can come of us having sex again—no matter how mind-bendingly good it was. My Sunday morning thoughts were only solidified by our encounter last night. Plus, watching him pine for something might actually be fun. If I can limit our interactions at the house and stay more than five feet away from him at all times, then I should be able to withstand his stupid fuck-me presence.

With that firm conviction ringing in my mind, I finish my morning routine and head to work, determined to put Tristan out of my mind and focus all my energy on the job that I'm lucky to have.

By the time lunch rolls around, I don't feel quite so lucky.

It's not often that I have days where I hate my job, but today is one of them. Most days I can coast by with minimal bad interactions, headphones in and typing away at whatever it is I need to research or write.

But today, it seems like someone has spiked the coffee with asshole juice. Everyone is ornery. I overhear more than one snappy exchange in the cubicles around me, as well as heated conversations loud enough to be heard through the conference room walls. It's not long before I'm on the receiving end of some of it myself.

Paul, the engineer that loves to not-so-subtly check out my legs, appears at my cubicle before I've even finished my first cup of coffee to grumble about some edits I made to his datasheet. Not long after he's gone, Cassandra appears in a whirlwind of high heels and too-strong perfume, demanding to know why her sales playbook isn't done yet.

I politely remind her that she only gave it to me on Friday, and that it's a twenty-two-page document that needs some serious touch-ups. Hardly a two-day turnaround time.

She glares at me before exiting with a huff.

I sigh and lean forward to hold my head in my hands, gently rubbing my temples. I can already feel the headache building.

"Long day?" I hear from beside me. I turn to see my coworker from the cubicle next to me peeking around our wall. A hint of a smile is tugging at the corner of his lips.

"Something like that," I mutter as I lean back in my chair. I stare up at the ceiling for a moment, debating asking my next question.

"What did you want to be when you were a kid?" I finally ask.

I can practically sense his wide-eyed surprise. My question is not one that's ever been included in typical workplace small talk.

"Umm, I think a fireman."

"And when you were in high school, getting ready to go to college?"

He frowns in concentration. He thinks about the question for a few seconds before answering honestly, "I wanted to create a non-profit for kids with trauma that need emotional support animals."

My eyes widen as I turn my attention fully to him. "Really?"

He swallows and nods, but doesn't go into more detail.

"Did you ever go into it? Or do you still want to?"

He nods again. "I obviously didn't have the means to do anything about it when I was in high school, so the plan was to go to college for business and then maybe figure something out. Then a job fell in my lap that I couldn't pass up and it just spiraled from there. I've been in tech ever since." He sighs and turns to stare off at some unseen target. "I always say I'll do it at some point. It's just... this job is too good and too hard to walk away from, you know?"

I wince but nod in agreement. "Yeah, I know what you mean. I think about the same thing sometimes." Then, in an effort to lighten the suddenly tense mood, I say, "Then again, some days Cassandra makes the idea incredibly appealing."

He lets out a relieved laugh. "Very true."

I grin at the only coworker that I don't hate. But before turning back to my computer, I pause, wanting to admit one last truth before we're shoved back into the daily grind of Corporate America.

"I hope you do it one day," I tell him honestly.

The smile slides off his face and the more serious expression returns. He swallows nervously but nods. "Me too," he says quietly.

The rest of my workday is fairly uneventful. The coffee continues to stay spiked and the people in the office continue to be on edge, but after Cassandra, the attitude seems to stay away from my cubicle, at least. I force myself to work through another two projects before deciding to actually stop working when I'm supposed to. At 5:00, I head down to the gym in the basement.

I end up running five miles, my conversation with my coworker running on repeat in my head. I rarely meet anyone in the workplace that regrets taking their job or that wants to be doing something else. Or maybe people are just better at hiding it than I realize, since I had no idea he felt that way. But most people seem to be enamored with the money and comfort of working a well-paying 9-5 where, for the most part, they can just coast through their work. Most of my coworkers will admit that they're not enamored with their jobs, but that they use the time and money gained from it to follow their real happiness outside of work. That's how people end up settling for this kind of job for the length of their entire career.

I never thought I'd fall into that same category. I even got a tattoo on the day I graduated college that was meant to signify that although I didn't know what I wanted to do with my life, I vowed that I would never settle and would find something that makes me happy and makes a difference. Settling was—and still is—my biggest fear, and I never meant to stay with something just because it's comfortable and easy.

Yet here I am, three years after that tattoo was inked into my skin, doing exactly what I vowed not to do.

I know I don't want to stay in this job, or in this industry. Not only am I not happy, but often I'm actually very *un*happy. I don't want to live like that.

But the idea of quitting without a backup plan, without knowing what I would do otherwise, is fucking terrifying. If nothing else, it would be hard to come by a job that pays as much as my current one does. And since I'm used to a certain level of comfort in my life—including rent that's not cheap—I can't exactly just leave my job.

I need... something before I can leave.

That frustrating conclusion has me itching for a drink by the time I've showered and left the building. When I see the lights of my favorite hole in the wall bar flashing at me down the street, an idea takes root in my head.

Slowly, almost hesitantly, I start to walk toward Andy's Dive Bar. It's one of the older bars in the city, and very out of place among the other up and coming bars surrounding it in the Business District. But somehow over the years Andy has managed to keep his bar the same dive that it's always been, never conforming to the pressure that's surrounded it.

It's also not a place I'd ever see any of my coworkers. It's too rundown for that. Not a lot of people know about Andy's Dive, which makes it the perfect place for what I suddenly feel like doing.

For the first time in years.

I order my favorite IPA before settling in at the table at the very back corner of the bar. Since it's a Tuesday night there are not a lot of patrons in the bar, just the usual couple of drunks sitting at the counter. I open my laptop with a deep breath.

Without letting myself think too hard about what I'm doing or why, I start writing. I write random ideas, scenes, plots, anything I can think of. It's a mess of words on my screen, but it's more than I've done in years. Typically, when I sit down to write, I get stuck because I start to think too hard. But tonight, with a few beers and the determination to avoid a life of regret, I let the words flow.

I sit there for hours. I barely take my eyes off the computer, doing so only to gesture for another drink every once in a while.

It's the freest I've felt in a long time.

For once, I'm not tense. I'm not stressed about work, or meeting deadlines, or feeling frustrated about having to do work that's not mine to do.

I'm not stressed about what I'm writing or whether or not it'll be a massive failure. I'm just... letting my brain take my fingers where it wants.

All of a sudden, I notice the bar has emptied out and the bartender is giving me dirty looks. I realize with a start that it's almost 11:00 and they're starting to close up.

"Sorry, sorry," I call out. I start to pack up my computer. "I'm leaving, I'm sorry. I didn't realize how late it was. Can I close out my tab?"

The older lady behind the bar gives me an angry glare before walking over to the register to ring me up. I pay my tab quickly and walk out of the bar.

It isn't until I'm getting out of the Uber a few minutes later that I suddenly remember that I'm walking into a house with a certain roommate.

"Fuck," I mutter under my breath. Wrapped up all my happy feelings, I completely forgot about everything with Tristan.

I take a deep breath to remind myself that I need to ignore him, that I need to keep my physical distance and act like I'm not borderline-obsessed with his glorious dick.

Just... stay away from him, I remind myself. Hopefully he's already asleep and I don't even need to deal with him right now.

But when I walk into the house, I find Tristan sprawled on the couch, flipping through channels with a bored look on his face. His eyes light with a mischievous twinkle when he sees me.

"Remy baby," he teases. "Where have you been? Curfew is 11:00."

I roll my eyes at him as I shrug my jacket off. "None of your business," I retort.

"Busy night at the library?" he guesses sarcastically. "Or maybe another Humphrey Bogart marathon at the local theater? My ears still hurt from listening to you yap about the last one."

I shoot him a withering glare. "Humphrey Bogart is an icon. I'm going to do you a favor and pretend you didn't say that, or else I might have to take scissors to all your hand wraps again. Do you remember the Jane Austen incident?"

I think I see him swallow roughly before saying, "Don't remind me. I had to use Jax's smelly wraps for a week because of it."

A self-satisfied grin stretches across my face at the memory. "Serves you right for insulting the mother of all romance by implying her literature is irrelevant," I chuckle as I hang my jacket on the coat rack.

"That still doesn't explain where you were tonight," he pushes again. "You're supposed to be at the gym on Tuesdays. *Naughty*."

I roll my eyes at his overbearing attitude. I'm sure he's assuming that I was trying to avoid him, and he's trying to call me out on it.

"Maybe I was getting dicked down," I mutter.

I manage to catch his horrified look for a split second before he covers it up. I hadn't meant for that to slip out, but his reaction was more than worth it. I grin and turn toward him with my hands on my hips, waiting patiently to see what he's going to respond with.

His face hardens but he still looks at me skeptically. "Not a chance," he decides. "Or if that's true, the poor sap did a piss poor job."

I scowl and drop my hands to my sides. "How on earth would you be able to tell that?"

There is nothing sarcastic about his tone as he answers. "Because if you had been pleasured right, you'd have sexy, freshly fucked hair and the most incredible pink, flushed skin. Not to mention, a sated smile."

My breath hitches. Suddenly, I'm flooded with memories of desperate hands and hungry moans and wet kisses. I squeeze my legs together to try to tamp down on the ache that's already started to build between them, but it doesn't help—I can't stop thinking about the last time I had freshly fucked hair and pink skin. And more importantly, about the person that made me that way.

"That's ridiculous," I choke out. "Sex doesn't always have to be like that. Plus, that's cheesy as shit, you sound like you're trying to quote a movie." I head toward the kitchen, wanting to get away from this conversation and those memories.

But I don't get far because he blocks my path, leaving only inches between us. I glare up at him.

"That's what you looked like the other night," he murmurs in a gravelly voice. A current of electricity shoots through me at the sound.

"Do you remember?" he says in that same quiet, deep voice. His expression is smug, but there's also a fire burning in his eyes. He twirls a strand of my hair between his fingers as he studies my face. "Do you remember when I ran my fingers through your hair? When I pulled it? Or when you came so hard that your skin got hot? Because I haven't stopped thinking about it since."

My breath catches at his admission. *He's been thinking about me?*

His eyes bore deep into mine. I can see the heat behind them, and I can't seem to tear myself away. I'm frozen in place, even as I see his face dip down.

He's smiling as he brushes his lips over my cheek. He's barely touching me—and it's infuriating. He continues down my chin, along my neck, until he reaches my ear. I feel his tongue dart out against my earlobe right before he nips it lightly.

I can't stop a hiss from leaving my lips. I was so dead set on never letting him get close to me again but now that he's this close, it feels like I've been drugged by his aura. Like the second I get too close to him, I'm enveloped in a strange trance that I can't break away from. I can't speak or move; all I can do is try not to hyperventilate.

"Remy..." he purrs, right before his lips touch mine.

I can't help my lips opening for him any more than I can stop my heart from beating. With a groan, he slips his tongue inside, and I shiver as it slides across my own. I wrap my arms around his neck and lean further into the kiss.

With a growl, he grips my ass and lifts me up. He spins and walks us to the kitchen island, then sets me on the edge. He pushes my thighs apart and slips in to stand between my legs. I whimper at the feel of his very big—very *hard*— length. I pull him closer so I can grind against him.

He groans and digs his fingers harder into my hips. In the back of my mind, I realize I'm most likely going to bruise —and with my next thought I realize that I don't care. In fact, I wish he would mark me in a better spot.

Without thinking about what I'm doing, I grab one of his hands and guide his fingers to wrap around my throat.

His eyes widen—and then darken with lust. The heat in

his eyes blazes, just like it had the last time he wanted to fuck me into the nearest surface.

"Filthy fucking girl," he growls, squeezing the sides of my neck. I can't help the moan that slips from my lips any more than I can help the wetness that I now feel between my legs. He kisses along my jaw, nipping and sucking. "I should've known you like it rough. Do you like it when I manhandle you? If I reached into your panties right now, would you be drenched?"

"God, yes," I moan, unashamed. I don't care about how it makes me look, or what we're even doing right now, all I can think about is how badly I want him to throw me around and fuck me seven which ways. I need his talented cock to douse this fire that feels like it's burning up every inch of my skin.

He reaches down to fumble with the buttons on my dress pants. When he finally gets them open, he squeezes my neck one final time before letting go to tug my pants down my legs. He leaves me in my thong, running a thoughtful glance along my body before stepping close again and ripping my blouse open. I gasp as my buttons fly everywhere.

And then I'm sitting in front of Tristan, exposed in my racy red lingerie set.

"Jesus," he gasps, gawking at my outfit. "You're like a sexy secretary fantasy come to life." He runs another hungry glance over my lacey bra and panties, then reaches forward to grab my hair so he can yank my mouth back to his. "I've always wondered what you were hiding under your work clothes."

My head drops back with a groan at yet another admission that he's thought about me. A surge of confidence runs through me at the thought that he's not as unaffected by me as I always assumed he was. He nips my lower lip before moving to my jaw, then down my neck. I gasp when I feel his fingers graze my pussy through my thong.

He groans when he feels how wet I am. Using only his pinky, he nudges the fabric aside, then slides along the length of my slit. He circles my clit tantalizingly.

He licks up the length of my neck, all the way over my chin and finally sliding his tongue directly into my mouth. I shiver in anticipation of feeling his tongue between my legs.

"I can't wait to taste your sweet cunt again," he growls against my lips. "Lie down."

I do as I'm told. I'm thankful he kept my blouse on because the granite counter is cold against my skin, and I'm glad my back isn't touching the surface right now. I try to focus on the feel of the cold counter under my ass and how it feels compared to my achingly heated core that's begging to be touched. I squirm impatiently when a few seconds pass and he still hasn't touched me.

He's standing between my legs, looking down at my body like a starved man about to devour his first meal. After what feels like an eternity, he reaches forward to touch my face. His thumb caresses my cheek before sliding across my lips—and pausing. The inferno continues to rage in his eyes as he stares at my mouth. I curl my tongue around his thumb and suck it into my mouth, my eyes never leaving his.

The motion seems to break the spell that he's under because he immediately growls and pulls his hand back. But instead of letting go of me completely, his finger continues its trail down. He runs it along the curve of my neck, between my breasts, then circles around my navel. He finally pauses when he reaches the lace of my thong. He glances at me once more before his face suddenly disappears from my view.

I gasp and arch my back when I feel his lips running over the fabric between my legs—he's not even touching my skin yet and I'm already ready to come out of mine. I feel his finger circle over my entrance, teasing what's to come. And just as I'm about to beg that he rip the rest of my clothes off and put me out of my misery, he yanks my thong off and hooks my legs over his shoulders before burying his face in my weeping cunt.

I moan at the feel of his hard grip on my thighs pulling me further into his tongue's assault. He circles my clit, occasionally pausing to suck on the small nub, before licking between my lips and thrusting inside my pussy. I whimper and tangle my fingers in his hair as he fucks me with his tongue.

Just when I'm about to explode in his mouth, he pulls away from me and stands up. I cry out at the loss and try to reach for him.

But he pushes me roughly back on the counter. With a mischievous smile, he slips first one, then two of his fingers in his mouth. And then, without breaking eye contact, he slides them inside me.

My eyes flutter closed with a moan, overwhelmed with the feeling of his fingers fucking me. His hands are big, his fingers long, and yet it feels like a tease—I need his hard length inside me in order to feel truly satiated.

He pulls his fingers out. But before I can voice my displeasure again, I feel his index finger pressing against my asshole.

I gasp as my eyes pop open. He hasn't taken his eyes off my face, and he's still wearing that mischievous smile. He gently starts to work his finger into my ass.

It doesn't take me long to relax and start wriggling down

the counter, silently begging for him to fill more of me. The grin on his face grows.

"I fucking knew it," he growls. "I knew when you moaned at my thumb on you the other night that you liked your ass being played with. God, that is so fucking hot." He starts to increase his pace, looking down at where his finger is moving in and out of me. "Maybe I'll fuck your ass some-time. Maybe, if you're lucky, I'll make you suck my dick before I push you down on my bed and take your ass. Would you like that?"

A sob breaks from my throat at the sheer eroticism of his words. I squirm on the counter, knowing I'm seconds away from losing control.

He studies my face for another moment before looking back down. "Maybe another time," he muses aloud—and then drops his mouth to my pussy.

He continues to finger fuck me as he circles his tongue. By the time he sucks on my clit, I shatter.

I scream at the force of the orgasm. The heat from my core explodes, expanding through every nerve of my body, every inch of my skin. As Tristan continues his delicious torment—never once slowing down or letting up on his intensity—my release continues to roll through me. I feel like I'm stuck in an undercurrent on the beach, with waves continuing to crash down on me until I can't breathe anymore and I stop fighting.

When my breathing slows and I can finally blink open my eyes, it registers that Tristan is still gently caressing my pussy, watching my face intently.

"Fucking beautiful," he breathes. Then he steps back and pushes his sweatpants down past his hips. He grabs his dick and squeezes.

Still shaking from the force of my orgasm, I push myself

up to a sitting position. My mouth goes dry at the sight of him roughly tugging himself. I try to reach for him, but Tristan pushes my hands away.

"Nuh uh, not today," he growls. "If you touch me right now, I won't make it inside your tight little body. Wrap your legs around me."

When he tugs my hips closer to the edge, I do as he says. I can't help the shiver of anticipation that runs through my body as he rubs the tip of his dick along my slick center. Gripping the edge of the counter with both hands, I wiggle to try to take him inside.

He chuckles against my skin as he lays kisses along my neck. "So eager," he mutters. "Luckily, I can't wait any longer, either." And with one long, slow movement, he pushes all the way in.

I whimper and squirm as I adjust to his size. He's just big enough that there's a twinge of pain when he first slides in, and it takes a few breaths until I can relax enough to enjoy myself. I probably didn't notice his sheer size the last time he took me because I was drunk then. But now, in this position, I revel in the feeling of being so utterly and completely full.

"Fuck, you're so tight," he moans. "I already don't want this to end."

I wrap my arms around his shoulders and nip his earlobe. "Fuck me," I whisper in his ear.

He groans and starts to move. He's still buried in my neck and he's got a bruising grip on my hips as he starts to thrust into me. And with every motion, I lose more and more of my mind.

"Oh my god, *Tristan*," I gasp. I grab at his arms, his shoulders, as I try to gain control of what's building inside me.

Even though I just came a few minutes ago, I'm already bordering on another overwhelming orgasm.

He pulls back a little so he can look at my face. When he sees my struggle, sees that I'm close, he growls in approval and kisses me roughly.

"Come for me," he whispers into my mouth. "Scream for me."

And when one of his thrusts hits the right spot inside me, I do. I scream as my orgasm erupts.

He smothers the sound with another hard kiss. He wraps an arm around my waist as his other hand braces himself against the counter. "Oh, *fuck*," he groans, increasing his pace. As my pussy starts to clench around his dick, he reaches his release, too.

I pant against his lips as my pulsing continues to drain him. When the sensations finally abate, he leans his forehead against mine, breathing heavily.

After a few moments, Tristan chuckles lightly and kisses the edge of my mouth. He pulls away and flashes me a playful smile. "You'll notice when you look in the mirror that my description of what you look like when you've been properly fucked is 100% accurate."

I scowl but can't stop the blush that flames my cheeks. "Shut up," I mutter. I hop off the counter and reach for my clothes.

I pull my thong on but I'm so skittish and confused in my post-orgasm haze that I abandon the idea of pulling on my pants and instead turn to bolt up the stairs.

But before I can make it more than a step, Tristan grabs my arm and spins me back to face him. He grips the back of my neck and pulls my face close to his.

"I hope this solidified it in your brain that this isn't stopping anytime soon," he growls against my lips.

My eyes go wide but I don't say anything. "I'm serious," he growls, nipping my lower lip. "Stop running from me."

"I—I don't—" I stammer, wide eyed and still completely clueless about how to answer.

When he realizes he won't get anything more out of me, he sighs and steps back to give me my space. Without another word, I run up the stairs and back to the safety of my own room.

12

REMY

So much for never sleeping with Tristan again.

I frown for the fiftieth time at my desk, unable to stop reliving last night. It has not been a very productive day. Honestly, I blame Tristan's hate-inducing personality. Everyone knows hate sex is the best sex.

I'm not really sure what's happening or what I need to do next. On paper I definitely shouldn't be sleeping with him, for multiple reasons: I don't want to date him, he definitely isn't interested in me, Jax wouldn't approve, he's only going to ruin me for other men... etc. etc. Any of the above reasons, even by themselves, should be making me run for the hills.

Yet somehow, I can't bring myself to regret the past few days. I'm fairly certain Tristan knows how to distance sex from feelings, so other than having him lord this over me for the rest of eternity, it most likely won't change much between us. Though that's not to say we should tempt fate by continuing to do it.

I make another vow to stay away from him, despite the tickle in the back of my subconscious that's practically cackling at the half-assed attempt. I shove that voice to the recesses of my mind and turn back to my work.

I somehow manage to focus enough to get through my workday, though I'm so eager to get a workout in that I'm practically bouncing in my seat by 5:00. Even the knowledge that I'll run into Tristan doesn't distract me from the idea of a good workout. Seeing him might even encourage me to punch the bag harder, since the idea that I shouldn't have sex with him again is enough to make me all kinds of sexually frustrated.

Despite the fact that I had two screaming orgasms not long ago.

Tristan must be in the gym office when I walk in because I manage to avoid him for most of the night. I only see him once when he's showing a new student around the gym. We share the briefest of glances in that one second, his gaze completely impassive when he meets my eyes. I can't read anything on his face—not regret, or longing, or arrogance. He's just... blank.

It further confuses my post-sex brain.

I should've known he's not as affected by our two nights as I am. Sleeping with women is Tristan's *thing*, the game that he's best at. Of course he's not walking around reliving a brief twenty minute affair. I'm an idiot for thinking he'd be pining for more.

I make my millionth vow to sign off of Tristan and move on from whatever these past few days have been. We need to just go back to normal and forget anything ever happened. I turn back to my heavy bag with renewed vigor.

The two hours of training easily puts me on my ass— which is exactly what I needed it to do. I'm finally tired enough that my brain has stopped freaking out about anything Tristan-related. By the time I get back to the house

I'm only spending every other minute wondering if Tristan regretted sleeping with me—instead of every thirty seconds.

He's nowhere to be found when I walk in the house. I see his bedroom door is closed when I go upstairs to shower, which probably means he's already asleep. I exhale the tightness in my shoulders when I think about having a little freedom in the house. Maybe I'll actually be able to take over the living room for a little while.

But when I reach the bottom of the stairs, I realize Tristan is in the kitchen, reaching in the fridge for a beer. I pause when he notices me and almost rush back upstairs when I see the look on his face. He turns his attention to me fully, his gaze locked on me as I take the last few steps toward the couch. In typical Tristan fashion, I have no way of knowing what he's feeling or what he's thinking when he looks at me. The one thing that's clear is that his intense gaze is trained completely on me.

I look nervously between him and the TV. "I'm starting to think you stay up later than I think you do," I mumble, wringing my hands.

With everything that's happened the past few days, I've discovered that I am now completely clueless about how to act around him. Before last week, I'd just order him around and not care about what he wanted or what he thought of me, but that seems like a rude approach to take once someone's dick has been in your mouth. At the very least, I just have no idea where we stand and feel nervous being anywhere near him.

He takes a swig from the beer as he rounds the island and throws himself on the couch. "Were you going to watch something?" he asks me, his voice devoid of the usual biting tone.

"I was going to watch the Best Fights of the Year series on

FightPass," I answer wistfully. "I randomly came across it today when I was on the app and wanted to rewatch some of the fights." I hesitate, unsure if he likes me enough now to sit and watch TV with me. "But I can watch them upstairs if you were going to watch something else."

He chuckles and takes another drink. "Just shut up and grab a beer. I'll find the fights."

I nod and walk over to the fridge. I decide to grab a sour IPA, one of the few things that Tristan and I can agree on. As much as Jax hates IPA's, I know Tristan always keeps the house stocked with some good sours.

Walking back to the couch, I hesitate again. It feels insanely weird to be willingly hanging out with just Tristan, and suddenly I'm debating if this might be a terrible idea.

"Just sit. I promise I don't bite." A sinful smile slides across his face as he looks at me. "Unless you want me to. I guess we haven't really explored that yet."

My stomach clenches at his words, but I scowl and plop down on the opposite end of the couch. I feel my face burning so I quickly guzzle some of my beer.

He scrolls to the section of the FightPass app where we can see the list of fights. "Any preference which one we start with?" he asks me.

I shake my head as I pull my legs up and curl further into the couch. "Nope. I don't care, they're all good."

He selects one and hits play. As the fighter introductions start, I sneak a glance sideways. He's lounging comfortably but his attention is laser-focused on the screen. Watching fights is like reading playbooks for him.

Curious, I ask him, "What were you going to watch?"

His attention slides to me. "I was going to rewatch the last few fights of one of the local guys."

"Because you think you'll fight him?" I ask.

He nods. "We've been running in the same circuit for years. He's been winning lately, and I keep hearing whispers of him getting called to the UFC, so I wouldn't be surprised if they matched us up soon to see which one of us should make the cut."

I tilt my head, studying him thoughtfully. I've seen and talked to plenty of fighters, but never anyone of Tristan's caliber. I've always been interested in what goes on in the brain of high-level pro fighters.

"Is it nerve-wracking for each fight to be higher profile than the last?" I ask. "I mean, every fight is the biggest fight of your career right now. Does that add more or less pressure for you?"

He shrugs, turning his attention back to the fight starting on the TV. "Pressure is pressure," he answers simply. "You never get used to the nerves. You just get better at dealing with them."

I want to ask more but I have a feeling he's uncomfortable talking about himself. Which seems really weird, since his usual personality is arrogant and obnoxious. But I take the hint and turn toward the TV.

We watch the first fight in silence. Well, not *silence*, since I'm incapable of watching a good fight without commentating and occasionally yelling, but I manage to keep my outbursts to a minimum and my attention away from Tristan.

But the IPA is starting to loosen my tongue and I can't stop myself from asking another question.

"What made you want to start fighting?" I blurt suddenly.

Tristan raises an eyebrow at me as he clicks on the next fight. "So inquisitive tonight, Remy baby," he drawls. I glare at him for his use of my hated nickname but wait pointedly for his answer. He sighs. "I didn't start training with the intention of fighting but once I got into the sport it seemed like a logical step. I just wanted to see how I would do in a real fight. Then once I started, I got addicted to the feeling."

For a moment he looks at me, as if assessing something. I shift nervously under his intense gaze, but he just continues talking. "People always say fighting is barbaric. And it is, but not for the reasons they think. It's not that it's too violent, because it's not—you've seen it, there's never been a death or serious injury in the history of the UFC. It's barbaric because it's primal and raw and there's no hiding anything once that cage door locks. It's honest. The most honest thing a human can experience. When that bell rings there's no trash talk, no social media, no one that can help you. It's just you and your raw physical abilities, trying to survive. You see people for who they truly are when they fight." He pauses and takes another swig of his beer. "With how fake everything and everyone is nowadays, I started to like the feeling of being that honest. And of exposing the frauds."

I stare at Tristan, wide-eyed, as I think about his answer. But before I can stop myself, I ask, "So if you hate fake people so much, why are all the chicks you date plastic as fuck?"

He chuckles. "I don't date in the classical sense of the word. I don't have to like someone to fuck them, Remy." He laughs again, shaking his head as he stands to get another beer. "Aren't you and I proof of that? You hate me, yet you still let me inside you. Twice."

"I don't—I don't hate—" I blurt out but think better of my startled confession and stop myself from finishing it. I look down at my hands, desperately racking my brain for when I stopped hating Tristan without realizing it.

"You don't hate me?" he purrs in my ear. I yelp—I hadn't noticed him leaving the kitchen to stand behind the couch. "Good to know. Sounds like my plan to fuck you into liking me is working right on schedule."

I scowl and shove him away from me. "Fuck you," I mutter. "Just because I don't plot your death anymore doesn't mean I like you." He laughs and takes his seat again.

I notice the beer in his hands and narrow my eyes. "You got yourself another but didn't think to ask if I wanted one, too?"

"Nope," he chirps happily, and cracks the can.

My eyes widen in shock before once again narrowing. "I lied," I growl. "I do still hate you. Guess your dick isn't that good, after all."

He grins. "That's too bad, I thought we were making some progress. Guess I'll just have to try harder. Should we try again right here, or would you rather I take you in a bed upstairs?"

I glare at him but turn away, feeling the blush light up my cheeks. "Jesus, can't you keep it in your pants for one night?" I grumble.

He chuckles and turns back to the TV, the second fight already halfway done. Part of me forgot what we were even watching.

I fume by myself and watch the screen for a little longer, giving him the space he clearly wants from my questioning. But once again, it doesn't last long.

"So, what's the plan for when your career ultimately ends? What's the secondary career?"

This time Tristan growls as he turns to me. "You're starting to push my limits, Remy. I'm getting very close to busying your mouth with something else."

My eyes widen again, and I shake my head to clear the

memory of Tristan fucking my mouth. The last thing I need right now is to give him the satisfaction of seeing how much that thought turns me on. Instead, I glare at him and growl, "Just answer the goddamn question, Tristan."

He sighs and turns back to the TV, clicking on another fight. I'm surprised to realize that means we've been sitting here for almost an hour already. And I haven't wanted to run away once.

"I'll most likely go back to my degree when I'm done fighting," he answers. "As tough as it was training, working, and going to school at the same time, I went to college for a reason. Some kind of career in business was always the backup plan. Or second career, since Jax's dad loves to tell us that there's room for—"

"—three careers in a lifetime," I finish for him. "Yeah, I've heard the speech too. He's not wrong. People don't usually stay in the same industry their whole life. Nor should they, I don't think." I take a sip of my beer, returning my attention to the new fight starting on the screen. "I'm surprised you have a backup plan after fighting. Most guys seem like they're offended when they're asked about another career. As if even thinking about doing anything else means they're not taking fighting 100% seriously."

"Most guys are idiots," he grunts. "If they think they'll be able to coach or open a gym and live comfortably for the rest of their lives, they're in for a rude awakening. Gyms don't often make a lot of money. It's common sense to have something else ready for when their career is over in their early thirties. Or mid/late thirties if they're lucky."

I nod, agreeing with his analysis. I come from a family of life planners, so I've never once been in a position where I didn't have potential next steps plotted in my life and career.

The fact that people live by the seat of their pants like that has always been baffling to me.

I sneak a sideways glance at Tristan. I knew he went to college and had some kind of a life outside of fighting, but I never thought of him as necessarily smart or accomplished. Not because I have a preconceived notion that fighters are dumb—they're not—but more so because he's so wrapped up in fighting right now that he rarely talks about anything else. Although now that I think about it, I remember Jax mentioning that Tristan had graduated from the Business School of Temple University. And that program is one of the highest rated in the country, so I should've known that he's not exactly a dunce.

I'm starting to realize I know very little about Tristan West.

We watch the third fight in comfortable silence. At some point I grab a second beer, nestling back into the couch cushions in my pleasantly buzzed state. I don't realize I've moved closer to Tristan until he reacts to my next question.

"What do your parents think about your fighting?" I blurt out.

This time, along with a deep growl, Tristan reaches out to grab my hair. He pulls, hard, until I drop my head back with a cry.

"You've officially progressed to questions that cross the line," he snaps. "When did I give you the impression that I would answer personal questions?"

"Play a game with me," I gasp suddenly.

He cocks his head and loosens his grip on my hair—enough for me to twist my head to look at him—but he doesn't let go completely. I vaguely feel his fingers twining in my hair.

"What do you mean, a game?" he asks in a guarded tone.

I turn to face him, forcing his hands to pull out of my hair. "The question game," I answer breathlessly. "We ask each other single questions, but you can never ask the other person something that they've already asked you. And we have to answer. I promise I won't get too personal," I say in a rush, feeling oddly desperate to get him to agree to my game. "But you can ask me whatever you want."

I have no idea why I suddenly need him to answer my questions. I just know that I need to know more about him.

When he's still skeptical, I tease him lightly. "So, what? You can stick your dick in my mouth, but you can't answer a few harmless questions?"

Instead of responding with a dirty comment of his own, his eyes drop to my lips—and immediately darken when his pupils dilate. I swallow nervously, clearly seeing the thoughts in his expression.

He pauses. "Seven questions. I'm not answering any more than that."

I nod quickly. "Deal."

"And before we start, I fuck your mouth."

I gape at his brazen words. When he sees my expression, he grins. "Good girl, hold it just like that."

I blush and turn away. When I still don't respond, he takes the beer from my hands and puts it on the table next to him. I watch him closely as he stands and walks to my side of the couch. As he rounds the corner, he gently guides my head to lay down on the armrest. I look up at him now standing behind me and swallow nervously when I realize what he wants.

And I yet again wonder how he can read our chemistry so well. Does he know this position is one of my favorites? Can he tell how eager I've been to suck his dick again? I clench my thighs to tamp down on the ache growing between them.

"Say yes," he mutters as he traces my lips with his finger.

I don't hesitate again. "Yes," I breathe.

He grins. "Good girl. Let's play."

13

TRISTAN

As I stare down at Remy, I resist the urge to pinch myself to make sure I'm not dreaming. I continue to trace her lips with my thumb as I try to wrap my head around the fact that she's sprawled in front of me, getting more and more turned on by the prospect of sucking my dick. I didn't miss the clench of her thighs when she realized what I was suggesting. I also can't forget how wet she got the first night when she dropped to her knees before me.

I stifle my groan as I let go of her lips and palm my cock straining against my sweatpants. Her eyes widen as they trace my movement. After a breath, she wiggles further up the couch until her head hangs off the armrest.

"Fuck," I groan. "You're so fucking sexy. Open your mouth."

She eagerly parts her lips. I push my sweatpants over my hips, freeing my cock. In a matter of seconds, I'm already rock hard. Which seems to be a common occurrence when Remy is around. I stroke my length a few times before stepping forward to touch my tip to Remy's tongue.

I practically combust when she moans and swirls her tongue around me. I watch, transfixed, as she sucks the pre-cum from my tip and licks her lips.

I gently press further into her mouth. She stretches around me, licking along my length and getting accustomed to my size. She wriggles further up the couch, trying to get more of me in her mouth.

I groan and grab the back of the couch with one hand to steady myself. I start to push in deeper.

The first time I hit the back of Remy's throat, she tenses up and gags. I pull back quickly. But before I'm able to pull out completely, she reaches behind my thighs and pulls me back into her mouth. She stretches her neck to try to take me deep again.

I pump into her mouth, and this time she doesn't gag when I go all the way in. Her hand behind my thighs coaxes me to continue fucking her.

"Fuck, I love watching you suck my dick," I groan. I can't get enough of the sight of her repeatedly taking my length into her mouth.

She moans when she hears my desperate praise. The sound vibrates against me and I groan as the feeling makes my dick swell.

She starts pulling me into her with more and more force. I oblige, fully fucking her face by this point, but I watch her expressions carefully for any sign that I need to pull back.

The moment I pick up my pace, she moans again before hurriedly pulling her tank top up over her tits. She cups them, then pinches each nipple.

"Jesus, Remy, you're gonna kill me," I gasp. "That is the hottest fucking thing I've ever seen." I lean down to tug one of her nipples with my teeth.

My dick slides out of her mouth when she gasps. I swirl my tongue around the bud and suck once, hard, before straightening back up.

"Don't stop. Open those pretty lips again." She does as I say, and I rub the tip of my cock around her lips before pushing back into her mouth. I groan when she goes right back to coaxing me to fuck her harder.

"I want you to touch yourself," I murmur. "Pull your pants down so I can watch you play with yourself."

She eagerly reaches to follow my instructions. She pulls her leggings down over her ass and immediately dips her fingers into her panties to feel the wetness between her legs.

"Thong, too, you little tease," I growl. "I want to see all of you. I want to see you make yourself come while I fuck your mouth."

She moans as a shiver runs through her body. But then she reaches down and does as I say. I watch in silent awe as she cups her breasts again, then trails one hand down her body, down her stomach, until her fingers reach their destination. She circles her clit a few times before moving further. In an instant, she's slid two fingers inside her pussy.

I grab her wrist and bring those fingers to my mouth. I suck the taste of her from her skin, just as she's sucking me now. She must have the same thought because she once again urges me to pick up the pace of my hips.

"So fucking sweet," I murmur. I guide her hand back to her pussy. "Touch yourself again. I want to see you come."

When she whimpers, I finally get a sense of her desperation. The last time she sucked my dick she got so wet that she exploded almost immediately after I next touched her. She's probably aching to come right now.

Sure enough, there's nothing lazy or playful about the

way she starts rubbing her clit. Her pace is hurried—frenzied. She starts to squirm as her orgasm builds.

I'm mesmerized by the sight below me and try not to increase my own pace as she nears her release. She's distracted enough now that she gives up trying to actually create suction around my dick, and instead just lets her mouth drop open as I continue to thrust in and out.

I can't stop myself from reaching down and sliding two fingers into her pussy, once again feeling my brain short-circuit when I realize she's drenched from just my dick in her mouth. The moan that she lets out at the feeling of my fingers fucking her reverberates around my dick and I swear I only hold my orgasm back by sheer force of will. I continue to thrust my fingers into her as she frantically swirls her wetness over her clit.

When I curl my fingers inside her, she drops me from her mouth and screams as her release tears through her. I groan and work my other hand over my shaft as I watch her explode beneath me.

That sight is what brings on my own release. I feel it barreling down my spine and I have just enough time to give her one more instruction.

"Open and stick your tongue out," I gasp.

Heavy-lidded and looking a little dick-drunk, she eagerly does as I say. Just as she opens her mouth, I explode, shooting my release all over her tongue. I watch as it drops to the back of her throat. I grunt through the overwhelming orgasm that Remy has once again brought on.

She swallows, her eyes sparkling up at me as she licks her lips.

I gape at her for another moment, then pull my sweatpants up and step around the couch to drop to my knees in front of her. I tug her to a sitting position before sliding my hand behind her head and gripping the nape of her neck. I press a heady kiss to her lips.

"You have the sweetest fucking mouth," I murmur against her skin. "You have no idea how pissed I am that we waited so long to start doing this." I sigh dramatically.

She laughs—a real, tinkling laugh—and pushes me away. I drop heavily to my spot next to her on the couch.

I take a deep breath to calm my still-racing heart. I watch as she straightens her clothes, then I hand her the beer that she had been drinking. I raise my eyebrows when she chugs half the can.

Seeing my surprise, she shrugs her shoulders and answers simply, "As good as you taste, I still prefer a good IPA as an aftertaste."

I bark a startled laugh. Shaking my head, I reach for my own beer. "Okay, now back to your question game." I settle back against the cushions and flash her an impish grin. "I actually did you a favor with that blowjob. If we hadn't started with that, I would've been distracted the whole game and every question would've been about sex. And *then* I would've fucked your mouth. So, this way, you actually get good questions and good answers. You're welcome."

She rolls her eyes as she tries to tamp down on the smile that's threatening to curl the edges of her lips. "Yes, thank you *so much* for fucking my face and coming in my mouth. How very *thoughtful* of you."

I chuckle and take a few gulps of my beer. I turn my full attention to Remy and study her thoughtfully. I'm trying to remember the last time I wanted to talk to a girl after an orgasm.

I'm coming up empty.

"Well, go on then. Ask away."

She tilts her head thoughtfully as she taps a finger to her lips, no doubt trying to make her first question a good one. Unfortunately, all I can think about is how swollen her lips look from my rough treatment of her—and how much I'd like to bite that plump bottom lip.

I swallow roughly and shift my hips, subtly trying to ease the ache of my hardening cock.

Unbelievable. I just came two minutes ago and she's already making me want to go again.

How am I so affected by this girl?

"OK, I'll start easy," she says, oblivious to my internal struggle. "What's the hardest part of fighting?"

I wince when the answer immediately comes to mind. "The day of the fight," I answer as I turn back to the TV. Incidentally, they're showing the fighters as they're warming up in the locker rooms. The scene on the screen is exactly the worst part about fighting. "The nerves are the worst. The week of the fight isn't bad because you're distracted by the weight cut, but the day of the fight—after you've weighed in—the only thing you can think about is how you're about to be locked inside a cage with a very large man that wants nothing more than to hurt you. It's a surreal feeling. And I don't care who you ask, every fighter will tell you that they question their decision to sign the contract during the hours before the fight."

Remy giggles even as she stares at me with wide eyes. "Seriously? All of you are scared of fighting? I didn't think you guys were scared of anything."

My brow furrows. "It's not scared, necessarily. It's more like we're in disbelief and questioning our own sanity. It's why I never judge people when they say our sport is crazy—

it is. They're absolutely right about that." I turn back to Remy with a feral grin. "But all those feelings go away as soon as the bell starts. And then the real fun—and my favorite part of fighting—begins."

She shakes her head with a small smile. She's been around fighting long enough that despite never having gotten in the cage herself, I know she understands my answer. A lot of people don't see MMA as a sport, they just see it as people beating the shit out of each other. But that couldn't be further from the truth. Fighting is the ultimate competition between humans: it requires skill, strength, speed, intelligence, and strategy, for starters. Nowadays you can't just be good at one aspect of this sport—you have to be really good at all of it. So even though on screen my sport looks like human cockfighting, it's actually the final exam of everything we've spent weeks, months, *years* training for. And being able to execute all of that hard work is exhilarating and actually incredibly fun.

I study Remy thoughtfully. "OK, my turn. Have you ever thought about fighting? You've done plenty of Jiu Jitsu tournaments, so what about taking a fight?"

She shrugs and starts playing with a thread on her sweatpants as she answers. "I've thought about it. Plenty of people have pushed me to try it over the years. Lucy tries to get me to take one every time she has a fight. But I just don't think I care enough about actually getting in the cage. I love training and studying the techniques, but I don't think I have it in me to want to hurt someone. I'm sure I would do fine if I actually did take a fight, but if the whole point is to physically best your opponent, and I don't really want to do that, then why would I do it?" She shrugs again as she looks up at me. "Maybe someday I'll want to experience what fighting is like but for now I just don't really have any inter-est. I'd rather watch you guys fight."

I hum thoughtfully at her answer. Most people have the opposite response—they brag about how much they want to fight, post it all over social media, but never put the neces-sary work in and usually end up dropping out of the sport after the brutal reality of their first fight. It's refreshing to hear someone that thinks like Remy.

She moves onto her next question. "Question #2: what would you be doing if you weren't fighting?"

"Like with my career or as a hobby?"

"Both, I guess. Although I assume they're wrapped in one for you, so fighting is either your whole life or nothing at all."

I nod. She's spot on in her assumption. I tilt my head and mull over her question. "If I wasn't fighting, I would've just used my business degree for something. Which is most likely what I'll end up doing after I retire, too. I would've figured out what industry I want to be in and what kind of work I like doing. I can't give you a more specific answer because I have no idea. Fighting has taken up all my head-space since even before college."

"What if it were just a hobby? What sport would you pick instead?"

I quirk an eyebrow. "How do you know I would need to pick a sport as a hobby? What if I enjoy chess?"

She looks at me in shock. "Do you like chess?"

I smirk and take a swig of my beer. "I do, actually. You don't need to assume I'm a dumb brute just because I like punching people."

"I didn't—" she sputters defensively.

"We're venturing into follow-up questions, which I believe is against the rules," I interrupt. She swallows roughly but nods. "What was the first thing you liked about training?"

A warm smile lights up her face and I can't help but think about how genuine her expressions are—and how contagious her happiness always seems.

"I liked how strong it made me feel," she replies honestly. "It's probably a cliché response as a chick but it really is empowering to be able to throw a good punch. It's so ingrained in us to be dainty and feminine that it's like a shock of cold water when you realize that a strength like this is actually practical. I push every woman I know to try a class at least once, just so they know what it feels like." She grins as she continues, visibly getting more and more excited now. "My favorite part is how nervous and awkward they are when they start, but then they slowly start to get into it and by the end they look like they're women on a mission. It's awesome."

Her answer is helpful from a gym employee perspective, since I can use that knowledge to make the right pitch to prospective female members. But it also surprises me—it's odd to think of Remy as anything but strong. Her physical strength is decent but it's her mental strength that puts the majority of grown men to shame.

"OK, enough about me. Next question is what was your favorite subject in school?"

I smirk. "History. My turn."

Her jaw drops open. "That's it? That's all I get? I gave you a whole dissertation as my answer."

I shrug. "It's not my fault you asked a simple question. Nowhere in the rules does it say I have to defend my answers."

She knows I'm right so all she can do is glare. I chuckle and think about what else I want to ask her.

"What's one thing on your bucket list?"

My thoughtful question surprises her. For a few seconds she just blinks, and I wonder if I've actually stunned her into silence.

"I've always wanted to go blonde," she mumbles. "I've only ever had brown hair and for some reason I've always wanted to see if I could pull off the hot blonde look. But everyone always tells me it'll look horrible and that I shouldn't do it. So, I don't know if I'll ever actually have the balls to go through with it."

"You're already hot," I blurt without thinking. She blushes and looks down, and I try to cover my compliment by adding, "But fuck what anyone else thinks. They shouldn't have any say in what you want to do with your life. If you want to go blonde, go blonde. Fuck, go hot pink if you want to. It shouldn't be anyone's decision but your own."

She laughs at my visual. "I don't think my office would appreciate hot pink hair, but I get your point." She contemplates her next question, then asks, "What's your top travel destination that you want to visit?"

"I loved Thailand and Brazil for the training but I've already been there so I can't put that on my list. I'd probably say Rome."

She looks at me skeptically. "Because you like history?" she guesses. I grin and wink at her, to which she rolls her eyes.

"My cousin lives in Rome," says conversationally, reaching for her beer. "Jax and I always talk about visiting, we just haven't gotten around to it. We always end up in a different European city."

I know how much Jax and Remy love traveling. I've been invited to more than one trip to Europe, but with fight camps it was never good timing. Plus I was never sure that being cooped up in a hostel or hotel room with a girl that hates my guts was ever a good idea.

Ignoring the temptation to get into a conversation with her about her traveling memories, I instead ask my next question. "What's your favorite book?"

I'm losing track of the amount of times I've shocked her tonight. If I were any other guy, I'd probably be offended by her shocked expressions that clearly imply she thinks I'm dumb as a brick. But I'm so used to people assuming that fighters are idiots that I can't summon enough energy to be outraged anymore. In fact, part of me actually enjoys the low expectations because it makes me feel smug when their assumptions are proven wrong.

"I'm not surprised because I think you're dumb," she says hastily, as if hearing my thoughts. "I feel like you think that I see you as a dumb brute just because you're a fighter. I don't. It's just... people don't ask that question anymore. They don't read. Or play chess. I feel like having academic interests just isn't as normal anymore outside of an actual intellectual career."

I shrug, caring less about what other people think or do than Remy seems to. I read because I like learning and exercising my brain. I don't feel any need to share my knowledge with anyone else if they don't ask.

Then again, I also don't care to socialize with people like Remy does. I will never understand how bubbly people have as much energy as they do.

"*Rooftops of Tehran*," she answers my question. "It's a coming-of-age story based in war-torn Iran and it's the most beautifully written novel I've ever read in my entire life. I read it once a year and it makes me sob like a baby every time."

I blink incredulously. "First of all, how can a book make

you cry? And second of all, how does it make you cry when you already know what's going to happen?"

She glares at me pointedly. "You're veering into follow-up questions. My turn to ask a question." She taps her lips thoughtfully before glaring at me again. "You have no idea how badly I want to ask you what your favorite book is. Something tells me you'd have a fascinating answer."

I grin and shrug my shoulders mockingly. I do actually have a fascinating answer.

She sighs but moves on to ask her question. "What's the worst female quality?"

Now it's my turn to stare in shock. I figured we'd get into sex or relationship questions eventually, but that's definitely not the direction I expected her to go in. Especially since she only has two questions left after this one.

I mull it over, wanting to give her an honest answer. I think about the women I've dated and fights or turn-offs I've experienced.

"Probably the inability to think logically when they're really emotional. Not that I think women aren't capable of that," I add hurriedly, anticipating her outrage. "But it's just a very female quality. I've had plenty of fights with women where they refused to see the issue logically because they were too caught up in feeling upset. It's definitely the most frustrating type of fight because there's no way to win or convince them otherwise."

She taps her lips as she considers my answer. After several moments, she nods her head in acceptance.

"That's it?" I blurt. "No rebuttal? No outrage that I dare to see women as emotional weaklings that are incapable of making smart decisions?"

"No, because that's not what you said." She pauses and then grins. "Also, that would prove your point."

I bark a startled laugh when I realize she's right.

"What's the most cringe-worthy thing a guy has ever said to you?" I ask her curiously.

She winces and starts picking with the thread on her pants. I'm starting to realize that twitchy hand movements are her biggest tell when she's nervous, and grin while I eagerly wait for whatever answer is making her uneasy.

"I had a guy repeatedly say the word 'wow' while I sucked his dick," she mumbles quietly.

I blink in shock—and then roar with laughter.

"Are you kidding me?" I gasp when I finally catch my breath. "Was he drunk?"

"No," she mumbles, still not making eye contact.

"That's the most ridiculous thing I've ever heard." I'm still chuckling when I reach over and tug her hair to get her attention. "Not that your blowjobs aren't the definition of wow-worthy, but I'd much rather tell you I think you look beautiful with your lips wrapped around my cock. Not 'wow.'"

She pulls her legs up on the couch and wraps her arms around her knees, but I don't miss the small smile that appears on her face. Suddenly, I wonder if she has any idea how sexy she is.

"How many girls have you dated?" she asks.

I raise an eyebrow. "Dated, or been in relationships with?"

"Um, either. Whichever one you want to answer."

I settle back into the couch cushions, debating what answer I want to give her. There are two different aspects to this question when girls ask it: either they want to know my body count—which is never a fun conversation—or they want to know how many girls I've been serious about. Which is also not a great conversation.

"I don't know how many girls I've dated, depending on your definition of the word. The majority of my experience with women is either a one-night stand or a casual hookup type thing. Not sure if I'd qualify either of those as really dating." I shrug awkwardly as I prepare to answer the second part of her question. "I had one serious girlfriend in college, but it ended when I went pro. Since then, I haven't really been interested in relationships. It doesn't seem to pair well with how selfish I have to be as a fighter."

I can see the wheels turning in her head as she considers my answer. I realize suddenly that I've never had this kind of honest conversation about relationships with a woman. I've never admitted that I am okay with being in this selfish phase of my life. I wonder if she's going to ask me more. But she seems to be resigned to the fact that we keep shooting down the other's follow-up questions, so she just nods in acceptance of my answer.

I think about the next question I want to ask her. We each have two questions left and there's a certain heaviness that's settled into the mood of the room—clearly calling out the personal nature of our questions.

"What's the longest relationship you've ever had?" I ask finally.

She sighs and meets my gaze with a resigned look on her face. "Six months."

My eyes widen in surprise. "You had a serious relationship in six months?"

"I see through people's bullshit pretty quickly," she mumbles with a shrug. "By the six month mark I already know if I'm going to get bored of them."

I frown when something occurs to me. "What about that pothead you dated a year ago? That seemed like it lasted a while."

She turns to me with a slight frown, as if surprised that I remember that. I'm a little surprised, too, but I don't take the question back.

"He... wasn't really a pothead. He was actually crazy smart. But he had really bad ADHD and needed to tame his own brain with something." Something flashes through my chest at her positive mention of the guy. I always knew she liked smart guys, so it shouldn't exactly come as a shock, but for some reason hearing her confirm it makes me annoyed. Especially since I know most people think I'm an idiot.

Oblivious to my inner turmoil, she continues her answer with a sigh as she drops her head back against the couch. "It was only six months, but it felt longer because he chased me for a while. In hindsight, it should've been a sign that he had to convince me to date him, but at the time, it felt nice to be chased. We ended up being really wrong for each other."

I'm not sure how to respond to that with anything other than *Good*, so I just stay silent.

"Okay, last question," she says quietly, raising her eyes to look at me. Actually, it feels like she's looking *into* me. And when she asks her question, I understand why. "What's your favorite quality of your mom?"

I wince and rub my forehead. Family questions always make me uncomfortable, which is why I freaked out on Remy earlier when she asked me about them. It's no secret that I don't have a great relationship with my parents. Jax is the only one I swallowed my embarrassment for and vented to about my clusterfuck of a family dynamic, and I'm certain he wouldn't have shared it with anyone, even Remy.

Since I'm sure she at least knows the relationship is rocky, I wonder if her question is meant to carefully broach the subject while keeping a light spin on it by asking me to focus on the positives. I study Remy for a moment, debating how much I want to tell her.

"Her kindness," I eventually mutter. "She has the best heart. Even with all the bullshit with my parents—them not accepting my career and putting my shithead brother on a pedestal just for having a respectable job—it's never come from a place of hate. She's just confused, and a lot worried." I laugh humorlessly. "In her own fucked up way, I think her hating fighting is actually her way of trying to protect me. She's only ever wanted what's best for me—even if she happens to be wrong. Her kindness is so all-consuming that she puts all of our needs in front of any of hers. There isn't a thing in this world that she wouldn't sacrifice if it somehow meant we could be happy."

I fidget with my beer as I avoid Remy's gaze. Even when I told Jax last year, we hadn't exactly sat around and talked about it. He just happened to catch me in a full-blown melt-down after my dad had called to tell me that he had no interest in coming to my upcoming fight. And oh 'when was I going to be done with this karate bullshit.' I still fume when I recall the memory.

"She'll come around," I hear Remy say quietly. I look up at her in surprise—I hadn't expected her to say anything. "I don't know your dad, so I can't speak for how much a douchebag he is or isn't, but if your mom is a good person then she'll figure it out eventually. She loves you. She just needs to see how important fighting is to you."

I feel a comforting warmth seep into my chest. I didn't realize how desperate I had been to hear someone tell me that until just now. I just assumed this is what it would always be like with my parents. But with Remy's words, I feel an ember of hope light inside of me.

Not wanting to ruin her declaration by responding to it,

all I manage is a gruff—but appreciative—nod. I finish the rest of my beer as I mull over my final question for Remy.

I decide on a family question of my own. "Were you always close with your sister?"

Remy smiles and rests her cheek on the couch cushions. "Always. Ever since she was a baby and I helped take care of her. There may have been a brief time in my early teens where I preferred my friends over her, but that felt normal. She was always my best friend." She grins cheekily as she straightens up and pulls her feet beneath her. "It helps that my parents raised us well and we both ended up being cool as fuck. Because to this day she's still the best person I know."

I roll my eyes. "Arrogant much?" I ask with an amused drawl.

Her grin widens. "I am about this."

I can't help the smile that pulls at the edge of my lips. "She is pretty cool, though," I admit. "Quiet, but seems like she has a good head on her shoulders." I grin when a memory surfaces. "I remember her telling off a guy that was hitting on her at one of the fights. She must've been, like, 17, but basically told the guy she didn't have enough time or patience for idiot boys. You almost bit the guy's head off when he kept pushing."

Remy practically growls next to me at the mention of it. "Damn right I did," she mumbles. "Men are idiots."

When I shake my head with a chuckle, she finishes the rest of her beer and turns to put the empty can on the table next to her. "OK, well my seven questions are up. I guess I'll—"

"What's your biggest struggle in life right now?" I blurt.

Her eyes widen. I mutter a curse, immediately regretting my outburst—not to mention the fact that I just broke several game rules—and begin searching my brain for a way to smooth it over.

But when I look up at her, she's opening and closing her mouth, each time trying to vocalize what I assume will be her answer. I guess she doesn't mind that I broke her rules. Maybe, because I opened up about my family, she feels like she can—or should—open up about this. I puzzle over what her answer might be.

She swallows nervously and tries again. I can barely make out her words, they're spoken so softly.

"I'm trying to decide if I should quit my stable, comfortable, and completely *horrible* job and pursue the career that I really want," she mutters eventually.

I hesitate—and then decide I've already broken the other rules, why not one more. "What do you want to be doing?"

When she looks up at me there's so much hope, so much vulnerability, that I suck in a sudden breath. I stare at her lips, desperate to hear her words. "I want to write novels," she finally admits.

I pause as I contemplate her answer. "And the self-employed part scares you?" I guess.

She looks back down, shaking her head. "I just don't know if I'm good enough. It seems insane to leave a stable job for something I'm not even sure I can *do*. But I hate what I do now. It seems like a bizarre alternate reality where I'm in the field I want to be in, only somewhere along the way I got lost and ended up in the worst possible version of the field. The writing I do daily is a mockery of the things I want to write."

She looks at me again, that same hope still shining through—this time mixed with a little bit of awe. "I've never told anyone that," she whispers, amazed.

"You've never told anyone you want to write books?"

She shakes her head, still wide-eyed and awestruck. "Not honestly. Sometimes I'll joke with Hailey that I write for fun here and there, but I've never actually admitted out loud that it's a real dream."

I think about her honest response when I told her about my mom a few minutes ago. I want so badly to appease her the way she did me, but I'm not exactly the motivational type. I'm not sure what to tell her right now.

I settle for the truth. "Well, you'll never know until you try. Would you rather live your life with definite regret that you never went after what you wanted, or would you rather live with some *possible* disappointment if you try but fail? That's really what it comes down to." I realize something and make a face at Remy. "Either way, your current job sounds like shit and you should probably quit anyway."

A laugh explodes out of her and I grin, feeling good about my pep talk.

She glances at me in between her fading giggles. "You're right. I've just been too much of a pussy to actually do it." She straightens with a determined look on her face. "Next week, I'm dying my hair blonde and looking for publishers for my book."

I chuckle and give her hair a light tug. "Good girl," I murmur.

Her eyes light with delight before she sighs contentedly and curls into the couch cushions. Her attention lands on the black screen of the TV.

"I forgot we were watching fights when we started all this," she murmurs. She peeks up at me through lowered eyelashes. "Can we start them over?"

Without a word, I turn back to the TV and press play. I

settle back into the couch as we slip easily into a comfortable silence.

I'm on the edge of consciousness, about to doze off, when I feel her against me. My eyes snap open and I turn to look at her. She's fallen asleep and without realizing it, is leaning into my body. As her head finds a comfortable spot on my shoulder she sighs contentedly and nuzzles further into my neck. I feel more of her weight settle on me as she falls into a deeper sleep.

I'm too surprised to even move. Tonight showed me what she looks like without furrowed brows and angry frown lines, but even a skeptically happy face is different from this. Now she looks peaceful. And breathtakingly beautiful.

Before I realize what I'm doing, I lift my hand to brush away the hair that's fallen into her face. I linger on her cheek, amazed at how warm she is, and how soft her skin feels. I feel like I'm stealing an intimate moment by looking at her in such a vulnerable state. But I can't help myself—I can't stop looking at her.

She's so different than what I thought she was. Before she moved in, I always thought she was Jax's annoying childhood friend who walked around with a stick up her ass. I always thought she was pretty hot but the bitchy comments and air of pretentiousness always far outweighed that fact. Especially after our first encounter, I never cared to take a closer look.

Now, I'm realizing my character analysis may have been all wrong.

She's not bitchy, she's just defensive and protective. And

she enjoys the banter with me, though she doesn't want to believe it yet. Even after she admitted tonight that she doesn't hate me anymore, we still kept up the verbal sparring. I'm realizing I actually enjoy the challenge and entertainment of it.

When I remember my conversation with the bride at the bar last weekend—where I found myself wishing she would snap at me a little more—I realize my thought process is entirely accurate. I do enjoy the banter with Remy.

And I can't really fault her for thinking I'm a dumb brute. Everyone thinks that. It's just a casualty of being a professional fighter. That combined with the fact that I'm silent—or rarely talking about anything other than fighting—means I can't exactly hold that assumption against anyone. But once we got talking and Remy realized I don't quite fit that mold, I could actually see the pleasantly surprised admiration light in her eyes. Instead of the shocked disbelief that I usually get.

As I sit there, stroking her cheek and staring at her, I feel ridiculously happy that she instigated tonight. Despite getting initially defensive at the idea of any kind of get-to-know-me game, I'm glad I got to dig into Remy's life a little bit. Even if that meant letting her dig into mine.

But even sharing the bad parts felt completely natural with her. Opening up about my family was never something I even considered with anyone—let alone a female—but for some reason I didn't even hesitate with Remy. I wanted to tell her about my life. I really wanted her to know me as more than just Tristan the Fighter.

The craziest part is I enjoyed the non-sex just as much as the sex. It's been a very long time since I've wanted to talk to a girl after an orgasm high died down, yet tonight I actually found myself looking forward to it. That's not to say I didn't enjoy her blowjob or the times we had sex. Because in all honesty, I don't even think there's a word for the level of mind-blowing that our sexual chemistry is. I could probably fuck Remy for the rest of my life and never get tired of her little moans, or the way she feels coming on my fingers. I meant it when I told her we weren't going to stop this anytime soon—days later and I *still* can't stop jerking off to the thought of fucking her.

But once we sat on the couch and started talking, I stopped looking at her lips as something I'd like to see wrapped around my cock, and started looking at them to see what she would tell me about herself.

I can't remember the last time I wanted a girl for conversation instead of just sex.

It's an unsettling thought. For years I've only ever wanted women for the purpose of taking the edge off—I could never find one that I actually cared to listen to. Most women just see me as a hot athlete to fuck, or an up-and-coming fighter to latch onto for social status. No one's ever cared to actually get to know me.

But Remy cared to ask questions. She cared enough to initiate a game, to actually *push* me to talk about myself. She could've jumped me if she just wanted sex, or she could've walked away if she didn't want anything to do with me. I half expected her to go back upstairs when she saw me down here. But she didn't, and instead we spent hours just hanging out. *Hours.*

And the craziest part is, I don't know which I want to do more of: fuck her or talk to her.

Her quiet snore snaps me out of my introspective state. I swallow nervously and look around, trying to figure out how I can move her without waking her up. But by now she's so deeply snuggled into my side that she's almost on top of me.

And judging by her dead weight I know she's in a deep sleep.

I know I should move her but something inside of me wants to let her sleep—to stay in this moment of peace just a little bit longer. So instead, I settle back into the couch with a sigh. My head drops gently onto hers just before I drift off to sleep.

14

REMY

I wake up with a content smile. I feel warm and tightly cocooned, like I'm wrapped in a cloud with the sun shining down on me. My body feels well-rested, too lazy still to fully wake up. I sit comfortably between the sleep and waking state. The whole sensation is so comfortable that I sigh happily and snuggle further into my cocoon.

The cloud tightens around me.

I frown, the sensation abruptly waking me. *Do cocoons move?*

I blink my eyes open. I'm still too close to whatever is wrapped around me, so I slowly pull back to analyze the wall in front of me.

My breath catches as I realize I'm staring up at Tristan's face only two inches from mine. He's snoring softly. His expression is so peaceful, so happy, that for a moment, I can't stop staring. It's such a different image from how I usually see him.

His arms tighten around me again and I realize that his body is my warm cocoon. He pulls me closer so all I can do is press my face into his chest. I feel his cheek against my hair.

I close my eyes and take a shaky breath. We must've fallen asleep during the fights last night and ended up tangled together on the couch. I'm shocked to be in this position but I'm even more shocked at how much my body is enjoying the feeling. I realize that the last thing I want to do is get up.

My relationship with Tristan has only ever consisted of arguments, sarcasm, and harsh insults. It feels bizarre to have a moment free of all that. With him unconscious, I'm free to experience him in a way that I've never even imagined. And my mind can't seem to wrap around it.

It suddenly dawns on me that I've been nuzzling into his chest for the past few minutes, entirely too comfortable with the feeling of his arms wrapped around me. I need to get up. I can't be in this position when he wakes up. It would be way too awkward for both of us.

I take a deep breath—ignoring the pang inside of me that hates that I'm about to pull myself away from this moment of perfection—and gently wriggle down and out of his arms. I roll off the couch, landing with a small thud. I jerk my head toward Tristan to see if the sound woke him up, but let out a sigh of relief when I see his eyes are still closed.

I watch, curious, as the expression on his face changes. Where only a moment ago he looked peaceful, now his brow is furrowed, and the corners of his lips have turned down. He looks confused, even angry. Somewhere deep in my subconscious I think about how I hate this change in him, and that I wish he would be happy again.

I realize then that he's probably about to wake up. So,

before he can spot me standing there staring at him, I bolt out of the room and head upstairs to get ready for work.

My workday is a clusterfuck of chaos. Between the constant stream of people stopping by my desk with nonsensical questions and my own jumble of distracted thoughts, I feel like I'm actually getting further *behind* on my work. By the time 5:00 comes around I'm ready to scream my frustration.

Typically, on days where I'm in a bad spot with my to do list at work, I stay as late as I need to in order to get comfortably caught up. But I feel so frustrated with work lately that I've officially reached a strong state of *fuck-it*.

Ignoring the surprised glances of my coworkers around me, I pack away my laptop and grab my gym bag from beneath my desk.

"Leaving already, Remy?" someone calls from behind me in a teasing tone.

I slow my determined march toward the exit and turn to see who called after me.

I realize from the lazy grin on his face that it was one of the sales guys. He's leaning against the front desk, clearly flirting with the giggling and doe-eyed secretary.

He straightens when he sees me turn around, his smirk still firmly in place. "I'm surprised. Isn't it a little early for you to be leaving?"

I continue to stare at him in sheer amazement at his set of brass balls. Even looking past his particular work habits, 5:00 is the official end of the workday. There's no reason anyone should be teased for leaving on the dot. Not to mention the company is flexible enough that plenty of people often leave at 4:30 or even 4:00—this asshole included.

"I'd say I'm more surprised that you're still here," I answer tightly. "Doesn't your workday typically end after a two-hour lunch? Or are you putting in overtime because Becca got a new haircut and looks really cute today?"

Becca shoots me a stupid, grateful smile at the same time that the smirk drops from his face. His brows furrow in anger, probably having never been called out for his lazy work habits that everybody knows about but is too polite to address.

I turn and continue toward the stairs, not wanting to hang around this place for another second. "Have a good night," I call behind me.

By the time I reach the gym in the basement, I've walked enough steps and taken enough deep breaths that I've worked through the majority of my enraged anti-work thoughts. I'm so over my own coworkers and the amount of work that's piled up on my plate—none of which I enjoy doing—that I know spending any more time thinking about it will only make the situation worse. I'll put everything work-related out of my mind, run a few miles, and then maybe I'll try to get a little more work done at the house.

I change into my running gear and start on the treadmill at a jog. It doesn't take long for my thoughts to go from angry, to forcibly meditative, to now puzzled and reflective.

Except now my frazzled thoughts aren't about work—they're about my night with Tristan.

I increase the speed of the treadmill to try to further distract myself from the confusing replay of our questions game. In just two hours last night, Tristan managed to completely change my view of him. And in just a few minutes this morning, my own subconscious reaction to him changed it even more.

I meant what I said to him about never thinking he was a dumb brute. But I also never really thought of him as more than a fighting-obsessed womanizer who only cared about himself.

Although, I admit the womanizing skills have been deliciously appreciated lately.

But to find out that he has intellectual interests, that he understands what a person's favorite book says about them, and that he's had a life plan outside of fighting since before he began, is not something I expected to learn about him. I also never thought about how fighting explains a lot of his apparent self-centeredness. I've seen how much time and energy goes into being a professional athlete, but I never really considered how selfish they have to be at that level. To be the best they can be, athletes need to center their whole world around the sport and devote every second, every resource, every last ounce of their energy.

It's no wonder he doesn't date seriously. He probably knows he wouldn't be able to give a girlfriend the time or attention she needs. In a way his player attitude actually makes sense now—something I never thought I'd say. I always assumed he just thought of women as interchangeable and didn't care to see them as more than an hour of pleasure. But maybe he's actually being considerate of their feelings by being honest with them that he can't offer a real relationship.

As I increase the speed on the treadmill, I can't stop thinking about my new feelings toward Tristan. I obviously don't hate him as much as I did a few weeks ago if I bent over for him—three times. Something about being in close confines with him has allowed us to see more of each other than we ever have in the past few years. We've never spent time together with just the two of us, and I'll admit that getting to know each other beyond a surface level understanding when there's always a horde of other fighters around us isn't exactly an easy task. It's no wonder we didn't really know each other.

I was also correct in my thinking last weekend when I realized our verbal sparring is actually proof of the sexual tension between us. It always has been, even though we never realized it. And fuck if the years of "foreplay" didn't set us up for a few seriously explosive encounters.

But where do we go from here?

By Tristan's own admission, he's not looking for a girlfriend. And I'm definitely not looking to be one. He's too focused on fighting and I'm... just not interested in being a couple. I like being independent. I like not having to consult someone else about my plans or worry that they won't like that I spend so much time around guys in the gym. God knows I've dealt with enough of that jealousy in past relationships. But I mostly just enjoy being by myself right now.

That's not to say I don't enjoy sex. I don't do sex with strangers, but I've had a few friends with benefits over the years. I'm not sure I consider Tristan a friend yet, even if I don't hate him anymore, but the benefits with him are definitely a thousand times better than with anyone else. Maybe hate sex—or barely-just-stopped-hating-you sex—really is the best kind.

I decrease the speed on the treadmill as I start to cool down from my 5-mile run. I feel appropriately winded, and my legs are screaming from the exertion and fast pace. My head feels ten times clearer than it did an hour ago, and I happily jog the last mile. Exercise endorphins are a wonderful thing.

I wonder if I'll see Tristan tonight. He's usually at the gym until late, so I don't know if I'll run into him again before I go to bed. I wonder if last night is making him consider the same things I just spent the last hour thinking about.

I snort. *Fat chance.*

He's probably surprised he allowed himself to be engaged in a series of personal questions. Maybe he actually enjoyed himself. Maybe I should actually consider us friends.

Well, maybe non-enemies with benefits is more accurate.

I slow my pace to a walk as I let myself come to terms with the fact that I wouldn't mind having Tristan on me again. Memories of his hands gripping my hips, of my tongue tangling with his, of the overwhelming feeling of him moving inside me, flash through my mind. A blush flames my cheeks and a light sweat breaks out across my skin—separate from the one I worked up with my hard run.

I shake my head to clear the distracting thoughts. Just because I wouldn't say no if Tristan came on to me again doesn't mean I'm going to throw myself at him the next time I see him. For one, neither of us wants to get involved, and too many encounters just increase the chances of something going wrong. So, it's probably smarter to not make this into a reoccurring thing. But for another, I don't want Tristan to think I'm just another desperate plaything. The last thing I need is him thinking he holds any power over me.

I exhale a heavy breath as I press the Stop button on the treadmill. Now that I'm calmer and have a clear head, I really do have work I need to finish. But I'm definitely not doing it at the office, since I'm actually more productive in a casual setting where I can be sprawled out on a bed wearing sweats with my hair in a messy bun.

The house is empty when I get home, for which I'm grateful. I'll get more work done if I don't have Tristan distracting me—both physically and mentally. I reheat the chicken alfredo I made earlier this week and head upstairs to shower and get settled for the night.

I smile happily when I finally flop down on Jax's bed, clean and full and comfortable. I force myself to resist the urge to snuggle into the pillows with a book and instead pull my laptop from my bag with a dejected sigh. I start in on a product marketing campaign.

It doesn't take long for my frown to reappear and my head to begin pounding again. I feel so *bored* doing this work.

I actually enjoyed the writing when I first started at the company. It obviously wasn't the kind of literature that I had loved studying in college, but part of me enjoyed the fact that I was using my skills to project a valuable technology product into the world. I even enjoyed the challenge of learning the marketing aspect.

But nowadays I just can't find it in me to care about what I'm writing. I don't enjoy doing technical research for a product I don't understand, just because the engineer was too lazy to write the datasheet themselves. I don't enjoy writing about the same product over and over again. And on top of everything else, I can't stand the fact that I care so little about what I'm writing, yet it eats up so much of my time—I feel like I'm expending way too much energy on something that, in reality, is just mindless grunt work.

I stick my pen through my bun and rub my eyes tiredly. I stand up from the bed and begin pacing around the room. I find myself remembering Tristan's last question to me.

What's your biggest struggle in life?

I can definitely appreciate that my biggest problem right

now is something as easy as not enjoying my job. I inhale a deep breath and take a moment to silently express my gratitude that I have a stable, well-paying job that I can afford to dislike.

But as soon as that moment is over, I think about how unhappy it really makes me.

This is not what I wanted to be doing with my life. When I realized after college just how hard it was to become an author, I accepted this job for the stable paycheck. But the plan was never to stay here for years. I should've used the first year to work through my writing process and get a few books ready to publish.

And yet somehow, after I failed so horribly at writing during that summer after graduation, I just couldn't get myself back into it. It was almost like I had scarred myself away from my own passion. I still read a lot and would jot down ideas in my journal, but I haven't given writing an honest shot in years.

Instead, I let myself remain stuck with writing blurbs about a technology I don't care about and will never use.

I wonder if Tristan is right. I wonder if the choice here is really between a life of definite regret from not going after what I want, and possible disappointment if I try and fail. Is it really that simple? Was I so scarred from my first try that I'll never attempt it again?

I'm so lost in my own thoughts that I don't realize Tristan is home until I hear him coming up the stairs. His phone rings just as he gets to the hallway. I don't think he knows I'm here because he doesn't shut the door to his bedroom before he answers. I can hear him clear as day even through my own closed door.

"Hey, Mom. I was actually just about to call you... No, everything's fine, I just wanted to talk to you about something... Where are you with planning your birthday trip? Is everything officially scheduled?"

I hear Tristan start to pace the hallway. Even his steps sound agitated.

"Okay, so everything is set then. Fuck... Sorry, I didn't mean for that to slip out. I'm just asking because I got offered a really big fight that weekend and it would be huge for my career if I could take it. A win would definitely put me on the UFC's radar... No, of course I'm not saying I don't care about your 50th birthday. I love you, and I would love to be there for you. I know how excited you are to get the whole family together for a weekend. But this is a really huge opportunity and—Mom, please stop crying. Please don't cry..."

Tristan's angry steps cease, and I can only imagine the frustration that I'm sure is plastered all over his face. I know his relationship with his parents is rough when it comes to fighting so I can guess how difficult this call is for him. To find out that you have a great opportunity that might catapult you into your lifelong dream, and then have to turn it down because your Mom wants you at her birthday party, sounds painful and unfair.

I meant what I said to Tristan last night. I really think his Mom will come around at some point—she just needs to realize how important fighting is to him.

Apparently, today is not that day.

"If it means this much to you then of course I'll come for the weekend. I just want you to be happy... But Mom, I need you to try to understand how big this decision is. I know you and Dad don't understand why I fight but I need you to want to support me anyway. I love fighting and Mom, I'm *really* fucking good at it. As in, I'm telling you I'm going to be one of the best fighters in the world one day. Will you be proud of me then? When I have a belt strapped around my waist? Or will you always just be waiting for me to grow out of my silly little karate phase?"

I feel my own heart breaking just listening to this.

"Fine, Mom, I don't want to talk about it now, either. We'll talk another time... Yeah, I'll be there for your birthday weekend... I promise... I love you too... Bye, Mom."

I'm still frozen in place when I hear Tristan's huff of frustration as he enters his room. I can't tell what he's doing in there, but I hear him aggressively moving things around.

I try to wait for him to go back downstairs or at least shut his door, but after a few minutes I decide it's ridiculous for me to walk on eggshells around him. Plus, I really need to get some water.

As softly as I can, I open the door and start to tiptoe down the hall. *I guess I was lying to myself about the eggshells.*

But it doesn't matter how quietly I walk because Tristan picks that moment to step out of his room.

He freezes when he sees me. I can tell by the way he looks at me that he realizes I heard every word of his conversation. And although he opened up to me about his Mom last night, I get the feeling that he wouldn't have wanted to share what just happened with anyone. I wince guiltily.

"I'll get out of your way," I blurt awkwardly. "I was just going to get some water."

I go to step past him but, per usual, he blocks my path. Except this time there's nothing teasing in his expression. No jokes tumbling from his lips, no smirks, no sleazy innuendos. He just looks deflated.

"You're never in the way," he says gruffly. His eyes bore into mine, clearly studying me for something. I shuffle my feet awkwardly.

"OK, well I'm going—" I start but he cuts me off.

"What would you do if you were me?" he asks suddenly. "What would you do if you had to pick between your dream and your family?"

My eyes widen in shock. Not just because I'm surprised he's letting me into a side of his life that I know he prefers to keep a secret, but because he's asking for my opinion, too. This conversation with his mom is clearly weighing heavily on him if he's desperate enough to talk to someone about it. He rarely even opens up to Jax about it.

I feel a pang of deep sadness for him.

I hesitate, knowing he's not going to like my answer. "I would give up everything for my sister," I answer softly. "Not just because she's my best friend, but because family— whether by blood or by choice—is the foundation of every-thing. Without them we have nothing." I cock my head as I study him, trying to figure out how I can say what I want to without seeming like I'm trying to push him in one direction or the other. "There will always be another dream, or at least another opportunity for the dream. Nothing is the end of the world but the end of the world. We're always changing, always re-prioritizing things in our lives. Something we didn't give a shit about last week might be important to us this week."

Something blazes in his eyes when I say that. I don't quite understand it, and he doesn't say anything out loud, but I can see his mind spinning a million miles a minute right now.

He looks so vulnerable, so much like a lost child, that part of me wants to wrap my arms around him and tell him everything will be okay. The moment is so surreal that I forget this is Tristan I'm talking to. Instead of our usual easy banter, this feels heavy, and real. I can't bring myself to look away.

I'm still locked in place when he takes a step toward me. His gaze feels like it's devouring my soul, the tension so thick I can barely breathe. And even though I've vowed multiple times over the past few days to never let him near me again, I can already tell my defensive walls are about to come tumbling down.

"Remy..." His voice cracks on my name.

And with it, cracks my resolve.

Suddenly all the games, all the power moves, everything that makes our relationship as vicious as it is, disappears. Suddenly, I couldn't care less about whether or not he has power over me, whether or not he'll consider this me surrendering to him. I've been lying to myself about how much I want him near me anyway, and right now it's obvious that I'm not the only one. He's clearly just as desperate as I am. Just as powerless.

And in this moment, the game of who's in control disappears, and we're left with only each other and the unbearable heat between us.

His lips crash down to mine. I kiss him back just as hard, giving myself up to him completely and sliding my arms around his neck as I open my mouth to him. The kiss charges an already overcharged tension between us, and we begin grabbing desperately at each other.

Tonight, neither of us has the power. Tonight, we both win.

15

REMY

Without a word, Tristan reaches under my thighs and lifts me up. My legs automatically wrap around his waist, our kiss never breaking. He turns and walks us to his bedroom.

As soon as we're in his room, he closes the door and presses me against it. I tighten my arms around his neck and angle my head, begging for him to deepen the kiss.

He does. With one hand now fisted in my hair at the nape of my neck, he slides his tongue across mine and kisses me with an intensity that I feel in every nerve of my body. A small whimper escapes my lips.

His mouth leaves mine and starts trailing kisses down my neck, under my ear, across my collarbone. He reaches down to quickly pull my tank top over my head. He kisses the curve of my breasts, biting lightly, before taking a nipple in his mouth. I moan, my eyes closing as my head drops back to rest against the door. I bask in the delicious way that he sucks and nibbles first one, then the other. With every tug of his teeth, I can feel the ache between my legs grow.

Just as I'm about to beg him to end his torture, he lifts his head and crushes his lips against mine once more. I weave my fingers through his hair, holding his lips tight against mine. I feel him pull us away from the door.

He turns to lay me on the bed. The second his body is flush and heavy on mine, the tension seems to spike.

He groans as he grabs my waist and grinds his hips into mine. I feel his dick, hard and thick, press against my center, forcing another whimper from my lips. I grab the hem of his shirt and pull it over his head, desperate to feel his skin against mine.

His weight settles back on top of me, and he kisses me again, flexing as he holds himself above me. I wrap my arms around his waist and run my fingers over his back, his hips, his sides, entranced by the smooth skin and ripples of muscle. I wriggle my hips underneath him, silently begging for more contact.

He growls and starts kissing down my body. He sucks my nipples hard enough to make me groan, then continues further down, leaving wet kisses across my stomach and causing a hard shiver to run through my body at his sensual touch. Without a word, he pulls my sweatpants and panties off.

He spreads my legs wide. He kisses the inside of my knee before slowly trailing kisses closer to my core—never looking up at me, his eyes too focused on the invitation in front of him.

I gasp and arch off the bed at the first swipe of his tongue.

He drops his forearm across my stomach to push me back down. His other hand wraps around my thigh as he anchors me in place, making me a slave to the pleasure that he's swirling around his tongue. He sucks on my clit before flicking it quickly, alternating the motions as my legs start to tremble.

I can feel the orgasm building under his mouth. I tangle my hands in his hair again, wanting to keep his head exactly where it is right now. It vaguely registers in my mind that I'm beginning to grind myself along his tongue, desperately trying to take my pleasure. I start to pant as I feel the sensations building.

When he sucks hard on my clit, my release explodes inside me. I gasp as the aftershocks roll through me, one right after the other.

His tongue slows as my body drops heavily to the bed. "Perfect," I hear him mutter with a kiss. I shudder, both from his touch to my oversensitive clit, and from the rush of pleasure at the tender gesture.

I tug his hair gently to bring him back up my body. He kisses me once before standing to peel the rest of his clothes off. I allow myself a moment to admire his naked body, mesmerized by the hard-earned muscles that look like they were chiseled from stone—that are just as effective as they are beautiful. My gaze travels over his chest and shoulder, at the black ink that reaches down to his elbow. I've always wanted to ask about the story that his tattoos tell.

I file that idea away for a future time because all conscious thought flies from my brain as he settles his weight on top of me. I moan happily at the feel of his heavy frame pushing me into the mattress. I cup his face and slide my tongue in his mouth, wanting to taste myself on him. He groans when I lightly suck on his tongue.

I can feel the tip of his dick pushing against my entrance. I want him to slide inside, to tamp down the desperate ache that needs to be filled. I wrap my arms and legs around him and silently beg him to enter me.

"Fuck, Remy, you make me so goddamn crazy for you," he mutters. I can't even find the energy to be surprised at that because right now I feel exactly the same way. I feel like I'm going to lose my mind if he doesn't start fucking me soon. But he must sense my desperation because in the next breath he pushes inside. I gasp as he fills me completely.

He groans and buries his face in my neck. Then he starts to move.

I close my eyes to heighten the feeling of him fucking me. His thrusts are deep, and the pace is already building me to another orgasm. I scratch my nails down his back as my breaths start to come quicker.

Tristan lets out a deep groan. "I don't think I'll ever get enough of the feeling of your pussy squeezing me," he whispers as he slides his tongue in my mouth. I moan when I feel his dick pulse with his desperation.

Suddenly, Tristan flips us until I'm on top, straddling his hips. I brace my hands on his chest and blink at him, momentarily startled at the sudden change in position. But when I look down and see his eyes blazing with hunger, I immediately sigh and circle my hips. He digs his fingers into my thighs with a hiss.

I rise up on my knees before slowly dropping back down, relishing the feel of his hard length inside me. I repeat the motion and moan when he's once again buried deep. Leaning my weight further forward into my hands braced on his chest, I increase the pace of my hips.

Tristan starts to drive into me, meeting each one of my motions with a thrust of his own. A whimper slips from my lips as I feel another orgasm start to build. Desperate for the release, I reach between my legs to touch myself.

"That's right, come for me," Tristan growls. "Let go. I wanna feel you come on my cock." I moan and close my eyes, feeling too overwhelmed to watch him as he watches me. And when his dick hits the perfect spot inside me at the same time that my nail slides across my clit, the fireworks explode in my body.

I drop my head back with a gasp. The orgasm rolls through me, every muscle clenching and every nerve tingling.

I shudder when the sensations eventually abate. Just as my eyes finally open, Tristan sits up and weaves his fingers into my hair at the nape of my neck. He presses a hungry kiss to my lips. "You are the sexiest little thing when you come," he growls against my mouth.

I wrap my arms around his neck, relishing the feel of our sweaty skin pressed together, and moan as he slides his tongue across mine. I love that I can feel how turned on he is through just a kiss.

Before I get a chance to start riding him, he flips us so that I'm on my back again. He doesn't break the kiss as he starts thrusting into me.

I whimper at the overwhelming sensations and desperately grab at his arms. Between his soul-melting kiss and the feel of his pelvis hitting my overly sensitive clit, I feel like I'm coming apart at the seams. I've never been fucked like this and I don't know how to handle it.

"Tristan," I gasp. "It's—it's too much, I—I don't think I can do it aga—*oh my god*." I moan as my back arches and my eyes roll back. He knows exactly which spot to drive into to ignite a fire in my body.

"Fuck that," he growls as he straightens. He's kneeling over me when he lifts one of my legs up on his shoulder and presses the other thigh flat against the bed. His pace never falters but the intensity of his thrusts increase with the new position. I gasp at how much deeper he feels.

"Come on, baby," he groans. "Give me one more." He lifts my hips a fraction higher to drive even deeper, even harder.

With the hand not flattening my thigh, he reaches up to pinch my nipple—hard.

I scream his name, yet another orgasm tearing through me.

My body tenses, light exploding behind my closed eyelids. I barely register the jerk of his hips as I struggle to keep any control over the convulsions racking my body. I don't know how many times I moan his name before I feel my soul settle back in my body. Slowly, still in a daze, I blink my eyes open.

Tristan has thrown my leg off his shoulder and collapsed against me. His fingers lazily trail through my hair as he breathes deeply against my neck. He's struggling to catch his breath.

I revel in the closeness for a moment while we both recover from our orgasms. I wrap my arms around his body and lightly run my nails up and down his back.

Eventually, he groans and raises himself up to lean on a forearm. He looks down at me with clear, assessing eyes. "You're so much fun," he says with a grin.

I roll my eyes, trying to hide my smile, and lightly shove him off of me. But before I can do anything other than sit up, he grabs my arm and pulls me back on top of him.

"Sleep here," he mutters, kissing the corner of my mouth.

I pull back in surprise. He wants me to sleep with him? *Since when is that part of the Tristan FWB experience?*

Noticing my shock, he rolls his eyes and tries to make light of the situation. "I know Jax's bed is uncomfortable as fuck. I have no idea how he sleeps on that thing."

I raise an eyebrow at him. "Why do you know what Jax's bed is like?" I ask, trying to contain the smile that wants so much to break free.

He growls at my implication and rolls over top of me. He

grips my hip and nips at my jaw. "Don't make me prove to you just how straight I am. Again."

I giggle as I try to swat him away. He sighs and lies back, tugging me into his side and wrapping an arm around me. He pulls a blanket up to cover us. I rest my head on his chest and after a few moments, tentatively reach forward to trace the lines of his abs.

When I threaten to follow the lines of the V under the blanket, he shivers and interlocks his fingers with mine.

The silence between us is a comfortable one. He turns my hand to study the lines of my fingers, the callouses on my palm, the tattoo on my wrist.

"Does this mean anything?" he asks, gesturing to the tiny elephant inked into my skin.

"I got it in Thailand," I smile, remembering that day fondly. It's by far my favorite tattoo. "I got it to commemorate my trip. They did it by hand with a bamboo stick."

"Did that hurt more than a normal one?" he asks, the surprise evident in his voice.

I shake my head. "Not really, it mostly hurt because it took longer. That would've taken five minutes with a machine, but by hand it took almost twenty." I pause, anticipating his next question. "And yes, I made sure they used a new stick. I actually watched them whittle it down. I don't know why people think I'm stupid enough to let them recycle a bloody tattoo stick and risk getting an infection."

He chuckles, and we revel in the silence for a few moments. But I've always been secretly enamored with the ink on his skin and can't help asking about his. He's got one stupid image on the inside of his bicep that I know he got when he turned eighteen, but the tattoos stretching over his shoulder and upper back are incredibly intricate and beautiful. I've gotten caught up staring at them at the gym more than once.

"Do you want to get any more?" I finally ask.

"Probably," he shrugs. "I'm sure I'll get the itch again. I've always wanted to get a full sleeve but I don't want to have to wear long sleeved shirts if I end up working in a professional job after I retire. I might just stretch the one on my upper back to cover more of my back."

I nod in understanding. Tattoos are becoming more and more accepted in the workplace but it's still well-known that people without visible ink have a better shot at getting hired than those with it. It's impressive that Tristan not only recognizes that, but sees its place in his future and plans for it.

I feel another surge of reverence for him.

"It's probably better that way anyway," I murmur, going back to tracing the ridges of his abs. "You would be way too hot with a full sleeve. Women would spontaneously combust around you."

A laugh rumbles through his chest, and a warmth spreads through mine at the sound. I smile into his skin. I've spent so much time insulting him that I never realized how much I would love the sound of his joy.

"You're one to talk. What's the tattoo on your ribs?" he asks me.

I cringe. "A stupid young one," I respond. "I got it on my eighteenth birthday. I was super into Buddhism and decided I really needed the saying of a Buddhist tea ceremony permanently etched on me in Japanese. I can confirm it means what it's supposed to, but it's still a silly thing to get inked onto your skin."

He laughs, probably understanding the pain of a stupid tattoo. "What does it say?"

I sigh. "It means 'each moment, only once.' Buddhists

believe every tea ceremony should be treated like it's the last time you'll ever see that person." I frown as something occurs to me for the first time. "Basically, it means YOLO."

A bark of surprised laughter bursts from him. I grin as I look up.

He holds my gaze as he starts to brush his fingers along my shoulder. "Can I see it?" he asks me.

I swallow nervously, suddenly aware of the intimacy of this moment. But I nod.

He gives me space to turn over onto my other side. I pull a shaky breath into my lungs as I settle into the pillow, now facing away from him. I tug the blanket down to my hips and tuck my top hand under the pillow, exposing my ribs and side boob to his heated gaze.

Several seconds go by before he leans forward to trace the Japanese kanji characters running the length of my torso. I shiver at the feel of his touch and I'm sure he notices the goosebumps that appear. I marvel at how gently his fingers brush across my skin.

When he reaches the bottom of the characters, he starts the path back up again.

"That... feels so nice," I sigh, basking in the heavenly sensation. "That's better than a massage. And a lullaby."

Sure enough, on his third path down the ink, my eyelids flutter closed. A soft moan escapes my lips at the amount of sheer contentment that I feel in this moment.

The next time he reaches the top of the tattoo, I vaguely register the feeling of his lips pressing against my shoulder before his fingers begin again. And although I drift to sleep with his skin brushing against me, it's the feel of his soft lips that I dream of.

When I wake, Tristan's room is pitch black and my bladder is about to burst.

I stifle my groan as I untangle myself first from the arm draped over my waist, then from the multiple sheets and blankets that Tristan pulled around us at some point. I slide off the bed and pad as quickly and as quietly as I can to the bathroom next door.

Sighing at the relief that comes from something as simple as peeing, I clean myself up and wash my hands. I smile when I feel the slight ache from last night.

I briefly debate sleeping the rest of the night in Jax's room, but quickly decide that Tristan was right about his bed—it really is horrible. I'll get much better sleep in Tristan's bed.

Even my subconscious rolls its eyes at my ridiculous lie.

I quietly slip into Tristan's room and try to get comfortable under the sheets without disturbing the bed too much. Eventually I settle on my side, facing away from the still-gloriously-naked man behind me.

Just as I'm drifting off to sleep, a heavy arm wraps around my waist and pulls me against a hard chest. I try not to yelp when I feel a very stiff erection press against my ass.

Tristan nuzzles into my neck, his breath tickling my ear. I glance behind me to see his eyes are still closed.

Instead of untangling myself and risking waking him up, I settle into the comfort of his body wrapped around me and close my eyes. Normally, I can fall asleep immediately.

Except, I don't normally have a sex god pressing into my back, heating my body and distracting my mind.

I can't help circling my hips any more than I can help how fast my heart is beating. A small moan escapes my lips as I arch my back and push my ass into the man behind me.

On my third repetition of that motion, I hear a sleepy

growl sound in my ear as a hand latches onto my waist. I feel Tristan press himself tight against my back, his dick twitching between our bodies.

I circle my hips again, silently pleading.

Without a word, he reaches down and slides inside me. A heavy moan sounds from my throat as I close my eyes and arch harder, desperate to take in more of him. I'm completely wrapped in a carnal, lust-drunk spell. I automatically reach back to grip his muscled thigh, my nails digging into him as I spread my legs and invite him deeper.

I hear a deep growl in my ear as he grips my hip and starts pushing into me. There's nothing slow or careful about his movements—he's just fucking me as hard and as deep as he can. We're both filled with the sudden primal need to possess our pleasure.

I whimper when he bites my shoulder. He pins me with his teeth and his hand on my hip, his hard thrusts never slowing. I feel the familiar ache of a growing orgasm deep in my belly.

With every thrust of Tristan behind me, I get closer and closer to my release. But just as I'm about to scream, Tristan presses me onto my stomach and flattens his weight on top of me, never once creating space between us or letting up on fucking me. I turn my head to the side and gasp at the feeling of him *mounting* me and taking what he wants.

With his teeth still pressed against my neck and his breath heavy in my ear, he braces himself on his forearm with one hand and arches my hips off the bed with the other. His movements are so carnal, so possessive, that I shatter without a second thought.

My scream is silent, caught in the sheets wrapped around us. As soon as my body starts shaking, I feel his hips lose their rhythm. The energy leaves our bodies at the same time.

He slumps against me with a groan. I'm too drained to even grumble about how he's too heavy on top of me—I'm just trying to get air into my lungs.

After a moment he seems to realize that he's crushing me. He rolls off of me with another groan, and I pout at the loss of his body heat.

I still haven't moved from my deflated position when he returns from the bathroom. He climbs back into bed, pulling the blankets over us, and tugs me once again into his embrace. He slides one arm under my head and wraps the other around my waist. He nips my earlobe before settling into the pillows.

"If that wasn't the most exhausting orgasm I've ever experienced in my life, I would tell you that your tempting little body needs to stay on the other side of the bed for the rest of the night," he murmurs in my ear.

I laugh quietly as I wiggle against his groin in teasing. He growls and slaps my ass lightly, then wraps his arm around me again.

It only takes me a moment to fall back asleep.

16

TRISTAN

I wake up to hair in my face and the scent of coconut in my nose. It takes me a second to realize who I'm holding so tightly.

I'm lying on my stomach with my arm curled around Remy's waist, pulling her flush against my side and burying my face in her neck. It's early so she's still asleep, her arm wrapped around where I'm holding her and one of her legs haphazardly tangled with mine. She's not quite snoring but I can hear the quiet little sounds she's making as her breaths escape from between her lips.

I pull away slightly to look at her face. This feels so different from when we fell asleep on the couch together.

I don't remember if we cuddled that night or how long Remy even stayed, since she was gone when I woke up. I think we spent the night there because I remember holding something—or rather, someone—in my sleep, but obviously I didn't get the full experience if I don't even remember it.

At that reminder, I pull Remy closer to me and nuzzle into her neck. The thought of experiencing her closeness and not getting to enjoy it makes me irrationally annoyed. I'm even more annoyed at the fact that I have to get up soon and that Remy will be the one waking up alone today.

I try to pull her even closer, my thumb starting to trail circles on her skin where I'm gripping her waist. I want to soak up another few minutes with her like this.

Last night was... a lot of things. Even though I told her a little about my family the night we sat on the couch, it's a whole other level of vulnerability letting someone overhear one of the worst conversations I've had with my family in a while. Even the memory of my mom's selfish cries makes my teeth clench.

But Remy didn't show any of the pity that I'm used to when people hear about my unsupportive parents. She just offered me her honest opinion and let me do with it what I wanted. She didn't awkwardly pull away—she just stood, strong and unflinching, with her painful truth.

In that moment I could've kissed her for her strength and her honesty. So, I did.

I don't think sex with Remy will ever not blow me away. The chemistry between us is like a pull that clearly neither of us can resist. We fit so perfectly together that it actually makes me angry that we waited this long to start doing this.

Only now, it's more than just sex.

I asked her to stay with me last night. I've never wanted to ask a girl to stay. I've never cared to spend more time with them after I've come down from my orgasm high. If they did stay it was only because I'm not enough of a dick to send them home when it's late. But I've never wanted to spend more time with them, or keep the physical touch going without having sex. I've never wanted to cuddle.

But last night—as well as this very moment—I can't seem to get enough of Remy's body against mine. It feels like there's a current running between us that's constantly pulling us together, an energy that's also hypnotizing me and demanding that I spend as much time around her as I can. Kissing her, touching her, talking to her.

It should probably scare me, but it feels so natural to want to be around her that I can't really bring myself to be freaked out about it. She's been in my life for longer than probably any other girl so there's already a level of comfort between us that I've never experienced before. And no matter how I look at it, I can't see wanting to spend time with Remy—in bed, out of bed, in the gym, everywhere in between—as anything but a good thing.

The sex isn't even on the forefront of my mind anymore —I just want *her*.

The thought makes my breath catch and my eyes shoot open.

I want Remy? Since when do I have any interest in a girlfriend?

My focus has been on fighting for years now. The whole reason I've stayed away from steady girlfriends—other than not finding anyone interesting enough to hold my attention —is because I need to be selfish to be a good fighter. 'Selfish' and 'boyfriend' don't exactly go together in a sentence.

Yet when I look at Remy, I can't fathom any of that. I just want more time with her. Surely, I have time outside of the gym to spend with another person? Is that enough to be a good boyfriend?

Does she even want a boyfriend?

I suddenly realize the insane turn my thoughts have taken. I frown and mentally shake the images from my head —of fight nights with Remy curled in my lap, of dinner in the city, of lazy Sundays between the sheets. I'm getting way ahead of myself here.

I gently slide away from Remy, trying not to wake her. I smile when I see her frown in her sleep at the missing weight of my arm around her.

Pulling the sheet up her body—and growling when her delicious tits are no longer visible to me—I exhale one final smile at the sight of her before quietly grabbing what I need for the gym. I slip out of my room a few minutes later.

I'm not sure how I get through my classes and private lessons at the gym today; I'm completely distracted with thoughts of Remy. I occasionally glance at my phone, debating texting her, but I give up on the idea when I realize I'm not sure what I'd actually say. I turn back to my students with a sigh.

It's almost 8:00 when I'm finally done working and teaching for the day. I once again think about calling Remy, this time with the idea of just flat out asking her if she wants to hang out. But the fact that I'm not sure what her answer would be has me discarding that idea, too. I still have no clue where her head is at with us.

I cringe. *Us.* When did I become that guy?

Apparently when a feisty little brunette gave me a listening ear and mind-blowing orgasms.

Sighing, I grab my phone to see who might want to hang out tonight. I never realized how much time Jax and I spend together until he wasn't around.

But a missed call and text message catch my eye. I open the message with a frown, wondering why Aiden would've called me.

Aiden: Hey man, people are gonna start showing up at the house at 9 if you feel like coming over. It'll be chill, just some drinks and maybe a fire out back. Text me if you need the address.

I completely forgot Aiden invited me to his party

tonight. I wince and rub my temple. House parties remind me of college kids, which I was never really a big fan of. Also, lots of talking. At least at the bars I don't have to make conversation, and I can slip out without being noticed.

But with a sigh, I decide this is probably as good an opportunity as ever to put some time in with the team. If Aiden invited me that means there's going to be a few others from the gym, so at least I'll have some people to talk to about fighting. I'm not big on socializing with the students since I enjoy being the stoic, no-bullshit coach that keeps his distance, but there is such a thing as too distant. An hour at a party will give me a chance to spend some time with them and prove I'm not a total asshole.

I tuck my phone in my bag and head for the showers, ignoring the little voice in the back of my mind that's whispering I'm only going to the party in the hopes of seeing one particular student.

I walk into the townhouse and immediately remember that there is a very valid reason that I don't do house parties. It feels like I've walked into the middle of Hipsterville.

There are people scattered all over the couches in the living room and crowded around the bar in the kitchen. I even notice the people smoking in the backyard through the open back door beyond the kitchen. I recognize a few people from the gym but for the most part, this is a party of freshly graduated, lost-in-the-world twenty-three-year-olds that are getting together to smoke weed and talk about problems they know nothing about. Not exactly my ideal crowd.

But when I spot Aiden in the kitchen, I plaster a smile on my face and make my way over to him.

"Hey man, you made it! Can I get you a beer?" Aiden gives me an overly excited fist bump, his grin stretching from ear to ear. I make a mental note that although I'm most likely going to have a terrible time here, it makes a big difference for team morality when I spend time with the guys. My smile becomes a little more authentic.

"Yeah, a beer would be great, thanks. Who's coming from the gym?" I look around the first floor, trying to decide who will be the easiest to spend the next hour with.

Aiden opens the fridge but looks thoughtfully over the door as he thinks about his answer. "Uh, Max's here somewhere, so is Lucy, but I don't think Remy is coming. Two of the new fighters are here too, Dane and Pete."

I try to ignore the pang of disappointment I feel when he says Remy isn't coming. I had assumed that she comes to events like these, seeing as she's such a social person. It wouldn't have been the worst thing to hang out with her in public—although I'm not sure I would've been able to keep myself from eye-fucking her.

I smile thankfully when Aiden grabs an IPA from the fridge. He pops the top off with a bottle opener then slides the beer across the counter to me.

"I also have a few friends here from Temple," he continues, crossing his arms and leaning against the bar. "Not sure if you'll know anyone but some of them graduated the same year you did."

I nod, deciding not to tell him that running into people I went to college with doesn't exactly sweeten the evening for me. I take a swig of my beer.

Someone calls for Aiden from the living room, at which he nods and then turns to me. "I have to go handle that.

Max's outside with the rest of the guys if you want to say hey. I know you're not exactly the mingling type." He clasps my shoulder with a big grin. "But thanks for coming anyway."

I flash him a very crooked, very guilty smile. *Busted.*

I make my way outside, immediately recognizing Lucy's ringing laugh. I find her sitting around the fire with Max and the two new fighters that Aiden had mentioned.

"Holy shit, you actually came!" Lucy exclaims in mock-shock. I roll my eyes and tug her ponytail before giving each of the guys a fist bump.

"Figured I'd bless you with my presence for a while," I tease. I sit down in the camping chair on the other side of the fire and take a swig of my beer.

Lucy rolls her eyes and fakes vomiting on my shoes. I wink at her with a grin.

I turn to the two guys across from me—Dane and Pete, Aiden had said. I've seen them at the gym and know they've just joined our fight team, but I haven't spent any time training with them yet. As much time as I spend at the gym, I typically don't remember anyone's name until they've either scheduled privates with me or they've started training with the fighters.

"So, I hear you guys are trying to get on the next fight card," I say by way of a conversation starter. Since I'm here I might as well use the time to get to know the new additions to the team.

They nod, eager to have my attention, and launch into a description of their training and fight goals. I smile and nod along, occasionally adding my thoughts and suggestions when they ask me questions. It makes me happy to see fighters just starting out being this excited about their train-ing. I've been in the game for so long that I've seen plenty of fighters burn out and lose their love for the sport. It's refreshing to be reminded of the excitement that we all start out with.

"Do you think Jax will fight again?" Dane asks me, as if sensing my train of thought.

I shrug and take a sip of my beer, enjoying the alcohol's pleasant hum in my veins. "I don't know," I answer honestly. "Nowadays I'm not sure he enjoys it as much as he used to. He's so good and could easily go further, but that would mean stepping in with a whole other caliber of fighters—fighters that have their hearts set on the UFC and are willing to dedicate their entire lives to getting there. I don't know if Jax wants to give everything up for that."

They all nod in understanding. The whole gym loves Jax, but we've all noticed that he's been less excited for his fights in the past year.

"Speaking of Jax, when does he get back from San Diego?" I hear Lucy ask.

I turn toward her. "This weekend. Sunday."

"And how has it been living with our darling Remy?" she asks with a grin.

I tense when I realize I have no idea if Remy has told anyone about us. I study Lucy for a moment but decide she's probably not close enough to Remy to warrant that kind of intimate conversation. I know Lucy sensed the tension between us last week, so I answer her question based on the assumption that that's why she's teasing me.

"Well, we're both alive and kicking, so as well as can be expected," I shrug.

"And there have been no other pranks? No other... incidents?"

I narrow my eyes at Lucy and decide she should be the last person to be told any kind of gossip.

But before I get a chance to answer, Max pipes up beside me.

"Speak of the devil," he murmurs. "Look who just walked in."

I turn my head toward the house—and feel my heart-beat stutter, just for a beat—when I see Remy walk through the door.

She immediately commands the attention of the crowd with her genuine smile and unassumingly perfect, *womanly* body. Her jeans are tight enough to showcase her very feminine curves, while her trademark combat boots contrast that with her "take no shit" aura. She's wearing a very cut-out white tank top that lets her black bralette peek through, the lace of which covers just enough of her breasts that it's not overly revealing, but entirely enticing. My mouth goes dry at just the sight of her.

She greets a few people before spotting our group, then freezes when she notices me.

After a moment she plasters a smile on her face again and walks over to us. "Hi," she squeaks nervously, looking at everyone but me.

I grin at how uncomfortable she looks. Clearly, she's never had to hide a secret about sex before, and I realize quickly that Lucy is going to see right through her.

I'm surprised to realize that I couldn't care less.

As much as I keep my personal sexcapades out of the gym and away from my job, I wouldn't mind stamping a claim on Remy. I don't enjoy sharing my women, for one, but I'm starting to realize I also feel a very carnal type of possessiveness when it comes to her. I should be the only one that wakes her up in the middle of the night with a screaming orgasm.

I shudder at the memory of last night—and then quickly

wipe it from my thoughts before I decide to drag Remy upstairs for a repeat performance.

"Hi, Remy baby," I tease with a grin. "Fancy seeing you here."

She finally looks at me with a quirked eyebrow. "I should be telling you that. Since when do you come to house parties?"

I shrug nonchalantly and gesture at the group with my beer. "I wanted to bond with the team." I'm rewarded with a grateful smile from Dane and Pete.

Before we can say anything else, Lucy cuts us off. "Actually, we were just talking about the two of you living in the same house. How's that been going?"

Remy whips her head to glare at a very smug—and very *smiling*—Lucy.

Instead of waiting for Remy to awkwardly stumble over some kind of non-answer, I respond for her. "It's been great," I quip. "We were able to lay down some new ground rules and now we're perfectly capable of hanging out around the house. We had a lovely conversation about it just the other night on the couch."

Remy's eyes go wide. I can tell by Lucy's barely-covered snort that she definitely understood my comment, but the guys might be too clueless to key into my hidden meaning. Remy's response will be what makes it obvious or not.

"Um, yeah. I just needed to scream at him a few times until he finally saw the value of my house rules. We're practically civil now."

Max chuckles from beside me, probably picturing how many screaming matches we must've had before we reached a truce.

Little does he know, the screaming was of a very different nature...

But it seems like the guys buy our lies. They start to ask her if she wants to head to the bar with them after the party ends here, but they're interrupted by someone calling Remy's name from across the yard.

She turns to the group that has since congregated near the grill. Based on the amount of Temple gear I see some of them wearing, I deduce that they know each other from college. She excuses herself from our circle and walks over to her friends with a big smile.

I try to rejoin Dane's conversation about the upcoming UFC fights this weekend, but I keep getting distracted by the sound of Remy's lively laugh. I can't stop myself from glancing over to where she's standing.

She's having an animated conversation about some kind of college memory with one of the girls. She's gesturing wildly, her facial expressions conveying every emotion during the length of the story, and every so often she throws her head back with a deep belly laugh.

She's absolutely radiant when she's happy. Her hair is blowing in the warm September wind and she occasionally brushes away a stray strand that's blown into her face. I realize I want nothing more than to tuck the hair behind her ear and kiss her so hard that she forgets her own name.

After a while she chances a look my way. While her friend is talking, she peeks a glance at me from beneath lowered lashes. I grin and wink at her, unashamed that she caught me looking.

Her eyes drop down again as a blush flames her cheeks. But she can't quite hide the small smile that tilts up the corners of her lips.

Finally sensing a lull in the UFC conversation around me, I use the opportunity to excuse myself from the group and make my way over to Remy. I decide I want to coax a few more blushes out of her, maybe see if I can convince her to sneak out of here with me. My nerves tingle with excitement.

Remy looks up at me with wide eyes when I reach her side. But just as I open mouth to make a teasing comment, I'm cut off by someone recognizing her as they walk by.

"*Remy*? Is that you? Holy shit!"

She turns startled eyes toward a man in suit pants and button-up. His dark hair is slicked back, and he's got a beer in his hands. His whole image reeks of Corporate America.

I narrow my eyes at him, something familiar nagging the edge of my consciousness.

"Jason?" she gasps. "Wow, it's been years. How are you?"

That's when it hits me. Jason started at Temple the same year that I did. We actually lived in the same freshman dorm building. At the time he was an awkward, nerdy kid studying philosophy. I think I heard he eventually used his degree to go to law school.

He grins at Remy and steps a little closer to whisper, "I know, right? Although God knows it hasn't been long enough to forget Lowe's class."

I put two and two together and deduce that Remy and Jason probably had a class or two together. They were both liberal arts majors, so they most likely spent time in the same academic buildings. Even though Remy is three years younger than us, I'm not surprised she was taking classes with juniors and seniors. Everyone knows she's a bit of a brainiac.

My pride at her being the polar opposite of my usual bimbo is soured by the fact that Jason has yet to acknowledge me and is now hanging on Remy's arm.

"Hey man, long time no see," I interrupt in a tight voice, trying to resist the urge to yank her away from him.

He turns to me as if just now noticing my presence. Both he and Remy are wide-eyed as they look at me.

When he doesn't immediately remember my name, I add coldly, "It's Tristan. We were freshmen together in Peabody Hall."

A flash of recognition appears in his eyes. He looks me over and then grabs my shoulder in an overly friendly gesture, a fake grin plastered on his face. "Tristan. Hey, man! How you doing?"

I resist the urge to rip his hand off of me. Instead, I force a smile onto my face and return the sentiment. "Great. Life's great. Funny running into you here."

At that he turns back to Remy. "Yeah, small world. Although I'm glad I ended up here tonight." Without taking his eyes off Remy, he leans in closer to me to whisper conspiratorially, "Because between you and me, I had the biggest crush on Remy in college."

A blush flames across her cheeks while rage threatens to silently tear me apart. I have never once felt jealous over a girl. I always thought if a girl wanted to be with someone else, then why would I waste any of my energy being jealous over someone that didn't want me?

But now, with Remy... it feels like I'll maul anyone that dares to touch her.

I swallow roughly in an effort to jam down my archaic feelings. Instead, I force myself to chuckle.

I might as well be invisible to him, though. With his eyes trained on Remy, he steps up to her and grips her elbow, tugging gently to lead her away. "Let's get you a drink. I want to hear about what you've been up to. Someone told me you work for a tech company now. I'm glad you ended on a realistic career instead of trying for that writing thing you talked about for a while..."

I see the flash of pain in her eyes even as she lets Jason tug her along. Rage toward this douchebag once again boils through my veins, this time for invalidating Remy's true passion. I'm just about to go after them and let all my caveman rage fly when a short blonde girl steps into my path. I freeze in surprise.

She's shorter than even Remy, with a huge smile on her face as she stares up at me. I realize then that she's the Temple friend Remy was talking with not long ago.

"Hi," she chirps happily. "I'm Anna. Are you friends with Remy?"

"Yeah," I answer hesitantly. "I'm Tristan. I know Remy from the gym." I can't help glancing to the other end of the yard where Jason is standing by a cooler with Remy, drinks in hand and talking animatedly. She's just nodding at whatever he's saying.

"Oh, that's cool," Anna continues, and I begrudgingly bring my attention back to her. "She mentioned she joined a gym a couple years ago. You definitely look like you work out." She shamelessly steps closer to run her fingers along my bicep.

For some reason my eyes snap over to Remy.

She's frozen, staring at Anna's hand on my arm. Her mouth ticks down into a small frown.

A satisfied warmth blooms in my chest. It doesn't seem like she's reacting with the same blind fury I felt when Jason touched her, but she definitely doesn't look happy. Maybe she really is starting to like me.

A smile tugs at my lips at that thought.

The motion seems to snap Remy's eyes to mine. For a tense moment we just stare at each other, everyone else at the party fading away until it's just her and I and the tension growing between us.

But then she breaks our eye contact. Her eyes jerk, once, to Anna, and then back to Jason. I can tell she's trying really hard not to look back at me.

The idea that Remy might be a little jealous simmers the burning rage that almost overtook me a minute ago. I turn back to Anna, the need to rush over to Remy dimming slightly. *Slightly.*

"Yeah, I do a couple pushups now and then," I tell her sarcastically.

She laughs, way too loudly. As if I just told the funniest joke she's ever heard. She grips my arm and steps even closer, her head thrown back with the laugh.

I wince, feeling a twinge of regret that I encouraged her flirtation on pure instinct. I take another peek at Remy.

She clearly heard Anna's laugh—everyone at the party heard her laugh—but she's still purposefully looking only at Jason. Even from where I stand, I can see the tense way she's standing and the hard frown on her face.

I sigh and take a step away from Anna. *I need to cut this off before it gets worse.*

But as I look at her, it suddenly occurs to me that Anna's exactly the kind of girl I would normally go for. She's pretty, feminine, small enough that I could throw her around in the bedroom—everything I usually look for.

But she does nothing for me.

I feel no attraction, no urge to turn on my charm. I don't feel anything that would make me want to spend another second around her. All I can think of is that she's not Remy.

Another wave of warmth surges through my chest as my morning thoughts return. *I want Remy.*

I chance another look at the target of my inner war, any warmth inside me freezing when I realize she's still talking to Jason. And now he's got his hand on her hip.

"Look, Anna, I'm sorry to cut you off but I have to go," I grit through clenched teeth. Without waiting for her reaction, I turn to make my way over to Remy.

Politeness be damned—I'm about to remove this guy's hands from his body.

But before I take more than a step, I see Remy disappearing into the house.

I don't see her in the kitchen or living room, so I make my way to the second floor. There are two girls waiting for the bathroom and a few hipsters smoking weed in one of the bedrooms, but no sign of Remy. I climb another set of steps to the third floor.

This floor only has two bedrooms and it looks completely empty of people. I frown, wondering how I could have lost Remy in this house.

But then I hear a toilet flush coming from the master bedroom. I hesitantly push the door open.

Remy is leaning against the bedroom wall, staring at her phone as she waits for the bathroom door to open. I step up behind her.

"Having fun?" I mumble in her ear. She yelps and turns around.

"Tristan," she hisses, clutching her heart. "What is your obsession with sneaking up on me? You're going to scare me to death one of these days."

I chuckle. "Distracted, are we? What's that pretty little head of yours thinking about?" I cock an eyebrow thoughtfully as I wait for her to answer.

She looks away quickly, seeming suddenly uncomfortable. "Nothing," she mumbles.

I laugh again. "You're a terrible liar, Remy baby," I tease her. "It's not a hard guess." The hunger in my eyes deepens as I look down at her and suddenly forget why I'm angry. All

I can think about is how beautiful she looked riding me yesterday, shining with sweat and not caring how wild she looked as she chased her orgasm. I swallow roughly and tamp down on the urge to adjust my growing cock.

She blushes at my words and looks away again. "I'm not thinking about anything," she says again, more firmly this time. "I'm just enjoying the party."

Now I remember why I'm angry with her. "Are you having fun with Jason?" I ask her, trying to keep my voice light and my fury not at all obvious.

She turns to face me fully. "Jason's great," she says, her face expressionless. "How's Anna?"

"Trying very hard to flirt," I respond curtly. She stiffens at my answer, her eyes narrowing. But I push past any talk of Anna and steer us back toward Jason. I need to know if there's anything between them.

"Were you close to Jason in college?" I ask tightly, trying to mask the jealousy in my words.

Remy's posture is still tense as a frown mars her pretty face. "Not really, but he was part of the study group," she starts cautiously. "He was the smartest one, so he helped us a lot. He was always around."

She seems to notice the way my jaw clenches at her comment because she relaxes her stance, a small smirk appearing on her lips. "He's a hard worker, too. He just graduated early from Temple Law. He was always very... *stimulating* to talk to."

It takes all I have not to slam her against the wall and fuck him out of her mind right then and there.

Instead, I swallow the growl in my throat and try to adopt a bored look. "I'm sure he is," I shrug. "I'm sure he's very *pleasing*."

A small frown appears on her face when I don't bite at

her taunt. She opens her mouth to snap back at me but then the bathroom door opens, and she never gets the chance.

We both turn to nod politely at the girl coming out of the bathroom, who smiles at us and walks out of the room. I wait until she's out of sight before spinning around and gripping Remy by the throat. I push her into the bathroom and lock the door behind us.

She's breathing heavily as I push my body against hers, flattening her against the door. I study her for a moment, my thumb gently rubbing circles on the side of her neck.

"Do you really think he'll please you as much as I do?" I murmur against her lips. I don't know if I'll ever get enough of her little gasps when I affect her like this.

"Yes," she moans.

"Liar," I chuckle. I brush my lips against hers, not quite kissing, but I'm desperate for more contact. "No one can make you feel like I do. You know it's true. Just say it." She shakes her head, refusing to admit to such a thing.

"No one can make you as wet as I can with just my fingers," I growl. The hand that's not on her neck begins tracing up and down her side, occasionally dipping under the edge of her tank top. She shivers, but I don't know if it's from my words or my touch.

"No one can drive you as crazy as I can when my tongue is in your pussy," I continue. "No one can make you come as hard as when I bend you over and take you from behind. No one." A whimper escapes her lips.

Suddenly the jealousy inside of me explodes. I crash my mouth down to hers, easily splitting her lips with my tongue and darting inside to caress hers. I feel like a madman, like I need to be inside her in any way I can. I kiss her hungrily, desperately.

When I pull away, we're both breathless. I tuck a strand

of hair behind her ear, letting my touch linger on her cheek. But the gentle moment is only that, a moment, because then I grip her hair roughly and yank her head back. She whimpers but turns her face up toward me, and I can hear her breathy little sighs as she tries to cover up how turned on she is.

"You're *mine*," I growl against her lips. "Your pleasure belongs to *me*."

My sudden possessive outburst surprises her just as much as it does me. I decide to ignore the insane, animalistic jealousy that's flowing through my veins right now and instead focus on the object of those feelings in front of me. Without waiting for her to respond, I quickly unbutton her jeans and yank them down her legs. I lean down to pull them the rest of the way off. When I stand back up, I grab her behind the thighs and lift her up against the wall. Her legs wrap automatically around my waist.

Fuck, it's like our bodies were molded for each other. They fit together so perfectly, so easily. Nothing ever feels awkward or uncomfortable. It's like our bodies know each other, even after such a short amount of time.

I unbutton my own jeans and free my cock quickly, knowing this fuck will be hard and fast. I feel too crazy from the jealousy, too desperate for her body around me, for it to be any different. I pull her panties aside and line up with her entrance. Even without any foreplay I can feel how wet she is.

"*Mine*," I repeat with a snarl, and thrust in with one stroke.

She whimpers at the overwhelming sensation. Her eyes are closed but she's holding tight around my neck as I fuck her, hard. I pound into her, letting my possessive emotions fuel my thrusts. My body's animalistic urges make me feel like if I can fuck her hard enough, maybe she won't ever think of anyone else.

"Say it," I growl against her lips. "Say you're mine." I lift her thighs a little higher around me and push even deeper.

She gasps at the feeling but shakes her head. She's too stubborn to admit anything. It's too early for us.

That knowledge temporarily tamps down on my jealous rage, and my forehead drops against hers. "Remy," I groan, even as my thrusts never slow. "Look at me."

Her eyes open and widen in surprise at the change in my tone. Her breaths start to come quicker, and her gaze darts over my face, searching for answers that I'm not sure either of us are ready for. I hold her eyes with mine, not letting her look away even when I feel her thighs start to tremble as her orgasm builds.

I lean forward and kiss her hungrily. I swallow her moans as our tongues tangle and my thrusts become harder. I pull away just enough to look at her when I sense we're both getting close, and immediately I'm drowning in her wide-eyed stare. Before, she didn't want to look at me, and now I know why—in our closeness, in this moment between us, she's completely open and flayed bare before me. I can see every bit of fear and lust and affection in her eyes. And I suddenly realize that I hope she can see the same in mine.

I hear her gasp just before her muscles clench around me, her eyes never leaving mine. Between our connection and the physical feel of her orgasm, my own release is immediately triggered.

"Fuck," I groan as I spill inside her. I can still feel her spasming around my cock. I keep pounding into her until I feel her sag against me, her body limp and exhausted.

We stay there for a moment, tangled in each other and

leaning heavily against the door. Our foreheads are touching and we're breathing heavily.

I hesitate for a moment before kissing her, knowing I was aggressive but not knowing how she's feeling right now. I set her down gently, keeping my grip on her until I feel her steady herself. I can see the blush on her face as she reaches for her jeans. She doesn't meet my eyes.

Just then there's a loud knock at the door. "Is someone in there?" a very stoned voice calls out.

I roll my eyes but watch as Remy pales. She pulls her jeans on hurriedly. "Just a second!" she calls out.

"Remy..." I start. I want to ask her to stay with me tonight. To get out of here so we can spend the night together.

But she's hell-bent on rushing out of this bathroom so she ignores me entirely, throwing the door open and pushing past the hipster from downstairs. I hurry after her.

"Whoa! Nice, dude!" The guy is stoned out of his mind and can barely see straight but he has a massive grin on his face from seeing the two of us leave the bathroom together. He holds his hand up in expectation of a high five.

I roll my eyes again. "Grow up," I grumble as I shoulder past him.

I don't catch up to Remy until we're back on the first floor but by then, Anna has already spotted her.

"Remy!" she calls out. She prances up to us and grabs Remy's hand. "We're heading over to the Barbary. You *have* to come! My friend Shane says it's the most entertaining drag show in the city."

"Oh. Umm..." Remy casts a nervous glance at me. I silently will her to understand that I want her to say *fuck no, I'm going home with Tristan.*

"Tristan, you should come too!" Anna exclaims happily.

"I'm... not really into shows," I say hesitantly. "Plus, I have an early morning at the gym tomorrow, so I'll probably just head home soon." Once again, I look at Remy to try to convey my silent message.

I think she's about to decline the offer when another girl from their Temple group bounces up to us. "Remy! Oh my god, I haven't seen you in so long! Please tell me you're coming with us to the Barbary. I'm only in town for this weekend so you *have* to come hang out with us."

I see Remy's almost imperceptible wince. But then she says, "I had no idea you were in town. Of course I'll come, that sounds like a lot of fun."

I try to keep the frown from my face, but I doubt I'm successful.

Anna practically beams with happiness. "All right, well I'm just going to grab my jacket and then we can head over there." She turns to me with a thousand-watt smile. "You sure you don't want to come? I'm happy to keep you company."

I smother the wince that threatens to take over my face from the obvious come-on. "Sorry, I'm just going to call it a night," I tell her. I swallow roughly and turn to Remy. "I guess I'll see you at home." She gives me a small nod.

I head toward the backyard to say goodbye to everyone from the gym. From behind me I hear Anna say, "Home? You guys live together? I didn't know you were dating."

"We're... not," is Remy's answer.

And I can't stop my heart from cracking a little bit at those words.

17

REMY

I can't stop thinking about Tristan's bathroom sex declaration.

It's four hours and way too many shots later, and I haven't once been able to focus on the show, or my friends, or the music we're now dancing to. I just keep replaying Tristan's words.

You're mine.

What does that even mean? Why would he say that? That makes it sound like we're so much more than just sex, but I know for a fact that Tristan is not interested in a relationship. He said as much when he admitted he's too selfish as a fighter to have a girlfriend. But then what did he mean?

And why did his words make me so insanely, ridiculously happy?

Something changed with us last night. Mentioning his family during the question game this week was one thing, but talking to me after his mom called him yesterday, letting me see his pain... that changed something between us.

And I don't want to fight it anymore.

I realize I like spending time with Tristan. I like asking

him random questions, and watching fights together, and lying in bed after sex. I like that he's so much more than everyone thinks he is, and that he only shows that side of him to a few people. I like the way his brain thinks. I like how protective he is of the people he loves. I like the way we fit together, both during sex and after.

I like *him*. And I want more.

I cringe at that thought, hoping Anna doesn't notice and think I'm reacting to whatever it is she's been babbling on about for the past twenty minutes. But she's so drunk that I doubt she'd notice even if I broke down and started crying. I chug the majority of my cocktail in an attempt to erase my thoughts from my brain.

I can't like Tristan. I can't want more. He's just not that guy—he doesn't do relationships. He's the playboy that sleeps with women and then turns them down when they inevitably want more.

And I've just become one of them.

I wince and finish the rest of my drink. *Fuck. I'm officially a statistic.*

I glance at my phone and realize with a start that it's almost 2:00 in the morning. Not only are they going to yell last call soon, but I also planned on taking class in the morning. I can already feel how tired and hungover that workout is going to be.

I quickly say goodbye to the girls, promising to call Anna again. Twenty minutes later my Uber is pulling up to the house.

I glance nervously at Tristan's window, but I can see even from here that the lights are off and the house is quiet. I can't decide if I'm relieved or dejected that I won't see him tonight.

With a tired sigh, I walk into the house.

I was right about the workout being horrendous. I drank so much trying to distract myself from my Tristan-addled thoughts that I might still be drunk even several hours later.

I haven't seen Tristan yet. I know he's here somewhere because Saturday is the day our training always overlaps, but he's not the one teaching our cardio bagwork class this morning and I haven't exactly found the courage to go looking for him.

Thank goodness it's not one of the pro fighters teaching the class because an hour at their intensity definitely would have made me puke. Even now, I'm struggling to keep the nausea at bay.

But a hard workout is exactly what my body needs. Not only do I sweat out the alcohol, but the physical exertion seems to immediately clear my foggy brain and sober me up. By the time the class is over, I feel great—though very eager for a nice, fat burger.

I leave the bag room and step into the mat room where the jiu-jitsu class is starting. My eyes lock with Tristan's immediately.

My blood warms just from his stare. The images of him fucking me into the bathroom door yesterday tumble through my brain until I'm squirming on the sidelines, my teeth latched onto my lower lip.

Based on the inferno blazing in his eyes that I now know to be his sign that he's turned on, I can tell he's thinking the exact same thing.

"Remy, you coming to do a few rounds?"

The question snaps me out of my lust-drunk haze. I turn toward the person who called out to me.

"Only if you don't mind the tequila leaking out of my pores, Coach," I grin.

He shakes his head with a chuckle. "Do a few rounds. I want you to do that tournament next month."

At that reminder the smile slips from my face, to be replaced with nervous energy. I nod and drop my bag. I'm completely distracted by thoughts of the tournament as I switch my soaking wet T-shirt for a skintight rashguard.

The nerves end up fucking with my flow. I do a round with Coach, and then three more with other students, but I'm so distracted by the memories of my mistakes from the last tournament that I end up second-guessing my every move. I huff my frustration at the end of the third round.

"Remy," Tristan calls. "Let's do a round."

I look at him in surprise but give a hesitant nod. Now that we're training and actually moving around on the mats, all memories of last night are gone. He slips easily back into a coaching role and I'm too focused on thoughts of the tournament to even be distracted by the feeling of his body against mine. We both love this sport too much to treat it with anything other than our complete dedication.

If I wasn't so fixated on my own inner turmoil, I might actually be pleasantly surprised at how easily we set our tension aside to focus on something serious.

I'm still slow and awkward in my movements, still thinking too much about how badly I fucked up the last time I competed. Tristan's letting me work a little bit and not capitalizing on it yet, but I can tell he notices my lack of focus.

"Just relax," he murmurs. "You're thinking too much. Just do what your body wants you to do."

"Easier said than done," I grumble. "You're not the one that fucked up at the last tournament."

"You did fine at that tournament," he says from his spot beneath me. He's on his back with his legs wrapped around me, holding me in his guard. I have my body angled low against his, my head pressed to his chest. "You were just nervous. You had that sweep lined up that you love so much but you second guessed it and missed the opportunity. You could've beat that girl easy."

My head pops up in surprise. "You saw my match?"

He doesn't break our eye contact. "I've seen all your matches."

Shocked, I can only stare down at him for a few moments. I had no idea he even noticed me.

Seemingly tired of the lull in action, Tristan takes advantage of my pause by flipping us over until he's on top. I land on my back with a grunt.

"You're too nice," he continues. "Too hesitant. You need to be cocky as fuck when you step on the mat."

I raise an eyebrow in question. "Is that your excuse? You're arrogant so you can win?"

A huge grin splits his face. "My winning record speaks for me. Clearly, the arrogance is doing something."

I focus back on what we're doing and try to grab one of his arms. "It's doing *something,* all right," I grumble under my breath.

He ignores my comment. "Just try it," he says, easily shifting to a more advantageous position beside me. "The next time you step on that tournament mat, pick a weapon and act like there's no way someone could stop you from using it against them." His face is no longer in my line of sight, but I can practically hear the grin as it stretches across his lips. "I'm sure you can find *something* you're good at."

I glare at his ribs that are currently in my face. With a sudden angry burst of strength, I push myself to a slightly better position. "You are such an ass," I hiss. "Is that part of your strategy too? Along with the ego?"

I was right, he's grinning from ear to ear. He looks incredibly pleased with himself. "Nope, that's just because it's fun to piss you off."

I shake my head, fighting the smile that wants to break free. Just then, the bell rings and our round ends.

Tristan gives me a little shove toward another student for the next round. "Cocky as fuck," he mutters so only I can hear.

I sigh and turn to my next partner.

The last few rounds fly by. And as much as I hate to admit it, Tristan is right. Being arrogant—even if I'm faking it—immediately causes my nerves to dissipate and stops my tendency to overthink. It allows me to freely move as I want, since I no longer think about *what if* every move is wrong. I just... roll.

I allow myself a quick glance at Tristan as that realization once again reminds me that Tristan was made for this sport. Not just because of his talent, but also because of his coaching ability. He was born to be a leader. He knows exactly what to say to any given athlete to help them in their training because he pays attention and he gives a shit. I shouldn't have been surprised that he admitted to watching me in the last tournament because that's the most Tristan admission there is—he's the guy you want in your corner because he always has your back.

I should've realized it sooner. I should've known when I watched him corner fighters and coach kids at tournaments.

I should've given him more credit a long time ago.

I'm starving by the time the hour ends. I turn toward Aiden and Lucy with hopeful eyes. "Burger House? I might eat my shirt if I don't get some food in me soon."

They laugh but nod in agreement. Aiden looks over my shoulder at Tristan.

"What do you say, big dog, wanna get lunch?"

I stifle a giggle as I hear Tristan choke on his water. "Big dog?" he splutters.

Aiden grins but shrugs, unashamed. "Just trying it out. No go?"

Tristan glares at him, every ounce the stoic fighter that you shouldn't fuck with. "No," he says firmly. "No go. And if you come up with any others, I'm putting you on bag drills for a week straight. One thousand kicks before you can leave, every night. On each side."

At that, Aiden winces. "Okay, okay, no nicknames. Jeez. I thought we were all friendly after last night." Tristan only glares at him again. "No burger then?"

Tristan glances at me before answering. "No burger. I have a kid coming in for a private lesson in a few minutes. Rain check."

I hide my frown that automatically wants to appear on my face when I miss an opportunity to spend time with Tristan.

And then internally shake the hell out of myself for acting like a teenage girl.

We shower quickly and then head out the front door, the gym already empty of students. But just as I'm about to follow Lucy out, I see a flash of movement in the mat room. I peek around the corner to see who's still working out.

Tristan is showing a little boy how to fall. It's the first lesson everyone in jiu-jitsu learns, since you will undoubtedly fall in this sport—a lot—and there is definitely a right way and a wrong way to do it. Tristan's showing him how to slap the mat with his palms when he falls.

The little boy, no more than five or six, is giggling as he

topples over. He's not listening to a word Tristan's saying, he's just happy to be throwing himself on the mats.

But Tristan isn't forcing him. He just lets the boy fall again—still the wrong way—before telling him, "Here, let me show you what you look like." And then he makes a funny face and exaggerates falling down, this time looking more like a fainting damsel than a well-trained athlete. The boy's giggles intensify into loud belly laughs at the sight.

With a grin, Tristan stands back up. "That looked silly, right?" he asks him. The little boy nods. "Let's do it the right way this time. Do you want to try?" Another nod. "Good. I want you to try doing it like this: fall on your butt and then slap the mat with your hands. Ready?"

Giggles subsiding, the little boy looks at Tristan with newfound determination. With his nose scrunched in deep concentration, he falls backwards, slapping the mats exactly the way Tristan showed him.

Tristan lets out a loud whoop. He grabs the little boy and throws him up in the air, offering them both a quick moment of celebration. Giggles once again sound through the gym.

Tristan sets him back down on his feet. "All right, show me one more time. Let me see if you can do it even better the second time."

"Remy!" someone yells from behind me.

I jump so hard I'm surprised my feet don't actually leave the ground. "What?" I hiss.

Lucy is staring at me with one eyebrow raised in question. "What're you doing?" she finally asks. "We're waiting for you."

I fight the urge to glance back at the mat room. "I, um, thought I forgot my phone," I stammer. "But I found it. So... I'm good to go."

Lucy's eyes narrow suspiciously but she doesn't say anything else. Just jerks her head for me to get moving.

Once her back is turned, I chance a quick look back at the remaining people in the gym. Tristan is grinning, looking completely at ease and happy. There's no tension in his shoulders, no cold mask on his face, no arrogance on his lips. He's just... happy.

A feeling of genuine happiness fills me at the sight. My heart swells with the emotion and it feels like it'll take over my entire body, filling every crack and crevice of my soul until nothing but my happiness at his joy remains. It completely overwhelms me.

The door slams behind Lucy, shaking me out of my daze. I hurry after her, so she doesn't come back in again.

Fuck, I am so far gone.

Lunch turns into drinks, which turns into a late afternoon and eventually more food. It's almost 7:00 when I finally get home.

Tristan's passed out on the couch when I open the front door. It looks like he had some fights on but fell asleep at some point. I don't want to wake him, so I tiptoe silently up the steps.

It's still quiet downstairs after I get out of the shower. I decide to take a catnap, the food and drinks after a hard workout making me practically sway on my feet.

Twenty minutes and a Red Bull later, I hear movement downstairs and decide to finally put my big girl pants on and stop putting off seeing Tristan. The last time it was just the two of us, he immediately fucked me into the nearest surface. Surely after that I shouldn't be too nervous to make small talk.

He's finishing his dinner and putting his dishes in the sink when I finally walk into the kitchen. He doesn't quite smile but he turns to give me his full attention.

"I'm going to head over to my new apartment to make sure the key works and to drop a few things off," I tell him nervously. "I'll take a few boxes now but move the rest of it tomorrow. I should be back in an hour or so."

"Want some help?" he asks me.

I glance at him, startled. I'm always surprised when Nice Tristan makes an appearance. Even with everything going on between us, I still don't quite expect him to go out of his way to be helpful.

Sensing my hesitation, he jokes, "The sooner I get you out of here, the sooner I can go back to making my Brussels sprouts." He grins as my nose crinkles in disgust. He knows exactly how much I hate the smell of his favorite vegetable.

"Fine," I concede. "Grab some boxes and let's fit them in my car."

The drive over to my apartment only takes ten minutes and we spend the entire time lost in our own thoughts. I still can't figure out where his head is.

When we reach my new building, I park the car and we each grab a box. I swing my front door open and take in the dark, now seemingly lonely, one bedroom apartment. I turn on the lights in the hallway and make my way to the bedroom. All of the boxes I brought are clothes and bedding, so we make quick work of unloading everything into one room before wandering into the main living area.

We haven't said a word to each other since we left the house. Between the silence surrounding us and the darkness of the apartment, I feel my nerves start to buzz. It doesn't help when I realize that there is no light in the living room.

"Shit, I guess I didn't notice there's no lighting in here," I mumble as I wander into the room. I make a mental note to buy a lamp tomorrow. It's almost 10:00 and dark outside. The only reason the room isn't just as dark is because of the wall of oversized windows. The lights from the city illuminate the room, casting a comfortable glow around me.

"I love this city so much," I say quietly as I step up to the windows. "It has such an addicting energy. Even when I was a kid, I could tell how much passion the city held. I've always loved the sights, the sounds, everything about it. I don't think I'll ever be able to leave it." I close my eyes and take a deep breath, as if I'm trying to inhale the feel of the city itself. "Isn't it amazing?" I turn back to look at Tristan, nervous that he's still silent.

But he's not looking out the windows. He's looking at me.

My breath catches as our eyes meet. His smoldering gaze feels like it's looking right into my soul, like it's trying to reach the secrets in the depth of my heart. He takes a step forward to stand in front of me, his eyes never leaving mine.

"You're so fucking beautiful," he says quietly.

My heart jumps into my throat. It's beating so hard I'm scared he'll hear it, and I focus on reminding myself to breathe. I can barely catch my breath under his intense stare.

He steps closer still and rests his hand on the side of my neck, his thumb gently stroking my cheek.

He studies me for another heartbeat, then gently pulls my lips to his.

The kiss is soft, and timid. It's like he's exploring me for the first time and trying to figure out what to make of me. It only lasts for a moment before he pulls away and gazes down at me again.

"Why does it feel so different with you?"

His question is what breaks us.

This time I'm the one that pulls him to me, but now there's nothing gentle about our kiss. He's kissing me hungrily, possessively. His hands grip me hard, one still on my neck and the other now wrapped around my lower back. I'm pressed so tightly against his body that it feels like our hearts are beating against each other.

I fist my hands in his shirt, wanting desperately to understand what he's trying to tell me. A whimper escapes my lips as he opens my mouth with his tongue and deepens our kiss. I don't think I'll ever get enough of him when he touches me like this.

He continues to grip my hips as he feathers kisses down my neck. My stomach flips every time his tongue touches my skin, and I start to pant.

I cup his face and bring his lips back to mine. My kiss is frenzied, wanting more than anything for him to feel what I feel. Wanting him to become just as lost in our connection as I am. I want him to kiss me back like he can't stand the thought of any space between us, because that's exactly how hopelessly I'm aching for him right now.

"Tristan," I whimper against his lips. His hand tightens on my hips in response to my plea. He groans against my lips and hurriedly reaches for the bottom of my sundress to bring it over my head. He pulls away only long enough for the fabric to pass between us, then he's right back to kissing me like it's the last time he'll ever taste my lips.

I reach behind me to undo the clasp of my bra, the fabric sliding down the front of my body. I toss it to the side as he pulls back to look at me.

He looks... awestruck. His eyes take in my swollen lips, the tiny red marks he's left on my neck, my bare breasts with their pebbled nipples. Only the panties I'm wearing hide any part of my body. His eyes take in every detail.

And suddenly I feel exposed—too naked. My subconscious recognizes that in the past I've always hidden my nakedness, that I would never really let my boyfriends see me this way. I would either keep my clothes on or just not give them the space or the light to pull away and really see me. It always felt too intimate—like they didn't deserve to see who I really am.

I step forward to press against Tristan so he'll stop devouring my body with his fiery gaze. But he gently grips my hips to keep me an arm's-length away.

My eyes widen, alarmed. But he's staring at me so softly, so tenderly, that my panic quickly subsides.

His hand drifts up to caress my cheek. "Don't ever hide from me," he whispers simply.

Everything around us, everything before and after this moment, fades away until it feels like the world is frozen and it's just him and I standing there, lost in each other. Nothing exists but this moment and his truth. His words, his gaze... I can't remember how to breathe.

He breaks the moment by stepping forward and kissing me as softly as anyone has ever been kissed. His sudden tenderness brings tears to my eyes, and I wrap my arms around his neck and will them not to fall. I've never experienced this level of affection from anyone, let alone someone as hard as Tristan—I've never felt it down to my very bones. Between his words and this kiss, I feel my heart swell with happiness.

He gently guides me down to the carpeted floor, onto to my back. He settles above me and props himself up on an elbow, continuing to stroke my cheek. His eyes never leave mine.

He opens his mouth to say something, then closes it. His expression is almost pained. "Remy..." he chokes out. But still he hesitates.

The right words don't exist—neither of us could say the right thing in this moment. Our verbal communication is subpar as it is, but our physical communication...

Our physical communication can say exactly what we can't.

I pull him down to me. "I know..." I murmur against his lips.

Something in him breaks. Maybe he understands that this is how we communicate best.

He's back to kissing me hungrily, his tongue sliding into my waiting mouth and his hands trailing desperately over my naked body. His lips move to my neck, then to my collarbone. I gasp as he continues further down, licking and sucking my nipple, gently kissing the curve of my breast. He does the same to the other side before making his way further still. He knows exactly where to kiss me, where to touch me, to elicit a response from my body. It feels almost as if his touches were meant only for me.

That thought lights a flame inside me, and my body automatically arches into his touch. Every piece of me is drawn to him, begging for more contact. I never want him to stop.

He slides down my body and parts my legs so he can kneel between them, holding himself up on his hands. I'm barely breathing by the time I feel him circle my navel with his tongue. His wet kisses trail across my stomach, closer and closer to the only article of clothing I'm still wearing on my overheated body. When his tongue finally slides under the edge, I gasp and arch my back off the floor. I'm going to come undone before he's even done anything.

He presses my stomach back down as he kisses the inside of my thigh. Then he reaches for the straps of my thong and slowly pulls it down my legs.

And just like before, he stares at me—stares at my naked body spread in front of him. Stares like this is the first time he's ever looked at me.

He leans down to gently kiss the inside of my knee. "You're beautiful," he whispers again, his eyes twinkling with awe, as if he can't get over the fact that in this moment, I am his.

Then he's kissing the inside of my thighs, closer and closer to the heat between my legs. His first lick of my lips has my back bowing off the floor again.

With a groan, he settles on the carpet below me and buries his tongue in my cunt.

It barely takes a few swipes of his tongue before my release shatters me.

I gasp at the sudden explosion of pleasure. Tristan's been able to get me off from the very first time we slept together, so it shouldn't surprise me that I just came so quickly, but something feels different now. It's like we're completely in sync—like we've eliminated any remaining barriers between us. My orgasm is a result of allowing myself to be completely vulnerable and open with Tristan.

Sex, even meaningless sex, comes with a certain expectation of trust. And I realize suddenly that I trust Tristan unconditionally. Maybe I always have.

That thought drives another wave of my orgasm through me. It should probably scare me, the idea that I'm giving him everything, but in this moment I can only sigh in relief, a content smile stretching across my face even as my whole body shakes, drained of all the energy my release has ripped from me. I run my fingers through Tristan's hair, his head still between my legs, still kissing me. I tug him gently, wanting his face near mine. He looks up at me with a hunger in his eyes, then slides up my body to brace a forearm next to my head.

I cup his face and pull his lips to mine—and groan as I taste myself on him.

He slides his tongue in my mouth, offering me a better taste. I take all that he offers, unable to get enough of our chemistry.

I realize suddenly that he's still completely clothed. I grip the edge of his T-shirt and let my fingers trail over his abs as I pull it over his head, then immediately begin to fumble with the button on his jeans. He brushes my hands away and quickly pulls off the rest of his clothes. In only a few breaths he's settled back on top of me, caressing my hair and kissing me softly.

I'm so lost in his lips that I barely register his hard length nudging between my thighs. I'm too wrapped up in our closeness, our mingling breaths, our body heat. I'm intoxicated by everything about him.

"Tristan," I breathe. Nothing else, just his name.

"I know," he whispers, just as I did, and slides inside me.

I gasp, my hips bucking off the floor and my nails scratching down his back. He growls at the feeling and starts pushing harsh kisses against my neck. His thrusts are agonizingly slow and deep. I tilt my hips to meet each one, silently begging for more.

I've never understood the concept of making love. I've never seen sex as anything but a physical expression of passion and I can't understand how it could be slow and emotional. Sex is about orgasms, which are brought on by friction and touching—not slow motions and declarations of love.

But in this moment, I know I'm as close to making love as I'll ever be. I don't think about my feelings for Tristan or what we might mean to each other, but I'm intoxicated by our closeness. This position, the way he's caressing me so gently... it's making me feel a passion and connection that I've never felt before. And for a moment, I even enjoy his slow, careful pace.

"Tristan," I moan in his ear.

Something in him snaps, and his thrusts become frenzied. One of his hands slides down to cup my ass and lift my hips. The shift makes him press against my clit with each thrust. I whimper, feeling my release start to build.

His face is still buried in my neck. Part of me wants to pull him away so I can look in his eyes when we finally give in to the sensations, but it all feels like too much—too intimate, too honest. I don't know if I could handle what he'd see if he looked at me right now.

As if he can read my thoughts, he pulls away to look down at me.

My eyes widen at the raw intensity in his face. His eyes are burning—burning a hole through my heart. His hand grips the side of my neck and he looks down at me with an almost pleading expression. *Pleading for what? What does he want from me?*

Before I can hazard a guess, he hits the spot deep inside of me that makes me instantly shatter into a million pieces. I open my mouth to scream.

Tristan captures my lips with his and smothers my sound. He holds me in an iron grip as the pleasure rolls through me like never-ending waves. I can't tell where one stops and another begins. I vaguely register his groan and the feeling of his hips jerking as he reaches his own release. Throughout all of it he never stops kissing me.

Eventually his movements slow and then stop. He pulls away from my lips and touches his forehead to mine. But I'm too overwhelmed to really look at him so I close my eyes and nuzzle my cheek against his. He places a tentative kiss on my cheek and rolls to the floor, never letting his hands leave my body. I find myself pulled against his side as he wraps an arm around my shoulders and entwines his legs with mine.

As his hand traces the tattoo on my ribs, I nuzzle deeper into the side of his neck. My fingers slide up his chest to gently run along his collarbone.

And the moment feels so comfortable, so complete, that neither of us spoils it with words. We lie there, wrapped in each other, watching the light from the windows dance across our bodies. And before long, we've both drifted off to sleep.

It's still pitch black when I wake, shivering. Honestly, I'm surprised we were even able to fall asleep without anything covering us.

I gently slip out of Tristan's arms and pad lightly into the bathroom. I clean myself up, taking special pleasure in the pink marks on my neck and hips.

It only takes me a few minutes to find the box with my pillows and blankets in it. I grab what I need and head back to the living room where Tristan is still sleeping.

I stand in the doorway and watch him for a moment. A warm smile lights up my face as I think about what we did only a few hours ago—and how it felt.

Subconsciously I've known for a while that my feelings for him were growing, even though I fought them. But I've seen so many new sides of him this past week that I don't think I could've stopped myself from falling even if I tried. The asshole that I thought he was turned out to be a front—just a small part of him. In reality he's everything I could ever want in a partner.

I ignore the small twinge of nervousness when I think about the fact that I don't know if he feels the same way. Actually, I don't know anything about how he feels. He's a closed book when it comes to emotions. I have no idea how he feels about me.

I push the thought to the back of my mind, to be dealt with at a time that's not 3:00 in the morning. Instead, I sit down next to him and spread the blanket over both of us. I'm just about to snuggle back into his chest when I see his head jerk with a frown.

His eyes are still closed so I know he's sleeping, but he keeps twitching, squeezing his hands into fists. It seems like he's looking for something.

"No," he whispers. "No, no, no..." His voice sings with an aching sense of sadness. "Remy, no..."

My heart stops at the sound of my name. But he keeps repeating those two words, and his thrashing is increasing.

"Shhh, it's ok, I'm here," I murmur as I hold his face in my hands. "I'm right here, I'm not going anywhere."

His eyes shoot open. I watch him wake up, watch as consciousness returns to his gaze.

"Remy," he mumbles as he reaches up to touch my cheek.

"I'm here," I say, stroking his hair. "I'm right here. I just went to grab a blanket and some pillows. Here, lift your head," I instruct softly as I slide one of the pillows under him.

But he ignores it completely and wraps his arms around me in a crushing embrace. He rolls me over his body until I'm on the other side of him, pulled tight to his chest. His face is only an inch away from mine.

He strokes my hair gently, his eyes never leaving mine. Then he leans forward to kiss me softly.

When he pulls away there's barely enough room for our breaths to pass between us. His forehead is pressed to mine and I can tell he's already falling back asleep.

Just as his eyes flutter closed, I hear him murmur, "I need you..."

18

REMY

I'm still floating above consciousness when I distantly feel the warmth leaving my back. I frown in my sleep, not wanting to wake up but already missing the comfort that heat provided.

Just as I'm about to slip back into dreamland, I feel the ghost of fingertips brush along my cheek. They're gone so quickly that I'm not even sure they were really there. I curl back into my pillow and fall back to a deep sleep.

By the time I wake a few hours later, the sun is high in the sky and shining light directly through my wall of windows. I blink my eyes open sleepily.

I stretch my arms over my head with a smile. I notice the small ache between my legs with satisfaction.

At the reminder of last night, the smile freezes on my face. I look behind me to confirm what I already know: Tristan is gone.

I sit up with a frown. *It's Sunday morning, where would he have to go?*

Then another thought pops in my head that instantly makes my heart drop into my stomach.

This is the second time he's bolted from a bed that I'm in.

I didn't question the night we spent together in his room because it was a weekday and I know he has really early sessions with some of his clients that want to workout before they head to work. But on a Sunday morning? I doubt anyone is working out.

Is he avoiding me?

Last night changed something for both of us. I should've already realized my feelings for him were growing but everything happened so fast that I wasn't sure until last night. I don't know what that actually means for us, but I do know that I want to try for something with Tristan. I'm not sure where he stands with his feelings but last night proved that he at least cares about me. The sex was too emotional for it to just be sex. I could see in his eyes that he felt something.

Except, I am currently naked and alone for the second morning after sex. *Am I reading too much into last night? Did I scare him away?*

The sound of my phone vibrating snaps me from my thoughts. I walk over to where I dropped it on the kitchen counter last night and see that Jax is calling. My mood immediately lifts at the thought of my best friend coming home today.

I answer the phone with a grin. "How hungover are you right now?" I ask by way of greeting.

A heavy groan sounds on the other end of the line. "You know me way too fucking well. I don't want to see another drink for the rest of my time at this job. Remy, I really feel like I'm dying."

I shake my head with a chuckle. Leave it to the massive 230 pound alpha to be a total baby about a little headache. "What time do you get in?" I ask Jax.

"I'm on my Chicago layover now so I should be home around 11:00. When I get home, I thought you, me, and Tristan could do lunch and I can squash any remaining feuding between you two that might've brewed this week. By the way, is the house still standing?"

My eyes widen and my breath catches when I realize I never thought about how this thing between Tristan and I might affect Jax. *Should I tell him the truth? Will he be angry?*

To be fair, Jax has only ever wanted Hailey and I to be happy. It's the reason he keeps his mouth shut about Steve. He sees that Hailey is happy—albeit confused—and he doesn't want to blow something up just because he knows Steve is a dipshit. He'll support anyone that brings us happiness.

But at the same time, I'm not even sure where Tristan and I stand.

I make a split-second decision to tell a white lie, just until there's something more to actually tell. Which, given Tristan's vanishing act and radio silence, might never happen.

"Yes, the house is still standing, and yes I will withstand Tristan for you. He's already survived ten days, what's another hour?"

"Good," Jax grunts. "In that case I'll see you in a few hours. I'm going to go puke in a trashcan now."

I'm still shaking my head when I hang up. But when I finally look down at my phone screen, I see I have a text notification.

Tristan: I had to leave early to help a friend move this morning and I didn't want to wake you. I was almost late, though. I couldn't stop staring at you. Who knew you're so cute when you're not yelling at me.

A huge smile breaks across my face. *He didn't run from me. He wanted to stay with me.*

Remy: Might want to figure that out before Jax gets home today. He might not appreciate you ogling his sister.

His reply comes almost immediately, which sends another burst of happiness through my chest.

Tristan: No promises. When you're yelling, all I can think about is how much I want to bend you over and hear you make that breathy little sound right before you come all over my cock.

A shiver runs through me at his erotic words. Who knew Tristan was so *dirty*? I quickly type my response.

Remy: Focus. Jax gets home at 11 so he wants to do lunch with us. Will you be home?

I ignore the part of me that beams at the domesticated sound of that question. *As if you're the darling wife welcoming your hard-working husband home with dinner and sex.*

I shake the thoughts from my head. *We are getting way too ahead of ourselves...*

Tristan: Yea I'll be home. I'll see your sweet ass then.

I can't keep the ridiculous smile off my face for the rest of the morning.

I sing softly to myself as I pack the last few things into my suitcase, a smile playing on my lips. My heart feels light, and happy.

I hear voices drift upstairs from the living room. Realizing Jax must be back, I pack away the sweatshirt I'm holding and head toward the stairs to greet him. I smile at the thought of seeing my best friend again.

When I reach the top of the stairs, I realize they're talking about me. And even though I know I shouldn't eavesdrop, I can't help but stop and listen. God knows I can't get Tristan to talk to me, so this may be the only way I can hear what he's thinking.

"...glad to hear you two didn't kill each other. How was it with her?"

"You know, the usual," I hear Tristan answer. "Bitchy as fuck."

I roll my eyes even though his answer stings a little bit. It's odd to think that he answered the same exact way he would have before I moved in, yet now I'm bothered by the response.

I hear Jax chuckle. "Obviously. Where is she now?"

"I think she took some more of her stuff over to the new apartment."

"Ah, okay. Oh, by the way, I meant to ask you if you're still seeing that girl, Dana. I was hoping you could set me up with her friend. The redhead?"

"Oh," says Tristan, and I hold my breath as I wait for his response. "Yeah, I still see her sometimes. I'll set it up."

My breath whooshes from my chest. *He's still seeing someone else? Could he have seen her in the past week, or is he talking in general terms?*

"Cool, thanks man," Jax responds. "You've been seeing her for a while, right? Is it anything serious?"

"Nah, not serious," I hear Tristan say with a chuckle. "You know me, I can't do serious. She's just one of many. I'm still just seeing what's out there and having fun. I doubt any girl would be able to hold my attention."

His words slide a blade into my heart. I grip the banister as my head starts to spin.

He's seeing other women? How could he possibly experience the kind of chemistry we have, and then turn around and look for it somewhere else? What else is he looking for?

I knew from the beginning that he wasn't the relationship type but after everything that happened, I thought he would at least lose interest in looking elsewhere. I thought he might be willing to take a chance with me. I thought we felt the same thing last night. I thought...

I shake my head, trying to clear the tears that are threatening to spill from my eyes. I should've known. I should've listened to my gut when I first felt my feelings grow. I should've reminded myself that Tristan is not a one-woman man. I knew better than to get attached, and I let myself fall anyway. I can't even really blame him, either. I knew exactly who he was when this all started.

I try to think of the signs that made it seem like he had become interested in me.

And then fight the urge to vomit when I realize all of them—every action, every glance, every word—happened either before or during sex. Even asking me to sleep in his bed could've just been so he would have someone to fuck in the morning.

I've never really had a fuck buddy or a one night stand so I have no idea what guys might say when they just want to get laid—no idea what lies they might tell to keep a girl coming back to their bed. Right now, it feels like everything Tristan said must've just been a part of his act to get me into bed. That must be his game with women: to make them feel loved and wanted in order to make them interested.

And I played right into it.

I've never been one to believe in "making love" but I never thought to treat the words spoken during sex as anything but truth. I didn't expect him to fall in love with me just from having sex, but I don't understand how he could say those things—how he could touch me adoringly, how he could kiss me so softly—without meaning it. How could someone lie that well?

I close my eyes, the tears finally spilling down my cheeks. My grip on the banister is so hard that my hands begin to ache, but even that pain doesn't register compared to what's warring inside me. A quiet, broken sob tears from my throat as my heart surrenders to the pain.

I never should have expected Tristan to be anything more than what he is. And I definitely shouldn't have let myself get attached to him, especially so quickly. I should have listened to the part of my brain that knew this would happen. The worst part about this is the fact that this pain is my own fault.

After a few ragged breaths I realize I need to get out of this house. I need to get as far away from Tristan as I can. Even though part of me wants to cling to him and convince him that we mesh perfectly, that he doesn't need to look anywhere else and that he should give us a chance, I also know that I will never be the girl that begs a guy to be with her. I have never understood how women could chase men. Why would I want to be with someone that doesn't want to be with me?

And Tristan clearly doesn't. If he's still thinking about other women and treating us like we won't last, then he's sure as fuck not interested in being with me in a way that matters. And his feelings clearly aren't even close to the depth that mine are. If I continue down this path with him, I'm only going to end up in more pain than I feel even now. I need to end this thing between us and get as far away from Tristan as I can.

I hastily brush the tears from my cheeks and stride back to Jax's bedroom. I stuff the last of my clothes in the half-filled box and tape it shut. Before I grab it to take downstairs, I take a quick look at myself in the mirror—and immediately wince at how I look.

My face is white as a sheet and my pink-rimmed eyes clearly show that I've been crying. I dig frantically through my bag for the concealer I rarely use, then apply it quickly to my under eyes. It hides any proof of my tears, but my face still looks like I've seen a ghost. I slap and pinch my cheeks to bring some pink into them.

Good enough. I only need to look normal long enough to rush out of here.

I grab the box and head for the stairs. By the time I reach the landing I realize that Jax is nowhere to be found, and Tristan is the only one sitting in the living room.

A warm smile lights up his face when he sees me. "Hey, I didn't know you were here. Why didn't you come grab me? I would've helped carry these." He stands from the couch and walks over to grab the box out of my hands.

I twist so he can't take it from me. "It's okay, I got it," I blurt out hastily. A flash of confusion appears on his face but disappears as quickly as it came. A small frown takes its place.

"Where's Jax?" I ask, refusing eye contact.

"He wanted to run out and grab some groceries," Tristan answers. "He said he wants to do a home-cooked lunch when he gets back."

"Oh, I was actually going to head out. I want to unpack and get settled and I don't want to take up your guys' space anymore," I babble. I glance nervously between the door and the box in my hands, wanting desperately to walk out of this conversation. "Just tell Jax I'll see him later."

Before I can move toward the door, Tristan's fingers grip my chin, forcing me to look at him. My eyes finally meet his and I see that they're flashing with anger. The frown on his face has deepened.

"What is going on with you?" he growls. "Why are you freaking out right now?"

I rip my face from his hands and glare at him. "I'm not freaking out," I snap. "I just want to go home. Ten days is a long time to look at your ugly face and I'm eager to get out of here."

I realize suddenly that my anger is actually making it easier to deal with the pain. So, I stand a little straighter and look directly at Tristan. "Although I guess we knew that nothing good would come of us being cooped up together. Maybe fucking was our way of not killing each other."

I'm being harsh. I know I'm being harsh. But the blade that sliced through me only a few minutes ago has evoked a fight or flight response, and I can't help the frantic fight that's coming out of me.

I study him closely, debating for only a moment if I want to put the nail in the coffin of my heartbroken tirade. When I see the shock and hurt flash across his face I almost don't —but then decide that it's either him or me, and he's already made his choice.

"Thanks for the dick," I sneer. "It's been fun, but I think we're done here."

Without waiting for his answer, I stride down the hall and through the front door.

19

TRISTAN

I stare wide-eyed at the front door as it slams shut. I'm so shocked at Remy's parting comment that I just stand there, blinking, for what feels like a very long minute.

There's an ache in my chest. Unthinking, I start to rub it. It suddenly feels hollow and cold.

Thanks for the dick, but we're done here.

Thanks for the dick? Is that all this was? A fuck?

How could she think we were just fucking? Last night was like nothing I've ever experienced before. I've never felt so connected to a person, or so obsessed with their pleasure. I almost fell to my knees when she stood naked in front of me yesterday, beautifully clothed only in moonlight. In that moment, I would've given her anything she asked for—my only thought was to make her happy. I could've skipped the orgasms and been just as happy doing anything she asked of me.

I don't think it's ever been just fucking. How could I have misread the situation so badly?

I shake my head with a frown, trying to physically straighten the muddled thoughts in my brain into some kind of order. Why does the thought of not having Remy around make me feel worse than a fifteen-pound weight cut the day before a fight?

I feel dizzy, like I might pass out. I reach for the banister to steady myself as I start to sway. I realize then that I've never before wanted to be more than a booty call to anyone. These thoughts of wanting to keep her, of getting jealous when someone else pays attention to her, of wanting to see her smile and feeling lighter in my own body when she does —these are all brand new thoughts to me. And it never fucking occurred to me that she might not feel the same way.

Jax walks through the front door and finds me wide-eyed and glued to the spot, gripping the banister with white knuckles. "Whoa, dude, what the fuck?" he cries. "You look like you just saw a ghost. What happened?"

I shake my head with a frown, once again trying to organize my own clusterfuck of thoughts. I let go of the banister and shove my hands into my pockets with a cough.

"Nothing, I just got a big fight offer," I lie quickly. "And then I had to turn it down."

Okay, so not a complete lie, just a few days late with the news.

And yes, a little lie about why I'm white as a sheet right now.

"*What?!*" Jax yelps. He braces his hands on his hips and aims a very angry frown in my direction. "What do you mean you turned it down?!"

I nervously run my fingers through my hair, turning my gaze to the ceiling. "They finally offered me Jenkins," I admit. "But I had to turn it down because I'm already scheduled to go to Myrtle Beach with Mom for her 50th birthday weekend. I tried to make her understand how big an opportunity this was, but she couldn't let go of the idea that I was picking fighting over her. She practically burst into tears when I mentioned not going." I wince at the memory.

Jax mutters a curse and starts pacing the hallway. "How does your family not understand how good you are?" he spits angrily. "Why do they still think you're just a kid playing at karate? It's fucking ridiculous to turn down a possible interview for the UFC for a goddamn *birthday party*."

Jax is seething, glaring at the wall as he tries to calm his thoughts. In this moment I'm once again reminded how good a friend he is. How hard he'd fight for me and how much he actually gives a shit about me. He might be more upset about this situation than even I was after the phone call with my mom.

That might be because you had Remy underneath you immediately afterwards.

I shake away the thoughts of Remy. I can't handle more than one life crisis at a time.

"This is bullshit," Jax growls. "So, you're really not going to take the fight?"

I wince and awkwardly rub the back of my neck. "I can't hurt my own mom, Jax. My parents aren't like yours. You know you'll always have them, no matter what happens to you or them. With my parents... with my parents this would be the last straw. It would break Mom's heart and Dad would cut me out." I hang my head, guilt seeping out of my every pore. "I can't do that to my own mother, man."

Jax sighs angrily and throws up his hands in defeat. "Yeah, yeah, I get it. It's the right call." He pauses and aims one more glare my way before dropping it. "But dude, your family fucking sucks when it comes to fighting."

I sigh in defeat of my own. "Yeah, I know. If I want to

make it to the UFC, I might have to break their hearts some-day. I know that. But... just not today."

He nods sympathetically before looking around. "By the way, where's Remy? I thought we were doing lunch when I got back. Is she back yet?"

A hot blade of pain pierces through my chest at the mention of her name.

"Uh, she left," I stammer. That blade twists further in my heart when I hear just how true those words ring.

She left me. Even though I never really had her.

Jax's brows furrow and he tilts his head, staring at me with an unspoken question. Of course he'd be able to sense that something is different.

I try to remember how I acted with Remy before this all started. All sarcasm and condescension, right? Some sexist jokes? A generally uncaring attitude?

Fuck, has it really only been ten days?

"She said she was tired of my ugly face and wanted to get out of here," I choke out hastily, remembering her parting words and swallowing the dizziness that threatens to knock me over at the memory. "She went back to the new apart-ment. Not sure if she'll come back, she seemed pretty over this house after being stuck with me for so long."

Jax nods in understanding, the skepticism finally leaving his face. I exhale my relief and purposefully ignore the pang of fear that slices through me at the thought of Remy never coming back—to the house or to me.

I'll deal with that issue later.

Jax finally pushes past me into the kitchen, unloading the groceries I didn't realize he'd dropped at the door when he first came in. I quickly reach for the remaining bags and help him unload the food.

"I've been living off fast food and hotel buffet bars," he

grunts as he reaches for the sous vide to make steaks. "I'm ready for some healthy, homemade food. Figured I'd make us some steak and vegetables. Maybe some eggs. And some bacon. And maybe a salad? I think Remy said she had some chicken in here that I could throw in a salad..."

I shake my head with a smile. I have never met anyone that can eat as much as Jax does.

"If I throw the steak in the sous vide then instead of lunch we can do an early dinner in a few hours," he muses aloud, staring at the cuts of steak he just bought from the store. I can already tell he's laying claim to the bigger piece, and that he'll finish it all. "I might throw these in and then unpack and work for an hour. I'll make the eggs and bacon while the meat is cooking if you throw the chicken Caesar salad together. Good plan?"

I nod, even though he can't see it because his mouth is still watering over the steak. "Yeah, that sounds good. I might go for a quick run while you work then. Dinner at 5:00?"

He nods and I stand from the barstool to head upstairs to get changed. I barely make it to the stairs when I hear Jax mutter to himself, "It's probably a good thing Remy's not here. I don't think we'd have enough food for her."

I swallow roughly as her name drives another stab of pain through my heart. I sprint the rest of the way up the stairs, wanting to be pounding the pavement and letting the wind and my own physical exertion drive any remaining thoughts of her from my aching brain.

***

Thanks to an exhausting six miles, I manage to keep my inner turmoil out of my brain and away from Jax's attention.

We make dinner and then hang out on the couch, chatting about his trip and our California friends that he was training with. Talking about fighting is an easy and welcome distraction, and when the conversation dies down, I turn some fights on to keep the topic going.

Eventually we decide to call it an early night. And even though I find myself yawning from the hard run I just put my body through, I can already tell I'm not going to be able to sleep tonight.

I say goodnight to Jax at the top of the stairs, ignoring the pang of agony that beats through me when I see him turn into what was Remy's room. I quickly shuffle into my own room and slam the door.

Except here, the pain magnifies. Because she was here, too. With me.

And of course, I hadn't realized it then, but I was already into her at that point. It probably started the night we sat on the couch and quizzed each other. Every question revealed a new side of her that I never anticipated liking so much. I always knew she was smart, and loyal to her friends, but that night I found out she was fierce, and passionate, and smart in a way that she was able to be both of those things yet still stay rational. I learned that she was unlike any woman I have ever known.

And that night she slept in my arms.

And the next night she helped me face the painful issue of my parents.

And then slept in my arms again.

The funny thing is, I'm not even considering the sex we've had. It's not that I don't think it's the most mind-blowing, passionate, addicting sex I've ever had—because it's 1000% that. In all honesty, I don't know how I'll be able to fuck anyone else after Remy.

I lean against my door, nauseous at the thought of sleeping with another woman. I shake the ugly thoughts from my head and instead sit down on my bed, dropping my head into my hands.

I'm not considering the sex because that aspect of our connection just seems like a cherry on top. It makes me think we're more compatible, sure, but sex wasn't the reason I kept looking for more time to spend with her. Maybe at first, but definitely not after the night on the couch. I wanted her around because I actually liked talking to her; I liked hearing what she had to say. And that's never happened with a female. Typically, I can't wait for girls to leave after the sex is over. But with Remy...

With Remy I found myself looking forward to the non-sex part just as much as the sex part.

I groan and throw myself on the bed. I'm definitely not going to be sleeping tonight.

Why did it take Remy leaving for me to realize I want to be with her?

I can barely function at the gym the next day. I slept, but I didn't sleep. I closed my eyes, but it felt like I had pulled an all-nighter when my alarm went off this morning.

I force myself to fake a smile and a high energy level when I teach morning classes, and later my private lessons. I must do a decent job with my acting because nobody mentions anything to me all day. It isn't until the evening classes start that my mask slips for the first time.

When I realize that Remy trains on Monday nights.

Fuck. Will I see her tonight? Will she treat me like she used to? Or will she ignore me and act like I'm nothing more than a fuck buddy that she got tired of?

I scowl and angrily shake my head clear of ridiculous 'what if' questions. Since when did I turn into such a girl? I'm Tristan fucking West, why are my palms starting to sweat with nerves over a girl I've known for years?

You're being ridiculous. Shape the fuck up and just do your job like you normally would.

Only, my nervous glances toward the door are wasted. Remy never shows up to her usual class.

By fifteen minutes after the hour, I realize I can't put off leaving any longer. I'm usually gone, or at least getting ready to leave, by the time the last class of the night starts. If I continue to hang around—desperate for a glance, a reaction, *anything*, from Remy—people are going to notice. I need to leave. She's obviously not coming.

I ignore my agitated brain that's trying to figure out what that could mean.

Relax. She might just be at work. Maybe she's sick. It could be anything. It's one day, calm the fuck down and stop reading into everything. Go home, you'll see her on Wednesday.

Only, she doesn't show up on Wednesday. Or Saturday.

I go from being desperate to see her, to frantic that something's wrong. It's not like Remy to not train, especially on Saturdays.

I debate asking Jax if he knows anything. If there's something going on, he'll know. But asking him about Remy will tip him off that something went down between us, so I need to phrase it in a way that doesn't make him suspicious. But I definitely need to ask because I'm going crazy with all the unknowns.

I find Jax in the lounge area, stretched out on the couch talking to one of the assistant instructors. I immediately relax at the sight—he wouldn't look so casual, or even be here at the gym, if there was something wrong with Remy.

"Hey, sorry man," I interrupt. Their laughter is cut short, and they turn toward me expectantly.

I try for a casual look as I plop down in the office chair behind the front desk. "Some people have noticed that Remy hasn't been here in a while. Lucy seems close-lipped about it so Aiden and the others just want to make sure she's okay. Any idea what's going on with her?"

Jax is silent for a moment as he stares at me with a curious expression on his face. I squeeze the armrests to keep from fidgeting—he can probably see right through me.

"She's fine," he finally answers. "She has a big deadline coming up at work, so she's been focusing on that, working late hours. Plus, she's been busy getting settled in the new apartment." He tilts his head and stares at me for another breath, and I think to myself, *he definitely knows.* "You can tell Aiden and the others that she'll be back when her schedule's not so crazy."

I swallow nervously but nod. *At least now you know she's fine. And her absence at the gym has nothing to do with you, you self-centered bastard. She's probably forgotten all about you.*

I try to ignore the vicious thought as it pops into my head. Because if that's true, my barely-contained heart is definitely going to disintegrate into pieces and I'll never be able to get through the rest of my day.

I take a shuddering breath and turn back to the computer to try to distract myself.

Even though I know I don't have a chance in hell at holding another focused thought for the rest of the night.

I don't have to go to the gym the next day. Sundays are typically my days off, though I often end up scheduling private lessons in the morning for some extra cash. But my day is empty of even that today. I don't have a single thing on my schedule.

Which means I have nothing to distract myself with. Nothing to do but to yet again let my brain wander down a hazardous path of 'why' and 'what if.'

My five-mile run this morning did nothing to drive away the perpetual ache in my chest. Sometimes, when I'm exhausted enough, my body is too tired to hurt and actually lets me shut down and sleep. It's the reason I've been over-training and running myself into the ground.

Numbness and physical exhaustion are better than soul-deep pain.

I'm just about to start calling gym people to see who wants to get an extra workout in at the gym when my phone lights up in my hand.

Mom is calling.

As always, I answer with a hesitant tone, since it's rare that she calls without a request. God forbid she calls just to say hi and to see how her son is doing.

"Hi, Mom. What's up?"

"Hi, honey. How's your Sunday?"

"Good. Relaxing. It's my off day so I don't need to be at the gym." I immediately wince when I realize I probably just walked myself straight into an invite to see the family.

"Oh, good," she chirps happily, and I can hear her clap her hands in delight. "Why don't you come over for dinner then? I thought we could spend a nice family dinner together. I'll even make your favorite dish for you."

I rub my temples tiredly. The last thing I want to do

when I'm this exhausted is deal with small talk with my own family.

Then again, fighting with my dad might be the kind of distraction I need right now.

"Sure, Mom, I'll come over," I sigh. "What time?"

She claps excitedly again. "Come over at 6:00. That will give me time to throw some chicken pot pie for you. Does that work?"

"Yeah, that works. Thanks, Mom. I'll see you then."

"Bye, honey," she chirps as she hangs up.

I turn toward the front door and the running shoes I had just taken off before Mom's phone call. With a sigh, I lace them back up for another run.

20

TRISTAN

When I walk into my parents' house, I realize that my dad and brother aren't lounging in the sitting room the way they normally do. I hear Mom in the kitchen but otherwise the house is silent.

I make my way into the kitchen and, sure enough, I find Mom bouncing around getting dinner ready.

"Hey, Mom." She startles, not realizing I had come in.

"Oh, my goodness, you scared me," she breathes, clutching a hand to her chest. "I didn't even hear you come in. You're going to scare me to death one of these days with the way you sidle in."

A strained smile tilts the corner of my lips as I remember hearing those same words not too long ago. Only that time, it was a feisty brunette that was saying them, and I was there to punish her for daring to think anyone else could have her.

I shake the thoughts of Remy from my head. Again. It feels like all I've been doing for the past week is shaking my head.

"Sorry," I tell her, kissing her on her cheek. "I'm too graceful for my own good, I guess."

She ignores my weak joke and instead pulls back to study my face. A small frown appears on her lips.

"You look tired," she accuses. "Like you haven't been sleeping. Or eating. Is everything okay?"

I try for a big smile. "I'm fine, Mom. I just had a long week with work and I'm tired. Nothing a good Sunday dinner and ten hours of sleep can't fix."

Her frown deepens as she steps closer to me. She grips my chin and turns my head to the side. "And you have a black eye!" she exclaims accusingly.

I pull my face from her grasp, avoiding eye contact and resisting the urge to fidget under her scrutiny. I don't feel like explaining that I'm so depressed, I've been throwing myself into training and going way too hard during every session. I've been running myself into the ground, and when I'm tired, I get sloppy. I'll probably have a few more injuries until I can get my mental shit together.

I knew Mom would notice but I couldn't bring myself to care—about the injury or about her inevitable reaction, which is exploding out of her right now.

She plants her hands on her hips with a disapproving glare. "When will you be done with this insanity? How can this be fun for you? You're always hurt!"

Before I can answer back, I hear my dad's footsteps on the stairs. I wince, knowing this argument is about to get a lot worse. Dad walks into the kitchen to find Mom and I glaring at each other.

"What's going on?"

Mom throws her hands up in exasperation. "He's hurt again. Look at him! It's ridiculous!"

Dad frowns as he looks me over. I grit my teeth and endure the scrutiny, fury starting to sizzle in my veins.

It was a mistake to come here—I should've known this would happen. I'm too exhausted and emotionally unhinged to deal with them right now.

"You look horrible," he finally spits. "You look like a bully that got into a fight in a schoolyard. No better than an immature schoolboy that can only solve problems with his fists." He gives me another once-over and scoffs, his words dripping with disdain. "Your mother is right. You need to end this ridiculous caveman phase of your life. I will never understand what on earth pushed you to this idiocy."

I clench my fists so hard that I can feel my fingernails ripping into my palm. I take a deep, stuttering breath to try to keep myself from exploding at the insult.

"I'm not a caveman, I'm a professional athlete," I begin calmly. "And it's not a phase. I'm on the verge of getting into the top organization in the world."

A pained expression appears on my mom's face. "How can it be a sport when you're just beating each other up? Not only in your fights, but every single day at the gym. How is that a sport? How is getting hurt fun for you?"

I shake my head, furious that we're having this conversation *again*. I've lost track of the amount of times I've tried explaining this to my parents over the years. "Mom, it's the oldest sport there is. Combat is the ultimate form of competition. I know it just seems like guys beating each other up, but it's not centered around pain like you think it is. It's about skill, and strategy, and grit. Can't you just accept the fact that I love this sport for reasons you don't understand?"

"Enough," my dad snaps, just as tired of this argument as I am. He's heard all of this before. "I've heard enough of your ludicrous justifications. It's barbaric, and you need to stop this right now. I won't have you disgrace this family any longer. Do you have any idea how it feels to hear our friends at the country club talk about how their sons are doing as lawyers, doctors, investment bankers? I spend so much time steering the conversation toward Scott that I'm pretty sure a lot of them think we only have one son."

I didn't think it was possible to hurt any more than I already am, but I'm immediately and brutally proven wrong when my already-butchered heart feels yet another slash of pain at my dad's words. I swallow roughly to try to keep the tears at bay.

"Honey," my mom says to her husband with a wince. She touches his arm in an effort to pull back his words.

But they're already out there, finally spoken. I finally get to hear my father's true thoughts.

I knew my parents weren't proud of me, but I never thought they were actually ashamed. I thought they just didn't understand. I meant what I said to Remy that night on the couch: I really thought my mom's concerns came from a place of love, in her own fucked up way. I didn't know they hated fighting—hated me—this much.

"Well, I'm sorry I'm such a big disappointment, Dad," I choke out. "I didn't realize your wish for my life was to do the normal, *boring* things that everybody else does, even if it makes me miserable. I guess I was stupid to think I could pick *one* thing that brings me happiness and maybe, just maybe, you'd be happy that I was happy."

I look between my parents, blinking back sudden tears. "You were amazing parents when we were kids," I say hoarsely. "You loved us and raised us with morals and work ethic, and Scott and I loved you. We still do. God, I love you both so much, even right now when you're breaking my heart." I choke back the sob that threatens to rip out of me.

I clear my throat and straighten to my full height, spearing them both with a hard look. "But somehow when we became adults, your warped vision of success began to fuck us up. I need you to know that in that aspect, you guys are terrible parents. I don't know if it's because you bought into your stupid country club mentality that only certain high-paying careers count as success, or if something else drove you to think this way, but either way you completely fucked over Scott and I when it came to our outlook on careers."

My mom looks away from me as tears start to well in her eyes. It's killing me to hurt her like this, but they've been hurting me for so long and they don't even realize it. I can't keep dancing around the truth, hoping they'll figure it out on their own one day.

Dad looks absolutely furious at my declaration. Rage boils in his eyes, and I think he wants to cut me off, but I don't give him the chance. "Scott bought into your bullshit and went into the finance world, probably because you sold him on the importance of making a lot of money. He's now just as much of an asshole as any other Wall Street moron. He's so obsessed with money that he looks down on anyone that makes less than six figures. So much for the morals you raised us with, huh?" A sob tears out of my mom as she claps her hand to her mouth, but I can't stop my rant. "But me... I was smart enough to figure out that this particular view of yours is bullshit. I picked a job I love, that I wake up every morning excited to do. See, despite your bullshit parenting, I figured out that there's only two things that really matter when it comes to a person's career: it should make you happy, and it should make enough money to support your family. That's it. Well, I make good money with this sport. Not with fighting, not yet, but with teaching, and helping others. This sport *helps* people. It helps them to feel strong, and confident, and brave. It's so much more than just black eyes and fist fights. Though I don't expect you to ever give a shit about that."

I look between my parents again. My dad is fuming, clenching his fists and visibly trying to keep from lashing out at me for demeaning his parenting skills. My mom is crying quietly into her hands.

It's the sight of my mom's tears that finally cools my anger and dulls my pain. Suddenly all I feel is sadness. I'm sad for them, for their warped view of the world that is keeping them from having a real relationship with their son. I might never know what made them this way, but I'm deciding not to accept their treatment of me anymore.

I let the hurt and sadness shine through my gaze, so they know that even though I'm being harsh, I'm not doing this to hurt them. I just need them to understand. "I don't need you to like fighting, or even accept it. I just need you to accept *me*. I need you to understand that this job makes me happy, that it makes a difference. And I'm good at it. God, I'm *really* fucking good at it. I'm going to be the best in the world one day, and I hope by then you'll be in my corner. But I can't take this any longer. I don't want to talk to you if all I'm going to get is condescension and disgust. I deserve better than that. As my parents you owe me more than that."

I shake my head sadly as I walk out of the house, but pause when my hand grips the doorknob, desperate to make them understand. "So... don't call me anymore. Don't call me until you can stomach the idea of having a conversation with me that doesn't involve shitting on my life or trying to convince me to take a job as a corporate snob. Just... try to be my loving parents for once."

I walk out of the house and away from my own family, at

least for the foreseeable future. I ache with the hope that it's not for longer than that. Because I meant what I said: I won't come back until they accept me as I am. I refuse to be shit on any longer.

I slump into my car, willing the sadness radiating through my body to somehow diminish into a more bearable pain. I've been sliced with so much heartbreak lately that I'm not sure how much more my mind and body can take.

I exhale a shaky breath as I back out of the driveway and leave my family behind.

The next week is even emptier than the last one. Not only has Remy still not come to the gym, but I also haven't heard from my mom. I definitely won't be the first one to reopen lines of communication because I meant every word I said to them, but it still hurts that she hasn't even tried to call me. I can only hope it's because they know I was serious and are rethinking how they've been talking to me.

I throw myself into work and my training sessions even harder than before, if that's even possible. My miles increase and my workouts on the heavy bags become longer and harder. I barely make it to my bed every night before I'm passing out from exhaustion.

Jax has to practically force food down my throat. It's not that I'm not eating, but I'm definitely not eating enough. He stops by the gym during his lunch break most days and drags me out to eat some kind of calorie-dense protein meal. Being a pro athlete himself, he can tell my strength is down by looking at how I move during my workouts. Just the fact that I'm losing rounds at the gym to people that I have no business losing to is proof of the fact that my body is rundown and my head's not in the game.

But he doesn't push me to talk about anything. He just shoves food down my throat and subtly lets me know that he's there if I need him. Every day that he doesn't question me, I'm reminded again how much Jax gets me and how grateful I am to have him as a friend.

I'm attempting to refuel after a particularly grueling Saturday morning session when I first try to talk to him. It slips out of me while we're both drifting around the kitchen making food.

"I confronted my parents," I blurt out suddenly. He straightens from the fridge and turns startled eyes toward where I'm standing by the stove with a skillet.

"About fighting?" he asks, his tone gently coaxing me to continue.

I nod. "I had a black eye when I showed up to their house and Mom went off about how I could think being injured is fun, and that I should just quit. Dad took the opportunity and jumped in about what a disgrace I am and how they can't tell any of their country club buddies about me or what I do." I laugh bitterly. "He said they talk so little about me that their friends probably think they only have one son."

Jax's eyes go wide. "He actually said that?" he breathes. I nod again. "Jesus Christ, that man is so messed up. What an asshole. You're his son, for fuck's sake."

I shrug tightly, trying to brush off the hurt feelings that try to envelop me at the memory. I've kept the pain to a dull ache all week, and I'm not about to drown in them now. I just want Jax to know why my head's been so fucked up.

"I told them they sucked as parents," I continue. Jax's eyes widen even further, and his jaw drops open. "I told them they need to get over themselves and get over the idea that only certain careers are socially acceptable. I tried to explain that I love this sport, and that I'm really good at it, and that they should love me enough to support me even if they don't understand that." I swallow the hurt that tries to make an appearance with the final piece of the memory. "I told them I don't want to talk to them until they can do that."

Jax winces as he puts the pieces of the puzzle together. "I assume they haven't called, then." When I nod in confirmation, he goes back to arranging his ingredients on the kitchen counter, shaking his head in disbelief. "I'm glad. It's long overdue that they hear the truth about how badly they've treated you. You did the right thing." He hesitates before looking over at me. "You know that, right? You did the right thing."

I squeeze my eyes shut and pinch the bridge of my nose. I know Jax is right, but the knowledge still makes my chest feel hollow. "I know," I say softly. I take a deep, stuttering breath. "It just sucks."

Jax nods in understanding. "I don't know about your dad, since he might be too far gone into his bullshit by now, but your mom will come around. She's not a bad person, Tristan. She'll figure it out. Just give them some time."

His words are so close to Remy's that the sudden, piercing reminder makes me suck in a sharp breath. I take short, shallow gulps of air as my heart rate begins to increase. I try to distract myself by returning to the eggs cooking in the skillet.

Of course, Jax notices the change in my behavior. I can't see how hard he's analyzing me right now, but I can sense his hesitation. He's trying to decide if this is the time he needs to push me, or if he should back off.

I can't decide which I want him to do, either.

NIKKI CASTLE

"That's not all, is it?" he finally asks softly. As soon as he asks, I realize I wish he hadn't opened that door.

But even I can admit a partial truth. "No, it's not. But the rest of it I just need to get over. Nothing worth talking about."

He nods, and for a second it appears like he won't push further, even though I can tell he wants the last word. In the end he can't stop from taking it. "Maybe you don't need to get over it," he mumbles before busying himself with the prep work in front of him.

I stiffen at his words. I haven't been able to tell if he's figured out that my mood has to do with his best friend. Something obviously happened while he was gone, but at the same time I doubt Remy is moping in a corner somewhere. So Jax technically only has the timing and my change in mood to go on.

But he's also the most observant fucker I know. And something about his words just now makes me think he knows more than even I do. I sneak a glance at where he's cutting up some vegetables.

Maybe you don't need to get over it.

Does that mean I can still salvage this thing with Remy? She made it pretty clear when she left that she had only been interested in me for sex. In that aspect she was obviously into me—you can't fake the kind of physical connection we had. But is it possible she wants more than that? Why would she say what she did if she wanted more?

I shake the tempting thoughts from my head. I can't bring myself to really hope that Remy has feelings for me. If I do, and it turns out that she's telling the truth about only wanting me for sex, I wouldn't be able to handle it. Even now I'm only barely staying above water because I'm stuck in a place where I know I felt something between us, but I'm also not 100% certain she wasn't just using me for my dick. I'm trying not to crash and burn but also trying to limit hope.

I once again swallow every emotion swirling around in my heart and go back to faking my normal, stoic self.

Another week goes by without seeing Remy. Eventually, I'm able to stop myself from checking the doorway every five minutes. My workouts are just as hard, I'm just as exhausted, and I'm even more confused than I was in the beginning.

Part of me is beginning to wonder if those ten days even happened. Did I misread the situation so badly that I made up everything that I thought we felt while Remy was living in the house? It would explain how easily she was able to shove me under the rug and forget I exist.

But the hole in my heart is still there, and it still aches. I still can't see a short brunette on the street without my breath catching. I still can't look at Jax's room—or sometimes even my own—without remembering Remy's presence in the house. I still can't wake up without a stab of pain that she's not there with me.

It's Friday afternoon and I'm finishing up my last private lesson of the day. I have another hour before open mat starts where I'll oversee the students that want to come in and train on their own. I decide to use the time the same way I've been using any free hour the past few weeks: I throw myself into a workout.

Within minutes my gloves are laced up and I'm pounding on the heavy bag. The sound of my fists hitting the leather reverberate through the room, though it's not loud enough to drown out my chaotic thoughts.

The harder I hit, the more the chaos in my head dulls. There's something so primal, so honest, about fighting that I've realized in the past few weeks that it's hard to feel sad while you're doing it. The only things you can feel are determination or anger. Or sheer numbness, if you're exhausted enough.

For the first time in weeks, my numbness melts to anger. Anger at these insane emotions that Remy stirred in me so suddenly. Anger at the confusion over our relationship—and lack thereof. Anger at the fact that I'm hung up on a woman that doesn't want me back.

How can it possibly feel this bad? We didn't spend *that* much time together. I shouldn't be so depressed over her rejection or so obsessed with the thought of making her mine. I shouldn't have reacted with anything but short-lived shock that she turned me down. How can wanting to explore the possibility of a relationship with someone cause this much of an ache in my body?

I realize with a shock that I'm in the same position that every girl that's ever wanted to date me was in—wanting more but getting rejected because the other person is only interested in sex. When I would break up with a girl, I thought I was only hurting her idea of our potential. I was just stopping the fairytale before it could get started and inevitably run off the tracks. It's not like I was letting them fall in love with me and then breaking up with them.

My eyes widen and I pull back from the punch I was about to throw.

It's... not possible.

I'm not that guy. That kind of thing doesn't happen to

me—I'm too rational and too focused on my goals. It's impossible.

...isn't it?

Did I fall in love with Remy?

I have no idea what love feels like. My girlfriend in college was nice, and we got along great, but I knew I wasn't in love with her. I was too glad for time without her when we were busy, and not sad enough when she finally ended it. I wasn't sure I was even capable of feeling love. How could I when fighting was always #1 in my book? How could I say I love someone when I would pick my career over them any day of the week?

Except... except that's not true.

I know I need to be selfish if I want to be the best in the world but right now, in this moment, I feel like I would walk out of a packed arena with a title fight on the line if it would get me Remy. I would pick her every second of every day and every week.

Because I'm completely, desperately in love with her.

"*FUCK!*" I scream in frustration. I let loose a barrage of punches on the heavy bag.

With every punch, I realize that's exactly what happened. Somehow during her time at the house, I fell in love with her. I may have even felt that way before she moved in, if I'm being completely honest with myself. Even when she hated me, I always loved how feisty she was, how she would go toe to toe with me and never just roll over at my feet. Being in close proximity must've shed the veil between us and forced me to see what I never wanted to admit to myself: that Remy is my perfect match. The sex just opened the door to our chemistry.

"Fuck," I grit through my teeth, throwing each punch harder than the last. It's an outlet for an emotion that I don't want to feel. I don't want to love Remy. Not just because she clearly doesn't want me back, but because love is a distraction I can't afford in my life. Even if she wanted me, too, a relationship would affect my focus and fuck with my strict game plan for becoming a world champ. If I'm this messed up over one fallout with her, the potential for these kinds of emotions to ruin me is astronomical.

I can't pursue this thing with Remy. And more importantly, I need to get these thoughts and feelings out of my head. They're already hurting my training.

Even the hardest bag workout I've ever done can't stop the anger from coursing through my veins. It's like once I gave my body permission to feel it, I accidentally let it take over. I'm shaking—both from exhaustion and fury—when I finally unlace my gloves and throw them into my bag.

On a whim, I grab my phone instead. I dial before I can second guess myself.

Aiden answers on the first ring. "Tristan, what's up? Are you at open mat? I'm heading over there now."

"Let's skip it," I tell him hastily. "I need a drink. I'll have Danny cover the gym for two hours. You in?"

There's a pause on the other end of the line. I take a breath and let him have it, since I already know how crazy I sound right now. I've never been one to skip the gym—*especially* for a bar—and definitely not in the past few weeks. I've been gym-crazed and haven't been out with the guys at all.

"Yeah, let's do it," he finally answers. "I'll grab Max, too. Let's try out that new bar on 21st Street. Wanna meet us there in thirty minutes?"

"Yeah, sounds good. I'll see you there."

Twenty minutes later, I'm nursing my second whiskey at the bar and internally cursing Aiden for his location choice. It's 5:00 on a Friday and this place is not far from the Business District, which means it's packed with corporate assholes that are finishing a week of desk work and looking to lose themselves in a different life for the next three days.

The alcohol muffles the hurt in my chest better than the workout did. I should've started drinking sooner. I realize now that this is probably the reason that drinking is a normal coping mechanism after a breakup.

I shake my head to try to clear those thoughts from my head. *It can't be a breakup if we were never together.*

With a growl I slam back the rest of my whiskey.

Maybe Remy was right to shut us down. Maybe it's better if we were only having sex. I can't afford a distraction when I'm so close to the UFC, and she would've been a very big one. It didn't take long at all for me to completely lose my head and my focus around her. If it's this bad after less than two weeks, who knows how deep I would've gone with any more time with her.

I'm glowering at the bar staff, waiting for another refill, when Aiden and Max find me. Aiden looks between me and the bartender with a questioning gaze. "What on earth did the nice man do to piss you off? He has liquor, we need to like him."

I turn my glare toward my teammate, but he only offers a grin before taking a spot next to me on a barstool. Max sits on the far side.

"So... what's up?" Max asks curiously. "We haven't seen you in weeks. Miss us?"

I shoot another glower at the bartender who still hasn't acknowledged my silent signal. "I just punched you in the face yesterday. How could I miss you?"

Aiden grins again. "Miss bonding with us over alcohol, then?"

I sigh in defeat. "Something like that," I murmur. "What's going on with you guys? Outside of the gym, I mean."

"It's funny you ask," Aiden chirps happily. I mentally groan my regret for starting this conversation, even as I'm subconsciously thankful for the distraction from my thoughts. "I think I've finally found a good work/school/gym balance. Gym is good, though you know that. Work is boring but easy. And school is great. I have one semester left and I'm stupidly excited for the criminal justice class I have to take for my thesis. Who knew I was actually smart with this liberal arts shit."

"None of us," I hear Max mutter. A smile tugs at the corners of my lips for the first time in weeks.

Aiden ignores the comment. "I'm also seeing this hot-as-fuck blonde that I met in my political science course this year. Hottest chick I've ever been with. Smart, too."

I raise an eyebrow in question. "Smart? What, you like this girl?"

Aiden chuckles and Max grins at the insanity of my question. I've been friends with these guys for long enough that I should know better than to ask that kind of question.

"Nah, it's not going anywhere. She's just fun to hang out with every once in a while when the stress gets bad. She's the same way—she's not looking for anything, thank god."

I swallow against a suddenly dry throat. I try once again to flag down the bartender for another whiskey.

"It's just better that way, you know? No pressure, no feelings, just great sex." Aidan lets out an exaggerated exhale and looks up at the ceiling for a moment. "God, the sex is so good. She's a total freak."

Max nods his agreement and I find myself doing the

same. Maybe it is better if it's just physical—God knows the emotional part of the past few weeks with Remy has sucked ass. There's a reason I never wanted more than sex with other girls. It's just so much easier than the chaos that comes with... everything else. It's probably a good thing that nothing came out of this thing with Remy and I.

I feel the choking grip on my heart loosen a little at the realization.

I look over at Max. "What about you? What's your love life look like?"

He grins sheepishly. "I'm... kinda back with my ex. Not, like, dating, but we've been fucking lately." Aiden lets out a groan and drops his head to the bar.

"Dude, you know she's going to start pushing for you to get back together again," Aiden mumbles into the wooden bar top.

Max scowls at his friend's head. "I know that. But I've made it clear that's not happening."

Aiden lifts his head so he can aim a glare at Max. "Yeah, because that worked out so well last time."

I start chuckling as I listen to their banter. I should've leaned on these two a lot sooner. For just an hour, I can forget the pain that's been threatening to tear me apart for the past few weeks.

The bartender finally slides another whiskey in front of me. As he turns to Max and Aiden to take their orders, I look beyond them to take in the rest of the bar.

With one look, my blood freezes and my heart drops. All the pain I've been trying to drive away with exhaustion and distractions comes right back to the forefront of my brain and multiplies tenfold.

Remy is sitting at the lounge section of the bar. With Jason.

Even though I can only see her from the side, I'd have to be blind not to recognize her body and her mannerisms. I can't quite see her face, but I can see that whatever she's saying has Jason grinning like a madman. He's completely riveted by her.

And why wouldn't he be? She's fucking gorgeous. She's wearing her work clothes and yet again looking like a sexy secretary with black heels, a tight black pencil skirt, and a white blouse. Her dark brown hair is lightly curled and hanging down to the curve of her ass, looking just as grabbable as her ass in that skirt. The outfit reminds me of the night I fucked her on the kitchen counter after I ripped off her work clothes and revealed the sexy red lingerie she wore underneath.

I desperately try to shake the memory before it consumes me.

At the sight of them together, the ache in my chest becomes an exploding bomb, piercing every corner of my soul with a pain so blinding that it feels like I can't breathe. I realize in this moment that I've been holding onto a false hope that she didn't mean what she said when she left. Like an idiot, I've subconsciously been trying to convince myself that she'd been lying, or trying to protect herself from me, and that's why she hasn't been around. It's the whole reason I haven't tried to contact her—I wasn't ready to hear her confirm what my subconscious has been telling me for weeks.

But at the sight of Jason next to her, I realize she really did only want me for sex. That's all I was good for to her. That's the only way she could handle hating me and living in the same house as me. While I was falling in love with her, she was just using me to get off. And now that we're no longer under the same roof, she's free to move on to someone else. Maybe to Jason, who she has more in common with and who she's never hated.

And I'm watching it happen.

I fight the urge to vomit as I turn back to the bar. I slam half my drink in one gulp, ignoring the wide-eyed look of shock on Aiden's face. I don't miss that he turns to see what made me angry, or the look of understanding that appears on his face when he puts two and two together.

All of the sadness inside me from the past few weeks suddenly morphs into furious pain. And I need an outlet before I explode and dump all of it on Remy.

Without thinking about what I'm doing, acting solely because of the anger coursing through my veins and the heartbreak tearing my chest in half, I look around the bar for a distraction. If Remy is moving on, then so am I. I'll be exactly the kind of manwhore she thinks I am.

I plaster my trademark smirk on my face and turn toward the blonde sitting only a few seats down from me.

21

REMY

It feels like I've run an ultra-marathon in the three weeks since I've seen Tristan.

No matter what I say to myself or which one of my training partners calls me, I just can't bring myself to go to the gym. I can't handle seeing Tristan right now. Every time I even think about him it feels like another little piece of my heart breaks off. So, I continue telling my friends that I'm busy with a work project and settling into my new apartment. Only Hailey knows the truth, though I suspect Jax knows that something is up.

Instead of my usual workouts, I've taken to running miles and miles after work. I run as far as I can and as long as I can until I collapse from exhaustion. It's only then that I'm able to shut off my brain and manage a few hours of sleep without thoughts of Tristan's words to Jax echoing in my head.

I can barely eat anything. Even with the immense calorie burn of my runs, I just don't have an appetite. I feel constantly nauseous when I think of Tristan with other women. It's a struggle to force food down my throat. Hailey has tried cooking me different meals in an effort to find something that I can keep down, but it's no use. I've lost ten pounds in the past three weeks.

The weight loss is visible in my face—I can tell I look haggard from the way Hailey frowns with concern every time she comes over. My clothes hang on me, where before they were tight. My idiot salad-eating coworker badgers me every day about what I'm doing to lose the weight. I can't bring myself to tell her it's just a natural side effect of having your heart shattered into a million pieces.

I also throw myself into work. I'm at the office by 7:30 every morning and rarely leave before 6:00. I really do have work projects lined up but in a normal week I'd have them done in only a few days. Now, I'm constantly re-reading, re-writing, second guessing all my work. I can barely focus on my computer screen half the time and end up zoning out for an hour before I realize I haven't typed a single word. I can't concentrate in any of my meetings, which only serves to aggravate the engineers when I meet with them. In the past three weeks they've all snapped at me more than once, scolding me for making them repeat themselves. I don't even have the energy to fight them on it. I just nod and make a note to figure it out myself.

My days are long and tense. My workload piles up due to my lack of focus, and the engineers get increasingly disheartened with the quality of my work. And as much as I hate my job, it still kills me to hear that my work is suffering. I double down and try even harder.

It's a vicious cycle. Every day the people around me grow more and more frustrated, and every day I try to push through the resulting chaos—unsuccessfully. Until one day it all comes to a head.

Cassandra rounds the corner to my cubicle with a furious look on her face.

"What did you do?" she snaps by way of greeting.

I turn away from my screen to look at her with dead eyes. "What do you mean?"

"I just sent you the email," she snaps, her eyes blazing with rage. "One of our competitors is threatening to sue us for copyright infringement on one of the playbooks that *you* wrote." She's gesturing wildly with her hands and she's not bothering to keep her voice down. The entire office can hear her scolding me.

I look at her email in my inbox, trying to blink away my confusion. I've never once had legal issues with my work. All I can manage in response is a weak, "what?"

"How could you fuck this up?" she continues yelling. Heads are starting to pop over the cubicles like prairie dogs, trying to see what all the fuss is about. "That playbook was on *my* product so now I'm being reamed out by my boss for *your* work! What is wrong with you?!"

I continue to stare at my screen in confusion. She's not wrong—this is a huge deal. Copyright infringement can cost companies a lot of money.

How did I miss this? What was I thinking?

Answer: I clearly wasn't. This non-breakup-breakup is officially ruining every area of my life.

I swallow nervously and finally turn toward Cassandra. She's got both hands planted on her hips and her eyes dance with angry flames, waiting for my response. "I'm sorry," I say simply. "I don't know what happened. How— how do I fix it?"

She throws her hands in the air, clearly exasperated. "Not my problem," she growls. "But *figure it out*. I'm not going down for your stupid mistake." And with that, she turns around and stomps away, people's heads quickly popping back in their cubicles in an effort to not give away that they were watching our scene.

I clear my suddenly very dry throat. A cold sweat rushes through my body as the nerves inside me skyrocket.

Fuck. How did I fuck this up? What do I do now?

Just then, an email pops up on my screen. My face pales further as I read through the body of the mail.

A meeting with the Legal Department at 8:00 on Monday morning. *Fuck.*

I drop my head into my hands and take a deep, shaky breath. *Think, Remy, think. What do I do now? Who can I talk to about this before Monday?*

The idea comes so quickly that my head shoots up with a jolt. I know a lawyer. I can ask him how deep the shit is that I'm in, and how I can get myself out of it.

I grab my phone and fire off the text before I can second guess myself.

A few hours later, I'm sitting in a crowded bar for happy hour, scowling at the massive amounts of corporate assholes that are all around me. Working in the business center of a city means the surrounding bars are all packed starting at 5:00. Like now.

My scowl deepens the longer I wait for Jason to show up. God only knows why he couldn't meet until now, or why it had to be in a bar. But I'm so desperate for his help that he convinced me without much trouble.

Finally, I see his gel-greased head bobbing through the

crowd. He's wearing his usual custom-tailored suit and, per usual, he reeks of money-obsessed Corporate America. His fake, used-car salesman expression splits with a grin when he sees me sitting on one of the lounges.

"Remy! There you are! I'm so glad you could make it." He roughly pulls me to my feet and into a hug before I can respond. He doesn't let go of me when he pulls back.

I try to fake a smile. "Thanks for taking the time for me. I just wanted to pick your legal brain for a few minutes if you don't mind, then I'll be out of your hair—"

"Fuck that," he interrupts happily. "I always have time for you. But let's get you a drink first. We don't need to talk about work just yet."

He waves over a waitress that's floating around the seating areas. He lets go of me with one hand so he can touch the girl's elbow with a flirtatious smile, whispering our order in her ear. I swallow the furious words that want to burst out of me at his assuming what I want to drink. Or that I even want to drink.

It doesn't even matter. I'll just ask my questions and then get out of here.

He turns back to me with a smile and guides me to sit down with the hand that's still holding my arm. "So, I have to confess that I'm surprised—though extremely happy, don't get me wrong—that you called. I knew when we ran into each other two weeks ago that we ended up back on each other's radars for a reason. I'm glad we could meet up tonight."

His eyes sparkle with excitement and I suddenly realize that this is probably not going to work out how I want it to. He thinks it's a social call, whereas I couldn't care less about fucking anyone else right now.

I shake thoughts of Tristan from my head before they can fully manifest. I try to focus on the hopeful, happy man in front of me, and how I'm going to let him down nicely while still getting the answers to my questions.

"I actually wanted to get your legal advice, if you don't mind. I have a problem—"

"Let's not talk about work," he interrupts with a wave of his hand. "We're at a bar during happy hour. Work should be the last thing we talk about."

I try to hide my wince. "It's kind of important. I wanted to talk in your office, but I know you're busy—"

Once again, he cuts me off. "My office is too stuffy. I can't have a real conversation with you there, not like I can here. I promise I'll answer your questions, but do me a favor and have a drink with me first, yeah?"

As if on cue, the waitress returns with our drinks. She hands him a beer and places a fruity cocktail in front of me. I can barely stop myself from rolling my eyes at the cliché girly drink that Jason just ordered me. Clearly, he has no idea who I am.

I sigh internally at the thought. *At least he's trying. He's trying to get to know me. I can give him some of my time before I bolt out of here; I can at least give him that.*

I sip the drink through the straw with a tight smile. He seems pleased with my reaction and leans back into the lounge cushions with a grin, pulling his ankle to rest on his opposite knee. He looks supremely comfortable as he stretches out his arm to rest along the top of the cushions behind me.

"So, how's life been since college?" he asks conversation-ally. "Other than working in the tech industry, what's Remy baby been up to?"

I smother my wince, both at the nickname and at the fact that we're actually going through with this small talk right now. But the faster I can get through it, the faster I can get my answers and get out of here.

"Life's great," I squeak. "I work a lot, and I still spend a lot of time with Jax, if you remember him. He was that guy that was always at my dorm."

Jason frowns. "Yeah, I think I remember some guy hanging all over you," he says hesitantly. "Are you two together or something?"

This time I let my wince show. This is the default reaction for both Jax and I when people assume we're together just because we're a guy and a girl. "God, no. He's just a really old friend."

Jason seems to relax at that. Unfortunately, it leads me straight into his next question. "So, are you seeing anyone right now?"

"N—no," I stutter, ignoring the sharp pain that pierces my heart. I force out a stronger response. "No, I'm not."

He reclines into the cushions again with a smile. I'm careful not to touch his arm where it's stretched behind me.

"But I spend a lot of time at the gym," I continue hurriedly, trying to keep any kind of opening away from Jason where he might ask me out. "I'm there most days after work and on the weekends."

A smirk twitches at the corners of his lips as he gives me a lazy—and very blatant—once-over. "I can tell," he purrs shamelessly. "You have a great body, Remy. Whatever you're doing is working."

I fidget nervously. I'm typically more than comfortable with flirting, but Jason is being so straightforward right now that it's coming off as sleazy. I try to breeze past the compliment.

"I got into martial arts in college," I say by way of explanation. "I started doing kickboxing and then it kind of spiraled from there."

"Like an aerobics thing?"

I frown. "No, it's a real MMA gym. I've been learning Muay Thai and jiu-jitsu for years."

His eyebrows shoot up and I think he looks at me with admiration, but then the sleazy smirk comes back. "Ooh, jiu-jitsu, huh? You should teach me some moves. Maybe we can roll together sometime—I promise I'll go easy on you."

It's his wink at the end that makes my blood boil. Not just for the sexualization of a sport that I love so much, but also because of his assumption that he could beat me.

With zero training.

Just because he's a guy.

Which, for the record, he can't. Jiu-jitsu is the skilled person's sport, through and through, and has nothing to do with size or strength. But even if we were only talking about kickboxing, I'd still beat the shit out of Jason. Especially with how angry his typical chauvinistic male argument just made me.

I'm trembling, actually *trembling* with fury, trying to figure out how to respond to this dumbass without completely driving him out of the bar. Only I never actually get to say anything because just then, I see Jason glance over my shoulder.

"Hey," he says in surprise. "What're you doing here?"

"Well hello to you, too," chuckles a deep voice from behind me. I turn to look over my shoulder and find another professional frat boy in a suit.

Jason stands up with a grin and gives him a bro hug. "I just never expected to see you in this area. You were working in NYC, last I heard. Are you just visiting?"

The suit—albeit a good-looking suit—shakes his head as Jason settles back on the cushion next to me. "Nah, I just transferred here for good. I got sick of the Big Apple, figured Philly would give me a better crowd." His gaze finally flicks to me and slowly, lazily, looks me up and down. He brazenly licks his lips as his eyes meet mine. "The view here is way better."

I shudder and look away, hating my physical reaction for most likely making him think I was turned on by him.

I don't even care. I just want to get this over with. I turn back to Jason and open my mouth, ready to launch into my legal problem.

"Remy, this is my friend Zach. We went to law school together. Zach, this is Remy."

I smile politely at the man now taking a seat across from us. He gives me a grin that probably tends to drop women's panties.

"Remy, huh? That's a sexy name."

I sigh and look around the bar, avoiding eye contact and trying to look bored. Anything to get this over with. "Thanks. I was named after a pornstar."

Jason chuckles tightly next to me. I can tell he feels the awkward tension radiating from me, so he leans forward to brace his elbows on his knees and instead gives Zach his full attention.

"So where are you working now?" he asks his friend.

I zone out as they start talking. I lean back in my chair with a scowl, internally trying to suffocate the scream that's threatening to break out of me. I throw back half of my drink in frustration. In this moment I hate the fact that my job is important enough that I need to wait for Jason to finish his conversation. Resigning myself to the fact, I tear my eyes away from him and turn to scan the bar instead.

And then very quickly wish I hadn't, when I catch sight of Tristan at the bar.

My breath catches, and my heart immediately begins beating a million miles per minute. It's been weeks since I've seen him, but at the sight of him, I'm transported right back to the time we spent together at the house. My heart aches at the perfect vision of him.

He looks amazing. He's wearing jeans and my favorite kind of simple black t-shirt that accentuates his muscular frame. His hair is slightly ruffled and he's laughing at something that Aiden said. He's leaning casually against the bar, just as comfortable and confident in his stance as he always is, looking nothing but carefree and happy.

Looking nothing like how I feel.

I've been trying so hard to make myself hate Tristan—hate being easier to bear than heartache—but I realize now that's nearly impossible when he's actually in front of me. Now, I'm having a really hard time remembering why I walked away from him. Now, at the sight of his smile and natural confidence, I'm only remembering our easy banter on the couch, his genuine encouragement at the gym, his sweet reverence in my apartment. I'm remembering how perfectly we fit against each other, how in sync our chemistry felt once we stopped fighting it.

I'm remembering how much I miss him. My chest actually aches from the intensity of it. I even miss the Tristan I had before all of this, because I realize in this moment that I must have always liked the excitement of our verbal sparring, and our fighting rounds both in and outside of the gym. Our dinners and fight nights at the house, which were comfortable and fun even if I convinced myself I hated the teasing. I must've liked it because right now I fucking miss it.

Maybe I was wrong about Tristan.

Maybe it's worth giving us a shot.

Maybe I pulled away too quickly.

My heartbeat, slow and depressed for weeks, stutters at the thought—at the terrified hope that that's true. That stutter feels like a jumpstart to my heart, and it starts to beat again.

The decision to approach him forms in my head without a second thought. I take a deep breath to steady myself.

But I never even make it to my feet, because an attractive woman joins Tristan at the bar before I can even get my feet moving under me. He wraps his arm around her waist to pull her close, his blue eyes twinkling mischievously and leaving no doubt about his intent. His usual cocky smirk appears on his face.

And I realize in this moment that somewhere along the way I fell in love with Tristan West.

There's no other reason for why this hurts so bad. It physically feels like he's ripping my heart out of my chest and having another woman stomp on it while he just stares and smirks. I feel the same blade that sliced through my heart that morning in the house now cutting up my insides. My stomach drops, and my core aches so hard that I can't help but wrap my arms around my middle. The pain from the sight in front of me feels like it's clawing its way out of my body, shredding me from the inside out.

I see the blonde throw her head back with a laugh, touching Tristan's chest as she does so. Tristan's smile grows when she doesn't remove her hand and instead presses closer against his body. He leans forward to whisper something in her ear, causing her to blush and giggle.

The knife in my gut twists deeper with every glance between them. My arms tighten around my stomach, as if trying to keep my insides from spilling out, whether from the blade or from the sickness that I feel.

I can't watch this. It's one thing to hear him reject me, but another to watch him move on right in front of me. I don't have the strength for this. I stand up, ready to tell Jason off for dragging me to a place like this for a business meeting.

He turns away from his conversation with his buddy and looks up at me with a startled expression. "You're leaving?" he asks incredulously. I restrain my urge to grab his collar and shake him for his daftness.

"Yeah, I have to get back to the office," I say quickly, grabbing my purse. "Sorry we couldn't chat. I'll call you next week if I still have questions." With barely a wave goodbye, I turn to walk—or *run*—from the bar.

Except, at some point Tristan has spotted me and decided he wants to come over to say... *something*. Anything out of his mouth will butcher me right now. I feel the anger start churning in my still-shredded gut, slowly and messily holding my body together.

With one hand in his pocket and his other arm slung casually around the blonde's shoulders, he's walked over to our sitting area and is looking at us with a tilted head and a curious expression.

"Remy, Jason, didn't think I'd run into you two here," he smirks. "Isn't it too early to leave the office? You can hardly be overachievers from a bar."

"Spoken exactly like someone who's never had a real job," I spit. I can't help it. I don't even mean it, but I hate that we've reverted to jabs about my nerdiness.

I also hate that he's touching someone else. My stomach churns again.

Tristan's lips thin as they press together at my comment.

But if he wanted to say something else, he doesn't get the chance because at that moment Jason comes up behind me and slides his arm around my waist. He tugs me against his chest.

"Aw, come on, Remy, that's not fair," Jason defends. I stiffen, both from his touch and from thinking I'm about to be ganged up on. "It's hard work throwing weights around and still having the energy to charm a lady. Give him some credit." I don't have to turn around to know he winks at the blonde and gives her a sleazy once-over. I can feel it in the way the girl blushes and turns her face into Tristan's neck with a smile.

Tristan's arm tightens around her and I know him well enough to see the fury now dancing in his eyes. Suddenly I flash back to the last time he was around Jason—and how much he seemed to hate him. But that had felt like jealousy. Only, that doesn't make sense anymore, seeing as Tristan is making it very clear right now that he's not interested in me.

Once again, I marvel at the fact that Tristan's actions were for the sole purpose of getting in my pants. I replay his possessive 'you're *mine*' declaration from the night of the house party when he pulled me away from Jason.

And fight the urge to vomit when I now hear it through this new understanding of him.

"It looks like I'm not the only one doing a little charming," Tristan observes, looking directly at me.

Jason chuckles and pulls me tighter against him. The closeness makes me sick, but I refuse to pull away and let Tristan think he's the only one that's moved on. "What can I say, I haven't been able to get Remy out of my head since we ran into each other a few weeks ago." He turns to nuzzle into my neck.

Tristan's eyes bore into mine even as I feel Jason's face against my skin. There is an intensity—a *fury*—that I've never seen in him before.

I hold his gaze, unwilling to back down. I don't shield my own anger from him, either. Let him see how much I hate him right now.

"Yes, you definitely seemed to make an impression on her at that party," Tristan drawls. The corner of his mouth ticks up in a cruel, condescending smirk.

The leash on my fury snaps. With every patronizing comment, I feel us dragged further and further back to where we were before I moved into the house. Where he's once again the arrogant, boorish womanizer that I always thought he was.

The realization that I may have been right about him hurts worse than the pain of losing the man I thought he was.

"Some of us need more than a quick fuck in a bathroom to keep us interested," I taunt. Without breaking Tristan's gaze, I interlace my fingers with Jason's on my waist. I don't miss the way his eyes flash down to the contact. "Jason understands that women are worth more than that, that they *deserve* more than that."

Tristan laughs mockingly. "It's cute that you think Jason wants anything more than to bend you over and fuck you into submission. I can assure you he doesn't want you for your mind." He looks me up and down with a scoff, as if disgusted by my very presence. My blood freezes at the glance before he's even finished his thought. "After all, the only thing men want from women is pussy. That's all most women are good for, anyway."

I feel everything in me freeze, from the tip of my nose

down to my toes. I inhale a sharp breath, trying to still my heart and stop my lungs in an effort to hold myself together, even as every piece of me wants to shatter onto the floor.

All the fight leaves my body. It seeps out of my pores as if I had sweat it out from Tristan's single blow. I'm left without any anger, without any urge for revenge, or disappointment that he could be so cruel.

I'm left with only pain—mind-numbing, agonizing pain.

I look at Tristan, uncaring that every last piece of my façade has fallen. I let him see my pain. I let him see what his words do to me. I'm so numb that I can't even manage any tears, though I would probably let him see those, too— let him see what those words can do to a woman.

Jason laughs awkwardly from beside me, taking a small step away. "Damn, dude, way to demolish any hope of a good night. For both of us." Sure enough, the blonde has pulled away from Tristan with an angry pout and walked away without another word. I don't blame her, because I can't bring myself to care about the fact that Jason just admitted he, too, only wanted me for the night.

Tristan doesn't react—to the girl leaving or to Jason. His eyes haven't left mine. Where his gaze looked both victorious just a moment ago, he's now studying me with a small frown. He straightens and takes a step toward me.

"Remy..." he starts, unsure. I can tell he's seeing the pain in my eyes, and thankfully showing at least a shred of humanity by seeming to care. His glance darts across my face, taking in the true depth of what I'm showing him, and I can tell he's realized he went too far.

"Remy..." he tries again, this time with a small break in his voice. He takes another step toward me.

I shake my head and look down. "Well, I guess you'd know better than I would," I say quietly. I take a deep breath, then look back up at him with a tight smile. "I'm sure you're right. I guess I was an idiot to think differently. Excuse me." I turn away from Tristan and make my way toward the exit.

"Remy, I didn't mean—" But I don't hear the end of it because I'm already out the door.

22

REMY

I spend the rest of the evening getting shitfaced in my apartment by myself. I've never been any more than a social drinker, but in this moment, I just want to escape from my reality—or at least dull the edges of it. Anything is better than feeling what I feel right now.

Tristan's parting comment plays on repeat in my head, and every time it does, I feel my heart splinter a little more. I can't decide what hurts worse: his words, or the fact that I was so epically wrong about him. I alternate between hating Tristan for being so heartless, hating myself for being such an idiot, and fighting the pull of a downward spiral of sheer heartache.

Occasionally I remember my work troubles, which spikes a welcome distraction of panic through my thoughts. I have no one to blame but myself for what happened and I'm fairly certain I'm getting fired on Monday. So, on top of everything, I'll be jobless.

I down another shot of tequila at the thought.

Jax calls me at some point but by then I'm already a few

shots deep and I can't bring myself to talk to anyone. I pour myself another shot as I let it go to voicemail.

Sometime later, I pull out my computer and attempt to write something. But I'm drunk enough by then that it's just an angry stream of consciousness that doesn't make any sense, and it barely provides any relief to my overworked brain.

I slam my computer shut and throw my head back against the couch, a single tear rolling down my cheek.

I somehow manage to sleep through the night, but after chugging some water and forcing down some toast, I go right back to sleep. My exhausted body happily gives into the blackness.

I wake several hours later, my head pounding with a vicious hangover and my phone beeping with incoming text messages. I groan and squint at the screen with one eye.

There's another missed call from Jax this morning but it's Hailey that's blowing up my phone right now. I frown and try to focus.

Hailey: I hate Steve

Hailey: I hate him so goddamn much

Hailey: I don't know what I was thinking moving in here

Hailey: I need to get out of this house

Hailey: Are you around this weekend? Can I come over?

My eyes widen at the texts. I always knew Hailey would reach the wakeup point eventually but I was definitely not expecting it with this much intensity. I immediately type my response.

Remy: Yea I'm home. I'm moping too so come join the party.

Her response comes quickly.

Hailey: I'm already on my way

I glance at the time. It's almost 4:00, which means I've somehow managed to waste almost an entire day. And yet, when everything from this week comes rushing back, the only thing I want to do is curl up under the covers and go back to unconsciousness.

That plan is indefinitely put on hold when I hear Hailey fumbling with her keys in the hallway. She opens the door with a bang.

We both stare at each other with raised eyebrows—me because of Hailey's whirlwind entrance and her because of my very obviously hungover and pathetic state on the couch.

"It looks like we both have some issues to work through tonight," she finally mutters.

"Damn straight," I agree gruffly. "Tequila is on the far-left shelf if you've reached that point."

Hailey shudders at the mention of alcohol. She's never been a big drinker, though I've also noticed that she's even more opposed to it since she started dating Steve. I've never gotten an explanation about why he hates drinking so much but it's obviously affected Hailey's feelings for it, too. I can't remember the last time I saw her actually drunk.

"No thanks, I'm good," she answers as she pulls her sweatshirt off. "I just need to vent." She plops down on the swivel chair next to me with a huff.

I sit up with a wince and say, "That's fine, but let me go pee. I've only moved off this couch once since 7:00 last night."

Hailey's eyes widen at that. I know she knows that I've been fucked up over Tristan, but it was never so bad that I didn't leave the house. She has no idea that everything imploded yesterday.

In typical caretaker Hailey fashion, she's waiting for me with two aspirin and a big glass of water when I sit back down on the couch. I give her an appreciative smile and swallow the pills. Then I lean back with a quirked eyebrow and stretch out my arms to rest on the back of the couch. I look at my sister expectantly.

She pulls her legs up to sit cross-legged on the seat and places her elbows on each knee, dropping her head into her hands with a groan. "I just hate him so much," she mumbles. "I don't know how I got into this situation."

"Living with him?" I ask tentatively.

Her head shoots up in frustration. "*Being* with him!" she exclaims. "Why did I ever start dating him? We don't even mesh. We never did." She sighs, the fight leaving her as quickly as it came. "I just feel like I'm starting to realize that he's Prince Charming on paper, but the polar opposite in real life. I feel like I was somehow *convinced* to be with him."

I don't bother correcting her—the right word is actually *manipulated*. She needs to figure this out herself before she can see Steve for what he really is.

I stay quiet and let her vent.

"He's just not the same person he was when we started dating," she explains, throwing her hands up in exasperation. "It mostly has to do with how he is with me, which is what made me think it was just the honeymoon phase. I thought maybe I just bore him now. But I've noticed lately that it's more than that. He's actually kind of mean. He used to *worship* me—he would give me compliments, buy me little things that let me know he was thinking of me. Now it seems to be the opposite. He rarely ever texts me during the day or does anything to let me know I'm on his mind, and when we *are* together, he says things about me that I hate. He tries to play them off as jokes but they're all just barely-disguised insults. He constantly brings up my past relationships, as if he's trying to make me out to be a whore for loving someone before him. And he makes subtle digs about my cooking, my career plans, even my appearance. But by the time I'm ready to be mad at him, he makes it seem like I just can't take a joke. Then he turns the charm on and ten minutes later I forget I was even mad. I get whiplash almost every day."

She drops her head back against the chair with a groan. "I couldn't figure out if it was just a phase or if he was always like this, but I'm starting to think this is just who he is. Which makes me wonder how I ever started dating him." She sits up with a wince. "And then how I get out of it."

I look at her with a sad smile. "I'll tell you the same thing I told you a few weeks ago. If he doesn't make you happy, he's not worth it. It doesn't matter if you live together, or if you've been together for years, or if you have a pet together. If you don't want to be with him then don't be with him."

She sighs and looks down at her hands. "I just feel like I only feel this way when he's angry at me," she mumbles. "Like today. I said one wrong thing and now he's giving me the silent treatment." I snort at that. If any guy I dated began acting like a teenage girl, they would immediately be cut loose.

Hailey either ignores it or doesn't recognize the ridiculousness of her comment. She turns to look at me. "That doesn't happen often, though. Most of the time we're fine. Our relationship is fine." I raise an eyebrow at the fact that she repeated the word twice.

A word that should not be used to describe a relationship that anyone should be in.

But again, she ignores me. Her expression becomes desperate. "How do you end a relationship where you can't exactly pinpoint a problem? There's no one thing I can say is wrong. I can't even give him a specific example of what he says that makes me feel bad. All I have to go on is my feelings. I can't end a relationship without a reason."

"Hailey," I say sternly. "You can do whatever the fuck you want. If you want to dump Steve because you don't like his haircut anymore, *do it.* You don't need a specific reason to get out of a relationship if it makes you unhappy. *That's* the reason. And it's more than enough."

She looks back at her hands, her face flushing pink with an ashamed blush. "I know," she whispers. She winces and rubs her temples with her fingers. "I'll do it eventually. I already know it's heading in that direction. I just need to do it." She sighs and looks up at me. "Let's move on from my shit and talk about you. What's going on? You look like you spent the night drinking from the bottle."

Now it's my turn to wince. "I kinda did," I admit. She raises an eyebrow and waits patiently for the rest. Ignoring the pang that slices through me at the reminder, I tell her, "I ran into Tristan at the bar last night."

Both of her eyebrows shoot to her hairline. "You saw Tristan? And you were at a bar?"

I nod stiffly. "Those are actually the two parts of this particularly depressive episode. He was flaunting another woman in front of me, and I was only at the bar because I'm being charged with copyright infringement and needed to meet with that lawyer Jason to see how much trouble I'm in."

Hailey's mouth drops open in shock.

"Yeah," mutter.

She continues to stare at me with wide eyes and a slack

345

jaw. "You... I don't... I don't even know what to ask about first."

I look toward my kitchen, debating grabbing the tequila again. Talking about Hailey's problem was a welcome distraction but now that we're talking about me, all the pain from yesterday comes rushing back—the issue at work, the sight of Tristan picking up another woman, and the hurt I felt when he implied that I was only good for a quick fuck. All of it brings back the bone-deep pain that makes my chest ache.

And I once again think about how this hurts way more than I thought it would.

So I tell Hailey everything. I tell her about my fuckup at work, and my upcoming Monday meeting with the company's lawyers. I tell her that I think I might get fired but that maybe that wouldn't be the worst thing because I'm realizing I hate my job. I even tell her I've been writing again and thinking about giving my dream a real shot.

I tell her about realizing that I'm in love with Tristan. About seeing him with another woman and feeling like my soul was being pulled out of my chest even before he put the final nail in the coffin. She sits next to me on the couch when I tell her that I don't understand how I could fall so hard when he clearly didn't. She holds me as I finally break down for the first time when I tell her that it hurts so fucking bad.

And we stay that way for the rest of the weekend. Hugging each other and crying, laughing and eating junk food, sleeping on the couch and watching trash TV. We ignore all phone calls from Jax and Steve.

We're just two sisters, holed up in an apartment for the weekend, comforting each other and readying ourselves to face the world again on Monday morning.

I look up at the building in front of me and take a deep breath. It's Monday morning and I'm about to walk into work.

And deal with my colossal screw-up from last week.

I breathe in again as I steel myself for the situation that's waiting for me on the 12th floor. I've been reminding myself all weekend that a) it was an accident that could've happened to anyone, b) I hate this job anyway, and c) I'm good with money and have enough saved to be okay for a few months. It isn't the end of the world if I get fired this morning. It definitely won't look good on my resume, but it's not the end of the world.

I've barely had enough time to set up my laptop before my boss appears in my cubicle.

"Remy, we're ready for you," he says without any kind of greeting.

I look up at Brian and swallow nervously. He's been my manager for about a year and a half, and while I don't exactly have anything bad to say about him, I'm not really a big fan, either. He's just kind of useless. Doesn't seem like he knows what he's doing, doesn't ever offer any feedback or help, never cares enough to ask how things are going. I don't think he's ever even asked me if I like my job. And he definitely never helped with career progression. He's just... useless.

"I'll be right in," I say with a nod. When he walks away without another word, I close my eyes and steady myself with a deep breath.

It's okay, you're okay. It was an accident, and you hate this job. Whatever happens, you'll get through this.

With those affirmations running on repeat in my head, I stand and make my way toward the conference room.

There are three people sitting around the far end of the conference table: my boss, my boss' boss, and someone else I don't recognize. I take a seat, my nerves buzzing with the intimidating position of being the only person on this end of the table while three powerful people sit across from me. I clasp my clammy hands together in my lap.

"Remy, good morning," my boss' boss Will Templeton starts out. "You know Brian and myself, obviously, but this is Sam Hancock, our company's corporate attorney. He'll be involved in this meeting for obvious reasons." I nod stiffly.

Mr. Templeton pauses to study me for a moment. I don't know anything about the man except that he's damn good at his job as the VP of Sales, so I have no idea how hard he's going to come down on me about this. But this moment of thoughtful attention gives me hope that he'll be understanding.

He smashes that hope immediately.

"Remy, you obviously know what this meeting is about. Our competitor has contacted us with a copyright infringement notice for a datasheet that you created. If they were anyone else or if this was any other situation, it most likely would've just been a 'Cease and Desist' request. But because they're a competitor, they're using this as an opportunity to hit us as hard as they can. This could potentially cost us *a lot* of money." His frown deepens. "Can you explain what happened here?"

I open my mouth to answer but I'm so nervous that my mouth is completely dry. I swallow and try again. "Unfortunately, the only answer I have for you is that it was an accident. I do a lot of research on the technology and that often means I end up on competitors' websites. The phrase must've stuck in my subconscious and I added it to the datasheet without realizing. I would never knowingly plagiarize anything, Mr. Templeton. It was a complete accident."

Brian leans forward on the table and clasps his hands in front of him. "Why would you need to do any research, Remy? Why aren't you just working with the materials the engineers give you? That should be more than enough to fine tune and make marketable."

My eyes nearly bug out of my head. I've been very vocal with Brian about my struggles with the engineers, so the fact that he's even asking this is unbelievable.

Useless.

"I rarely receive enough information from the engineers to create an entire datasheet," I answer delicately. I've never been one to burn bridges or throw anyone under the bus, so I need to be careful about how I answer this question and the inevitable next one.

Even though I'm dying to rat out those lazy mother-fuckers.

"I'm not sure how that's possible," Brian argues with a glare. "I talked to Cassandra on Friday and she said she gave you plenty of information to work with for that datasheet."

I'm grinding my teeth so hard that I'm surprised I haven't bitten through my own jaw yet. I have no idea how to respond to that without calling both my boss and a valued employee a blatant liar.

Brian continues his scolding. "And anyway, why aren't you checking your work before you pass it to the Creative team to get published? How did a mistake like this get all the way through to publication?"

By now, my words have taken on a sharp edge. "I triple check everything I create," I say tightly. "But this is the exact reason I've asked for another person on my team, so it goes through quality control and so I'm not the only person—"

"I can't hire someone just to check your work," Brian interrupts.

I stare at him for a moment in complete disbelief. *He really hasn't ever listened to a word I've said.*

Either that or he's just trying to save face in front of his boss by using me as a scapegoat.

"I don't need someone to check my work, I need help in general," I say firmly. "None of the other marketing teams are made up of only one person. The company has grown significantly in the past year, which means marketing demand has increased, and I'm not able to give each document the attention it needs because of that. Every document should have at least two eyes on it to avoid situations like this. And with the engineers not providing enough information, the time spent on these documents is—"

"We can't hire anyone else right now," Mr. Templeton cuts me off. My eyes widen at both the rude interruption and the blatant effort to shut me down. "We can revisit that idea at another time but for right now, we need to deal with the issue in front of us. And going forward, I expect you to pay closer attention to your work."

A red haze clouds my vision and I'm sure they can see that I'm seething. But I'm so beyond caring that I just nod.

Mr. Templeton turns to the lawyer on his left and motions for him to begin.

The lawyer opens the folder in front of him before fixing me with a firm stare. "The first step here is obviously to remove that datasheet from the website and anywhere else that we can pull it down. Our team is handling that. The good news is that the competitor caught it quickly, so your customers haven't had a chance to share the document very widely. That might work in our favor—they might not be able to claim damages or much of a loss of revenue. I'm going to push for a settlement so that this doesn't make it to litigation, but if they find any way to prove that this was willful, or if they really want to push this to the max, they might take us to court for statutory damages. It is *imperative* that you do not talk to anyone about this. You say one wrong thing to the competitor or their lawyer, and we get taken to court for hundreds of thousands of dollars. *Do not talk to anyone without me present.* Do I make myself clear?"

I glare at him. I know he needs to talk to me this way, but I hate it anyway. "I understand."

He nods in approval and turns back to Mr. Templeton, who fixes me with a stern look. "Make sure you do as Sam says. This is costing us enough money as it is, so we don't need anything making this even worse. Please let myself and Sam know if anyone tries to contact you about this." He motions to Brian. "For the time being, you will submit all of your work to Brian for approval. Please check your work going forward. You won't be let go because of this, but I expect that it won't happen again."

I'm so furious that all I can do is give a stiff nod. I know I made a mistake and that they need to do damage control, but I'm being treated like an incompetent child. Not to mention this could've been avoided if my boss cared to listen to any of my suggestions. And on top of all of that, I should be *grateful* that they're not firing me. I can barely hold back my angry sneer.

Brian is the last to chime in. "You and I will meet again later today to discuss this further." *To further scold you and to talk about your punishment* goes unsaid. But the message is clear: even though companies hire lawyers and have money set aside for exactly these kinds of issues, I'm still going to be severely punished.

The meeting ends abruptly. At some kind of unspoken signal from Mr. Templeton, all three men stand and exit the room, leaving me sitting in shock at the conference table.

I didn't exactly expect someone to tell me *'it's okay, it could happen to anyone,'* but I can't help but feel hurt that there wasn't a single positive message or appreciative comment throughout that whole meeting. No one to tell me I do a great job otherwise, or that the company is perfectly equipped to handle this kind of thing. After all, copyright lawyers exist exactly because this is a common issue.

Instead, I once again feel like I'm undervalued by my company, and like the only purpose I serve is for others to bash me. It's the same story with my boss, the engineers, even the people that sit in the cubicles around me that don't care enough to talk to me unless they're teasing me for one thing or another. I'm completely unappreciated in every part of my work. Even though I'm damn good at my job.

Eventually I stand from my seat and go back to my cubicle. I spend the rest of the day on autopilot, working normally while my brain is lost in very different thoughts.

I think about my dreams in college. I think about my career up until this point. I think about my 5/10/20 year plan and where I want to be, and what I want to be doing.

I think about what makes me happy, and what makes me miserable. I think about the fact that I spend almost sixty hours a week doing something that I absolutely hate, and only eight hours a week in the gym being actually happy.

I think about what a horrible ratio that is.

I'm lost in my thoughts all day. I'm quiet throughout my entire existential crisis—as I work, as I go out for lunch, even as I talk to coworkers. I dissect and analyze everything in my life for my entire Monday workday.

Brian sends me an instant message at 4:00 to come to his office. I no longer feel angry or hurt—I just feel calm and sure of myself. I close my laptop and make my way to his office.

"Have a seat, Remy," he says by way of greeting. I close the door behind me and sit down in the chair he indicates. My calmness remains even as my boss leans forward on his desk, a smug expression appearing on his face as he clasps his hands together and gets ready to deliver what is most likely a verbal lashing.

"As you're aware—" he begins.

"I'd like to give you my official two-week notice," I interrupt, much like he and his boss kept interrupting me this morning.

Brian's eyes go wide. He clumsily leans back in his chair, looking physically taken aback.

I wait patiently for his response.

"Remy, just because you're in trouble doesn't mean you need to make any rash—"

"That's not why I'm doing this," I interrupt again. "This is not me trying to get away from any kind of legal consequence. I will still deal with my mistake. But I no longer want to work here, so I'm giving you my two weeks' notice."

He stares at me, wide-eyed, for a few seconds. I'm sure this isn't the way people usually resign, so it looks like he's struggling to figure out what to say to me.

"But... why?" he finally asks.

"Because I'm unhappy. I don't like what I do." I spear him with a steely glare. "And without trying to burn any bridges with this company, I have to admit that I did not mesh well with anyone here."

He swallows roughly, and I'm sure that he caught my not-so-hidden meaning. Despite his comments this morning, he knows how unsupported I am and how much the engineers take advantage of me. Not to mention he has to be aware of his own role in this game. Or lack thereof.

"I'm resigning, that's all there is to it. Let me know what you need from me to get it done." I stand from the chair and turn to leave.

"Quitting like this won't get you a recommendation from this company," he blurts out as I reach the door. "And it's the only job you've ever had, so it won't be easy getting another job in the industry."

I turn to face him, my hand on the doorknob and a sad smile on my face. "If I'm lucky, I'll never even look at this industry again." I leave his office without a single glance back.

I had already packed my tote bag before walking into Brian's office, so I grab it now and walk out of the building, not saying a word to anybody. I can practically feel people's surprised glances follow me out—it's only 4:00 and no one has ever seen me leave even a minute before 5:00.

But right now I don't give a flying fuck. I feel too good, too free, for the first time in a long time. I don't want to spend another second of the day being unhappy.

Part of me wants to go to the gym, not caring that I would probably run into Tristan. But for some reason the rest of me doesn't find the idea of a workout appealing. I know I need to deal with the gym issue soon—I will never be the kind of girl that quits something solely because of a boy—but that day is not today. Right now, I feel myself wanting to do something new and exciting. Something that I've always wanted to do but have put off for one reason or another.

And maybe it's my current 'fuck everybody' mentality, but I find myself pulling my phone out to run an internet search. A minute later, I hear my call ringing out.

"Hi, my name is Remy. Do you by any chance have any availability for a cut and color today?"

23

REMY

I try to remind myself for the millionth time that I love Jax's parents and already promised them that I would be there to celebrate their anniversary.

Every part of me dreads going to this party. There isn't a chance that Tristan doesn't go, which means I'll definitely run into him at some point tonight. My only hope for that not happening is if Mr. and Mrs. Turner invited enough people to actually fill their massive house. For the first time in my life, I'm hoping for a crowded party.

I turn to the mirror again to study my reflection. Even in my miserable state, I can admit it's a shame that I'm not more excited to wear this dress. A few weeks ago, Hailey helped me pick out a cocktail dress specifically for tonight, since Jax's parents love to throw formal parties. It's a simple design, a solid burgundy piece of satin that reaches all the way to the floor. But with a subtle neckline, backless design, and a thigh high slit on one side, the dress is clearly a show-stopper. I run my hands over my hips where the fabric hugs my curves.

I added my silver ankle strap heels and a pair of dangly

silver earrings. My newly blonde hair is curled and tucked back on one side with a single silver clip. I find myself wishing, more than anything, that I felt as beautiful as my reflection looks staring back at me.

My phone buzzes with a text message.

Jax: I'm here

I grab the nude lipstick to touch up my color and tuck it into my black clutch next to my phone. With a final glance at my despondent reflection, I take a deep breath and head downstairs.

Jax is parked in front of my apartment building, scrolling through something on his phone as he waits for me. And even though I often see him dressed in suits for work, I still smile at the sight of him. He will always be the center of attention in any room, but especially when he's dressed in a fitted black suit.

He looks up from his phone as I'm walking down the last few steps to the sidewalk. A small part of me takes pleasure in his double take when he sees my outfit. His jaw drops and he doesn't take his eyes off me as I round the car to open the passenger door.

"Jesus Christ, Remy," he exclaims as I take my seat. "You're a fucking bombshell." He's openly gaping, though after a moment he clears his head by shaking it and shooting me a small glare. "But you do realize that showing up looking like that is not going to help us convince Grandma Birdie that I shouldn't be swooning over you and begging you to marry into the family, right?"

I flash Jax a tight smile as I carefully arrange my dress around me. "I don't think anything is capable of convincing Grandma Birdie to give up on her idea of us together. It doesn't matter what I wear. But thank you. You're quite a showstopper yourself, as always." I turn to Jax with another smile, even though I can feel that it doesn't quite reach my eyes.

This whole evening is going to be painful if I don't start faking my smiles better.

Jax studies me closely for a moment. Even if I were the greatest actress in the world, he would still be able to tell that I'm miserable. And once again I think about how thankful I am for his friendship, for him understanding that I need space and not pressuring me for an explanation.

Without a word, he leans over and gently kisses my cheek. "You really do look beautiful," he says softly. He turns to face forward, ready to take us to the suburbs. But he pauses and, without looking at me, says, "Whatever it is, it'll work out in the end. If it hasn't worked out yet, then it's not the end."

I look out the window and try to will my tears not to fall. He doesn't wait for my reaction before he pulls out into traffic.

My wish for a packed party is pretty close to reality. By the time we pull up to the large house, there are two dozen cars parked on the property and multiple couples walking up the long driveway. Jax weaves my hand through his arm as we start the walk toward the party.

I take a deep breath when we step through the front door. I know a lot of the Turners' family and friends, so my plan is to busy myself with as many people as possible.

So as to avoid the temptation of looking around for a certain person.

Sure enough, it doesn't take long for Jax and I to be stopped by his family members. I let go of Jax's arm in an attempt to keep the older women in his family from yet again assuming that we're dating, but I don't get very far before he grabs a hold of my pinky. He never looks away from the conversation that he's engaged in, yet I get the feeling that he's trying to physically anchor me to his side to convince himself that I'm nearby and in one piece. I smile gratefully at the back of my best friend's head.

We make our way through the rest of the house, stopping to chat with a few more people, before we open the back door and step out into the stunning backyard.

This is the main location of tonight's party. On a September evening it's still on the warmer side, but not hot enough that it's uncomfortable. On one side there is a bar area set up, complete with a bartender decked out in a vest and bowtie, along with several wine and liquor options. Partygoers mingle around the nearby high tops with their drinks. On the other side of the massive yard, the Turners' party planner has arranged a few sofas and loveseats for comfortable seating. Both sides of the yard are filled with happy, laughing guests.

In the middle of the yard is the dance floor, where a few children are already twirling in circles. And if I know anything about a Turner family party, that dance floor will be filled with many drunk and boisterous guests before the night is over.

Along the perimeter of the property and stretching overhead, beautiful string lights twinkle and envelop the party in a soft glow. Between the physical ambiance of the setting and the sounds of children's giggles floating through the air, it's a beautiful and wonderfully welcoming party. My heart aches at the feel of it.

"Oh, there you two are, I've been looking all over for you. It's about time you made it here!"

Jax and I turn to see his parents walking toward us with big smiles. His mother, a beautiful fifty-year-old woman that is more elegant now than ever before, pulls me into a tight hug. She looks stunning in a simple white dress. When she pulls back, she keeps hold of my hands and smiles down at my outfit.

"Darling, you look spectacular! That dress looks like it was made for you." She tugs me closer to whisper conspiratorially, "Don't let Grandma Birdie see you. We only recently started to make progress with convincing her that you two are just friends."

Mr. Turner winks and pulls me in for a hug of his own. "If I'm being honest, I'm on Grandma Birdie's side. I have no idea what could possess my son to think there is someone better than you out there."

"Dad, *come on*," Jax groans. "You would think after a decade we'd be over this joke already. I am this close to never bringing Remy to the house again."

His mom gasps and grabs my arm. "You'll do no such thing. Remy is as much a part of the family as you are."

I smile my first real smile of the night. I am loved and taken care of by people that aren't even my blood family, and for a moment I remind myself that if this is the kind of love I receive in my life, I should be grateful.

I cover Mrs. Turner's hand with my own. "You look wonderful, by the way. I can't believe you've been married for twenty-five years. Every time I look at you, I think you should have a toddler running around, not a grown son that acts like one." She blushes and swats away my compliment with a smile at the same time that I hear Jax huff in outrage.

I smile at them—my second parents, whom I love as much as my own. "So, what's the secret? How did you get to twenty-five years and still look at each other like teenagers in love?"

At that, Mrs. Turner finally lets me go. She floats over to her husband to press a kiss to his weathered cheek. He smiles at her with the same tenderness I see him give her every day of their lives.

"I think the secret is finding the right person," she answers without taking her eyes off her husband. "I think if you wait for the person who makes you so happy that you can't stand to be without them for even a minute, who you love so much that it makes any problem thrown your way worth fighting through—then everything else fades in comparison. Everything else will work itself out because you've found the other half of your soul and nothing else matters. You've already achieved the main purpose of life."

I turn away to blink the tears from my eyes before anyone can notice. Mrs. Turner's words pierce a knife through my already aching heart. They remind me of the person that it physically hurts me to be without.

Because what if you find your other half and they don't want you back?

I don't voice my question out loud. Instead, I smile again at the love-struck couple and shove my pain to the back of my mind.

"I hope you put that in your speech tonight," I tell her honestly. "Because that almost just made me cry."

I feel Jax grab my pinky again as Mrs. Turner titters over my compliment. I squeeze him back in a silent thank you for his wordless support, once again reminded of the amount of love that I'm surrounded by.

I look between Jax's parents. "I think I'd like to get a drink, if you don't mind my sneaking away for a minute."

"Oh, honey, of course. That's what it's there for. Enjoy

yourself." Mrs. Turner waves a hand at the bar before turning to Jax and launching into an animated conversation about a friend's daughter that she wants to set him up with.

I make my way over to the bar while trying to keep from making eye contact with too many people. I inevitably get stopped by an aunt along the way, but eventually I find myself in front of the bartender.

"Can I have a glass of red, please? Whatever the current Turner favorite is." I smile at the eager young bartender and leave some cash in his tip jar. Before long I'm sipping a delicious red wine that I forgot to ask the name of and turning back to the party. In the past fifteen minutes the entire backyard has filled with people, laughing with each other and drifting toward the dance floor. The sounds of happy partygoers almost drown out the 80's hits that the DJ is currently playing through the speakers. I smile and look around the yard.

And freeze when I notice a face on the other side of it.

My heart sinks to the bottom of my stomach when I recognize the blue eyes and tousled brown hair. It looks like he'd already noticed me because he stands rooted to the spot as he studies me with a thoughtful expression. He's wearing a black suit and white button-up shirt, looking absolutely sinful with the buttons around his neck undone. He's got one hand in his pants pocket and is holding a glass of clear liquor in the other. His piercing gaze never leaves my face.

Before I can decide if I want to ignore him or run from him, the music cuts out.

"Good evening, everyone, and welcome to the 25th anniversary celebration of Mr. and Mrs. Turner! How's everyone doing?"

A cheer goes up in the crowd. There's probably close to a

hundred people at this party, with more now streaming into the backyard. People continue to pass in front of me as they fill the space around me, occasionally blocking my view of the man across the yard. But regardless of the jostling and blocked views, we never look away from each other.

It vaguely registers in the back of my mind that the DJ is talking, still working the crowd into a frenzy. None of it registers because I can't seem to take a deep enough breath into my lungs.

Tristan looks calm, almost thoughtful. He doesn't look worried about the fact that we're face to face for the first time since we shredded each other at the bar. His lips are pressed tightly together and there doesn't seem to be anything playful or flirtatious in his eyes, but other than that he looks just as handsome as he always does.

He doesn't look like he's lost sleep or like a part of his heart has been ripped from his body. He doesn't look like I feel. He looks fine.

When Mrs. Turner's voice comes through the speakers I finally come to my senses and tear my eyes away from Tristan. Jax's mom is standing on a small stage near the entrance to their house, looking over the crowd of people spread out in her backyard. I hear her say something about long-lasting love, but nothing is properly registering in my brain right now. I try to steady my breathing by looking for Jax.

But no matter how many different directions I turn, I can't find him. I automatically glance in Tristan's direction and lock eyes with him again—he still hasn't looked away from me.

I feel my skin flush as the panic starts to set in. I have to get out of here. I can't handle his eyes on me, can't stand the possibility that he might try to talk to me. Every time I look at him my heart aches all over again, his words from the past few weeks running on loop in my brain. I have to get out of here.

I silently beg Mr. Turner to speed up his declaration of love to his wife. He's also standing on the stage now, his arm wrapped lovingly around Mrs. Turner as she gazes adoringly at him. Just the sight of that is almost enough to make me interrupt their speech by making a run for the house. But I control myself, just barely, and keep myself glued to where I'm standing. As much as my body is screaming for me to look to the other side of the yard, I keep my gaze trained on Mr. Turner.

Finally, after what seems like an eternity, the Turners step off the stage and the music resumes. It feels like someone hit play on the party as the many sounds come back to life and people start dancing again. I don't notice any of it.

I leave my wine on a nearby high top and make a mad dash for the house.

───

I run down the stairs, trying so hard to get away from those blue eyes that I trip on the last step. I catch the banister before I can fall on my face but keep running. I need to get away from this place before I really start to break down.

I need to call an Uber, but I can't be standing out in the open as I wait; some family member will undoubtedly see me and want to chat. I spot the study to my left and duck inside before anyone can see me.

I take a deep, quivering breath as I try to compose myself. I still feel like I can't breathe so I rush over to the glass doors behind the desk and pull them open. The fresh gust of air feels so calming that I step out on the small terrace to lean on the railing. I close my eyes and begin counting my breaths.

I only get to three before I feel another presence in the room. Without even turning around I know he followed me in here.

"Don't," I say, my voice breaking.

I feel him pause his steps toward me. "Remy..." he starts. I shake my head, eyes squeezed shut, desperately wishing he would stop talking. That he won't make us do this right now.

"Remy, I didn't mean what I said," he says quietly. "You're so far from a quick fuck that it's laughable I even said it. I don't know why I did. I just got so angry when I saw you with Jason..."

A startled laugh slips from my lips. It's such a misplaced reaction that Tristan stops talking and waits for me to explain what could possibly be so funny. But I shake my head again and fall quiet. I can't believe he's still playing the jealousy card. Part of me is almost impressed by the fact that Tristan is fighting this hard to keep his booty call.

The power of a good pussy, I think bitterly.

"Remy..." I feel his hesitation before he starts again. "I'm sorry if I made you feel less than. I shouldn't have said it. You're worth so much more to me."

"Please stop," I whisper quietly.

He interprets my response as a good sign and takes a step closer. "Please just talk to me. Please tell me you didn't mean what you said at the house. It's killing me thinking that's how you really feel. Why are you trying so hard to push me away?"

And with that, the flimsy wall that I've tried to rebuild around my heart the last few weeks disintegrates into dust.

I spin around, tears now freely flowing down my face.

"Because," I choke on a sob, my heart breaking for what

feels like the millionth time, "I'm in way too fucking deep, Tristan. I can't go a single minute without missing you so much that it hurts. It feels like my heart is being shredded in my chest every time I even hear your name, and I can't ever catch my breath. I can't *breathe*, Tristan." I shake my head and look down at where my hands are nervously gripping my dress, unable to look at him as I admit the part that will break me all over again. "I can't do this," I whisper. "I don't want to do this anymore."

But then it occurs to me that I'm not the same girl I was a few weeks ago. I'm no longer lying to myself about what does or doesn't make me happy, and I'm not going to be ashamed of something that I know is the right decision.

So I lift my gaze to meet Tristan's, unwilling to back down from a fight even though I know I've already lost. His eyes are bluer than I've ever seen them, yet they still don't give anything away. I have no idea why he's here or what he's thinking. But it doesn't matter, because I'm going to lay the truth at his feet anyway.

I look at him, strong and unflinching. "I know that I was just a piece of ass to you, but I guess I'm just another stupid girl because somewhere along the way... I fell for you. And I can't do this anymore because I love you, but you don't love me."

A deadly silence falls on the room. I'm not sure what I expect him to say, but the longer he's quiet, the more cracks splinter in my hopeless heart. When it feels like it's going to fall into irreparable fragments, I suck in a breath in an effort to keep myself whole for another minute, and turn to walk out the door.

"No," I finally hear him whisper. "No, no, no, Remy, no. You have it so wrong."

He rushes across the room to gently grab my wrist and

spin me back to face him. He touches my chin until I reluctantly look up at him and blink away my tears. "Remy, listen to me. I am so, so sorry if I made you feel like you weren't special to me. I thought my feelings were obvious, and I actually thought that it was you who wasn't interested. I didn't want to push you if it wasn't what you wanted." His hands grip my wrists, gently caressing my pulse-point as he looks at me with a raw emotion that I've never seen in his eyes before. It feels like he's begging me to understand and believe him. "I didn't expect it to happen like this, so it took me a while to understand what I was feeling, but... I love you. I just didn't know it until you left."

He smiles a sad smile as he cups my face and brushes away my fresh tears with his thumb. "The truth is I can't stop thinking about you, either. Every morning when I wake up, I have a split second of pure bliss where I think I'm waking up with you in my arms. And every morning, I'm wrong, and it feels like another part of me dies inside. Because I can't be without you now that I know what I was missing. I don't ever want to be without you again. Please... please tell me you feel the same way."

His voice cracks on the last sentence. He stares at me with a desperate hope, the vulnerability etched all over his face. He looks like he's waiting for me to either mend his heart—or ruin it completely.

I'm struggling to believe the words coming out of his mouth. It's almost too much to hope for. After everything that happened, it feels like a mistake to let myself hope again. Because I can't be broken like that again. I wouldn't survive it.

But his words are there, hanging between us. He wants me. He loves me. I know he's not lying because I can see it in his face. He really does feel as strongly as I do, and he's asking me if I want to be with him. If I want us to be together.

The right words don't exist in this world to express what he's silently begging me for. So, I answer the only way we know how to communicate: I kiss him.

I press my lips to his with a broken sob. He responds instantly and wraps an arm around my waist to pull me tight against his body, his other hand fisting in my hair. Our kiss is passionate and hungry. It feels like we've been physically starved of each other.

He pulls back just enough to look down at my tear-stained face. With a smile and a look of pure adoration, he gently kisses my lips, my nose, my eyelids, my cheeks. He kisses away the tears on my face.

The whole thing is enough to make me want to burst into tears again. I tighten my arms around his waist and bury my face in his chest.

"It's okay, we're okay," he mumbles as he strokes my hair. "We're okay now."

He holds me as I cry silent, heavy sobs. He holds me like he never wants to let me go.

"I'm sorry again about what I said last week," he mumbles against my hair. "I couldn't understand why you'd pushed me away, and then it felt like you picked Jason over me. I don't think I've ever felt as much rage in my life as when I saw you two together. I just snapped." I shake my head and burrow further into his embrace, and he tightens his grip around me. "I meant what I said the night of Aiden's party. You're mine. I just didn't know how to make you understand."

"Why did you—" He pulls away slightly so I'm not mumbling my words directly into his chest. But I can't quite bring myself to look at him, so I nervously keep my eyes down and fidget with the edge of his suit jacket. "Are you still seeing other women? Why did you tell Jax you'd never be able to settle down?"

"Is that why you pulled away from me?" he startles. His fingers grip my chin and lift my face to look at him. His eyes widen in shock. "You overheard me talking to Jax the day he got back?"

I nod weakly.

"Jesus," he winces. "You never should've heard that." He shakes his head, wrapping his arms even tighter around me. "I didn't mean a word of that. I haven't even thought of anyone else since you threw that girl out. Jax just has this really annoying habit lately of giving me very long and very obnoxious 'how to be a good boyfriend' speeches whenever he thinks I'm getting serious about a girl. I think he's just trying to pass on what he learned from his last breakup. But it's incredibly annoying. When I said those things, I was just trying to keep him from going off on his rant. I didn't mean a word of it. I'm so, so sorry that you heard it."

I consider his answer, then nod in understanding. The breath he must've been holding whooshes out in relief at my acceptance. He kisses my forehead and squeezes me tight again.

"Maybe subconsciously I didn't want to hear his speech because it was too much to hope that I was actually in a position to hear it," he mumbles against my hair.

"What do you mean?"

"Maybe I really wanted to be a boyfriend—a good boyfriend—but didn't know where you stood with us."

I lean back to look at his face. He looks vulnerable and hopeful. I stand up on my toes to place a light kiss on his lips. "It's okay, we got there eventually."

A wide grin splits his face, and any remaining sadness disappears. He looks absolutely joyous.

But then a thought occurs to me and one side of my mouth twitches up in a smirk. "I guess now you'll have to actually hear the speech. What's on his list anyway?"

He throws his head back and laughs loudly. "You don't want to know."

I pinch his waist and he swats my fingers away with a scowl. "Come on, just give me one," I nudge.

His eyes start to twinkle mischievously. He leans down to whisper in my ear, "Well, step one is to make sure she comes until she's limp in your arms. *Then* you fuck her until she can't even scream your name..."

I shiver at his words—at the thought of him doing exactly that.

He nips my earlobe before kissing it gently. "Let's get out of here," he whispers. "It's been far too long since I've seen you naked. And you look absolutely *edible* in that dress." He pulls back with a smile and runs a strand of blonde hair between his fingers. "Not to mention this new hair is a goddamn showstopper. You look like you were always meant to be blonde. I can't believe you finally did it."

A huge grin stretches proudly across my face. "Quit my job, too. I figured I'd do all the classic breakup things that girls usually do."

His eyes widen in surprise and a delighted smile appears. "You did? Holy shit, Remy, that's incredible!" He cups my face and kisses me enthusiastically before leaning his forehead against mine. "I'm so proud of you," he whispers against my lips.

I smile—an honest, happy smile—and grab his hand to lead him outside. We're almost to the front door when we run into a tiny old woman with a bird pinned to her hair.

"Remy, honey, there you are. I've been looking for Jaxon to see if he's slipped a ring on your finger yet." She pauses as she notices Tristan. In all her seventy-five-year-old worldly experience, she looks over every inch of him. And when she finally turns back to me, I see a knowing twinkle in her eye.

"Although, if that's the one you've got your eye on then I can't exactly blame you. Jaxon doesn't hold a candle to him."

I laugh a blissful, teary laugh, throwing my arms around her and pressing a kiss to her weathered cheek.

24

TRISTAN

I don't know how I don't get pulled over on the drive home, because I definitely break one or four speed limits on the way. By the time we reach Remy's apartment, I feel like I'll die if I don't get my hands on her.

We tumble into the apartment, a mess of sloppy kisses and wandering hands. I push her up against the wall the second the door is closed.

I can't stop kissing her or running my hands all over her body.

I can't get enough of her taste, her smell, the feel of her soft skin.

I can't get over the fact that her urgent kisses mean she's just as desperate for me as I am for her.

My hands slide along her sides before dropping down to squeeze her ass. "God, I missed this ass," I groan. I feel her smile against my lips.

I reach down to her thighs and lift her up against the wall, her legs automatically wrapping around my waist. The motion shifts the slit on one side of her dress, and I greedily run my hand across her exposed thigh. When I grind my hips against her center, she lets out a moan that damn near drives me out of my mind. With a growl I pull her away from the wall and walk us both toward the living room.

The city lights shine through the wall of oversized windows and dance across the floor. The last time I was here there was no furniture, and Remy and I were in a very different headspace. And although I plan to worship her body the same way I did that night, everything else feels like it's changed.

We reach the couch but instead of laying her down, I gently coax her legs to unhook from around my waist. She obliges, sliding down my body and standing in front of me with wide, trusting eyes. That look is enough to make me want to drop to my knees before her and promise her every piece of my crippled, shattered heart. A large part of me is still in shock that she picked me—that she loves me.

For a moment, all I want to do is stare at her. I want to absorb every single detail of this night. Tonight is the night she became mine, and I want to make it one we'll both remember.

I cup her face in my hands, my thumbs stroking her cheeks lovingly as I try to memorize every detail of her face. Her beautiful, wide green eyes. The pink tinge to her skin from the heat of the moment. The bee stung lips from hungry kisses. I commit all of it to memory and I smile at how goddamn beautiful she is.

"You're so perfect," I murmur, pulling her lips to mine. My kiss is gentle. Adoring. I want her to know exactly how infatuated I am with her. She grips my dress shirt with both hands, clinging to me as if my kiss makes her physically weak in the knees.

When I slide my tongue in her mouth to deepen the

kiss, she lets out a small whimper. That sound undoes the last of my restraint.

With a growl, I slide my hands down her side to grip her waist and pull her flush against me. Eventually I tear my mouth away from hers and start to kiss and nibble along her jaw, over her ear, down her neck. When I get to her exposed collarbone and the sultry neckline of the dress, a pained sound rumbles through my chest.

"This fucking dress," I growl into her skin as I continue to kiss across her shoulder. "I couldn't take my eyes off you tonight. All I could think about is how sexy you are in it. And that I don't understand how it's possible, but that it's somehow going to look much better on the floor." I feel the shiver that runs through her under my lips. I smile at the knowledge that I can affect her so easily.

I nudge her hips gently. "Turn around for me, baby," I whisper against her skin. She does as I ask, letting go of her death grip on my shirt and spinning slowly to face the windows. Now it's my turn to shiver when I see the backless design of her dress and the amount of skin that's visible to me right now. "Fuck," I mutter under my breath. I trace the length of her spine with a shaking finger as I absorb every detail of the sight before me.

Once I've looked my fill, I lean forward to gently press a chaste kiss to the back of her neck. "You're so fucking beautiful," I murmur against her skin.

I stare at Remy for what is definitely not a long enough amount of time. I feel like I'm unwrapping my Christmas present and I want to draw this out as much as I can. I run my finger along the curve of her neck and over her shoulders, and I revel in the feel of goosebumps appearing on her skin. I slowly slide the straps over her shoulders.

The dress pools at her feet. From over her shoulder, I see

her nipples pebble once they're exposed to the cool air. I can't contain the groan that rumbles through my chest when I realize she's completely naked.

"No underwear? You dirty, dirty girl," I growl in her ear before nipping her earlobe with barely contained restraint. She lets out a whimper and arches her back to grind her ass along my hard length.

I grab her hips and pull her even tighter against me. Trailing wet kisses along her neck and shoulder, I let my hands start to wander along her ribs, teasing a light graze along the side of her breasts. I hear her breath catch at the touch.

I can sense the moment she runs out of patience for my teasing and light touches. Which is fine by me, because at the sight of her naked it feels like I'll die if I don't get inside of her within the time span of my next heartbeat. I'll save the drawn-out sex for round two.

She spins in my arms and kisses me, hard. Her hands start to hurriedly undo the buttons on my shirt. I let her work on my clothes while I cup her face and kiss her tenderly, unable to get enough of her taste or even wrap my head around the fact that she's here with me.

When she finally gets all the buttons, she yanks my shirt off my shoulders and down my arms, tossing it on the floor next to her dress. It doesn't take her long to undo my belt and pants, and then those are on the floor, too. We tumble back onto the couch in a mess of limbs and rapidly beating hearts.

I settle between her legs. I slow our kiss, pulling away just enough to kiss first her top lip and then her bottom, before lifting my head so I can look down at the vision before me.

The moonlight from the windows is spilling across her

face, illuminating her wide eyes and swollen lips. She looks at me with a love so raw, so complete... that for a moment, I can't get enough air to my lungs. I cup her face with one hand and rub my thumb across her cheek, over her lips. I stare at her in wonder.

She lifts her hand to run it through my hair. When she fists her fingers at the nape of my neck and pulls my face to hers, I kiss her with every ounce of emotion inside of me. I kiss her until we're breathless and panting.

Eventually I leave her lips to start trailing kisses over her body—down her neck, over her collarbone, across her breasts. I suck a nipple into my mouth until Remy's arching off the couch with a cry, then I switch to the other side and repeat the same motion. I don't think I'll ever get over how responsive she is to my touch.

When I continue my trail of kisses beyond her breasts, I barely get to circle her navel with my tongue before Remy reaches down to cup my chin. "No," she gasps. "I need you inside me. *Now*." She tugs my face to further emphasize the desperation of her request.

I immediately slide back up her body and return to kissing her delicious mouth, bracing myself on my forearm. I continue to nibble on her lip, stroke her tongue with mine, even as I reach down to fist my cock in my hand. I twist along my length a few times before grinding against her clit. The motion elicits a tortured whimper from Remy's mouth, and I swallow the sound greedily.

"Tristan," she gasps. In her agony, she digs her fingernails into my shoulders. "Please, I need you. I need you inside me right now."

I shudder at her words, and I know in my bones that she feels the same desperate need to be close to me as I do. As I have since the night she first stayed in my bed.

I slide into her with one deep thrust, making us both groan at the feeling of my cock filling her so fully. I grip her hip with one hand and drop my head into the crook of her neck, my eyes squeezing shut as I try to both absorb the perfection of this feeling and force myself to make this last. Remy's hands slide from my shoulders to once again tangle in my hair. After what feels like the longest breath, I start to move.

I had been so wrapped up in my heartbreak, I almost forgot what it felt like to be so consumed by Remy like this —her scent in my nose, her damp skin against mine, her moans in my ear. The way she grips me like it would physically pain her to let me go. The way she clenches around my cock, as if I'm the only one who can make her feel like this.

I turn my head to press my lips against Remy's jaw, her cheek, her lips. I sink into the kiss like I wouldn't allow myself to do the last time we were in this apartment.

"Remy..." I murmur against her lips, my thrusts never slowing.

I feel her smile against me. Her hands run over my shoulders to cup my face, and she kisses me gently. "I know," she whispers. Just like last time.

Except now, we can say what we didn't know or couldn't verbalize last time.

"I love you," I say. I tell her with my words, my kisses, my body. I tell her everything I should've told her the night we spent here.

A single sob breaks from her throat. Her legs tighten around my waist and she wraps her arms around my neck, running her fingers through my hair. She grips me tightly as she tells me, "I love you. So much."

My heart explodes with happiness at her words. This is how it should've been a few weeks ago. We should've known that this thing between us was more powerful than just sex —we should've recognized that something bigger than us was pulling us together, fitting us perfectly together.

I've never thought about whether I believe in soulmates, but I just know that she's it for me. If these last few weeks taught me anything, it's that life without her is unbearably empty.

I tangle my fingers in her hair and tighten my grip on her hip. I coax her mouth open with my tongue and stroke against hers, at the same time that I start to thrust harder, deeper. Remy's answering gasp makes me growl and hitch her hips up higher.

"I want you to come with me," I murmur against her lips. "I want to feel you come on my cock. Can you do that for me?"

Her fingers tighten in my hair and she nods eagerly. "I'm close."

I can tell she's about to explode when she starts grasping at my shoulders, my arms, as if she's trying to anchor herself before she flies away.

Sure enough, she gasps, "Tristan, oh my *god*." The sound of my name on her lips almost undoes me, and only from sheer will do I hold off my orgasm for a few seconds longer.

Instead, I increase my pace, angling my hips in a way that I know I'm hitting her clit on every motion. Remy's nails dig into my skin as she continues to squirm beneath me, my name still falling from her lips like a desperate prayer. I kiss her one more time, pouring every ounce of raw emotion inside of me into her body.

"Come for me," I whisper against her lips.

I feel her orgasm tear through her the second the words leave my mouth. She gasps, her body tensing, right before her pussy starts spasming around my length. The feeling immediately brings on my own release. I groan as I empty myself inside her.

The sensation of finding my pleasure at the same time as Remy is unlike anything I've ever felt before. The feeling of wanting to be as close to her as possible is one thing, but experiencing the epitome of pleasure—brought on by our chemistry and love for each other—is the most incredible thing I've ever felt. I tighten my grip on Remy as we ride out our orgasms, wishing this would never end and knowing I'll be addicted to this feeling for the rest of my life.

When the feelings of ecstasy finally fade, we're both breathing hard and clutching each other even harder. I bury my face in the crook of her neck and tighten my grip on her. I stay inside her, not wanting to break our connection just yet.

Eventually I pull my head back to look down at her. I study the sated bliss on her face as I run my fingers through her hair. "I should've known this was something the first time we had sex," I remark thoughtfully. "I never knew it could feel like this."

She smiles, her fingers tracing the shell of my ear and running lightly down the side of my neck. "I didn't either. I didn't think chemistry like this existed." She pauses as something occurs to her and a grin splits her face. "Although, I have to admit, I'm glad you're this good at fucking because we definitely wouldn't have gotten together if you weren't. I would've ditched you after the first time. And if I counted correctly, I think it took us 5 rounds of sex to fall in love."

I chuckle and push my hips forward, my still-hard dick hitting deep enough that it makes Remy gasp and the smile fall from her face. "Remember when I said you need someone to tell you when you're being stupid? Well, you're being stupid."

I watch in fascination as arousal lights a blush on Remy's cheeks. And I know in that moment that it's going to be a long, exhausting night for both of us. It's possible I won't be able to peel myself away from her even days from now.

After a few heartbeats, she settles and begins distract-edly playing with my ears again. "I think I started falling in love with you the night we sat on the couch," she says thoughtfully. "You were nothing like I thought you were." Her eyes snap to mine as she hurriedly tacks on, "Not that I thought you were a dumb brute—I didn't. I never thought that. I feel like you thought I was a judgmental bitch before I even moved into the house. But you were so quiet and fight-focused that I didn't know anything about you except that you were arrogant and you had a different woman in your bed every weekend. But I never thought you were stupid."

I wince at her words. I always knew in the back of my mind that my womanizing days would catch up with me, but I never thought I would actually care. But right now, I feel the strange need to explain myself.

I pull out of her and settle on my side against the couch cushions, holding her tight against my body so we're still facing each other. I run a finger down her side and over her hip when she throws her leg over me. "Remy... I'm not proud of the fact that I've been with so many women," I begin. I can't quite look her in the eyes while I say it, so I focus on my finger running along her skin. "Partly because it seems ridiculous to think about it now, but also because it took you from me. I hate that I told Jax what I did, and I hate that you believed it so easily. I just never liked anyone enough to keep them around, so women just became stress relievers. I know I said it before but I'm sorry if I ever made you feel like you were just a booty call."

A warm smile lights up her face and she cups one side of

my face. It feels natural to turn and kiss her palm. "You don't need to explain anything to me. It *was* hard to know how you felt about me—and whether or not it was just sex between us—but I think that was just because we were both guilty of not being upfront about it. The Jax thing was just a misunderstanding. I don't care about any of that."

I feel my heart explode with admiration and happiness at her admission. My lips stretch into the most content smile I've felt in weeks. I lean forward to kiss her, weaving my hand into her hair and holding her to me as I press my mouth against hers, taking my time memorizing the shape of her lips. I never thought I would enjoy kissing someone as much as I do with her.

Eventually I pull back. I continue stroking her hair, not wanting to let go of our contact. "You're different than I thought you were, too, you know. Not that I ever thought you were a—what did you call it? A judgmental bitch? Maybe a little bit of a know-it-all, but that's not a bad thing." I grin as she frowns and lightly slaps my shoulder. "You weren't that far off with your assumptions about me, though. I *am* arrogant and selfish. I have to be for fighting. All the other stuff that people assume about me because I'm a fighter... I never fault anyone for it because I never take the time to prove them otherwise. So, I don't blame you for thinking the worst of me."

Then a huge grin splits my face. I realize I have the perfect opportunity now to tell Remy the secret that I've always wanted to share with her—the one that I've always wondered if it would shake her opinion of me.

She narrows her eyes suspiciously at my suddenly gleeful expression. "What?" she asks hesitantly.

"There is one assumption that you were wrong about, though. Wanna know what it is?"

She pulls back to get a better look at my face, and I watch her eyes dart over my face as she tries to find some hint about what I'm going to tell her. "What?" she asks suspiciously.

My grin widens. "I'm not sexist. Not even close. I admire women more than a lot of men I know, so I would never look down on them or make assumptions about what they can and can't do."

Her suspicion changes to confusion. "But what about—"

"The first time we met?" I finish, knowing exactly what she's thinking about. "Yeah, I wasn't being sexist. A new ballet studio had just opened up next door, so we had been getting women at the gym all day long that were looking for the school. I think they had the wrong address listed on their website. By the time you came in that night, I had directed about thirty women to the studio. You looked exactly like the other girls had looked: nice clothes, wide eyes, and a ballerina bun in your hair. So yes, I assumed, but it wasn't from being sexist like you always thought."

Her eyes widen as I talk. By the time I'm done, her jaw has dropped, and her mouth keeps opening and closing. She clearly doesn't know how to respond. After a few seconds—during which I grin gleefully at her speechless-ness—her mouth snaps closed, and she looks at me with an incredulous expression. It's almost like I'm watching her brain rework the very foundation of her opinion of me.

"Why didn't you tell me that?" she finally asks.

I finally let myself chuckle at the situation—at the memory of Remy yelling at me after I directed her to the ballet studio. "Because I liked how feisty you were. I only ever met women who threw themselves at me, so hearing you tell me how you really felt and not pulling any punches was a breath of fresh air."

She glares and slaps my shoulder again. "You're so cocky," she mumbles. My grin widens.

"Don't get me wrong, you being feisty also became incredibly annoying when you loved to point out my playboy ways and shit on me every chance you got. But it was attractive at first. And you'll never convince me that I was wrong about it being your defense mechanism because you were so attracted to me.

She gapes at my blatant arrogance, and I can't help the raucous laugh that bursts out of me at the sight. The sound startles her out of her shock because she turns a full-force glare on me and shoves my chest with both hands. "You're such an *ass*," she growls.

I laugh again as I roll myself on top of her to pin her to the couch. She tries to wiggle out from under me, but I keep her caged in with my hips and arms. Instead of letting her escape, I lean forward to press my lips against hers. At first, she's stiff with anger, but I continue to kiss her as I wait patiently for her to relax. After a few seconds, I feel her sag into the couch. She grips my arms as her mouth starts to move against mine.

"I wanted you, too," I murmur against her lips. I nip her bottom lip before pulling away to look down at her. "You were one of the hottest things I had ever seen. I just didn't want to admit it because I knew you didn't want me, and because you were Jax's little sister. You were off limits. But I always wondered if you were a freaky little thing under those professional clothes." She rolls her eyes at my statement but doesn't correct me. My blood suddenly heats at the knowledge that I get to see just how freaky she can get now that she's mine.

Oblivious to the filthy thoughts now running through

my head, she says, "We still have to figure out the best way to tell Jax. I have no idea if he's going to be upset."

I lean down to nuzzle her neck and press a kiss to her shoulder. "I'll tell him. If he's angry then it'll be at me, not you. But I'm pretty sure he already knows because that motherfucker is a psychic or something. He can read me like a book."

At that, Remy chuckles. "Me, too. It feels like he always knows what I'm thinking." Her expression turns thoughtful as she studies my face for a moment. "Right now, he only knows that I've been miserable for the last few weeks. But I think as soon as he sees that I'm happy, he'll understand. That's the only thing he's ever wanted for me, anyway."

A smile lifts the corners of my mouth at the thought of Remy being happy. But then the first half of her comment hits me and the smile drops from my face. I cup her cheek and gently caress her skin with my thumb. "I was miserable, too," I tell her softly. "I don't ever want to feel that way again. I don't ever want to be without you again. Please tell me I won't have to be."

She holds my face in her hands and forces me to look at her—forces me to see the raw truth in her expression. "You and I will never go through that again. It's you and me. That's it. We're it."

I exhale a ragged breath at her promise. I didn't realize how much I needed her to say it until just now, and I feel the grip of uncertainty loosen around my heart. Joy takes its place.

I lean down to once again press my lips against hers. She returns the kiss eagerly, as if we're using it to seal the promise of "us."

"I love you," she murmurs against my mouth. I sigh at the perfect sound of those words on her lips.

"I love you," I tell her. I've never said it to anyone except my mom, and I take the time now to roll the words around on my tongue, testing their weight, checking how they feel. They feel like the greatest words I've ever spoken. When she smiles, I decide I love her happiness just as much as I love the sound of those words coming from her lips.

I start to kiss her again, and now that the talking seems to be finished, it doesn't take long for our breathing to become ragged and our bodies to start grinding against each other. I groan when she slides her tongue in my mouth.

But then my phone starts ringing on the other side of the room. I freeze when I recognize the ringtone.

Remy notices and frowns. "What?"

"It's my manager." I untangle myself from her and quickly pull my pants on before rushing across the living room to grab my phone.

"Jimmy, what's going on?" I ask nervously. I glance at my phone screen to see it's almost 11:00. "It's late on a Saturday night. You got a fight for me?"

"Boy, you are about to fall at my feet and worship the ground I walk on," Jimmy's loud voice sings across the line in his obnoxious South Philly accent.

My breath hitches. If Jimmy is calling late and sounds this happy, it has to be big news. I can't even respond to his greeting, I'm so nervous to hear what he has to say.

"Brandon Allen just got injured and had to pull out of his fight in two weeks," Jimmy says softly.

I frown, racking my brain for that name. "Brandon Allen, isn't he that guy that had that big knockout a few months ago?"

Jimmy stays silent on the other end of the line.

I freeze, the pieces of the puzzle clicking into place. My heart starts pounding.

"That knockout was on the UFC highlight reel," I whisper. "He's supposed to fight Kevin Holladay in two weeks." I whirl around and stare at Remy, my eyes widening and my heart feeling like it's about to jump out of my damn throat. She looks just as shocked as I feel. "Jimmy, are you telling me you got me a fight in the UFC?!"

His chuckle breaks through my temporary shock-induced blackout. "I did," he confirms simply.

"Holy *fuck*," I breathe. "That's a big fight. Holladay has been in the UFC for a while. He's beat some big names. That's... that's a big fight."

I can practically hear Jimmy grinning through the phone. "Yup. They're looking for a last-minute replacement and I told them I got just the crazy bastard to make it happen." He sobers and continues seriously, "They've been looking at you for a while. You accepting this fight is your interview into the UFC, kid. Do you want the fight?"

My eyebrows shoot to my hairline at the ridiculous question. "Please tell me you know me well enough that I don't need to answer that. Did you already tell them yes?"

"I did," he confirms again. "Get some rest, kid, the biggest fight camp of your life starts tomorrow."

I stare at my phone in disbelief after our call ends. I think I'm forgetting to breathe but I can't tell because I'm still convinced my heart is going to jump out of my chest. Eventually I raise my eyes to look at Remy.

She's got a hand covering her mouth as she stares at me with wide eyes. She doesn't speak, just lets me digest the last few minutes at my own pace.

"I got a fight in the UFC," I whisper finally. "I... I made it. It's finally happening."

Remy chokes on a sob at my words. I don't know if it's

the sheer happiness written all over her face, or me saying it out loud, but it shakes me out of my delirium.

A massive grin stretches across my face right before I launch myself at her. She shrieks as we tumble back onto the couch.

"Remy baby, holy shit! I'm in the UFC!" I thump on the cushions, making Remy bounce into the air with uncontrollable giggles.

I settle on top of her and brush a few strands of hair out of her eyes. She smooths her face into a look of mock outrage. "Speaking of, we need to talk about that," she says seriously.

The grin slides off my face.

Her frown deepens and she grips my chin with her fingers. "Just because we're together, doesn't mean 'Remy baby' is now an acceptable nickname."

I can't help the ridiculous smile that stretches across my face again. "I make no promises." Then after a moment, "So we're together, huh?"

The corner of her lips twitch. "Well how else am I going to be a WAG?" she teases.

I growl and reach up to grip her hair, pulling her head back to bare her neck for me to nip. She moans at the sudden contact.

"And don't think that just because we're together, I'm going to start going easy on you," I murmur against her skin. I pull her hair a little harder. "I'll still spank you when you're being an ass."

She moans at my words and starts squirming beneath me. I hiss at the feel of her body moving against mine, already feeling my dick getting hard again.

"I think I'll punish you in the bedroom this time," I growl

as I kiss up the length of her neck. When I reach her earlobe, I circle it with my tongue before nipping lightly.

"*Tristan*," she whimpers, and it's such a sweet sound that I wonder if it will ever not make me want to fall at her feet and give her the world.

I quickly stand up and pull her to her feet by the shirt that she put on at some point during my phone call. Sinking my hand into the hair at the nape of her neck, I kiss her as hungrily as I've ever kissed her—like I haven't tasted her enough, and like it'll never be enough. I groan when she deepens the kiss and touches her tongue to mine.

At the sound, she pulls away suddenly and braces her hands on my chest. "Wait, w-wait."

I can barely see through the dizzy spell of lust that's wrapped around us; can barely focus enough to hear what she wants to say. I growl and try to tug her lips back to mine.

She pushes on my chest, more forcefully this time. "Tristan, wait. Shouldn't you call Coach? And Jax? You only have two weeks, right?"

Since she won't give me her lips, I lean into her neck again. I zero in on the spot where her neck meets her shoulder, nipping and sucking happily.

"It's late," I murmur between kisses. "I'll call them in the morning. Tonight is probably the last time I can focus all my attention on you until the fight and I don't want to waste a second of it thinking about other men."

I grab her hips and spin her around to face the bedroom, pulling her tight against my body. She shudders when she feels me push my hard length against her, clearly signaling my intentions. "So why don't you stop talking and take your smart little mouth into the bedroom before I busy it with something else." I trace her ear with my tongue before kissing the spot right beneath her earlobe. "Although, now that I think about it, I think I might do that anyway. I've been wanting to be rough with you for a while now. Maybe I'll take your ass afterwards, too. I told you I would do that sometime, remember? Would you like to suck my dick and then have your ass fucked, Remy baby?"

She's so turned on that I can feel her trembling, and the only response she can give me is a desperate whimper. I place one last kiss on her shoulder before gently pushing her toward the bedroom. "I want you naked and on your knees. You have one minute. Go."

I grin when she practically bolts for the bedroom. I give her a minute to catch her breath and follow my directions, then I slowly make my way into the bedroom.

25

REMY

I'm on my knees waiting for him when he walks into the room.

The sexiest smirk twitches the corners of his lips, making me squirm in anticipation. I bite my lip and squeeze my legs together in an effort to relieve some of the pressure that started building the second he told me what he wants to do to me.

It doesn't help. He hasn't even touched me yet and I'm already about to start begging.

He makes his way across the room and stops in front of me, reaching forward to run his thumb over my lips and forcing me to look up at him. "Remy baby," he murmurs in a deep voice, "how bad do you want to suck my cock right now?"

My breath catches at his words. I've had guys talk dirty to me before, but never like Tristan. Never in a way that sets my skin on fire and makes me stop breathing.

"Bad," I breathe. I swallow and try again. "Please... I want you in my mouth. Please."

I hear him suck in a breath of his own. His eyes blaze with passion and I know he's just as affected as I am.

He brushes the back of his calloused knuckles against my cheek. "You're so fucking pretty when you beg," he murmurs.

My gaze drops to his pants, only inches from my face, and my eyes immediately widen when I realize he's already rock hard. I can see his entire impressive length pressed against his black slacks. I squeeze my hands into fists, desperate to reach for him, but also wanting to see where he wants to take this. I lick my lips and squirm impatiently.

A low growl rumbles through his chest at the sight of my tongue. He must be just as impatient as I am because he quickly strips out of his pants and steps closer to me, gripping his length and tugging slowly. I can't take my eyes off of the sight.

I feel his fingers curl around my chin and lift my face to look at him. He studies me for a moment, the inferno burning in his eyes, before he leans down and places a tender kiss on my lips. When he pulls away, still bent over and only inches from my face, he whispers, "Open your mouth and stick your tongue out."

I do as he says without any hesitation. With a final look of appreciation, he spits on my tongue and presses the smooth head of his cock inside my mouth.

My moan vibrates down his length at the erotic gesture, the manly taste of Tristan mingling with a faint aftertaste of his tequila from earlier. His hips jerk forward at the vibration of the sound. I eagerly take more of him in my mouth, licking the underside of his shaft before wrapping my lips around him and sucking hard.

"Fuck," he hisses as he grips the back of my head. "You're so fucking good at that. Take me all the way, baby."

The sound of his desperate command sends another rush of arousal to my core, and I relax my throat so I can take him deeper. I look up when I hear a ragged breath fall from his lips. Sweat is glistening on his skin, dripping down his chiseled abs and reminding me that I'd want to lick every inch of his glorious body if I wasn't already so invested in what I'm licking now. His muscles strain as he continues to fuck my mouth. The look of pure, male hunger on his face is driving a powerful bolt of lust through my body, drenching me even further and making me want to please him even more. I reach forward to grip his thighs as I take him down to the base, my eyes never leaving his.

His head drops back with a string of curses, and I feel him grow even harder in my mouth. I hold him deep for a moment.

He focuses back on me as his other hand reaches down to cup my chin. Between that grip and the one he still has on the back of my head, I'm powerless to move my head as he starts to fuck my mouth.

I moan happily at the sight of him taking his control back. His look of desperation, of *wild* passion, is the sexiest fucking thing I've ever seen. I can't stop myself from spreading my thighs and sliding my fingers over my clit.

He groans at the sight and fucks me harder. My eyes start to water at the intensity, which only makes him crazier. At the sight of a tear rolling down my cheek, he pulls out with a harsh breath.

"Get on the bed," he growls. "On your hands and knees."

I scramble to do as he says. I try to look over my shoulder at him but he's already next to me, already pushing my face down to the bed. With his hand on my neck, holding me in place, I whimper at the feeling of his other palm sliding over my ass cheek. And even though I know the slap is coming, it still makes me jump.

"Look how wet you get when I'm rough with you," he murmurs appreciatively. "You're already drenched and I've barely even touched you." His hand slides over my other cheek. "Tell me, is it being spanked that makes you so wet? Or having your mouth fucked? Or is it knowing that I'm about to take your ass?" Another slap lands on my skin.

I twist my face into the covers, panting heavily as I spread my legs and arch even harder, desperate for some kind of release. Just his words have me flying toward the edge, and at the first touch I know I'm going to lose it.

His hand leaves the back of my neck and trails down my spine. I whimper when he reaches my lower back, as he slides further and runs his fingers between my ass cheeks. Just before he touches the puckered entrance, his other slides between my legs and begins gently rubbing my clit. I gasp and push my hips back, begging for more contact, for something to finally fill me.

I hear his deep chuckle behind me. His touch against my pussy stays the same lazy tempo, but the thumb on my ass starts to slowly move in gentle circles.

"I'm not usually one for teasing but I can't quite get enough of the sounds you make when you're this desperate for me." His fingers continue at the same slow pace. "I knew the first time I fucked you that we would be the perfect match in bed. Our chemistry is too good. I get off on the power, and I know your strong, independent personality begs to give up your control to me when it's just the two of us like this."

He pauses, then removes his hand from my clit. I squeak in protest, pushing back for more, but then I feel him shift his weight and press his lips against my ear.

"Am I right?" he breathes against my skin. "Do you want me to take control and be rough with you?" He pulls his thumb away.

I nod, panting, desperate for him to stop teasing me.

I yelp when his hand drops a slap onto my ass. "I need your words, Remy," he growls.

I start panting, wriggling my ass in the air as my desire builds to nearly unbearable heights. "Yes," I gasp. "Yes, I want you to take control. I want you to be rough with me."

Still, he doesn't give me what I want. What I *need*. Just as I open my mouth to start begging, I feel his wet thumb slide in my ass.

"Oh my god, *Tristan*," I gasp.

I can practically hear the grin in his voice. "I love when you say my name like that." He straightens and shifts behind me again, his thumb never moving from where it's pressed inside me. When he rubs his cock between my lips, coating himself in my arousal, I think I'll die of anticipation.

Finally, he presses his head against my entrance. When I try to shift my hips back to take him inside me, he stills me with a firm hand on my waist. To emphasize his point, he drops another slap on my cheek.

"Don't move," he scolds.

Slowly, so slowly, he presses inside me. I fist the sheets in my hand in an effort to stay still. It isn't until he's seated all the way that we both exhale a groan of relief.

Then, his thumb starts to move.

As he fingers my ass, he also starts to fuck me, increasing his pace with each thrust. His dick and his thumb move in tandem, and I'm held powerless by the orgasm that's already growing so quickly inside me. My whole body heats as it rolls toward me.

"That's it, come for me," he growls as he drives deep into me. "Come all over my cock, baby."

He pushes his thumb even deeper and the feeling of that is what undoes me. I scream at the force of my release.

"Good girl," he mumbles as he slows his pace. I vaguely feel him pull out of my ass while my body sags into the bed. But just as I think he's going to give me a moment to catch my breath, I feel something cold replace his thumb.

"Oh *god*," I whimper, realizing he just spit on me. He spreads the wetness around and inside of my ass, even as he continues to slowly fuck me.

"I love that you're so wet right now," he murmurs thoughtfully. "I don't even need to use lube on you. You just came so hard that my dick is already drenched from you." To emphasize his point, he pulls out and slides his length between my ass cheeks, moving easily because we're both covered in my release.

I turn my face into the bed and fist my hands in the sheets again. I'm desperate for him, for his cock to finally fill me, but I'm also oversensitive right now and a little nervous about his size.

He must feel me start to tremble because he reaches down to grip my arms and pull me upright so that my back is against his chest. He wraps an arm around my waist and murmurs sweet nothings in my ear as he kisses along my neck, soothing me and giving me a chance to calm down.

When he feels me steady myself with a deep breath, he plants one last kiss along my jaw before reaching down to press the tip of his dick against my puckered hole. Slowly, gently, he shifts forward to push past the tight ring of muscle.

I gasp at the feeling. He pauses, giving me a chance to

adjust, and then reaches around me to start rubbing circles on my clit.

That feeling is the perfect distraction. As his fingers make my nerves start to tingle, he gently presses in another inch. And then another.

I drop my head back against his shoulder with a moan. I grip the arm that's banded around my waist, desperate to cling to something in the onslaught of overwhelming sensations.

Tristan pulls out slightly, then pushes back in, just a little bit deeper. He starts to increase the intensity of his fingers on my clit. The feeling is so distracting, so powerful, that I can already feel another orgasm start to build. I dig my nails into Tristan's arm.

"Good girl," he murmurs. I'm held so tightly against his chest that his lips are close enough to whisper his dirty words directly into my ear. I shiver at the feel of his breath on my skin.

"You take my cock so well," he murmurs, his fingers continuing to fly over my drenched cunt. "I've been thinking about how you'd look in this position since the very first night I fucked you. You look just as hot as I thought you would." I whimper at his words, digging my nails in even deeper. "How does it feel, baby? Do you like my cock in your ass?"

That question is what ruins me. This whole thing is so taboo, his words so vulgar, that a rush of heat immediately runs through me and demands more of it. I arch my back with a moan and press my ass against him, taking the last inch of him inside.

"*Fuck*," he hisses. The hand that was wrapped around me now grabs my waist with a bruising grip, even while the fingers of his other hand stay buried in my pussy. Then he starts to fuck me.

I reach one arm above my head to grip the back of Tristan's neck and arch my body. "Fuck me," I gasp. "You feel so good, I need you to fuck me. Fuck my ass, Tristan."

Another string of curses falls from his lips as he picks up his pace. I feel my release building, knowing it's about to completely consume me.

And as he thrusts deep at the same time that his nail slides across my achy and swollen clit, it does.

My orgasm explodes through my body, filling me with a kind of pleasure that I didn't even know existed. I'm completely powerless as it rolls through me and all I can do is cling to Tristan's neck as he continues to fuck me through it.

It vaguely registers that his hand has moved from my pussy to grip the front of my neck.

"You're so fucking perfect," he growls in my ear. "But I want you to come again. I want you to come from just my cock in your ass."

He squeezes my neck, and it feels like that's all I'll need to do as he says. But then his grip tightens on my waist and his thrusts become harder, deeper—his fucking has become primal and desperate.

This side of him is the sexiest side, and definitely my favorite in bed. This animal side of him. I love when he owns me like this. And he was right before, about my wanting to give up control in the bedroom and let him take what he wants.

And right now, he wants to fuck me into submission.

This explosion shatters me just as much as the last one did. I was already weak from that one so this one absolutely ruins me. I hear Tristan's loud curse at the same time that I feel his hips jerk, and then he's filling me, fucking us both through to the very end of our orgasms.

I'm trembling in his arms by the time he stops moving. He places a soft kiss on the arm that's still gripping the back of his neck, then he gently slides out of me and lays us down on the bed.

He settles behind me and pulls me tight against his chest. "I might not be able to fuck you that hard again until after the fight so I'm glad we got to do it tonight. I've been distracted thinking about doing that since the first night I had you." I turn over to face him and find him grinning down at me. "Definitely surpassed expectations."

I lean forward to nip his chin. "I hate you," I mutter.

His smile only grows wider at that. "Pretty sure that's your way of saying 'I love you,' so I'll take it."

I shake my head with a smile. Then I realize something about what he just said and look up at him with a small frown. "I know you need to focus on the fight now. The last thing I want to be is a distraction so whatever you need, wherever you want me to go, I'll—"

He cuts me off with a kiss. When he pulls away, he gives me a hard look. "You're not a distraction. I always thought having a girlfriend would split my focus, but that's not going to happen here. I don't know if it's because you're in the sport and you understand it better than most people, or if you and I just mesh that well, but having you around could only be good for me. I want you with me through all of this. You're stuck with me, Remy baby."

I roll my eyes at the nickname, but a smile still stretches across my lips. He just smirks and starts to rub circles along my lower back.

I trace his collarbone and run my fingers along his chest, already watching his eyelids droop with exhaustion.

"I'm proud of you," I whisper. "I always knew you'd make it, even when I hated you. And you're going to be champ one day, and I'm going to be right there next to you, telling you again that I knew you'd make it and that I'm so fucking proud of you."

For a moment I think he's already asleep, but then his arms tighten around me and he presses a kiss to the top of my head.

"I'm such an idiot for not seeing what was right in front of me all this time," he murmurs as we both drift off to sleep.

It doesn't occur to me that Jax might be home until we pull up in front of the guys' house. By the time Tristan turns the car off, I'm practically fidgeting in my seat.

"What if he hates us for not telling him?" I blurt. "What if he hates the idea of us together? I knew I should've told him what was going on. I can't handle Jax being mad at me, it'll kill me."

Tristan chuckles and lightly tugs on my hair. "Stop panicking, he's not going to hate us. Jax doesn't hate anyone. And he might not even be here. You know how he gets at his parents' parties, he probably passed out in their pantry last night."

"I don't think I'm that lucky," I grumble. But then I sigh in defeat and reach for the door handle. "Fine, let's just grab your gym stuff and get this over with."

As we walk down the sidewalk, a quick glance at the stark contrast between what Tristan and I are wearing soothes my nerves enough to force a giggle out of me. He raises an eyebrow at me in question.

"I'm wearing leggings and a sweatshirt, which is totally acceptable for a Sunday morning," I laugh, "and you're wearing a day-old suit, looking all kinds of rumpled and sexy. I'm just enjoying the fact that you're the one doing a walk of shame right now."

Tristan grabs my hand and yanks me against his chest. I gasp in surprise, but automatically settle against his body. He fists his hand in my hair and grins down at me. "How could anyone possibly be ashamed of spending the entire night inside your sweet little body?" he whispers against my mouth, leaning forward to bite my lower lip. Another gasp escapes me, which he immediately swallows with a heated kiss. I cling to his white button-up shirt, wrinkling it even more than it already was. It's all I can do to hang on as Tristan kisses me so hard that you'd never guess we spent the last twelve hours in bed together.

I'm panting by the time we break apart. "Okay, we should probably go inside before I start fantasizing about dragging you into the alleyway again."

Tristan keeps me pressed tight to his body with the arm he has wrapped around my waist. He cocks an eyebrow, a mischievous sparkle flashing in his eyes. "Again?" he asks with a smirk.

I swallow roughly and I'm sure that I'm blushing right now. "Yeah. That kiss in front of Sabrina gave me all kinds of dirty thoughts."

A grin stretches across his face. "Remind me to dive further into those dirty thoughts later tonight. I can't wait to hear what else you thought about over the past few weeks."

I roll my eyes and push myself away, but I can't stop the edges of my mouth from twitching into a small smile. I turn to continue walking toward the guys' front door. "You need to focus on the fight. Stop thinking about fucking me."

Tristan sighs but lets me go. "Fine. But don't think I'm going to be celibate for the next two weeks. That would make me even crazier." He emphasizes his point by slapping my ass.

I cover myself with my hands and shoot him an angry glare. He just smirks at me and tosses his suit jacket over his shoulder.

I realize as I climb the steps to the house that I've completely forgotten to be nervous about Jax. Until now.

I swallow nervously as I unlock the door. Tristan must feel the shift in me because he places his hand on the small of my back in a comforting gesture. His touch forces me to take a deep breath and push open the door.

Jax is sprawled out on the couch, a blanket covering his half-naked form, and he's scrolling through Netflix with a sleepy gaze.

We all freeze. For a moment, we all just stare at each other, trying to wade through the confusion of the sights before us: Jax sleeping on the couch, and Tristan and I walking in together wearing what are clearly morning-after clothes.

I want to ask the first question, but I can't find the breath when Jax's eyes narrow at us. I can practically see the wheels turning in his head. Even Tristan is tense beside me as we wait for his reaction.

After a few seconds he gives us a stiff nod and then turns back to the TV. "It's about time," he grumbles. "I thought you two would never figure it out."

My mouth opens in shock. I had a feeling Jax guessed what was going on, but I didn't think he knew before even we did. Leave it to him to beat everyone to it.

Something occurs to Jax and he turns to shoot a glare at Tristan. "Although I gotta be honest, dude. Even though I love you like my own brother, I have to warn you that my allegiance lies with Remy. So don't fuck her over. Because I'd hate to have to kill you after everything we've been through."

Tristan lets out a startled laugh. "Fair enough," he concedes.

With that, it feels like the whole room relaxes. I let out the breath I didn't realize I was holding.

But then I remember my own confusion, and my frown reappears. "Why are you sleeping on the couch?" I finally ask.

My gaze narrows when Jax looks away quickly and starts fidgeting with the remote in his hands. My friend is a confident, larger-than-life stud, and I can probably count on one hand the amount of times I've seen him look self-conscious. This is one of those times.

"I gave Hailey my room last night," he finally answers. "She... got into a thing with Steve and needed a place to crash. I didn't want to put her on the couch."

My frown deepens, and I reach to pull my phone from my pocket. Glancing down at the blank screen, I say, "Why didn't she call me? What kind of thing? What happened?"

Jax rubs the back of his neck nervously. "They broke up. Hailey ended it."

My mouth drops open for the second time in five minutes, at the same time that Tristan stiffens next to me and mutters, "Good."

"Why didn't she call me?" I whisper in shock.

At that, Jax finally looks at me. "I don't know if she was going to call anyone. I called her when she didn't show up to Mom and Dad's party and that's when she told me. She was drunk as shit. I wasn't going to leave her alone in that house, so I picked her up and brought her here. She might still be passed out."

My heart drops as I gaze up the stairs to where my little sister is sleeping. I've always known Steve wasn't good for Hailey—and it's probably not a secret that I've pushed her multiple times to reevaluate her relationship with him—but no one ever wants to see a loved one in pain. I just hope she doesn't shed too many tears over the asshole.

"I'll go check on her," I say softly. Then I remember why Tristan and I are here, and I turn to Jax. "What're you doing today? Can you go to the gym with Tristan?"

Jax turns to Tristan with a confused look. "Training on a Sunday rest day? I figured you'd be done with that now that you're not moping over Remy."

I try to stifle my giggle as Tristan glares at his best friend. "I was not moping," he growls.

I squeeze his hand. "I ran myself ragged, too," I reassure him. Then a thought occurs to me and I perk up with a giddy smile. "Holy shit, I just realized I can go back to the gym now. I don't have to avoid you anymore. Thank fucking God, I missed punching Jax in the face."

Jax glares at me. "Fat chance you'll land anything," he grumbles. Then he turns back to Tristan and his questioning look returns. "So why are we going to the gym on a Sunday?" he asks again.

Now it's Tristan's turn to grin. "Because I have a fight in two weeks."

Jax raises his eyebrows in surprise. "Against who?"

"Kevin Holladay," Tristan answers smugly.

There's a moment of supreme shock, and then... chaos.

"HOLY SHIT, DUDE, WHAT THE FUCK!" Jax explodes. He shoots upright as he stares at Tristan in disbelief. "Jimmy got you a fight in the UFC?!"

He jumps up and shoves his friend, but Tristan just continues to grin. Jax makes a move to shove him again—

clearly being unable to handle news of this size without any kind of physical outlet—but then he stops and frowns. "If you're fucking with me, man, I swear to God..."

Just then something creaks behind us and I turn to see Hailey coming down the stairs. I suck in a breath as I look her over and try to figure out how she's doing.

She's drowning in one of Jax's shirts and she looks exhausted, but it doesn't look like she's been crying. By first glance, I wouldn't guess that she's a heartbroken woman the day after a breakup.

"Why is Jax screaming at 8:00 in the morning?" she asks with an adorably sleepy smile. She stops on the last step and leans on the banister, waiting expectantly.

Tristan is the first to break our stunned silence. He clears his throat and says, "I got a fight in the UFC."

A pause, and then... chaos.

"HOLY SHIT!" Hailey screams. "Are you *serious*?! That's insane, congratulations!"

"Thanks," Tristan says with a grin. Then he turns to me with a skeptical look. "You know, I'm starting to feel a little hurt that my own girlfriend didn't react by screaming. Everyone else seems to think it's screech-worthy news."

I shoot him a glare and swat his arm, but from behind me I hear Hailey gasp, "Girlfriend? What the hell happened last night?"

I look back at her with a hesitant gaze. "I think I need to ask you the same thing," I say softly.

She swallows nervously but only nods in answer. I turn back to the boys with a quirked eyebrow. "So... gym? I'll stay here with Hailey. And you should call Coach."

My words snap them both into action. Tristan nods once and then squeezes past Hailey to get ready upstairs.

Jax moves to follow his friend but he stops next to Hailey

on the first step. He looks like he wants to say something but instead, he just presses a kiss to her temple. "I'll be back later, don't go anywhere," he finally murmurs quietly.

Hailey looks up at him with wide eyes and nods, a faint blush staining her cheeks. I make a mental note to ask her about Jax's exceptionally protective behavior.

Jax continues up the stairs and for a second, Hailey and I just stare at each other.

"It sounds like we have a lot to talk about," I mutter. She exhales a nervous laugh.

By the time the boys come back downstairs, Hailey is already making us some breakfast. Tristan walks over to where I'm sitting at the kitchen island and wraps his arms around me from behind, leaning forward to gently nip the side of my neck. I smile and turn my head for a real kiss.

"If we could not make PDA a habit, that would be great," Jax grumbles when Tristan finally ends the kiss. I only roll my eyes in response.

Tristan adopts a somber expression as he pulls away. "Okay, let's get the fuck out of here. I'm not going to beat Holladay from the couch."

Jax immediately matches Tristan's seriousness and nods firmly. "Let's fuck this shit up."

"Good luck," I call out as they head toward the front door.

Before Tristan closes it after him, he grins and flashes me a wink. "That's what you're here for. Why do you think I went after you so hard?"

I glare at him and immediately reach over the couch to grab one of the pillows. I launch it at Tristan's head but, per usual, he's too quick for me.

Some things will never change.

EPILOGUE - REMY

Three years later

I'm sitting cross-legged on the hotel bed, my computer in front of me and several loose-leaf sheets from my notebook scattered around me. I also have about several pens tucked into the messy bun on top of my head.

When Tristan walks into the room and sees me, he grins. "That frazzled, huh? Usually you only have four pens lost in your hair."

I blush and pull the pens out. Even after publishing two bestsellers, I'm still just as chaotic with my writing process as I was in the beginning. Each pen is a sign that I'm so lost in my thoughts, I've forgotten I already have one available to me in my hair.

Once it's free of all writing tools, I shake my hair free of its tie and smile at my husband. "Well, you look a little better than you did twelve hours ago."

He snorts and rolls his eyes. "Just a little." He throws his bag on the ground and launches himself on the bed, ignoring my squeak when he crushes all my notes.

Twelve hours ago, he was leaving our hotel room to cut the last few pounds before weigh-ins. He's never been a big fan of huge weight cuts before fights but cutting even ten pounds in twenty-four hours will make a man grumpy.

"Everything go okay?" I ask as he settles his head in my lap. I lean back against the headboard and start to run my fingers through his hair.

"Yup. Got the last few pounds off this morning and weighed in right at 185 at weigh-ins. I feel great. I'm glad I didn't do a huge cut this time." He reaches up to twirl a strand of my still-blonde hair around his finger. "I hung out with the guys for a while so I could rehydrate and snack, and then we went out for a late lunch. Found a great steak-house not far from here. I'll probably pass out early tonight but at least I'm in the eye of the storm for the rest of the day today. Nothing to do but relax and enjoy my wife. Then tomorrow the stress starts back up again."

I smile down at him. "You're going to do great. My fight gut is telling me we're coming home with that belt tomorrow."

He grins and tugs on my hair. "Your fight gut, huh? Well God knows that thing has never been wrong." He sobers and looks around the hotel room. "Are you hungry? Did you order anything today?"

I shake my head. "I haven't been hungry lately. I think I'm so wrapped up in this new book that I forget to eat sometimes. I'll order some room service tonight."

He nods at my answer, then stands up to grab his bottle of Pedialyte to rehydrate with. He takes a few swallows before leaning against the hotel dresser and facing me.

"Did you talk to my parents today?" he asks.

I smile at the knowledge that his parents are no longer a stressor for him. He wouldn't have brought them up on a day like this if he were anything other than comfortable talking about it. God knows it was a long road, but his parents have finally accepted the fact that Tristan chose his own path in life. They might not understand it—even now —but they do respect it. And they've stopped trying to convince him to quit fighting and take a corporate job.

"I talked to your mom a little bit ago," I tell him. "There's two tickets for them at Will Call tomorrow night so they'll be sitting with me. Your mom is nervous, obviously, but I think your dad might actually be a little curious about the fight."

At that, a surprised smile appears on Tristan's face. I decide not to tell him that his idiot brother is still blowing up my phone, begging for tickets for him and his golf buddies. Scott is still the same spoiled prick he always was, and the only reason he wants tickets now is because he likes bragging that his brother is fighting for the UFC Middleweight Title of the world.

Some things might never charge. We just need to focus on the things that have.

I watch Tristan cross his arms and stare across the room. I can practically feel him zoning out, distancing himself from any thoughts of the fight. He likes to distract himself the night before his fights, so we talk about everything and nothing. It gives his brain a chance to relax before everything changes when he wakes up the next morning. I smile and wait for whatever random topic is springing to his mind right now.

"I think I want to change my schedule at the gym," he starts. He's still staring out the window with a dazed look in his eyes. "It was hard balancing my training with teaching during this fight camp but it's going to be ten times worse after I win this belt. Coach suggested I pick between teaching classes and offering privates."

I nod my agreement. Tristan was always a hard worker, but his training camp got *insane* before this title fight. And they say that winning the title is actually easier than keeping it so he's not wrong about things getting harder after tomorrow. He spreads himself too thin by teaching so much. I make a mental note to thank Coach for somehow talking some sense into Tristan.

"Privates are the smarter financial decision, though it would probably be good for gym appearances if I kept teaching at least one class a week." Tristan cocks his head in thought, mulling something over. I lean my head against the headboard and close my eyes, relaxing into the sound of his stream of consciousness. I will never get tired of listening to him talk. "I could keep Mondays on my schedule. I'll use it as my rest day and teach the MMA class at night. Maybe I'll even teach the kids class at 5:00. They're actually easier than the adults to teach."

"God knows you're going to need the practice," I mumble.

But then my brain catches up to my mouth and my eyes snap open when I realize what I just blurted out. My eyes dart to where Tristan is still leaning against the dresser.

He's no longer unfocused or staring into the distance. His normal, piercing gaze is back, and it's fully directed at me. I don't see confusion or shock in his eyes—I just see him studying me, trying to dissect the words that just left my mouth.

I press trembling fingers to my lips, as if I can keep any more secrets from spilling. "I'm sorry, I didn't want to tell you before the fight," I whisper. "I didn't want to distract you."

At that, his eyes go wide. His gaze immediately drops down to my stomach. After a moment, he meets my wide-eyed stare with a shocked look of his own. "You're... you're pregnant?" he asks.

Fingers still pressed to my lips, I nod.

After he proposed, it was like a switch had flipped in his brain. I watched him realize he no longer needed to be the perpetual bachelor, and instead could have the life that he never knew he wanted. That he now felt he wouldn't be happy without. He wanted the wife, the kids, the house in the suburbs. He would get so happy when he'd talk about being a dad someday. And it practically ruined my ovaries to hear him talk about what he wanted to teach them, and what kind of parent he wanted to be. He was already so excited.

So, although this is sooner than we planned, I know the joy that's about to erupt out of Tristan the second he gets over his shock.

I drop my hands into my lap and tell him with a broken sob, "You're going to be a dad. We're going to have a baby."

My tears seem to snap him out of his daze. He strides quickly over to the bed and pulls me over to the side of it so he can kneel on the floor between my legs.

"Why are you crying?" he asks softly as he thumbs away my tears, his look of shock being replaced by one of awe.

At that, a wet laugh breaks out of me. I reach forward to run a hand through Tristan's hair, wanting more contact between us in this moment. "Because I'm pregnant and emotional. Get used to it."

He turns his awed look down to my stomach. Slowly, tentatively, he places his hand on me. My tears threaten to overflow again so I try to distract myself by pressing my hands over his. "You're going to be a dad," I whisper again.

Finally, *finally*, a smile appears on his face. Then it

stretches into an ear-to-ear grin. And suddenly the whole room fills with his happiness and I think I might drown from the feeling of it.

"You're going to be a mom," he says simply. And just hearing those words makes the reality of everything crash down on me. Another broken, happy sob tears from my throat as I throw my arms around his neck.

He stokes my back and murmurs soothing words in my ear, comfortable with the silence that allows us both to deal with the news in our own way.

I can sense when something occurs to him because his fingers freeze in their path along my spine. Sniffling, I pull back to look at him questioningly.

"When did you find out?" he finally asks. "Were you really going to wait until after the fight?"

I laugh at the absurdity of it—at the fact that I thought I could keep this from him. "I only took the test two days ago. You probably didn't notice but I've been an annoying grump the past week and I haven't really had an appetite. That's why I took the test."

Tristan winces and buries his face in my neck. "Fuck, baby, I'm sorry. I should've noticed. You shouldn't have to do anything alone."

I wrap my arms around my husband and turn to smile against his hair. The fact that he's upset he missed the signs is such a pure sign of his love for me that I feel like I fall for him all over again in this moment.

"Tristan, you're about to walk into the fight that you've spent your entire adult life training for. I didn't want you to notice me. I wanted you to focus on yourself." He breathes a ragged exhale against my skin but nods as he pulls back to look at me again.

I start running my fingers through his hair again. "I definitely wasn't going to tell you while you were worrying about cutting weight, but I thought I could at least make it until after the fight, so I wouldn't distract you. So much for that plan."

Tristan smiles and shakes his head. "It probably would've been a little jarring if you told me right before I walked out to the cage, but you could've told me any other time. You didn't have to hide it from me." He wraps his arms around my waist and pulls me tight against his chest. "I love you. And I love our baby. This could only make me happy."

Warmth blossoms in my chest at his words. I smile and lean forward to press my lips against his. He tightens his grip on me, intensifying the kiss and letting me feel every ounce of his happiness.

Just like it still does even three years later, it doesn't take long for our kiss to carry us away. He coaxes my lips open and slides his tongue against mine, drawing a heady whimper out of me. I try to press closer to him, but I just end up rocking my hips against him.

Tristan pulls away with a strangled curse. He leans his forehead against mine, both of us panting from the heated kiss. "I am going to fuck you so hard after this fight is over," he growls. "We're not leaving the bed next week. It'll be like our honeymoon all over again."

I shiver at the memory of our trip to the Maldives. Our hunger for each other never died down so we really did give the honeymoon suite a run for its money. We came back from that trip more exhausted than when we left.

A thought makes Tristan frown. He turns to me with suspicion and asks, "Do I need to fuck you differently now that you're pregnant? Do I need to be gentle now?"

The idea of Tristan doing anything other than fucking

me into whatever surface he has me on is laughable. I actually giggle at the thought, which makes him even more suspicious.

I smile at the loving, protective man in front of me. "No, you do not need to be gentler. The only thing that's going to change in our lives is my lack of coffee and the possibility of constant tears."

He stares at me with wide eyes, as if he's hearing the news all over again. He shakes his head to clear himself from his daze. "Fuck, this is so surreal," he mumbles. "I'm not really sure what to do now."

I wrap my arms around his neck and force him to look me in the eyes. "Now, you go win that belt," I tell him firmly. "That's the only thing you focus on for the next twenty-four hours. Everything else we can figure out later. You've been waiting for this moment your whole life and you are going to show everyone exactly why you're the best goddamn middleweight fighter in the entire world. You and I both know that belt is coming home with us tomorrow. So that's what you focus on. Sex and food and baby talk can wait a few days. We're not going anywhere."

Riveted by my words while I'm talking, by the time I finish Tristan lets out a ragged breath and nods once. I can practically see his resolve hardening as he mentally vows to focus on the fight for the next twenty-four hours.

But not before burying his face in my hair and tightening his arms around me again. Not before he whispers, "I love you so goddamn much. Sometimes it actually hurts."

My tears threaten to overflow again. But this time it's from the amount of happiness filling my lungs that I never knew was possible—as opposed to just pregnancy hormones.

So, I let the tears fall. I let them fall, and I hug my

husband as I think about how happy I am and how thankful I am for this life that we've created.

Now, we just need a championship belt.

ACKNOWLEDGMENTS

I've wanted to write a book for so long that I think I'm still in shock that I've actually reached the point of writing an Acknowledgement.

I have so many people to thank. My husband, who has not only supported this dream but has also tirelessly volunteered to test out certain scenes with me. I appreciate your sacrifice, babe.

To my sister, who was my sounding board throughout this entire process and who never complained about my million phone calls when I needed to know immediately if an idea was shit or if a scene was too dramatic. This book would have turned out to be a completely different story without your help.

To my parents, who have supported every single one of my dreams without hesitation. There are so many parents like Tristan's and I thank my lucky stars every day that I never had to deal with that when I was fighting.

And to my friends, my editor, my readers, *everyone* that has supported me throughout this insane journey, all I can say is, *THANK YOU!* Without you, a book is just some ink on a dead tree. Thank you for taking a chance on a debut author and for bringing Tristan and Remy's story to life. I love you all more than words can describe.

ABOUT THE AUTHOR

Nikki Castle is a 29 year old wife and bulldog mom who writes steamy love stories about alpha MMA fighters and the women that melt their badass, playboy hearts. She spends her days working for a technology company and her evenings running a Mixed Martial Arts (MMA) gym with her husband, who is also a retired fighter.

Nikki has been writing in one way or another since she was a teenager. She pursued an English and Philosophy degree in college, and finally decided to sit down and fulfill her longtime dream of writing an entire novel when quarantine began in 2020.

Nikki loves to hear from readers on Instagram or through email. Message her @nikkicastleromance or nikkicastleromance@gmail.com!

39940703R00250